"PUMP UP THE FORGE," MYRDDIN SAID. "WE HAVE WORK TO DO."

He selected several long thin rods of soft and hard iron and thrust them into the fire to heat. As Arthur watched, Myrddin, Nithe and I struck the hot iron in turn, fashioning the several rods into a single bar. This was hurried crafting. We had it shaped within half a dozen heatings, a record for us.

"Who is it for?" Arthur asked.

"For you."

Arthur's eyes glowed in the forge light. At age fifteen, having his own sword was a goal just less desired than owning his own horse. "This isn't for fighting," Myrddin said. "Would I fabricate a fighting sword for anyone, let alone you, with so little care? This is for looks."

It was evening when we finished work. The sword was a handsome four feet long. Arthur stepped out into the yard fronting the smithy and grasping the sword with both hands set it swinging around his head. I knew it to be as heavy as my great sledge, but in his hands it seemed no weightier than a willow withe. With shining eyes he brought it back to Myrddin.

"So you approve," said Myrddin dryly. "I am glad. Now we must build a nest for the bird." He picked up the great hollow anvil from its post. . . .

IN THE SHADOW OF THE OAK KING

First book in the story of Dragon's Heirs

COURTWAY JONES

POCKET STAR BOOKS

New York London Toronto Sydney Tokyo Singapore

This book is a work of fiction. Names, characters, places and incidents
are either products of the author's imagination or are used fictitiously.
Any resemblance to actual events or locales or persons, living or dead,
is entirely coincidental.

A Pocket Star Book published by
POCKET BOOKS, a division of Simon & Schuster Inc.
1230 Avenue of the Americas, New York, NY 10020

Copyright © 1991 by J. A. Jones

ISBN: 0-671-73404-0

First Pocket Books paperback printing May 1992

10 9 8 7 6 5 4 3 2 1

POCKET STAR BOOKS and colophon are registered
trademarks of Simon & Schuster Inc.

Cover art by Teresa Fasolino
Map and decorations by Harry Leippe
Interior design by Sofia Grunfeld

Printed in the U.S.A.

Acknowledgment
and Dedication

This book is based on tales contained in Sir Thomas Malory's book *Le Morte d'Arthur*. My retelling of the tales has been read by Carroll L. Riley, the anthropologist; Brent Locke, the writer; and Lilian Fuller Jones, who sometimes teaches dumbbell English. The book has gained much of grace and accuracy from the attention I paid to their suggestions. I expected it of them, as my three oldest friends. What I did not expect was to find such treatment from Knox Burger, my agent. He not only brought me this lovely new prosperity, but found me advice from Sam Weintraub on how to keep it. I also wish to thank Harry Leippe, who invented the fifth-century Romano-Celtic calligraphy to dress the book up and drew the map to help locate the adventures of the protagonists. And finally I am happy that Pelleas and his friends were adopted by Claire Zion and Dudley Frasier at Pocket Books, so that they came into print. I am grateful to all these splendid people, and in acknowledgment dedicate this book to all of them!

DRAMATIS PERSONAE

One of the most difficult things about trying to base a book on Malory's *Le Morte D'Arthur* is that Malory made nearly everyone in his story related to everyone else and chose names for his characters that seem much alike. It might help to think of these folks as being from different tribal groups even though some of them, like Arthur, are related to at least two, and sometimes three, such units. Arthur had relatives (father's side) from Armorica, in what is now Brittany in France (Lancelot and his kin), relatives from among the Gaels through his mother, Igraine the Gold, and among the Britons through his father, Uther Pendragon.

The names used here come chiefly from Malory, except for a few minor characters I either made up or gleaned from other sources on the Arthur myth. The following list identifies most of those who appear in this book.

BRITONS OF THE ISLES

Anna	Arthur's wet nurse, wife to Ulfas
Arthur	High King of Britain, son of Uther Pendragon and Igraine the Gold (baby name: Bear)
Brastius Red-beard	Warden of the North
Cador	Duke of Lyoness
Cathmor	Archdruid of Britain
Ector	Arthur's protector as a child, Kay's father
Gorlais	Duke of Cornwall, husband of Igraine the Gold, father of Morgan

DRAMATIS PERSONAE

Hilda	Lady of the Lake
Kay	Arthur's seneschal, son of Ector
Lot	King of Lothian and the Orkneys, husband of Morgause
Myrddin	Arthur's tutor, master smith, guardian of Nithe
Nithe	Hilda's daughter, friend to Arthur and Pelleas, Myrddin's ward
Samana	Arthur's first wife, daughter of Cador
Uther Pendragon	Arthur's father, High King of Britain

BRITONS FROM OVERSEAS

Balin	Knight, Hilda's killer
Ban	King of Armorica, father of Lancelot
Blamore	Cousin of Lancelot
Bors	Cousin of Lancelot
Ector de Marys	Cousin of Lancelot
Lancelot	Queen's Champion, son of Ban

GAELS

Aggravain	Son of Lot and Morgause, enemy to Guenevere
Gaheris	Son of Lot and Morgause, killer of Morgause
Gareth	Son of Pelleas and Morgause
Gawaine	Son of Lot and Morgause, cousin and close friend to Arthur
Igraine the Gold	Wife to Gorlais and Uther, mother of Arthur and Morgan, sister to Morgause
Mordred	Son of Arthur and Morgause
Morgan	Daughter of Gorlais and Igraine the Gold
Morgause	Wife to Lot, mother of Gawaine, Gaheris, Aggravain, Gareth, and Mordred

DRAMATIS PERSONAE

PICTS

Brusen	Mother of Pelleas, sister to Pellinore, wife to Pelles
Elaine	Mother of Galahad, lover of Lancelot, daughter of Brusen and Pelles
Ettarde	Niece to Pellinore
Grance	The Lion of Grance, guardian of Guenevere
Korlac	Chief of hunters in Strathclyde village
Lamerok	Son of Pellinore, lover of Morgause
Pelleas	Son of Uther Pendragon and Brusen, High King of the Picts, lover of Nithe
Pelles	Old king of the Strathclyde, husband to Brusen, father of Elaine
Pellinore	High King of the Picts, brother of Brusen
Pynel	Knight of the Poisoned Apple
Ulfas	Boyhood friend to Pelleas
Viki	Adopted daughter of Pelleas

SAXONS AND JUTES

Horsa	Jute Chief, father of Rowena
Hjort	Saxon chief of Arthur's mercenaries
Guenevere	Queen to Arthur, daughter of Rowena
Rowena	Queen to Vortigern, mother of Guenevere

INTRODUCTION

Most scholars are agreed that Geoffrey of Monmouth invented the story of King Arthur in the thirteenth century, building on tales of a hero, or heroes, who lived before his time. His book was immensely popular and attracted imitators who added to the legend until Sir Thomas Malory brought the body of texts together as *Le Morte D'Arthur* in the fifteenth century.

Today most readers are familiar with at least the main outlines of the story and can identify the six major characters: Arthur, Guenevere, Lancelot, Merlin, Mordred, and Morgan la Fey. Few, however, have read Malory. They would be surprised to learn that he portrays Arthur as passive to the point of idiocy, Guenevere as vain and hysterical, Lancelot as conceited and snobbish, Merlin as devious and cruel, and Mordred as brave and charismatic. They would probably recognize Malory's portrayal of Morgan la Fey as vicious, scheming, and manipulative, much as her reputation is today. Malory had a low opinion of women.

When I was old enough to read the story for myself I was not yet old enough to understand it; I know I didn't like parts of it. I didn't like reading that Merlin foretold a baby born on May Day in the year of Arthur's crowning would rise up to depose him. Since the baby's identity was shielded from Merlin's foreknowledge, he counseled Arthur to have all the babies born to noble houses collected and drowned. It was done. I was also uncomfortable with whatever it was Guenevere and Lancelot were up to, something I strongly suspected was one of those things my parents would disapprove of, but didn't talk about, at least while I was around. I thought then I could have managed the story better. I wanted my heroes and heroines to be strong.

Many years later, after retiring as an anthropologist and community developer, I reread Malory (Keith Baines' presentation of the Winchester Manuscript) and I found myself with much the same feelings. I was sure I could do better by the characters. I started reading everything, both fiction and fact, that I could find on the period when the story was supposed to have taken place, the generations immediately following the departure of the Roman legions from Britain in the early fifth century. Happily, I found the correspondence from John Steinbeck to his agent and to his editor that is printed along with his unfinished "The Acts of King Arthur and his Noble Knights." Steinbeck evidently stopped writing the book when his correspondents evinced disappointment with the work in progress he had submitted. They had wanted him to use the Malory framework and develop new insights into the story. That's what I decided to do.

I encountered a number of problems, mostly arising out of the fact that Malory wrote in the fifteenth century about the fifth century, in thirteenth-century terms. For example, he has men riding around on huge horses while clad in full thirteenth-century armor, something that obviously had not come into being in the fifth century and had gone out of style in the fifteenth.

My anthropological background helped me to find some solutions. There remain some problems. Malory features Saracens in his story. Saracens did not exist until after the rise of Islam (seventh century) and were but little known in England until after the Third Crusade (twelfth century). They were certainly not in existence in Arthur's fifth century. I substituted Picts for Malory's Saracens. Picts were as troublesome in the fifth century as the Saracens were later. Unfortunately, no one, including anthropologists, knows much about Picts!

Again, Malory has druids in his story, and so do I. I am sorry to report that no one knows much more about druids today than they did in Malory's time. For the most part, however, I was able to keep anomalies to a few that were mechanically useful, like inventing copper coinage with Arthur's likeness to facilitate a market economy in my story, when markets were probably restricted to barter after the Romans left Britain.

The murder of the innocents to protect Arthur's throne and the betrayal of Arthur's trust by Lancelot and Guenevere are here, but handled differently from Malory's account. He was an old cynic, who probably had it wrong, anyway.

Other than that, I have tried to keep events within the compass outlined in Malory's work, though I have added a few themes from other places. Even the giants of Geen are to be found in Malory in a tale of Arthur killing one on the top of Mont-Saint-Michel, for example. And, I admit I have given everything else a twist to make the story come out the way I wanted. So be it.

The Isles

ORKNEY ISLANDS

HEBRIDES

CALEDONIA
WOLF MOUNTAIN
ANTONINE WALL
ALPS
STRATHCLYDE
HADRIAN'S WALL

SCOTTI

EIRE

MAN

MONA

YORK

CHESTER

LINCOLN

NEW AVALON

CAMELOT

CAERLEON

BATH

LONDON

THAMES

TINTAGEL

CORNWALL

CASTLE GRANGE

EXETER

JUTES

ANGLES

LYONESS

ECTOR'S ISLES

ARMORICA

BRITONS

Part I

The Fosterling

453~468

It is the final year in the life of Attila the Hun, scourge of Rome. In Britain, in a Pictish village on the banks of the Clyde River, a young boy is playing ball. Far to the south, in Castle Tintagel, a baby is waiting to be born.

CHAPTER I

Any Gael who can feed a bull to breed his neighbor's cows can be a king. My father's bull grazes fat and free in our summer pasture, servicing the dun cows with no more ceremony than the Picts breed their women. Each spring at snowmelt his people follow my father, Brastius Red-beard, to this narrow valley, with the high hills close about, and set up their linen tents where the sod is too thick for Pictish plows to turn. He does not acknowledge me, bred by a small, dark, Pictish woman, but his eye seeks me out even before he inspects the grass.

I live in our palisaded village year around with my mother, Brusen, and her second husband, Brig, a man of little account: he has no tattoos. He dyes linen with the woad we boil down from wild mustard. It stinks, and the stink clings to him as closely as the dye does to his hands. The warriors will not let him raid with them. They say the smell of him would alert the enemy a mile distant. If he cannot kill and eat a man, he cannot be tattooed, and my mother cannot color the skin around her eyes. She feels the scorn of the other women keenly. When I am grown, I will dedicate a kill to her and relieve her of this shame.

I asked her once why she would marry such a man. She said she chose him when she came to this valley with a child and no dowry to attract a more eligible one. She could earn a dowry selling

3

herself to the Gaels when they come each spring, but she would need a man to collect the fees or the Gaels would take without paying, as is their practice in other things. Brig will not help her, and I can understand this, for she is very pretty still, and would leave him if she found a better man.

Brig would make me work with the dye if he could, but he has no control over me. He would also forbid me to eat at table and bar the door at night against my return from play. He cannot. It is my mother's house. Men do not own houses. I will not become a woad dyer. I am almost eight, by Samhain reckoning, though my mother tells me this is my eleventh winter. I am no shorter than Brig and as dark and as broad. The man I believe to be my true father is Brastius, the cattle-king, and when I am in full growth I will force him to acknowledge me because I will then be as tall as he, with a Pict's added strength.

We had been playing hurley and were gathered in argument, which is as much a part of the game as the running.

"The game is not over until the bell stops ringing," Gawaine insisted. He is leader of the boys among the summer people and is tall and red of hair and hasty of temper like his father, proud King Lot. The Gaels bring a priest when they come to summer pasture, and the priest has decreed that we cannot play ball in the commons after summons to prayers. He says it distracts God to have the game going. He may be right. Lud, the Long-handed, god to the Picts, sometimes appears in disguise as a boy to play hurley. I know little of the Christian god, served by the Gaelic priest.

"The bell has stopped," I replied sternly. "We have won, five goals to three. Pay your forfeit."

I was not ready for the sudden stinging pain across my shoulders, but my retaliation was swift enough. I dropped to one knee, whirled, and struck Aggravain, Gawaine's sullen brother, over the ear with my hurley stick. The blow stopped him from grinning at the success of his sneak attack. My stick is split chestnut, with a natural curve at the end, light and strong, and the edge of the blade cut him,

4

drawing blood. He staggered back, clutching at his head. I didn't hit him hard, but I hurt him more than he had hurt me, and that gave me satisfaction.

I turned back to Gawaine and held out my hand.

"The forfeit," I demanded coldly. Gawaine untied his belt-knot and handed me belt, knife and sheath. Without even drawing the blade, I passed it over to Ulfas, my second-in-command, short and dark like all Picts, but sturdy and brave. I knew Gawaine's knife was bright steel, and mine black iron, but a leader must be generous to his men. Besides, the gesture would annoy Gawaine. I held Gawaine's eyes with mine.

"I would rather be a bastard and call no one brother than be of proper birth and have a brother such as yours," I said. Gawaine did not reply, but his face was white with anger as he stomped off, followed by snot-faced Aggravain, sullenly holding his ear and blubbering. The Picts had not ventured near, except for Ulfas, until Gawaine and the other Gaels left. Picts will fight, but they like to choose their own ground, and the commons is too open.

"Is this mine?" Ulfas asked, "Mine for real?"

"I have no need for it," I replied. "Besides, I do not want something not freely given. Gawaine is a poor loser."

"He hasn't had much practice at it," Ulfas observed, inspecting the blade critically.

"Come on, we'll be late," one of his brothers called back to him, and waving the knife in thanks, he ran off. I touched my back where Aggravain had struck me.

"Does it still hurt?" a voice asked inside my head. I froze. This has happened before, though more when I was younger. My mother warned me that children who hear voices in their heads are chosen as sacrifices for the Oak King. She told me when she heard voices as a child she had learned to imagine herself in a room with a door and shutters on the window. When she closed both she could keep the voices out. I shut myself in and turned around to see a man rubbing down a great ox in the shade of the boundary tree. He straightened up, and sudden fear wrenched my guts. It was the god of the Gaels, the Oak King, the child-eater! The strength went out of my legs, and I crouched with one hand wrapped around my knees, and the other warding off evil with the sun-sign of Lud.

"Are you afraid of me, boy? They say the Oak King has red hair, and a red beard. Mine is brown, streaked with white. They say the Oak King has pointed teeth decaying black. Mine are white and even. They say he has claws instead of fingernails. Look at my hands, boy!" This last was said in a tone of command, and I chanced a glance at the hands he held in front of me. They were very big and muscular, but the nails were blunt. I looked up at his face, and in truth his hair and beard were brown and white, not red. He was smiling, and his teeth were white and even. His eyes were kind. He was dressed in a blue tunic, that came to his knees, brown Gaelic riding trousers and had shiny brown boots that reached to just below his tunic's edge. A gray fur cap crowned his head, making him appear even taller than he was. Not even my real father, Brastius Red-beard the cattle-king, was as tall.

"I didn't hear you come into the valley," I said.

"Did you not?" he replied. "You seemed very intent on what you were doing." It was true. When I am playing, the world could catch fire, and I would not notice unless the flames interfered with the game.

"Even so, I should have," I said, and walked around him out of reach to better look at the wagon. I wasn't sure about him. Only shamans wear beards among the Picts. All the young men among the Gaels, who fancy themselves warriors, sport mustaches. Their settled men wear short, trimmed beards and the druids long ones, but this man was not a Gael. His eyes were brown like mine, not blue like theirs.

I hate being as frightened as he had made me, but no one was expecting me at home so I decided not to leave. I admired the wagon. It was painted blue, red and gold. I had never seen anything so fine. It was very strongly built, with iron straps reinforcing the sides. The wheels were spoked and rimmed with iron and looked overdelicate to carry such weight. There was more iron on this

6

wagon than in the whole valley, except for the long spears of the warriors. I was looking at the undercarriage, which appeared to be suspended from two long iron braces, when a voice spoke.

"We don't allow dirty boys to touch our wagon."

I looked up and into a pair of clear gray eyes made somber by black brows with frown lines between them.

"I have not touched your wagon," I declared, truthfully, and added, "and I'm not dirty," which was a lie.

"You have cow dung all over your face and in your hair. You smell bad." That was probably true. Cows graze on the commons we use for a playground, and I had slipped more than once. I looked up at the tall man who was watching the exchange with some amusement. "You don't even have any clothes on!" she continued, scolding.

"Do you let her talk that way to strangers?" I asked.

"Her mouth is her own," the man said. "I have very little influence on what she says, or to whom."

"Well, someone should teach her manners," I observed. "Not everybody is as polite as I am. She should know that no one wears clothes when they play hurley."

From the corner of my eye I saw her pop out of sight only to reappear at the end of the wagon, and jump to the ground. She came up to me indignantly, and I saw she was only a child of seven or eight, perhaps, and dressed exactly like the tall stranger, boots, cap and all. The Picts make such dolls for their children. I laughed at the thought and she kicked me in the shins so hard it brought tears to my eyes. She stamped away to face the man before I could recover from my surprise enough to object.

"You tell that dirty boy to go away and stop bothering us," she demanded.

"He isn't bothering me," the man said mildly and suddenly put a hand out to push her back gently. "You remember what I said I would do if you kicked me again," he warned in a grave voice.

"I don't believe it," she replied, but she didn't kick him. It must have been a powerful threat for she didn't seem to me to be a person easily cowed. I resisted rubbing my shin as I had resisted rubbing my back when Aggravain hit me. It is unmanly to show pain. She had hurt me more than he had. I decided to ignore her, but I put on my tunic, pulling it from where I had wedged it in a branch of the boundary tree.

I returned to my inspection of the wagon. "Please, sir," I said, "There is something here I do not understand."

He walked over to me, leaving the little girl to stand alone.

"How does this work?" I asked, and I pointed to the strip of iron from which the wagon box was suspended.

"It works to cushion the shock of the bad road," he said.

"I can see what it's for," I said coldly. "What I don't know is how it works. How can that thin piece of iron carry that load?"

"Ah," he said, raising his eyebrows again. "You understand the principle?"

"Of course," I said. "It's not difficult. The leather straps allow the wagon bed to move side to side slightly and to bounce up and down when the wheels hit a rut. The thin iron springs up and down as the load shifts."

"So it does. To my knowledge there has never been a wagon on springs before, and my surprise is merely that the device was so obvious to you."

"I'm not stupid," I said. "What I don't know is why the iron doesn't bend permanently or break off under a heavy load."

"Because it's layered," he said, and I stooped to see it more clearly, always keeping in mind that I might be kicked by the small girl if I offered a target. Sure enough, I could see the lines running the length of the strip. It was layered.

"We use a strip of soft iron and one of hard, another of soft and another of hard alternating so it will be stiff without bending but bend without breaking."

"You beat them together while they're hot?" I asked.

"Precisely. It is necessary to reheat for every layer and beat to meld one piece into the next."

"It must take a long time," I said.

8

"It does. If I weren't doing it for myself I would not have done it at all."

"You're a smith?" I asked, astounded. I had never seen a smith. The valley had never had one before, so far as I knew. I was pushed firmly to one side, and Brastius Red-beard was there. I had never stood so close to him before. He gazed at me searchingly for an instant, and I felt suddenly shy. While he was almost as tall as the stranger, he was not nearly as broad, so that he appeared slight in the other's presence. Brastius was dressed much like the other man, for it is cold in early summer in our valley, except that he wore fur leggings attached to his sandals and held up by a strip of hide fastened just below his knees. This was a formal meeting for he also wore a plaid across his left shoulder with the five colors of an under-king. It was only attached by a bronze fibula, so it wasn't an honoring occasion. I learn these things for when I become a king myself.

"I am Warden of the North," Brastius said. "If you are truly a smith, we would welcome you here."

"I am that."

"Can you make weapons as well as tools?"

"At need, I can. What use do you have for weapons here?"

"We have no trouble with the Picts, who are our neighbors, but with raiders from the sea, who fall upon us and carry away our cattle and our women," Brastius replied.

"Against that need I will make weapons," the smith said. "I will need iron. I was told in the markets in London that you mine bog iron in this area for trade. Is that true?"

"Yes," said Brastius. "More than you can possibly forge. It is the reason we come to this valley for summer pasturage rather than some other."

"I see also the smoke from charcoal makers in the hills," the smith continued.

"Those are Pict fires. They make charcoal and trade it for milk and cheese with us in the valley. We can get it for you."

"No, I will trade with them directly. I do not desire to have my

9

roof burned down over my head because someone is angry about being denied access to my work."

"At what rates will you trade?"

"Ten to one by weight for both iron and charcoal."

"You will have much work. We do not have such prices in the southern markets, and lose the time in transport as well."

"I have found that true wherever I go, and yet I make a good living from the smithy. That brings me to my next problem. I would like a place to work far enough from your village to avoid interruptions from small boys."

Brastius turned to look at me, and to avoid being sent away I said, "There is a cave down by the sea that is dry, and has a small spring near it."

"That might do," the smith said. "I would like to keep my own eye on the sea for your raiders. Cold iron draws raiders like dung draws flies, and I don't want my throat cut for a handful of tenpenny nails."

"I know the cave the boy means," Brastius said. "It has been used in the past to store ship's goods, but we have no sea trade now. It is dry and large enough to store your wagon. You follow this cart path to the first turnoff, and it will lead directly to it." The smith nodded, and Brastius continued, "I will have the council confirm it, but that is merely a formality." He held out his hand palm up and the smith placed his open hand on it in a gesture of agreement. Brastius left, and the smith picked up the little girl, who was watching the whole interchange, and lifted her to the high seat. He stepped up himself, unwrapped the reins from the cleat to which they were attached and clicked his tongue at the oxen to get them moving.

"Why do you use such huge beasts to haul such a small wagon?" I asked, easily keeping pace with them. "You would move faster with horses, even our small hill ponies."

"Why should I wish to move faster?" the smith asked, reasonably. There was no answer to that. I'd want to move faster, however. The smith drove to the level place in front of the cave and stopped.

He got out to inspect the place, tasting the water that came from the small spring first of all. It was as I had said, a good place to be. I like it and often sleep there in summer to avoid the flies and smells of the village. In the winter the dung piles against the north wall of every house give welcome protection against the winter wind, but in the summer their smell is most unpleasant. I guessed he decided to stay when he began to unharness the oxen, and I helped him, patting the docile beasts who gazed at me with great dark eyes, unafraid.

"Will you use them to plow a field this spring?" I asked. "They are half again as big as any draft animals here. You'll have to ask for land on the hillside, however, where the grass is not so thick."

"I do not farm. I will trade iron for our food." He stopped to consider. "Perhaps others might wish to borrow them to work the plow?" he asked, tilting his head slightly to watch me for reply. I nodded.

The smith turned the animals loose, slapping them on the rump to move away from the wagon. "Will you eat with us?" he asked politely.

Before I could give answer, the small girl said, "Make him wash first."

I ignored her, as before, not wishing to encourage such behavior. "I will eat later," I said. "I have rabbit snares set which I must look at. Usually I come back here to cook."

"You do your own cooking?"

"When I do not work, I do not eat at my father's table except to prove I can once in a while. Sometimes the charcoal makers feed me when I work for them, but mostly, I find my own food. Today I promised to play ball against the Gaels, so I set the snares before full light. I will eat well."

"You are still welcome to eat with us."

"I thank you, but if I do not go to the snares before dusk, the foxes will get my rabbits. If you like, I will share them with you."

"Fresh game would taste good. I do not hunt."

"I will return before sundown," I said. I trotted along the shore until I rounded the point and was out of sight of the cave. When I was sure I would not be spied upon, I stripped and plunged into the sea, the cold water shocking me to a bitter reflection that small girls have big mouths. The sea sluiced most of the cow dung from my face and hair, but to be sure, I scooped a handful of sand from the beach and rubbed myself with it, shivering in the slight breeze. It was not a long bath.

I make my snares of rabbit gut cut in long, thin strips and tanned in urine. They are light and tough and the urine smell masks any scent from my hands that would make wild animals wary. I use a simple loop tethered to a stout piece of brush anchored next to one of the small paths in the brush where I know rabbits live. The loop catches them around the neck as they run through from either side and chokes them as they struggle against the restraint. Rabbits die quickly in my snares, not screaming as they do when a fox catches and bites them. Two of the snares had rabbits, both young and fat, and unless the smith was very hungry, it would be enough. The girl couldn't eat much.

I held them up as I came into camp, proud of my catch. The smith had a fire going in a stone circle and a stack of dry wood for fuel. A savory stew was already simmering in an iron pot. The smith took my rabbits and had them cleaned and cut up in a fraction of the time it would have taken me, although I work fast. He added the cut-up meat to the stew to cook, watched carefully by the small girl. None of us spoke as the rabbit meat cooked in the stew until the smith spooned it out into wooden bowls, serving me first as a hunter should be served. The little girl did not say anything, perhaps warned by the smith, but her face expressed disdain for me. The message was clear. Hunters do not bring in rabbit meat.

I was finishing my second bowl when I saw the smith looking over my shoulder at the meadow. A delegation of men was coming from the camp, led by Brastius Red-beard and the priest. The priest had not shaven the crown of his head in months and his long black tunic was dirty. There were men from the Pict village with them, hanging back so as not to appear too interested. They had donned tunics in deference to the Gaels, who wear them always when not bathing or fighting.

The priest spoke to us first. "Are you Christian or a devil worshiper?" he asked.

"Neither."

"Don't quibble. Are you a follower of the Oak King? We permit none such amongst us." Brastius looked uncomfortable. Every one of the summer people were followers of the Oak King, although they were nominally Christian. The Picts did not even pretend to be Christian.

"Smiths are exempt from religious duties," the smith said gravely.

"That is why they are not permitted to live among Christian men nor marry Christian women," the priest replied.

"That is not the reason, but so be it. I will live outside the palisade and avoid your tents. Your daughters and wives would be safe from me in any case," the smith said coldly. "I am a citizen of Rome. Why would I wish to marry among barbarians such as you?"

"What about the girl?" the priest asked, intimidated by the smith's haughty manner, but not wanting to back down before Brastius and the others.

"Has she been baptized?"

"Not to my knowledge. Her mother was not Christian, and when she abandoned her no one but me was willing to take responsibility for such a small child. She will have no value as a worker for some years."

"The church is not content to have her in the care of one who is not Christian," the priest declared.

"The church will have to live with its discontent, then, because I do not choose to give the child up, and no force available to you is likely to be able to take her from me."

At this point Brastius interfered, and said to the priest, "This is no real concern of yours, Father, and I will thank you not to drive this smith off. We need him here." The priest turned color, and walked away, anger showing in the very set of his habit.

"We have a proposition to put to you, smith," Brastius said. "We will buy your weapons as I have said, but this village has another need. Will you consider taking an apprentice? One from the valley here could learn rudimentary ironwork in a few months, so, when you leave this winter, the Picts would be able to get their iron utensils repaired after a fashion."

"Do you speak for the Picts?" the smith asked in a mild tone.

"They depend on us to deal with the outside world," Brastius said in a slightly pompous voice.

"If I can choose my apprentice, then, I will," the smith replied.

"We would have no objection."

"Very well, it will be this boy," he said, and pointed to me. "Will his family allow it?"

"No one speaks for me, but me," I answered.

"All boys talk so," one of the older Gaels said scornfully.

"Will any man here speak for me?" I asked, looking him in the eye. "Some say my father is a Gael. Does one of you acknowledge me?"

"You are insolent, boy," the man said, pushing through the circle to confront me. It was proud Lot, King of cold Lothian, father to Gawaine and Aggravain and angry, perhaps, about my cutting Aggravain's ear with my hurley stick. He is new to the valley, having brought only his immediate family and some young bulls for trading. He thinks well of himself, being the only person who saw fit to wear his five-color plaid on this mission. I could see his red beard was dyed. His young wife, Morgause, drives a light wicker chariot behind two small, active ponies up and down our road with little regard for the lives of children, dogs or fowl. Often enough one or another gallant rides the drawbar, balanced between the two ponies, usually drunk and loud. Ulfas and I had spied on her bathing in the sea with the young men once. Shameless, she was, about allowing them to handle her. She is tall, red-haired like most Gaels, and proportioned like a Pictish earth god-

14

dess. I follow her around when she is not watching, imagining
how it would be to have her as the young men do.

"What is your name?" Lot asked.

"Pict mothers give their children scurrilous names to avoid the
attention of your Oak King," I said. "Mine named me Dog's-
brother."

"It fits," he sneered. "Discourtesy to elders also attracts the Oak
King's attention, Dog's-brother."

A sudden stillness fell on the group, which I perceived, and well
knew the reason. The threat was obvious, but there was something
other in his voice than mere warning. It was confirmation of what
I already feared must be true. The Gaels had selected me for the
Oak King sacrifice! I shrank behind the wagon and crawled underneath it to hide my face.

The Oak King is a god worshiped by the Gaels, an old god
who came before the Great Mother brought men the knowledge
of planting and harvesting of crops. The Picts turned away from
the Oak King many generations past, but the Pictish shamans
remember and help the Gaels to honor him. The shamans say the
Oak King permitted the Gaels to drive the Picts from the rich
valleys to the south because they no longer give him the first fruits
of the chase or the blood of their young men. Now, when the
Gaelic druids make sacrifices to him, often enough it is Picts who
bleed, Picts who have offended Pictish shamans.

"Would you take more than one apprentice, smith?" Brastius
asked. "We would also have a young Gael learn what he can of
your art."

"It is called art only if it is very good or very bad," the smith
replied. "I will teach the craft to another."

"Let it be Lot's son, Gawaine. He is well grown, quick to learn
any new skill and knows his place when he is with men." Lot
looked at me haughtily when I peeked out from under the wagon
as Brastius spoke, but I made no rejoinder. The smith could think
as he wished about me.

"It is done, then. Men call me Myrddin."

15

"You are Uther's smith," Brastius said in surprise.

"I am no man's anything," the smith said with anger in the tone of his voice. "I have worked for Uther, but I have also worked for many other men, as I saw fit."

"He may come to this valley for Beltane," Brastius said. "We do not want trouble with him over your services." I was listening underneath the wagon. Beltane is the festival for the Great Mother, honoring the spring and new life. There was no danger in it for me.

"There will be none. He expects me to be here," Myrddin replied. "But even if this were not so, I come and go where I will, when I will, respecting no contracts except those I make myself. I will be here until Samhain, and after, if it pleases me." Samhain is the Oak King's feast and comes on the day of the first full moon after the first killing frost. Samhain night would see me stretched on the black stone in the oak grove, trussed like a young pig for the druid's knife, if I could not escape. I shivered in fear.

"So be it," Brastius said, and reached out to touch palms again to show agreement. The smith clasped his, in return.

King Lot walked away with the other men, saying over his shoulder, "Gawaine will be here in the morning."

I crawled out from under the wagon, still shaken. The girl and the smith were watching me.

"Why did you run away, Dog's-brother?" the girl asked, frowning.

"You heard what that haughty man Lot said," I replied, defensively.

"How does the Oak King know about you? You're only a boy!"

"Oak King Child-eater knows everything," I said. "He might be listening to us now, unseen." I looked around, nervously.

"I don't believe it," she scoffed.

"No? The hunters tell the boys in their care stories that prove it. Sometimes, when we are practicing in the woods, they sneak up behind one of us, and grab us the way Oak King is supposed to do when he comes for you. I've wet my pants in fright like a baby, when it happened to me."

"That's cruel," she said.

"Perhaps it is, but you learn to listen, and to believe in the Oak King."

"Has the belief made you a better boy?"

"Do you mean have I changed, because I fear what may happen to me if I don't? No, I haven't. That's why I'm frightened now. I had a chance to escape his attention, and I didn't take it."

"There must be lots of boys worse than you."

"No, there aren't. I'm the worst boy in the village. Everyone says so."

"You sound proud of it."

"I'm just trying to tell you that I really believe I'm in trouble," I said, miserably.

"Do you know Gawaine?" Myrddin asked, breaking into the conversation.

"It was he whose knife I won," I replied.

"Does he smell as badly as you do, Dog's-brother?" the girl asked.

"What name have you?" I replied.

"They call me Nithe."

"That's no Christian name."

"I know it. I'm named for my mother, Neithe, and my father, Ninian. A neithe is a goddess of streams and lakes. My mother is one."

I looked at the smith for confirmation of this and was surprised to see him nod gravely. "They say her principal home is either in, or near, the Usk River in Wales, but her name is Hilda, not Neithe," he said. "Anyway, a neithe is not a goddess, but a simple water sprite, according to those who profess to know about such things. This one is called Nithe because she was wet all the time as a baby, and Nithe is as close as she could come to saying Neithe."

"Are you Nithe's father?" I asked, wondering why else the child would be with him.

"No, her father's name is Ninian, like she said. Mine is Myrddin."

"Bishop Ninian?" I asked surprised. "The Pope's missionary to the Picts?" That was the only person of that name I could recall.

"Yes. Nithe's father and mother had a falling out over whether or not she should be baptized, and they agreed to give her to my care until the matter should be settled between them."

"But I didn't know priests married," I said.

"They don't. They didn't. That's part of the problem."

"What about Gawaine?" Nithe demanded, interrupting.

"He doesn't smell. All Gaels bathe daily, sometimes twice," I answered her. "Only their priests go dirty. They say bathing is vanity, whatever that might mean."

"You're not a Gael," she stated flatly.

"No," I replied coldly. "I am a Pict. My mother is a Pict. She tells me my father is a king, and I suppose she knows, but I have not been acknowledged by any of the Gaels. I bathe whenever I feel like it."

"Do you know who he is?" she asked.

"My father? Yes, I think so. His name is Brastius. He is one of the Gael cattle-kings."

"Do you ever see him?"

"Of course. You just saw him yourself, the man with the long red beard. He has sworn not to cut it as long as he serves as Warden of the North for Uther, the High King. He is the chieftain of the summer people here, except for the visitors like King Lot." I looked at the smith. "Do you still want me for an apprentice?" I asked. I was thinking of what would happen at Samhain.

"What do I have to do with Brastius, or Lot, for that matter?" he replied, and that was all the answer I got.

Gawaine came next morning early, and we helped the smith build a forge of river stone held together with mud and a shade of willow and chestnut branches tied to a frame of young oak to stand under while he worked. The wagon we pushed back into the cave, and emptied of most of its contents so there was room on the wagon bed for him and the girl to lay out sleeping pallets. We took turns driving the oxen down to the water and out to the pasture, and I came to love the gentle beasts. Gawaine, arrogant as ever, was contemptuous of them, preferring the bulls his father kept as being more spirited.

We ate well that summer. There is always food for hunters, but everyone eats well in summer, even children. Were this not the case, Gawaine and I would still have feasted. The smith received so much of his payment in food for the weapons and tools he made that he could have fed several more workers. There was great demand for the long leaf-blade spears the Gaels prefer, along with saxeknives with blades as long as my forearm. We made bosses for the centers of their wooden shields, and rims to fit around their edges. The Picts wanted iron arrowheads with the broad blades that would open a great wound and bleed a stag to death. The hoe was the tool most commonly purchased, though there was call for an occasional plowshare. They were expensive, for they weigh as much as twenty pounds.

The hard work pumping the bellows for the forge put new muscles on both of us. My friend Ulfas joined us some days and was welcomed by Myrddin, though Gawaine held himself as aloof from him as from me. He does not like Picts. There is so much to know about how to bring the fire and the iron together so it can be shaped, that the fear of the Oak King receded in my mind. Myrddin showed us many secrets. I made a knife of my own, as did Gawaine to replace the one he had lost at hurley, and we learned how to keep them sharp on Myrddin's great round grindstone. I regretted the end of each day.

Beltane came and went, but Uther did not arrive. We heard he was at war in Cornwall over stealing someone's wife. Myrddin seemed to know something about it, but only shook his head when I tried to question him, and I gave it up. I was merely curious, anyway. What was Uther to me?

Ulfas told me Uther and his people were Britons, people who spoke a language much like that of the Gaels. He said it was easy to tell them apart. The Gaels are tall, red-haired and blue-eyed. The Britons are shorter and more compactly built, with straw-colored hair and gray eyes. They do not bathe daily as the Gaels do, so they sounded like more sensible people to me.

Half a year had passed since Beltane, and Samhain was only a few days away; preparations for the harvest festival were made as they had always been made, and as they would be made when these women were all with the Oak King. They baked great pasties filled with fruit and wine-soaked meat, and fermented tubs of mead, enough to get the entire village drunk for three days. I started wondering where I could hide.

One morning, in the midst of this, a stranger came to the forge. He was but of middle height, but strongly built and richly dressed in a long tunic of Roman purple with gold thread worked into the collar and sleeves. He had a plaid over his left shoulder, secured by a huge gold broach, and wore a heavy gold torque around his throat. I counted the colors in his plaid, as I always do, and there were seven! This was the plaid of a high king! This man was not a Gael, but a Briton!

"Greetings, Myrddin," he said.

"Greetings, Uther," the smith replied, wiping his hands on a piece of waste linen before grasping Uther's arms with his hands. "You look well."

"Marriage has always agreed with me," Uther said. "This time is no exception."

"How is Igraine?"

"How should she be?" Uther answered in a cynical voice. "To her, one master is much like another. She is compliant."

"I wished better for you," Myrddin said. "What of Gorlais?"

"Dead," was the grudging reply.

"Well," Myrddin said with a sigh, "I suppose it's best, maybe even for him. It can't be pleasant knowing that one's wife prefers another man."

Uther was not listening. He was watching me. "You are the one the Picts call 'Dog's-brother'?" he asked me.

"I will take a new name after Samhain," I responded.

"What would that be?"

"Pelleas."

"You will call yourself after a Pictish king? Old King Pelles?"

"My mother tells me my father is a king," I said defiantly, looking him in the eye.

"A king, but not King Pelles," he said. He reached over and touched me, lifting my face to his. Ulfas was right. I could smell that he had not bathed recently. He was a Briton, not a Gael. I was not prepared for what happened next. His eyes were a very bright blue, with reflections from the forge, and suddenly within my head the words formed, "You are my son."

"No!" I cried, but I did not speak the word aloud. Nevertheless, he heard me, and smiled.

"Oh, yes, Pelleas," the voice in my head continued, "you are my son. You can both hear and speak with your mind. There are not many of us."

I backed away from him and fled. He knew about the voices. I was sure my secret was exposed to the Oak King! I did not return until after dark and found Myrddin and Nithe waiting up for me.

"Why are you in such particular fear of the Oak King?" Myrddin asked me.

"I am not under the protection of the hunters like the other boys are," I replied.

"Why is that?"

"I let a wolf out of a trap. The hunters use wire snares to catch wolves. They make a simple loop, like my rabbit snares, and attach it to a sapling bent over and held down by a notched stick. When the wolf takes the bait attached to the stick it releases the sapling, and the wire, which has been hidden on the ground, catches a foot more often than not as the sapling springs straight. Sometimes the wolves chew one of their own feet off to escape, but this one was truly caught. A hunter bragged at the supper fire that he was waiting for morning when he hoped the wolf's mate would be with him. That way he could kill them both. Hunters eat apart, so all the young men of the village heard his tale, even us young boys, who are sometimes allowed to sit outside of their circle and listen."

"What did you do?"

"I went out before daylight and found the wolf. The wire was stoutly anchored and the wolf had pulled it tight, cutting into his leg. His paw was badly swollen. I tossed him a rabbit from one of my snares and slowly untwisted the wire from the sapling, releasing the tension. The wolf stood up on three legs while I crawled to him, not wanting to loom over him in a threatening way. He watched as I loosened the wire on his leg, sniffed at me, picked up the rabbit and loped off on his three good legs."

"Why did you do that?"

"No reason, I guess. I like wolves. I didn't like the hunter, a mean man with hard hands, a man named Korlac. I would not like you to make wire for the hunters," I added.

"What happened next?" Myrddin asked, without responding to my request, which is often the way with him. It didn't mean he wouldn't heed me.

"Korlac found me before I could get back to the village and beat me with his unstrung bow. It was heavy and as tall as I. He might have killed me for I could not escape from him, but before that happened a tremendous growling broke out around us, and Korlac dropped his bow and fled. I was hurt and too dazed to move. I must have fallen asleep for I gradually became aware that it was fully light and the wolf and his mate were sniffing and licking me. When I opened my eyes they walked off into the woods. They must have watched over me during the night, for I found where a boar had come, smelling the blood on my legs and back, and had been turned away.

"I picked up the bow, which had been bitten in two, limped back to the village, went to the hunter's fire and dropped the bow in front of Korlac, who had beaten me. I told him, 'I bring you a message. Stay out of the woods.' I have not been back to the hunter's fire since."

"They threatened you with the Oak King?"

"They didn't have to. Even my mother fears for me. I have been shunned by everyone but the boys who play hurley. Everyone is equal on the hurley field."

"What do you think the Oak King will do to you?" Nithe asked.

"I don't like to talk about it," I said.

"Perhaps I can help," Myrddin said.

"There is no help. I think they will come after me tomorrow, so I'll wait until everyone has seen me at work, and then I'll slip into the woods. If I live past Samhain, they can't touch me."

"Why not?"

"I'll take my proper name at Samhain and after that I will have to consent to the sacrifice, or commit some crime deserving of it. I am not that bad."

"Won't they track you if you try to hide in the woods? I've been told the Picts hunt at night."

"They won't follow where I plan to go. I know where the wolves meet. I'll go there and take my chances."

"I wouldn't be afraid of the Oak King," Nithe said stoutly.

"Would you not?" I said, stung by her tone. "The Oak King eats children alive, even girls."

"Why?"

"The truth is he needs to eat souls to keep himself alive. If the Oak King eats you, you are not reborn, but live in him forever, conscious of the fear all the time. He needs that, too."

"He sounds dreadful!"

"He is dreadful. I watched a boy I knew die on the black stone last Samhain. I crept up in the dark to the edge of the oak grove and spied on the druid as he cut the boy's stomach open. The boy screamed one long scream, took a deep breath and screamed again and again until there was no blood left in him and he was dead. It took a long time."

"Was the Oak King there?" Nithe asked, not so bravely this time.

"I don't know. After the first scream I ran away, but I could still hear him screaming in the dark."

"Saxons go to live with Odin when they die. That's better than being reborn like a baby. Do you remember being reborn?"

"You know babies don't know anything when they're born. How could they remember last time they were alive?" I asked.

"Are all Picts reborn, except those the Oak King eats?" she asked, insatiable for new information.

"It's not just Picts the Oak King eats, but Gaels, too. Children that die before they have a Samhain name are not reborn. Warriors who have their hearts eaten by enemies are reborn as women, but the problem is not that kind of thing. The problem is being alive inside the Oak King, and participating in his tearing the souls out of living people. You feel their pain, as you did your own, and it never ends. I will die with the wolves rather than live with the Oak King."

"Are you sure of this?" she asked doubtfully.

"No. How could I be? I know the shamans tell us that it is worse than can be imagined and my imagination makes it so terrible that I think about it all the time. The closer it comes, the worse it gets."

"If the shamans know so much why don't you ask them for help?"

"They'd just laugh. They are the ones who select Pictish boys for the Oak King sacrifice. They wouldn't see the point. Shamans don't get reborn. They join the Oak King when they die. They like the pain." I could only speak in a whisper, for shamans sometimes can hear long distances. They do not like to be talked about.

"Will you help him, Myrddin?" Nithe asked.

"I will try," he replied.

I was grateful for it, but I would seek out the wolves.

CHAPTER

II

I have bad dreams that I do not like to talk about. The hunters said we will know when it is truly the Oak King who has caught us. The Oak King does not let go. In my dreams, when I am caught from behind, it is Oak King Child-eater. I never see his face clearly, but I know what he looks like, tall and fierce-eyed with a straggly red beard framing a mouth full of rotten teeth. I can feel his hands on me as if they were real, biting into the flesh of my arms like eagle claws. I wake shaking in terror, and sometimes I do not immediately realize where I am. I often hear the voices in my head, when I am still half-asleep, and I am even more confused. Every night I stay awake as long as I can, but always, eventually, I fall asleep. Now, I also fear the hunters who, I am sure, will look for me on Samhain night. It was with this fear that I fell asleep.

They did not wait for the full moon that would not rise until tomorrow's evening. They came for me this very night, and had me bound and gagged before I was fully awake. They were not gentle, and when I heard proud King Lot's voice among the others, I knew why. This was not a dream. When my eyes became accustomed to the dark I could see they were carrying me into the forest away from the village. There must have been Picts guiding them because the Gaels cannot see at night as we do. Samhain is a festival honored among the Picts only because the shamans fear the Gaelic gods.

A great bone-fire lighted up the meadow at the edge of the cliff over the sea. The men dropped me outside the circle of light, and I watched in horror as they cut down a man who had been hanging by his feet from the branch of a great oak like a butchered hog, and bleeding into a gilt caldron. They threw his body into the bone-fire, shouting to the Oak King to bless the harvest, and danced drunkenly around the blaze. I sniffed. They had been drinking mead, made from fermented honey. I had had some once. I lay ignored for hours until the moon was overhead.

I could smell meat cooking in the bone-fire, rank meat none but a god could eat. I strained to move my head so I might watch, hoping, as the night deepened, that I had been forgotten. Unbidden, the vision came of a snared rabbit awaiting the coming of the hunter, dreading his arrival, but preferring that to the waiting.

Black-clad shapes shuffled by, moving between me and the edge of the woods, exhorting the sweating men and women coupling there to greater efforts, in honor of the gods. Their high-pitched voices mumbled old Celtic words I but half recognized, words heavy with ritual power from a distant past.

Off in the dark someone began to beat a hollow log raised from the ground and braced to keep from rolling. At earlier Samhain feasts I had watched the drummers in admiration, but now the regular thump seemed to control the rhythm of my heart; both speeded up as the keening voices shrilled higher and higher, until the drumbeat suddenly stopped, and my heart lurched in my breast. The silence was broken by a scream so unexpected that I struggled to my knees to flee, but there was no feeling in my bound legs, and I pitched onto my face, scratching my cheek on the sharp gravel.

The shuffling march of the dark figures came near me again, hesitated, and moved on. This time, when the drum increased in tempo to match the rising voices, the scream after the agonizing silence was much closer. I found difficulty in getting enough air in my lungs, being able only to pant in shallow breaths. Perhaps I fainted in my distress for only gradually I became aware of the approach of the dark walkers. The voices shrieked from all around me, and for the first time I could distinguish individual words: moon, knife, kill, blood! The drumming of my heart was so loud that I didn't hear the hollow log at all, and when cold hands clutched me, both the voices and my own heart stopped for a moment. The scream that sounded, wild with fear, was from my throat.

"Bring him to the altarstone," a deep voice commanded. It was Uther. Lot and Brastius picked me up and carried me, unresisting, into the dark under the trees. I knew the place. It was uncanny, and I never entered it while hunting, a glade in an oak grove, centered by a long, low, black stone. The trees are old, with restless leaves even in the absence of a breeze. The moon shone down into the clearing, silvering the rock, but there were dark spots that did not catch the light, and as we came closer I could smell fresh blood. They laid me, not ungently, faceup on the stone. A coldness emanated from it, and I thought I felt it stir beneath me.

"It is time, Uther," a dry, harsh voice intoned from the shadows. "You owe a life to the Oak King."

"I give a life," Uther said, to the unseen speaker. "This is my son. He will be my surrogate." Uther stepped into the moonlight near the stone.

"Is he willing?" I shook my head violently.

"What difference does that make?" Uther asked harshly.

"None, unless he is of age. He appears almost full grown."

"He was walking before he was presented to the sun for I knew not of him, and the shamans would not act in the absence of a father until then, believing him to be a Beltane child. The presentation was a moon less than eight years ago. He will not take a name until after Samhain," Uther said.

"Then he never will. Hold his head while the seer opens his belly. He will divine your future in his writhings."

"I need not that. Let one of your priests hold him."

"No. He is your surrogate. You must hold him, while his life force seeps away. How else will the Oak King know it is your debt he pays?"

"I have done this before, Druid. No one has asked me to participate."

"Then you are lucky to be alive. Do not tempt the Oak King to pay himself twice." There was a moment's silence, and the dry voice continued, "Are you sure you have the stomach for this, Uther?"

Uther bent over me and took my head in his two hands, looking into my eyes. His face was in shadow, but I saw the clearing's central fire reflected from the surface of his own eyes. "What kind of a son would you make if I let you live? Would you defy the Oak King with me, standing behind me, guarding my back?"

I could not speak. My throat was swollen from screaming and my mouth too dry to articulate words. I nodded frantically. A tall shape came into the light behind him, a man I did not recognize, wearing the red, hooded cloak of an arch-druid. I looked desperately back at Uther, trying to force words out. They would not come. Uther stood upright, no longer looking at me. I could sense he had made up his mind with a finality that would not yield to appeal.

"Do it, Cathmor. What are you waiting for?"

"I was waiting to see if you had enough courage to face the Oak King in your own body. I further see I am wasting my time."

"You are not immune from my power, Druid."

"Nor you from mine, High King. We do not have to permit the substitute." After a long moment of silence, during which neither man moved, the arch-druid turned to someone behind him and spoke again. "Take him, Myrddin."

Myrddin came to me, to where I lay trussed on the stone. He looked at me and turned his head to speak to someone hidden behind him. "Give me the potion I asked you to hold," he said.

A short, hooded figure carefully handed Myrddin a small goblet. Myrddin sniffed at it and turned to me. "I would spare you if I

could, boy, but you were born to this destiny. Hear me carefully.
You must drink this, all of it. Then I shall have to hurt you
dreadfully, but you will fall asleep, and wake tomorrow free from
pain. I promise it."

He came up to me while I tried to escape by inching backward,
but Uther's strong hands held me fast. Myrddin sighed, and gently
forced my jaw down while he poured the liquid into my mouth.
It tasted of mint, and was cool and soothing to my throat. I
swallowed it convulsively, feeling it heal as it went down. I also
recovered my voice.

"You will not eat me?" I asked, gasping as air once more freely
moved into my lungs.

"I will not eat you," he assured me.

I searched for some device to postpone the sacrifice.

I shouted, "Let me confess before I die! I don't want to go to
hell!" There was a silence.

"Is he Christian?" Myrddin asked.

"What difference does that make?" Uther asked, annoyed. "This
is no Christian sacrament!"

"Are you baptized, boy?" Myrddin continued, ignoring Uther.

"No," I said.

"He doesn't have to confess if he's not baptized. He's going to
hell anyway." I recognized Lot's voice as much by what he said
as by the tone of it.

"Why do you say that? If his intent is to be a Christian, and
he has not been either baptized or confirmed, why isn't he an
innocent? I think he should confess if he wishes. What harm can
it do?" That was Brastius' voice. I could see no faces but Uther's
and Myrddin's.

"Augustine says that unbaptized children burn in hell, eternally,"
Lot insisted.

"We Romans of Gaelic heritage know better," Brastius said. "A
child without a Samhain name is not reborn after he dies, but he
does not live in torment. I say if this child wishes to confess, that

he may do so." No one responded, so I tried to remember what I had been told of Christian confession.

"First," I said, "I wish to confess witchcraft." There was a sudden stillness that was almost palpable. "Once," I continued, "I was in the woods practicing stalking like the hunters taught us, and came across the shaman with his chamber pot taking a dump. He was the one who was pestering my mother. I waited until he was fully occupied, squatting and grunting before I took a small stone and broke the pot with my sling. It was a great shot." I heard muttered laughter. Shamans hide their body function products so other shamans won't be able to use them in witchcraft.

"When the pot broke," I continued, "it splattered everything all over, and he had to scrape it up and build a fire over the spot to cover everything. He also tried to spy me out, but I was hidden so well it was impossible. When he left I knew he would double back and watch, so I waited until it was dark. I heard him leave a second time, when he got tired. Then I went back where the broken pot was and searched out a small piece of shit clinging to a leaf."

"How did you do that in the dark?" a voice asked. It was Korlac, the hunter.

"With my nose," I said. There was more quiet laughter.

"Go on," Brastius said.

"I picked the leaf and took it to the oak grove. I used my knife to split a deadly toadstool and slipped the leaf into the slit. Then I said, 'If you ever bother my mother again may your prick rot off and your balls swell up and burst.' Then I went home." There was open laughter now, only stilled by an angry outburst from the shaman.

"What are you laughing at? If it were you he cursed, would you laugh?" When it was silent again, he asked, "Where is that toadstool, boy?"

"I could show you," I said, hoping he would insist and perhaps I could escape.

"You may not leave the black stone while the moon shines,"

30

Myrddin said, with a trace of regret. I thought that he might be trying to tell me something, perhaps that I could not only put off the moment of sacrifice, but cancel it completely if I could but talk until the moon no longer shone down upon the stone.

"The next thing I wish to confess is feeling lust," I said.

"At eight?" Lot asked incredulously.

"He has seen eleven winters," Brastius said. "I felt lust before I was that old, aye, and satisfied it too. Let him speak."

"I felt lust," I said, "when I saw Morgause sporting in the sea and on the beach with three young men a week ago. They were all naked, and they had her one after another all afternoon while she laughed and laughed. I wanted to go down and join them, but was afraid." So much for proud King Lot! I heard laughter in the dark.

"I felt envy," I went on, "when I saw the priest use Gaheris like a woman and give him a fine new hurley stick for payment. I wanted the stick, not the priest," I added.

"He's making this up," Lot burst in, his voice shaking with anger.

"How do you know?" Brastius asked. "Does it make sense that he would make up this kind of a thing when his immortal soul depends on a true confession?"

"This one? This one no more believes in confession than I do. He doesn't even use the correct formula."

"I'm inclined to agree," said Myrddin. "If we do not get on with this the pain-easing draft I gave him will wear off, and it will go harder with him under the knife. Turn him so I can reach the area under the heart, and I'll start the cut."

"I have more," I shouted. "Let me tell more!"

Uther expertly rolled me over on my side as Myrrdin said, "This will hurt, and I am sorry for it."

Before he had finished speaking Myrddin slipped the sickle knife into my side. I felt the edge grate along the bone as the most incredible pain completely took my breath away. Up to now I had not believed this could happen. Blood spouted in an arc, splattering his white garment.

"Cut his bonds so that he may move freely," Myrddin said, and in a moment I was clutching at my belly, trying to stifle the pain. I still couldn't breathe.

"Enough. Leave us now. I must talk with the Oak King." This last statement was enough to clear the circle of the watchers. No one seeks the presence of the Oak King.

I was handled roughly. My hands were dragged away from my belly, and a cool compress placed over the wound. The pain subsided.

"Is he dead?" a small voice asked. It was Nithe.

"No, but it's a close thing," Myrddin answered. "Help me get him into the sack before he bleeds any more." As he lifted me I suffered a wave of nausea, and I vomited. Myrddin swore.

"It's not his fault," Nithe said.

"I know it's not his fault! I'm not cursing him," Myrddin replied, crossly. I felt leather slide up my back as Myrddin gently eased me into the sack. "Now, get in there with him and hold that compress in place, or he will be dead," he said grimly. There was a quick scurrying and a small presence adjusted itself against me. Nithe wedged herself so she could press on the compress with both hands. The sudden rush of pain made me faint briefly, and their voices faded out, still quarreling.

"I don't know why you let them hurt him like this," Nithe was saying. I vaguely heard Myrddin grunt as he lifted the sack with me and Nithe in it, and walked toward the noise of the revelry. The motion made me nauseous again and I fought to keep from vomiting all over myself and Nithe.

Moments after, I heard Uther speak. "What news, Druid?"

"You have a new heir, High King. Igraine carries it in her belly. What's left of this one is mine." Without waiting for a reply he started walking again, but I heard Uther's voice follow, mocking.

"Eat him in good health, Druid."

I heard no more, but in my barely conscious state one thought

32

was clear, perhaps because it had so central a place in my mind. It was not that I had survived, for I could not think that clearly, but that I had been acknowledged. My father was not Brastius Red-beard, a petty cattle-king, but Uther the Pendragon of Wales, High King of the Britons! I was glad he was not a Gael, if only to avoid the incessant bathing they do, but I wondered what kind of father was this to lay me on the black stone to pay a debt he owed the gods.

CHAPTER

III

ime stands still in a Pict village on the night of Samhain. Not even children wander away from the light of the bone-fires before dawn. The smell of meat sacrifices is a reminder. The new year can be started only through the agency of men, and the shamans have told us to start new life as part of the process. On this night women seek out dancers and lead them to the light's edge to couple, choosing whom they will without regard to marriage rules. Women are encouraged to take man after man so the life flow will warm the earth and the door between the worlds through which the dead come on this one night will close again. Never have we failed in our duty.

On this night when the dead walk among us, living men may be lured away to join the dead and not find their way back to the land of the living by dawn. Such men disappear, and the village remembers them with dread. They may return to lure others away, even those once dear to them. There is much jealousy of the living among the dead.

I did not like jolting along in Myrddin's wagon in the dark, gazing at the stars overhead. They seemed to move if I stared too intently at them. My side hurt, but I could not recall exactly why. Nithe cuddled beside me, wrapped in a tanned wolfskin, giving off heat like a charcoal fire. I tried to shift away from her in the

34

crowded wagon. but she reached out and fastened her small fist in a loose fold of my tunic. holding me close. Her face was pressed against me so that I wondered how she breathed. How could a person sleep under a Samhain moon?

I wondered about what had occurred this night. having time to think about it. going over it step by step. preferring that to spec-ulations about the walking dead. Uther. the High King. had spoken to me. mind to mind. calling me by my chosen name. Pelleas. and acknowledging me as his son. About that I could recall two things. He had said there were few of us who could mind-speak. and he claimed me so he could send me to the Oak King in his stead.

Ah! Was I dead? My mind was fogged from the minty draft forced on me lying on the black altarstone. But. I could see in my mind's eye Myrddin's face bending over me as he slit open my belly. I gingerly touched the spot where the knife had entered my side and found a tight bandage with a sore spot underneath. I wondered again about Myrddin. I had been afraid that he would discover my voices and give me away for the Oak King's sacrifice. I was right! If Uther could talk to me mind to mind. why not Myrddin? I pictured myself inside of Myrddin's head. a dark cave with shelves loaded with interesting pots and bundles. I pictured myself sitting. with my knees drawn up. He must have felt me probing.

"Hello. Pelleas." he said. his voice quietly sounding inside my own head.

"Did you know I could do this?" I asked. in wonder. my fear overcome by my curiosity. I had never done this willingly before!

"I suspected it. but you resisted my attempt to find out. so I did not press you."

"Why did you spill my guts for the Oak King?" I needed to know this immediately. though I was too weak to flee. It is not knowing things that bothers me.

"I didn't. I made a small hole in your side. slipping the curved blade around your stomach and stopping short of your spleen. If

35

I had not done so, a lesser seer would have opened your belly with little chance of recovery."

"But why?"

"Uther, the High King, was supposed to reign but eight years, after which his life should have been forfeit to the druids. They would read the future of the people in his twisting and thrashing around while he died. To escape that, he sent a son as a blood surrogate. He has done it before."

"Why didn't you tell me?"

"Would anyone have been able to find you for the ceremony if I had?"

"Of course not."

"So you've answered your own question. I knew I could carry you through the sacrifice without killing you, and I knew that was your only chance. The hunters would have found you and brought you in dead had you run."

He was right. "Why doesn't it hurt more?" I asked.

"You drank medicine of such power that by tomorrow only a slight tenderness and a thin scar will remain."

"It wasn't supposed to be until full moon, tomorrow night," I said, still aggrieved.

"Cathmor, the arch-druid, had someplace else to be tomorrow night. He authorized the early observance," Myrddin replied.

I thought about this for some time, not making much sense of it in my fuzzy mind. Finally I asked, "Do you talk to anyone else like this?"

"Of those you know, only Uther and Nithe," he replied. That was interesting. I wondered if he could hear me when I talked only to myself.

"Can you?" I asked.

"Can I what?"

"Hear me when I talk only to myself?"

"Only if you speak loudly, and even then I wouldn't. It isn't nice to pry into a person's thoughts."

I agreed. Lots of things I think about I don't want anyone else to know. I wondered if my voices were only eavesdroppings.

"Does Nithe know about me?" I asked.

"I do now," she said, aloud.

"I thought you were asleep," I said.

"I was until you started thrashing around. Why can't you lie quiet?"

"You don't have to be so close," I said.

"Yes I do. It's cold."

"How come you don't mind-talk if you can hear me doing it?" I asked.

"I can do something else," she said, and I was flooded with such a strong feeling of being laughed at that I wondered why there was no sound. Abruptly the feeling changed to one of terror.

"Stop that, Nithe," Myrddin ordered sharply. "You have no idea how far that sort of thing travels. Everyone within half a mile will think the dead are upon them this night."

"I'm very powerful," she said smugly.

"You're very naughty," the smith said reprovingly.

"She can project emotion, but not words," Myrddin explained to me. "She understands mind-speech perfectly, but has no capacity to speak." It was silent for a while until Nithe's regular breathing suggested she had fallen back to sleep.

"Is Uther really my father?" I asked.

"Yes," Myrddin replied. The creaking of the wagon and the plodding of the hooves of the great beasts that pulled it did not interfere with the sound of the voice in my head.

"I thought it was Brastius," I said.

"I know."

"Why didn't you tell me?" I asked.

"You didn't ask."

"Would you have told me if I did think to ask?"

This time there was a silence, and then Myrddin admitted, "Probably not; it was no part of my concern."

37

"Did you know Uther planned to substitute me on the druid's altar?"

"I feared it. That is one reason I stayed in the valley. If you were spared this year, you would have been safe, because the substitute must not have reached his ninth year to be acceptable. As I said, Uther has done this before. He is fortunate in the fact that the Oak King used to demand the sacrifice of the High King every year, but in these days of grace, only every eight years. Uther is old himself, and has avoided the sacrifice by having many sons to take his place."

"Why not one of those who has known a father's love and might understand, rather than me?"

"He has only daughters living. You came as a welcome reprieve."

"How did he know about me?"

"From King Lot, I imagine. It is no secret here except, apparently, from you."

"Why does Lot hate me so?"

"You are a Pict. When you defeated his sons, Gawaine and Aggravain, in hurley, a sport the Gaels, like himself, claim to have invented, you brought yourself to his notice. He is touchy because the Britons, like Uther, look down on the Gaels, having driven them from the best lands when they came here, much as the Gaels drove out the Picts. Lot likes people in their places, that's all. By his reckoning, Picts are supposed to acknowledge the superiority of the Gaels. You don't."

That was true. "Is there another son in Igraine's belly, like you said?" I asked, not out of interest, but out of fascination with the process of mind-speech.

"She is at least pregnant. Whether the child was of his making or of her husband Gorlais, gossip doesn't say. Uther married her within a few days of Gorlais' death, and she was pregnant then."

"What do you think?"

"I think it is at least likely to be Uther's. He went to war with Gorlais to get her, and she went to Uther willingly enough when it was over."

"He took a kingdom to war to get a woman?" I asked.

"Well, there was also Tintagel Castle and its lands, which are now his, but he mostly wanted the woman, to control the child. It is the first he has sired in years, and will be necessary to him eight years from now, if it's a boy, and if he lives to face the Oak King again."

"Will you save him as you did me?" I asked.

"It depends on Igraine. She is from one of the old Gael families. Children belong to the female line among the Gaels. She may not allow him to be sacrificed."

"Igraine is Gawaine's aunt," I said.

"Yes."

"He says the family is Roman."

"Well, he would. Gaels figure everyone descended from a common grandfather belongs to the same family. That grandfather was Ambrosius, brother to Uther's father. He was a Roman citizen, though born a Briton, who took a Gael to wife."

"He speaks Latin."

"Are you still talking about Gawaine?" Myrddin asked.

"Of course."

"All educated people do."

"I do," Nithe said suddenly. She had been eavesdropping. The niceties didn't impress Nithe much.

"So will Pelleas," Myrddin said.

"Do I have to call him that?" Nithe asked. "I like Dog's-brother better."

"Call me Pelleas," I answered, "and I don't see the need for Latin. I speak Celtic and Pictish and that's enough."

"You will learn Latin, and Saxon as well," Myrddin insisted. "Smiths travel from place to place and have customers who speak many languages. It is a necessary part of a smith's training."

I wasn't sure about that.

"I'll help you, now that you are one of us," Nithe said. "I am good at languages." Oddly enough, that was reassuring.

"Are you a druid?" I asked, starting a new conversation.

39

"No. Druids are men among the Britons and Gaels who have spent years memorizing ritual to become lawgivers, seers and bards, and who take oath to serve their dread God of the Woods, the Oak King. I have undergone the training, but have taken no oath. At need, I know what druids know, but I am not enrolled among them, and do not serve the Oak King."

"Are you a Briton or a Gael?" I asked.

"I am a Roman. My mother was a Briton. My father was something quite else."

"Does Uther know that?"

"That I am not a druid? No. It is better that no one knows it, particularly where we are going, maybe as far as Lyoness."

"Why?" Nithe asked.

"To hide. No one would look for us in that place. Pelleas is supposed to be dead, and it might come true in earnest if either Uther or the druids find he is still alive. Our need is to escape their attention."

"Uther would harm me?" I asked.

"Oh, yes. He believes in the old gods, and would deem it most unsafe to cheat the Oak King."

"Don't you?"

"I think it most unsafe to cheat Uther. There is no Oak King."

"How can you say that? How can you say that on Samhain night?" The thought terrified me. Surely the dead would hear and come after us.

"The dead do not walk," Myrddin said.

"People have seen them," I said.

"They have not."

"They say they do," I insisted.

"That is a different matter."

"Aren't you afraid of anything?" I asked.

"I am not a fearful person. I try not to put myself in jeopardy needlessly, but that is caution, not fear."

"You sound like a Christian," I said accusingly.

40

"You must have a wider acquaintance with Christians than I do," Myrddin said.

"Don't you believe in anything?" I asked.

"Of course. I believe the sun will rise tomorrow unhindered by Samhain's passing."

"You don't believe the shamans?"

"About coupling at the edge of the firelight to start time swinging back through winter toward spring? No, I don't believe that."

"But it has always worked," I said.

"It will work when the practice is long forgotten. In the meantime, shamans are the exception to the rule that women must seek males for coupling on Samhain Night."

"It's a great honor to be chosen by a shaman," I said.

"Who says so?"

"They do."

"They would. Shamans are generally old and ugly, and no woman, not under some kind of duress, would look at one in that way. Shamans invented the practice to indulge their sexual appetites."

"They are forbidden sex any time but Beltane and Samhain," I said.

"You seem to be well informed for one so young."

"I was chosen by one of the shamans to be an apprentice, but my mother wouldn't let me go," I said. "I heard him and my mother argue about it."

"Your mother has extraordinary courage to defy a shaman," Myrddin observed.

"She's not from here. Her soul is safely hidden in her home village."

"That accounts for it, then. But even with the fear that people have for shamans, if they insisted on exercising their power sexually any more often, all the women would revolt. As it is, you don't find women seeking the honor of coupling with a shaman," he said dryly. That was true.

41

"They smell bad," Nithe remarked. "I won't sleep with one even when I'm grown."

Nithe seemed very intolerant of the way people smelled, I thought. As I considered this, I fell asleep, worn out by the experiences of the last six hours. I usually do not talk so freely with folk. I decided it must have been something in the minty drink Myrddin forced on me.

I woke up to the smell of food cooking, and sudden panic when I recalled what had occurred the night before. I peered over the edge of the wagon and Myrddin and Nithe looked up and smiled. I was not reassured. The sun was shining, and the pain was gone, as Myrddin had promised, but I felt wary.

I looked around me from my seat in the wagon. I had never traveled outside of our valley before and everything was new to me. Our village is in the hills west of the Clyde. We had journeyed east through the night and were camped on the banks of a stream.

"Is this the Clyde?" I asked. My voice was raspy from the screaming last night.

"Yes."

"It's not much," I said disparagingly. I had always thought the Clyde would be broad. How could a stream I could spit across keep the sea full? I know sometimes the waves slip over the world's rim and water falls into the void. I wondered what would happen to the sea if the Clyde dried up.

"This is near its source," Myrddin said. "We will leave it soon."

I got out of the wagon and sat across the fire from the two of them. Nithe brought me a trencher with slices of bacon broiled over the fire, good dark bread, cheese and a flagon of cool water from the river. She looked closely at me, but didn't speak. I felt as edgy as a roe deer who has left the shelter of the woods to graze.

Myrddin harnessed the oxen to the wagon and Nithe cleared up the remains of the meal, sluicing the trenchers in the small stream. I did not help either of them.

When all was ready, Myrddin turned to me. "Aren't you coming with us? It is unsafe for you to stay. If you are found you will be given to the druids to do with as they will. You would better have died on the stone."

"I don't know," I said.

"Are you concerned about what happened on the stone last night?"

"Of course," I said. It was a stupid question.

"You may not appreciate it yet, but I saved your life. I am truly sorry it was necessary to cause you so much pain, but there will be compensations. You will heal faster from other injuries in the future, because of the medicine I gave you."

"He's afraid," Nithe announced. "Who needs a baby, afraid of the dark? Let him stay." She climbed into the wagon and turned her head away from me disdainfully. Myrddin looked at me and shook his head sadly, and followed her, picking up the reins and clucking to the oxen to move forward. I let them go a few steps and rose, running, to slip over the back of the wagon. Neither of them acknowledged me. Little wisps of laughter escaped from Nithe from time to time, so they knew I was there. She thought she had tricked me. She hadn't. I was coming anyway.

We turned east and the land rose around us. There were mountains to the south and before us, but Myrddin followed a track that led us surely onward, and that evening we came upon another stream flowing from the south and turning east in a great bend just where we encountered it.

"What river is this?" I asked.

"It's called the Tweed," Myrddin said. "We will go along its bank for several days, cross it, and continue nearly to the sea."

"Why don't we just go south?" Nithe asked.

"Uther will be on that road within the next few days, not to mention Cathmor. Are you eager to meet either of them again so soon?"

It was as he said. The oxen walked about twelve Roman miles a day, according to Myrddin, and the path followed the river so it was longer than going cross-country on horseback. Still it was

43

interesting. Myrddin knew many things about the country we were passing through, and we moved so slowly there was time to ask many questions. Nithe sat on one side of him and I on the other. She asked three questions to one of mine.

At the end of the sixth day we came upon a Roman road running north and south. Myrddin said it was called the Ermine Way because of the trade in furs. It ran from Antonine's Wall in the north to Exeter in the southwest, across the length of the island. I was sorry not to see Antonine's Wall, for it ran from the mouth of the Clyde east to the sea as a barrier to keep Pictish wolves from Roman sheepfolds. Our village had been south of the wall, so it had not worked.

I marveled at the road. "How long has it been here?" I asked. It could have been laid down a week ago, it appeared so smooth, extending north and south as far as my eye could stretch.

"Several hundred years, at least," he said. "Romans build roads like they build walls. In fact, you might say they dig a ditch some four feet deep and build a wall in it."

We followed the road south for days until I could make out a wall that moved over the land like a great snake. I could see forts along its edge every mile or so, like beads on a string, and it looked impossible to cross.

"We are not going there, are we?" I asked, pointing at the obstacle that loomed in our path.

"That is Hadrian's Wall," Myrddin said. "It was built by an Emperor of Rome to protect his lands from raids by the fathers of your people, much like Antonine's Wall. However, it has only been defended by crows since Maximus pulled the legions into Gaul before Uther's time. There is naught to fear. The gates stand open."

And so they did. Furthermore we found a good stone-paved Roman road on the other side which hastened our journey south. We drove slowly, stretching the autumn season as we rode south, the oxen plodding the same two miles an hour they had covered since we started. This was richer country by far than the land where

44

I was raised, but not as beautiful. There were prosperous villages with markets along the route, centered on dirt roads running east and west. The people were Britons, but you could see Saxons from the west coast trading in the markets.

We had traveled for two months when the first deep frosts chilled us, and Myrddin declared we must rest for a time. We stopped in a nearly deserted Roman town with good stone buildings still standing, a town he said the Romans called Bath. Only a few peasants lived on one edge of the town, their huts clustered about a small tavern. It had hot springs and we warmed ourselves gratefully and had been there several days when the messenger found us.

"Be you the druid, Myrddin?" the man asked.

"Some call me that," the smith replied.

"I be sent by Uther, King, to fetch you to Tintagel."

"What is his need?"

The man turned his head carefully and spat before replying, "Lud, would I know? I'm sent to fetch." The man's scorn was warranted. Myrddin did not make distinctions between persons based on their condition as the run of men do, and treated everyone with unfailing courtesy. I had seen him display irritation only to those who might consider him an equal. While I liked him for it, it confused some people, and offended a few who were proud of some small distinction they had achieved. This man was a messenger. He did not need to know why he was sent with this or for that, only where he was to go, and whom he was to seek. He took pride in his objective ignorance. It was a badge of professionalism.

"Very well," Myrddin said. "Is there any time constraint?"

"Time is it? Uther, King, said be there by Auld St. Deere or not at all."

I thought of the rhyme, "Auld St. Deere, worst day of the year." It came nine months after Beltane and produced a crop of babies without fathers. Although babies are generally welcome among the Picts at any time because they are hard to raise, and are valuable, when grown, for their labor in the fields and with the herds, those born of the Beltane feast are considered unlucky. Gods come to lie with mortal maidens at Beltane, and their offspring tend to be ill-omened.

"Is Igraine that far along?" Myrddin asked.

"She looks ready to me," the messenger said, willing to give an opinion on his betters from his own observations. "Beltane was over before Uther took her to wife, but she and Gorlais were guests at Uther's Beltane feast." He sat by the roadside to inspect his feet, paying but little attention to us now that he had delivered his message. I was surprised to see him shod in leather as Uther had been. I still went barefoot.

"I see. How are the roads?"

"Passable. The mud is froze deep enough so oxen can pull a wagon over it. We have a fortnight," he added, consulting a notched stick.

"Still, better to be early than late," Myrddin said. "We'll be on the road by dawn tomorrow. You can rest your feet a day or two before you start back and still be able to report us a week before we arrive." Myrddin gave the man a small coin which he bit before touching his hand to his forelock and departing for the tavern.

"Is Igraine going to have a Beltane baby?" Nithe asked, looking wiser than her years.

"It looks like it," Myrddin replied.

"Why are we sent for?" Nithe continued with her questioning. Myrddin smiled. It was like Nithe to assume that a royal summons from the High King would include her.

"I'm not sure," Myrddin said. "It may be that Uther wants to move the child away from the court. A child of royalty with no sure father would be an unending source of intrigue. Its chance for survival would not be high, and Uther needs a son for the Oak King in eight more years."

"You told Uther it was a boy. What if it's a girl?" I asked.

"It is well known that the gods can change the sex of an unborn child."

46

"I never heard of that," I said.

"Perhaps Uther hasn't either, but he will not be so quick to admit ignorance," Myrddin said.

We drove over hill roads toward the sea, to Tintagel, not Lyoness. Myrddin was out in his reckoning for the weather warmed, and the roads were considerably worse than the messenger had claimed, but perhaps a man on foot could more easily avoid the quagmires that delayed us. As it was, we barely reached our destination by the appointed day. Still, while it was slow, it was pleasant. I felt no pressure to be anywhere on time, despite the king's summons, as the deep cold of winter had not yet set in. I was content only to be out of the hands of the druids. The nights were still bearable, sleeping in the open, and the days were wonderful, with brisk, light winds to keep the oxen from becoming overheated, though I wondered if we would not have been better off with hill ponies after all.

We arrived after dusk, and Myrddin left us in the wagon at Tintagel Castle's postern gate. We could see lights from a window high in the keep. Once or twice a woman cried out in pain from up there. Nithe slept wrapped in her wolfskin, and I dozed, waking as the oxen shifted their feet, more patient than I. I heard the gate creak, and Myrddin came to us with a bundle well wrapped in a fold of his cloak. He handed the baby to me, still damp from the midwife's bath.

"Take him under your plaid against the cold while I drive," he told me. I braced my back against the side of the wagon and held the baby against my chest, sheltered. He seemed asleep, which was a good thing, for I know not what I would have done else. Boys do not tend babies among the Picts. The wagon creaked as Myrddin settled his weight and with a gentle clucking to the oxen started us moving off. I may have slept before dawn but I was awake when the sun rose, shining dimly through the winter overcast. The baby opened his eyes as I took him out to look at. His stare was blank.

"Is he blind, Myrddin?" I asked.

"He sees very little as yet," Myrddin said. "It will be some months before he recognizes your face."

Nithe stirred and sat up suddenly. "Let me have him," she demanded, and I surrendered the baby to her care with no argument. The baby looked at her with the same blank gaze, but Nithe said, "He is aware, Myrddin."

"Truly?" Myrddin asked, and brought the wagon to a halt reaching out for the child. He examined him carefully before giving him back to Nithe and guiding the oxen to a grove beside the road to make breakfast.

"Well?" Nithe demanded.

"I agree. He is aware. It would seem to put who his father is beyond question. Gorlais was never one of us, nor is Igraine. It had to be Uther."

"Do you mean he can mind-speak?" I asked.

"Not yet, of course. He may never be able to do that. He can be reached much as Nithe can, however, but has no language yet. We will see."

"If he is Uther's son, he is also my brother," I stated.

"Yes."

"Give him back," I told Nithe. "I've never had a brother before." She surrendered the baby to me without comment, and I felt no self-consciousness in holding him this time. I marveled at it. A brother.

We drove into Exeter by afternoon, and the baby was beginning to fuss. I guessed it was hungry, for I was, and we had nothing to feed it. Myrddin went straight to the market at the edge of the town as one sure of his way.

"We will be able to hire a wet-nurse here unless things have changed since my last visit," he said. Myrddin pulled the wagon to an area reserved for buyers and we got down. I was stiff, but Myrddin reached for the baby so I could stretch the kinks out. He gentled the baby quiet. We must have looked odd, I thought. Myrddin stands a head taller than other men, even the Gaels, and is broad to boot. His long hair and full beard contrasted with the pink, bald baby whose face peered out from under the beard. Both Nithe and I have black hair, but my skin is also dark whereas hers is translucent, like a Saxon's. No one looking at us would think we belonged in the same family.

I had never visited a big market and the noise and smells were almost overwhelming. There were folk everywhere buying and selling goods, for some of which I could not imagine a use. Ignoring displays of baked stuff that set my mouth watering. Myrddin led our little procession up to a man standing before a cart on which a plump young woman sat, stripped to the waist. Her full breasts were oozing milk and the baby may have smelled it for he commenced to cry strenuously. At the sound, she looked up, milk now spurting from her breasts.

"Looking for a wet-nurse for that baby?" the man asked.

"Yes." said Myrddin. I said nothing, but that's no way to haggle. He should have said he wanted to sell a baby.

"Hand it over." the man said, and taking the baby gave it to the woman. She guided the baby's mouth to a nipple and the crying abruptly ceased to be replaced by a slurping sound as it nursed.

"See how it takes to her?" the man said. "For only seven gold pieces, your search is over."

"That's a high price for a meal." Myrddin said. "I could buy three cows and a calf for seven gold." I nodded. That was better.

The man stared for a moment and guffawed, slapping his knee. "That's a good one, master."

"Would you like to come with us?" Myrddin asked the young woman.

"Here now, she's got nothing to say about it. She's my property, branded legal and all. You make your deal with me and she'll do anything you say. Anything at all." he repeated slyly, sidling up to Myrddin and nudging him sharply with his elbow.

Nithe ignored the interchange, watching the girl nurse the baby. The baby was covered with fine, golden hair, and not just his head, for he had no hair to speak of, but his whole body was covered with fuzz.

"I shall call him 'Bear,' " Nithe announced.

"Is he yours, then?" the girl asked with a quick smile. Nithe looked at her teasing face a moment, and smiled back.

"I'm only seven, but I know where babies come from," she said, moving closer. I followed her, and for the first time saw the girl's back. Nithe was staring at it with fierce concentration. It was a mass of raw welts as if someone had beaten her with a whip, very hard and very long. Nithe turned back to the peasant who was haggling with Myrddin, reaching into the little purse that hung from her belt. It contained seven gold pieces that Myrddin had given her for her birthday, one for each year of her life, and which she had shown me once a day over the many weeks I had been with her. She walked up to the peasant and flung the coins at his feet.

"There's your money," she said. "I'll buy her." The man looked at her with amazement, and stooped to retrieve the coins. He turned to Myrddin.

"You heard her, master, she gave me full price." Myrddin shrugged and looked at me for an explanation.

"It's her back," I said. "It's been cut to pieces."

"And why not?" the man said. "She's a slut, whoring around and getting pregnant. Serves her right."

"Where is her baby?" Myrddin asked.

"Ah, it had no father. You know how those things are. Well?" Myrddin nodded grimly and the man turned to Nithe and said patronizingly, "She's yours, little mistress. She'll give good service or send for me and I'll touch her up again to remind her of her duty." He raised his cudgel and the girl cringed, bending over Bear to shield him from the blow. Before it landed, Myrddin grasped his wrist and sent the stick flying. Nithe jumped between the girl and the man with her belt knife drawn as I watched.

"How dare you?" she cried. The man stretched out a hand, and she slashed at it, nicking a finger. He yelped and stuck it in his mouth. took it out. looked at it doubtfully and glared at Nithe. I moved beside her.

"You cut me." he said reproachfully.

"If my arm were longer. I'd have killed you," Nithe said. her voice choked with anger.

"She is a princess in her own country." Myrddin lied. "Those of us who serve her are aware of her temper and do nothing to provoke it." That last part was true.

"Well, she's not in her own country now." the man blustered.

"How fortunate for you." I said. following Myrddin's lead. "or you would have lost more than a few drops of blood."

Myrddin turned away from the man and addressed the girl. "We will go when you are ready," he said.

"Not while the baby's eating." she replied firmly. her eyes on Bear. who was already fastened greedily to her breast. The man drifted off. grumbling. retrieved his stick and walked away. glancing over his shoulder at us from time to time. When he judged he had reached a safe distance. he made a rude gesture and half ran to lose himself in the crowd. No one but me was watching.

"You surprised me." Myrddin said to Nithe.

"The baby likes her." Nithe replied.

"How do you know?"

"His mind is aware. like I said. I can tell he likes her." Not only could Nithe project emotions with her mind. evidently she could receive emotions of others as well. As we left. I made a resolution to guard my feelings around her. or I would have no secrets.

The girl's name was Anna. When she was satisfied the baby was full. she insisted that Myrddin buy her some strips of soft linen to diaper and swaddle it. saying it would be a stinking mess to travel with else. She seemed sure of herself for one who had been so abused. but what she said was plain sense and Myrddin gave her a few handfuls of nails to barter for whatever she needed. She was much better at it than he was.

She had a sunny nature. and soon took over the role of cook for the company. claiming it as her right. She was not as good with sauces as Myrddin, according to him, but I was used to simple fare and I liked her food better. I also liked her. She kept Nithe away from me and managed the baby to Nithe's satisfaction, a duty I would not willingly have sought. Myrddin exchanged several knives for a warm cloak with a hood and gave it to her. She was more grateful for having a possession of that quality than for the salve he rubbed on her back, easing it of pain overnight. She would do anything for him, without complaint, another performance I could not match.

The truth is, Myrddin is sometimes testy and given to arbitrary and unusual demands. He made me bathe daily, as if I were a Gael, and did so himself so that I could only make faces at the cold water instead of complaining. I could not see the use of it, for we did not sweat, riding in the wagon. I took to walking alongside of the oxen, talking to them, both to ease my legs and to give me something to wash off in the evening.

We traveled to the port at the mouth of the Exe River to look for boats, and Myrddin found one to his liking, eight paces long and four wide. It was made of oxhide, sewn with linen thread and waterproofed with wool grease. There was no deck, and I thought the boat would soon be filled with water coming over the side, but it looked dry enough at dock. There was one mast with a square sail, hanging from a yard no wider than the boat. A steering oar was lashed to a rig fixed to the stern, and it looked clumsy, but not different from the boats the Picts use for fishing. As with the Pict boats, this one had oars as well. I like boats.

I stripped to the waist and dove under the boat to inspect it while Myrddin haggled with the owner. It was clean-bottomed, and newly greased. Myrddin dislikes haggling, and parted with both oxen and the wagon in exchange for the boat. He ended up buying extra linen sails, oak water casks and watertight food and clothing chests. He knew what I thought of that. Since I kept my mouth shut about it, so did he, but he was grumpy with unvented spleen.

We slept aboard to accustom ourselves to the movement of the sea and sailed the next morning with the tide.

"Where are we going?" Nithe asked. I had wondered too, but would not ask, to avoid the possibility of being snubbed. She always spoke her mind, regardless of consequences.

"To Ector's Isle in Lyoness," he replied, in a voice which did not invite further questions, though there was no one to overhear. I wondered if anyone had marked our passage, and whether word would drift back to Uther or the druids that a tall Pictish boy was in Myrddin's company. I had felt safe in the wagon for we had spoken to few folk, but in a busy port were many extra eyes and ears. They could be listening and looking for anyone. Even me. I touched the pink scar that ran across my belly and hoped there would be no druids on Ector's Isle.

CHAPTER IV

We sailed southwest along the coast, bordered by cliffs where I could see eagle nests high up in the rocks. The great birds soared in the air, stooping at the sea and often as not flying off with a fish in one claw back to the cliff to eat. There were no young to feed at this season. Instead of turning when we got to land's end we kept sailing in the same direction into the open sea. Nithe's face had the stubborn look she assumes when things do not please her, but Myrddin merely looked remote and preoccupied. I caught Anna's eye and she winked and hid a smile by bending over Bear. Even Myrddin called the baby that now, although he resisted it at first.

There was an offshore breeze that took us southwest at the rate of a man walking fast. Even so, the sun was past noon when we first sighted breakers and finally several small islands. Myrddin steered toward one of the two larger ones and pulled the boat into a natural harbor. I jumped out and splashed ashore, hauling on the bowline, and dragged the boat up the gravel shingle until it rested on its oak skid.

"This is Ector's Island," Myrddin announced. "It is part of Lyoness," and glared at Nithe when she giggled. She resumed her stubborn expression. It was a long way from anything, and I could in some part understand Myrddin being depressed and foul of mood from the necessity of spending time in such an out-of-the-way spot. Since the need to stay hidden was as much on my account as Bear's, I did not comment on it. Nithe was silent out of policy.

It was good to be someplace, however, and I liked what I could see of this. There were flowers everywhere. The air was warmer here than on the mainland, and the smell of the warm sea breeze was exhilarating. It seemed a good place to hide, and I hoped Uther never found out I was with Myrddin's party. I knew I could not survive the terror of another night on the black stone. Uther would not allow it.

Out of the shadow of the cliff a stout man limped toward us. He was dressed simply in sandals, a woolen tunic and short cloak and was accompanied by several workmen similarly attired. They soon had the boat well up on the beach once Nithe, Myrddin, Anna and Bear had debarked. I looked at him and his men closely. They worked like disciplined men, crisply and attentive to duty, and I realized these were Romans, probably soldiers who had taken discharge here rather than return home. Their leader must be Ector, who, Myrddin said, had been wounded fighting beside Uther, and who had taken service with him when the Romans discharged him as unfit for duty.

"We saw you coming from the headland," the leader observed in good Welsh, paying scant attention to Myrddin to whom the words were addressed. He was looking at Anna, who seemed to be oblivious. He turned back to Myrddin. "Welcome," he said, belatedly. "I had word from Uther to expect you and to prepare quarters for your party."

"My thanks, Ector. A small house with room for a smithy would do nicely," Myrddin replied.

"We were hoping you would consent to do a little iron work while you're here," Ector said.

"I could hardly expect guest status for the next eight years,"

Myrddin said dryly. At the look of surprise that crossed Ector's face, Myrddin continued, "I can see you are not aware of what Uther really wants. We are to stay here until called for, and that probably means until the baby is old enough to be fostered in Armorica. Eight years is about what he has in mind."

"No, Uther did not indicate what he expected. The messenger said you would have full instructions."

"You now know all that I know. It won't be so bad. I can find enough work to pay our way even in an isolated place like this. I brought iron and tools along with that in mind."

"Then, you are doubly welcome. Come with me and I'll bring you up to Lady Ellen. My men will carry your gear." He had not looked at me, but I planned to stay with the boat until Myrddin called for me, anyway. I was correct in this, for Myrddin nodded to me.

"Pelleas," he said. "Help unload. You know where everything is. Pelleas is my apprentice," he said to Ector as they walked off up the cliff path, followed by Nithe and by Anna with Bear. Their voices carried to where I worked with the men, choosing what would be needed right away, and what could safely wait.

"He's a Pict, Myrrdin," Ector was saying. "We have rules about that. Pict raiders stop off to join with the bloody Scoti and Allacoti and then come cruising down our coasts burning and plundering every spring as soon as the March winds start, and just as regularly. We watch the smoke rise from village after village on the mainland, and wonder if they'll turn back before they reach here or not. This place is too small to hide in, and too big to defend with the men I have. I'll be damned if I'll have a Pict opening my doors from the inside to let them in. I don't even want him on the island!"

I paid no attention at first, but I suddenly noticed the men were staring at me and nudging one another. Ector was talking about me!

"He's my apprentice," Myrrdin said as I looked in vain for a place to hide my face. "I'll be responsible for him, and anyway,

56

he's only half-Pict. Look at the size of him at nine, if you have any doubt of that."

"Nine? He's nine like I have nine balls! Why he's nearly as tall as I am!" That was true. "Half Pict! What's the other half, Geen?" He snorted with laughter at his own wit, though I had no idea what a Geen was.

"Why not?" Myrddin replied. "Anyway, I speak you truth. There are reasons associated with our being here which require his presence that I can't explain, but which are compelling. He must stay. Trust me."

"Stay, is it? Well, have him stay away from me, that's all I ask," Ector said as they reached the crest of the hill and further words were lost to me.

From then on I was known as "the Geen," by all of the islanders. Nithe continued to call me Dog's-brother occasionally when she was pleased with me for some reason. Anna called me Pelleas, as did Myrddin to my face, and "that boy" when speaking about me, but no one else gave me my name.

Myrddin came back with Ector to look over the amount of goods Myrddin had brought with him, enough to set up his smithy with stock for a year or more. The great anvil was still in the boat, for I would not let the men move it, fearing they would drop it through the bottom. Myrddin moved it easily.

"I will set up my smithy near a spring, if you have one here. I need the pure water to temper the iron. I'll live near it with my household, the better to safeguard my stores against theft, if that's agreeable."

"There are no thieves on this island," Ector said, and then added, glancing on me, "at least until now."

"Perhaps it's only that there has been nothing worth stealing until now," Myrddin rasped back, irritated, at last, by Ector's remarks. That night he camped with me on the beach, allowing only Anna and the children to take advantage of Ector's hospitality. The reason he had given then was security for his goods, but no one had been deceived. Ector would not let me under his roof. Before it was dark, however, Nithe, Anna and the baby came back down the cliff. Nithe refused to stay with Ector without Myrddin, and Anna followed her, explaining to a scandalized Lady Ellen, Ector's good wife, that she was Nithe's property. Myrddin did not send her back on hearing her story, which surprised me. He sets great store on people obeying him.

We were a tired and silent group, and went early to bed, sleeping on the boat, which we launched to rock gently at anchor. The only sound was Myrddin muttering to himself on "the intransigence of country gentry being matched only by the stubbornness of girl children." The next morning Ector's bailiff appeared and took us to a sheltered site near the cliff edge where a small spring sparkled in the sunlight.

"This is the place," Myrddin said. "We will build here. Have some timbers brought, if you will," he said to the bailiff, "and we will pay for them with iron tools. I would also like the help of some laborers, skilled in carpentry, whom I will hire for coin or goods, as they please." The bailiff was evidently instructed to comply with Myrddin's wishes without debate, for he said nothing past a grunt of assent.

Workmen arrived before noon with several wagonloads of squared timber, and we had the frames for two small buildings up by dark. Within two days' time we filled the space between the bracing timbers with stone and mud, and a week later the thatched roof was in place. One of the buildings was for sleeping and storage, and the other for cooking and smithing, with a porch under which the anvil was set near the spot he planned to build a forge. The structures were removed from one another by ten feet of space to keep the thatch in the sleeping and storage room from catching fire and burning us up as we slept. There was no fire in that one, ever, save for a lamp at night.

The only iron in either building were hinges that swung the doors, an innovation much admired by the workmen. They asked to be paid in hinges, and nails to fasten them to the doorposts of their own houses.

Our sleeping arrangements were as private as Myrddin could make them. Bear slept with Anna, and Myrddin, Nithe and I had each our own cubicle built into the wall, with a curtain to seal us off from each other's eyes. There was not much modesty shown, nor much curiosity, but the rule set down by Myrddin was that when the curtain was drawn others did not intrude.

I drew my curtain against faces that showed sympathy and concern a few days after we arrived. I could hear a hurley game in progress one warm afternoon, took my stick and ran to join in, as I would at home. But, when I dashed onto the field, the boys set upon me, wrested my stick from my hands and broke it over my back, sending me away in tears of rage. I already knew the bruises would heal overnight, a lasting effect of the minty draft Myrddin gave me on the altarstone, but there was no medicine to cure the hurt inflicted by the names I was called. "Dirty Pict," it was, and "Geen." I crept in to my cubicle and pulled the curtain, shutting off the questions.

"He can't do that!" Nithe objected to Myrddin.

"He has done it," Myrddin said with finality.

I did not come out to supper, sunk in my private misery, but when night had fallen I got hungry. Anna had saved me some stew and kept it warm by the fire. She went to get it, but returned immediately with blood streaming down her face. Folk in the night had waited for someone to go outside, and thrown rocks as soon as the lighted doorway gave them a target. Myrddin stanched the blood and washed the wound, which was not deep. Comforting Anna and calming Nithe at the same time, one would think nothing had happened beyond a slight domestic mishap until one saw his face. His eyes were fierce. It was all I needed by way of permission. I covered the lamp, took my sling and my bag of river-washed pebbles and was out the door unseen by those outside. They were taunting, now, with "dirty Pict" and "Pict-lover" being the names most commonly used.

I slipped into the shadows where I could not be seen, and got behind them, where they were silhouetted by the light of the half-moon. They were right. I am a Pict, and I have a Pict's night eyes. The stones I threw were not big enough to kill a man, but they could break teeth. I yelled to turn them, a dozen or so of the same boys and young men who had driven me from the hurley field. They could not see me, but I could see them, and one by one I found them with my sling. When they rushed where they thought I was, I was already in a new place. Finally they fled, and I followed them, marking each one at least once before they scattered to their homes. When they turned their dogs loose, I was waiting, and sent them off howling on three legs. I was king of the night.

I came in briefly to tell Myrddin they were gone, but that I would stand watch outside. He grunted in assent and then found it necessary to explain to Nithe why she could not join me. I grinned as I went back into the darkness, climbing a tree where I could see down the path toward the village. I thought about it, and decided I would have liked it better if I had been allowed to play. The Gaels had always treated us as if we were inferior to them, but since we could beat them at hurley, none of us boys really believed it. This was different. These Romans hated me.

I came to breakfast early, sleepy from being up all night. "Do you want to know what I've been doing?" I asked.

"Anything I wouldn't have done?" Myrddin asked.

I considered the question. "No," I decided.

"Then it's not necessary," Myrddin replied. I ate and retired to my cubicle. I was awakened by angry voices.

"I tell you he attacked my people!" a voice shouted. I peeked out. It was Ector.

"And I'll tell you something," Myrddin replied. He loomed over the other man, his hands clenching and unclenching at his sides. "I am not answerable to you. My people are not answerable to you. We are Uther's guests, not yours. Do you really think you will be allowed to stay here if I report to him that you have so little control over your people that they assaulted his son's nurse, and could possibly have killed him?"

"What is this you are saying?" Ector replied, stepping back to gaze up at Myrddin's eyes.

"If you wish to know, and to escape sure and merciless punishment, you will bring those who attacked the inhabitants of this house to me before the sun sets. And now, if you please, leave me. I find I do not have as sure a control over my own temper as I might wish." He didn't shout, but there was no need. Ector turned and left. I grinned as I went back to sleep.

I had risen and was straightening out stock in the storage area near the smithy when next Ector appeared, leading the boys from the hurley field. I was gratified to see they all bore marks of my sling. They stood in a loose group behind Ector, facing our hut.

"I am here, Myrddin," he called out. "I have brought with me those who were attacked and injured by the wild Pict you harbor. What have you to say to them?" The boys had eyes only for me as I continued to work, ignoring them. Their faces were sullen, and only threats delivered by Ector before they arrived served to keep them from attacking me anew.

The door opened and Myrddin came out, dressed in the long, white, hooded robe I had seen last in the oak grove. He carried a golden sickle in one hand, which I remembered well. As he walked toward Ector, he and the boys stepped back in alarm and I found myself moving into the shadows away from him. Myrddin turned and came toward the smithy, stopping under the great oak that sheltered it before turning again and facing Ector and the boys.

"Hear me, then," he said, his deep voice heavy with emotion. "Each of you must swear here and now on this anvil, to Weyland Hammerhand, the warrior's god, that you will protect the heir of the High King, and those in his service, with your lives. This trust comes to you by command of Uther the Pendragon of Britain. Your fathers swore such an oath to him. Will their sons do less to his son?" He had them. Even Ector stepped forward.

As he spoke, Anna came quietly to his side, carrying Bear. She was simply dressed, with her hair flowing over her shoulders and her eyes downcast. Bear was naked, his eyes open and looking around. The picture they made together of vulnerable mother and child appealed to the boys in a way that made Myrddin's words understandable. Of course they would protect them! Nithe had followed Anna, at her own insistence, but kept her peace as she had promised Myrrdin.

"This is your future king," Myrrdin said, "and his nurse and sister. Each of you will kneel before him, touch his hand and swear allegiance." They crowded up, each wishing to be first, and Anna raised her eyes and smiled at them. It was enough. One of them had thrown the rock that cut her scalp the night before, but they would shed their own blood for her without a thought from this time on.

Next, with Anna watching, Myrddin cut each boy's hand with the point of his sickle and dripped blood on the anvil. Anna handed Bear to Nithe to hold, and draped a leather baldric attached to a sheathed saxeknife over each initiate's shoulder, kissing him in the process to conclude the ceremony. It was most effective. I wished I could have been one of them, though I feared the sickle.

"Take these boys home and train them to be warriors," Myrddin instructed Ector. "It is time they stopped playing boys' games and took on the responsibilities of men."

Ector gave Myrddin a look that I interpreted as one of admiration mixed with dry chagrin. Myrddin had solved the problem of the boys' hostility at no cost to himself. Ector would have to find the time to train the boys, not Myrddin. He led them away, shaking his head.

Myrddin went back into the house, dressed in work clothes and joined me in the smithy. He brought a pail of soapy water with him and proceeded to wash the blood from the anvil.

"I thought you said you were not a druid," I said, still disturbed by his appearance with the golden sickle-knife.

"I am not," he said in a tranquil voice, much pleased with himself, I thought from the tone.

"How could you administer an oath to Weyland Hammerhand, then?" I asked.

"I administered no oath," he said, glancing at me sideways.

I realized he spoke the truth. He hadn't. "Who is Weyland Hammerhand?" I asked suspiciously.

"I haven't the faintest idea," he answered, humming a tune I did not recognize.

He put an end to the questioning by asking if I thought the mud with which we had stuck the stones of the forge together would be dry enough to risk a fire. Consulted in this fashion, I dropped the subject of druidry, and entered happily into talk about smithing. I really do know a lot about mud.

I had hoped to have seen no more of the boys, but every evening one or two would come to sit under the tree with Anna. What they talked about I do not know, for I paid them no attention. I believe Anna talked very little, being content to smile from time to time, showing no preference for one over another. It amused Myrddin and suited Nithe for she had Bear to herself for once. I looked at Anna with new eyes. She was very pretty.

The smithing went well. We were busy almost from that first day. We had to make hinges first, to pay the workmen as we had promised, and by that time Ector's bailiff had brought in everything from the manse that needed fixing. Ector also wanted a stock of weapons for an armory that Uther had requested be built against the possibility of Saxon raids, although there had been none in anyone's memory. The fisher folk wanted nails, fishhooks and tie-rings for their boats, and Myrddin taught me to make them. The tempering of fishhooks is a nice art. If they are made too hard they break; if the iron is left too soft they will twist so that the fish escape.

I was so busy that I almost didn't mind not having any friends my own age. Myrddin had affairs that took him to see Ector and he often went to inspect the training of the boys at Ector's request.

He brought them blunted weapons to get them used to the weight of the real thing, both spearheads and swords. They could be sharpened to be used in reality should the need arise. They used shields and helmets from the new armory, and we made extra cap bands and nose pieces, shield rims and bosses as the training exercises wore out the armory stock.

In the smithy, when work slowed down, Myrddin showed me tricks I would not expect to learn until I had spied them out for myself. Each morning I rose early, as did Anna, she to her kitchen and I to the smithy to blow up the fire. We would eat together in companionable silence, hot soup made the previous day and day-old bread toasted over the coals. Her ear was always tuned to Bear and at his first cry she would leave to bring him into the warm kitchen to feed. He ate greedily, making noises of content-ment. When she changed his diaper afterward I would leave, driven out by the sight, to her amusement.

Spring gave way to summer, summer to fall, and it was winter again, the difference being that Bear was nearly two, walking and into everything. Myrddin was forced to put his harp and all else of value up high on shelves, or hung from the beams with thongs, or tied in bundles in hard knots so Bear's hands could not examine them. Myrddin finally built a small house for himself on the edge of the cliff overlooking the sea when he discovered he could keep his things safe from Bear in no other way. Myrddin also liked to meditate from time to time and needed the quiet. In truth, he was not cut out for family life, and I wondered at his continued patience with us all. Nithe would not be parted from him, however, and carried her pallet over herself as soon as he left the smithy, bedding down in a corner of his new house. For the rest, Bear was free to explore, always under Anna's tolerant eye, and overseen by Nithe, who bossed him unceasingly. He paid her absolutely no mind, but it relieved the rest of us from her ministrations.

He liked me, and often as not insisted on sitting on my lap rather than Anna's or Nithe's of an evening. I felt the honor keenly. He spoke to me in Pictish, a few words only, but understandable. He spoke Jutish to Nithe, who was raised with them until Myrddin took her. He spoke Latin to Myrddin and Welsh to Anna. How he was able to learn so quickly to distinguish one language from the other I did not know, but Myrddin said he associated the sounds with the speaker. Perhaps that was so.

I became aware I was continuing to grow when Anna remarked on it one morning at breakfast. "Are you any kin to the master?" she asked. She never referred to Myrddin by name.

"I don't think so," I said.

"I wondered why he came looking for you, then."

It had never occurred to me that he had come looking for me. I frowned, recollecting. I remember he said he had stayed for fear that I would be chosen for the Oak King but nothing about why he had come. I shook my head, and looked at her.

"Well, it's just that you look like him. Your hair and eyes are darker, maybe, but the color of his could have faded with age. You're built just like him, and the way you have patterned your walk after his make you look like father and son." She giggled at some vision she had of us.

"But he's enormous!" I objected.

"You're growing," Anna said. "You stoop when you come in the door now." The workmen had made the house after the ones they were familiar with, and the doorways were tall enough for them. "Let me measure you, and we'll keep track," she suggested. And so we did. Anna stood on a stool and measured me against the wall, scratching a mark with my belt knife on the day after each new moon through the winter and spring and the spring after and I grew the width of her forefinger every time.

If Bear was two, I was thirteen in real years, although only ten by Samhain count. I had noticed other changes in myself, hair around my crotch, under my arms and on my chest and my voice was uncertain in the high register when we sang with Myrddin's harp of an evening. I could talk about this to Anna, who never laughed at me when I confided in her. She said I ought to look for a girl. I didn't know where. I was not welcome at the manse, and the fisher folk kept to themselves, discouraging visitors. No women ever came to the smithy.

Two years passed before Myrddin decided we needed a dependable supply of charcoal and pig iron as the stocks we had brought with us became diminished. He sought out the leaders of the fisher folk and struck a bargain with them to trade fish and finished iron goods in Cornwall for the materials he needed in exchange for products of the forge. He spent much time traveling with them, accumulating stocks, and we saw little of him. With nothing to do, I was able to spend more time with Nithe and Bear, and found Nithe with a problem. At four Bear had discovered the sea, and was not happy far from it. She was afraid he would drown.

All Picts swim, at least those of my village. We were close enough to the sea there to bathe daily if we chose, and did so in clement weather. I understood the attraction it had for Bear. The water is warmer here, and it is possible to stay in it for hours without becoming too chilled if you are swimming. Bear was delighted with the new skill, for he took to it as naturally as walking, or running, rather, for he never walked. Nithe was apprehensive, but would not allow it to be said she was afraid, and before summer was over, the three of us spent much time in the water.

Almost from the first days I had traded hooks to the fisher folk to keep our boat repaired, thinking we might need it again to flee from Uther, and not wanting to see it rot. Now that I had no fear of Bear or Nithe falling overboard, I took them out boating, teaching them to steer, and handle the sail, though they were too small still to do more than help. They learned to read wind and water in our sheltered bay, and would sit beside me on the thwart, one on each side, pulling with me when I rowed.

When Myrddin came back and we began smithing again there seemed to be no reason to discuss this, so we didn't. Bear and Nithe were gone all day, out from under foot, and we were busy.

One morning, however, when I blew on the banked coals to light the fire, Myrddin entered and said, "Let it die out, and clean the fire pit. There isn't anything in the island left to mend."

"We can make new things," I said.

"What new things? We have enough horseshoes for every horse in Lyoness over the next three years. There isn't a farmer or a fisherman on this island who hasn't replaced his leather door hinges with iron ones from our forge, and I've pounded out tenpenny nails until I see them in my sleep. Let us do something else for awhile."

Bear came running into the smithy with Nithe chasing him. He got to me before she could catch him, and lifting him high above her head, I stood him on my shoulders, out of her reach. He balanced easily, holding on to my raised hand.

"It's not funny, Bear," she scolded, arms folded over a fat stomach. "Anna says you have to take a bath this morning."

"I did yesterday," he objected.

"A real bath, Bear, with hot water and soap!"

"Let's go sailing instead," Bear said.

"That's what we'll do," Myrddin exclaimed. "First, however, I must teach you to swim. Then, when I am satisfied everyone can survive falling overboard, we'll do some sailing."

"I can swim already," Nithe said.

"Me, too," said Bear.

"Actually, they're both right," I said. "Bear insists on playing on the beach and begging rides from the fishermen, so I taught him months ago. Nithe wouldn't let him in the water alone and learned along with him."

"I didn't need to learn. My mother is a water nymph," Nithe objected.

"Well," Myrddin said, with a raised eyebrow, "if you swim we can make plans. Let's examine the boat and see what repairs are needed."

I was embarrassed. "The boat needs no work," I said. "The

fisher folk have kept it up in exchange for hooks. I sail it sometimes when there is nothing else to do."

"We go with him," Nithe said.

"Why was I not told of this?" Myrddin asked.

"I didn't think you'd be interested," I replied, knowing that was not the truth, and wondering if he would show one of his rare bursts of anger.

"Have you been fishing, too?" he asked in a calm voice.

"No," I said. "We don't go far out enough for that."

"Good! Then there is still something left for me to teach you. Nithe, ask Anna for food to take along and we'll spend the day on open water. You take a quick bath as Anna wishes, Bear, and join us on the beach." They scrambled to obey.

Myrddin is a master sailor and knows the sea in all its moods. We sailed and fished in any weather through the seasons, the four of us, learning to live on the water without fear. I am not timid. Wild things in the woods have never frightened me, and even the Oak King no longer held any terror for me, but I had been less sure about the sea. However, it became as familiar as the land, and I took pleasure in being out on it.

We browned in the sun, with Myrddin and me stripped to our breechclouts and Nithe and Bear naked to the breeze. Now and then one of us would jump into the sea and swim around the boat in sheer exuberance. Time stood still for us and we were happy, working, playing and storytelling, but we grew, me and Nithe and Bear. Only Myrddin seemed unchanged.

I measured myself against Myrddin, frequently, lifting what he lifted, rowing when he rowed. He knew it, but ignored it. Though I was not his equal yet, I hoped to surpass him when a few more years knit my sinews more tightly together. Time and work at the forge had changed my body from that of a boy to that of a man. Fishing, however, was not work. We caught only enough for our household, using lines with hooks, rather than nets, knowing the fisher folk would not welcome our competition.

"The weather's blowing up," Myrddin said on one gusty day in late summer when we had been out since dawn. "A squall is coming, and I'm too hungry to spend the night trying to get in against the wind. Reef the sail and let's start rowing toward the lee side of the island."

Nithe and Bear lowered the sail while Myrddin and I manned the two sets of oars. We moved well against the waves, and I felt no anxiety. I didn't care if we did have to spend the night at sea. It was then that Nithe spied the overturned coracle. She and Bear sat on either side of the steering oar, holding our course steady, though Myrddin and I could direct the boat well enough without that.

"Look, Myrddin," she cried. "People are clinging to that boat. They'll drown!"

"Steer for them," he ordered, gesturing with his lips to where she was pointing. When we got close I saw a blond head disappear beneath the surface and, shipping my oars, dove over the side, swimming strongly toward the spot. By the time I had reached the girl and lifted her up, the boat was beside us, and Myrddin took her from my upraised hands, her long hair wound around her face and shoulders like a shroud.

I turned to the coracle and found a fisherman still clinging to it. He would not loosen his hold, panicky at the thought of drowning, and I had to guide the coracle to where he could transfer his grip to the side of the curragh himself. Our freeboard is so low that it took little effort to tumble him into the boat after that. As an afterthought, I dove under the coracle and found a line hanging loose in the water. I gave the line into Bear's hand, and rolled the boat over. Coracles are very light, being only greased oxhide stretched over a frame of split ash. I rocked it back and forth until most of the water was cleared and it bounced on the waves before I heaved myself back into the curragh.

Bear had tied the line to the stern-thwart. He and Nithe were having trouble keeping the curragh's bow facing into the waves, so I unshipped my oars and started rowing back toward shore. Myrddin was working over the girl as her father watched.

"She's coughing, master. She's alive!" the man cried. At his voice, the girl sat up convulsively and stretched out her arms blindly. The man held her tightly, half in shock himself, and she sobbed without stopping. Myrddin joined me at the oars and we brought them in safely.

On the beach the man turned to me and said, "That was the bravest thing ever I saw, the way you went after my daughter. You must come to the house so her mother can thank you."

"It's not needful," I replied, realizing it may have sounded sullen even as I said it. I was only surprised, and not used to folk outside of my family speaking to me.

"Yes it is," Myrddin interrupted. "I'll bring him myself."

"Why?" I asked, after they left, and we were dragging the two boats above the reach of the tide. "There was nothing to it."

"He thought there was. The fisher folk don't swim."

"But I don't need thanks for such a thing," I insisted.

"He's one of the leaders of the fishermen on the island. He will praise you to his people and maybe this Pict nonsense will die out for good."

"It doesn't bother me," I said untruthfully.

"Well, it does me," he growled, and I let it rest.

CHAPTER V

Myrddin said the man's name was Bran, but that I was not to call him that, or anything else, as names are given only as pledges of friendship or other obligation, when, true to his word, we called on the family the next day and I was invited into a house not my own for the first time on the island. The floor was cut into the earth so as to be below the frost line to take advantage of the earth's natural heat in winter. We did the same at home. The main room was big, perhaps five paces across, enough to hold a dozen men seated comfortably on furs of seals and fox skins sewn into robes.

The girl hid her face on seeing me, but not because I was a Pict. She was merely shy, and had been told by her family how I had saved her life. She appeared to be about my age with the fresh good looks that distinguish the young fisher folk here. I had noticed her more than once before on the beach helping to unload the fish after a successful run.

Myrddin and I sat in a circle of men on the floor and ate pork as a change from the fish which was their usual fare, I guessed. I was placed on Bran's right, the seat of honor, and Myrddin on his left. The girl served me first and I glanced at Myrddin. Anna always serves him first. He smiled.

The girl sat behind me, brushing up against me as she helped me to more food, or filled my wooden tankard with beer. I was very conscious of her warmth and smell and the soft pressure of her body, and had trouble concentrating on much else. What the others thought of this I had no idea, but no one seemed to notice.

Bran addressed me in Pictish, and I responded, surprised.

"I had not thought to hear my language again," I said. "You do me much honor."

"The fisher folk are Picts descended from the old tribes," he replied. "Ector and his men have been here but a few years, and know little about us. Over the years the Gaels fled here, pursued by Britons, and the Britons pursued by the Romans. Some of them stayed and intermarried, and we use several languages at need, but we do not forget who we were. Mostly we just keep to ourselves."

The family's acceptance of me went far in changing the behavior of others toward me, as Myrddin had predicted. The fisher folk greeted me when I met them on the beach or the path. Ector's people still ignored me, for the most part, even when scolded by Anna, but no overt hostility was shown me even by them. I took to visiting Bran's household and sitting under the oak that shaded it, to talk with the girl.

The better I knew her, the more beautiful she came to be in my mind. She was tall for a person of this stock, and I suspected one of the Gaels who took refuge here in generations past had been an ancestor. Her hair was red, but a darker shade than that usually found among the Gaels, more like a roan horse in color, and she was funny. She teased me for my sober ways, making light of concerns I had about people not liking me, so that I came to have a better opinion of myself. It was a joy for me to be with her, and I took to spending every minute I could in her company, all but neglecting my duties at the forge. Fortunately work there was light, and Myrddin was tolerant of my absences, happy to see me in good spirits at last. No one else noted unless I missed story hour, but that happened rarely, for her family retired early at night. They had no lamps such as Myrddin owned.

She confided to me that she did not like her name much, being called after her father, who had no sons. Bronwyn, it was, which I thought very pretty, and said so. I was aware of the trust shown me in revealing her name, and gave her mine in return. She said her family wished her to marry to bring a man into the family to help her father, but that no one she knew interested her. They were not pressing her, however, for she was still very young.

"Your family will not arrange a match for you?" I asked.

"Oh, no," she said. "My father would never bid me marry at all if I did not wish it. It is my mother who has spoken to me about it, for she thinks he works too hard. She feels guilty because she has not given him a son. Still, he has many brothers and cousins, and owns his own boat. There are always people who want to go with him. Even I do, sometimes, though maybe not again," she added, shuddering.

"I have two years to serve in my apprenticeship," I blurted. "I will not be free to marry until it is over." I made no promises, but I kissed her for the first time that evening; and went home making plans.

While I was discovering what a girl was, Nithe and Bear were discovering soldiers. Myrddin took them down to review Bear's soldiers, for such they were, and both the children were made much of. The young men fashioned wooden swords for both of them, and wooden shields, and Myrddin was persuaded to make small helmets for each of them. They insisted on going back again and again, and when they were given small hill ponies of their very own they joined their soldiers every day. The boat was forgotten in the excitement of the new experience, and we went no more sailing. Myrddin told me that the children drilled, undergoing the same exercises the young men did, and with less fatigue at the end of the day.

Things changed between Bronwyn and me. A growing trust developed, and affection past the physical attraction we felt for one another. I told her things about growing up, and my isolation here on the island, that I had not even told Anna, and she confided that she feared she would never be able to leave the island and see something of the world as she dreamed of doing. I did not plan to become intimate with her, but it happened, and as naturally as the sun shines. I had talked her into learning to swim, for I could not bear the thought of her vulnerability in the water. She knew a secluded beach where her efforts would not attract attention, for swimming is thought unnatural among these people. They believe if the sea god wishes to take you, resistance is not only useless but impious as well. How they thought I had rescued her in the first place I do not know.

She made easy progress, for she trusted me, and I carried her from the water as she became chilled one afternoon, holding her close to warm her. She had only a tunic on, a light affair that clung to her body as a second skin. I kissed her, and rubbed her back to bring warmth to it. The rubbing became rhythmic and she pulled me down into the warm sand where we made love for the first time. It was a revelation. There are few secrets among the Picts, and certainly none of this nature. Virility is highly prized by men and demonstrated on ceremonial occasions publicly. What women think of it I do not know, but they at least permit it. I had experimented with village girls from the cradle on as all boys did, to the amusement of the elders. What I didn't know was that it could be like this.

That evening I spoke to her father and mother in her presence, and we were made handfast, pledged to one another until I was free to marry at the end of my apprenticeship. I didn't even think of asking to be released from it, for I still had much to learn, and Myrddin was the best teacher in the world. It was with a new seriousness, however, that I went about my duties at the forge. I told him why, and he grunted in approval.

"Bran and his family are of good stock," he said. "You have made a fine choice." And he clapped me on the back in congratulations, smiling.

I do not know what precautions Bronwyn took not to become pregnant, but I know I didn't worry about it one way or another.

74

I would have welcomed a baby. We found a piece of land watered by a small spring, situated between the smithy and her family's house. I enlarged the spring's mouth, cleaned out a pool and lined it with rock to store the flow, near one of the big oaks I planned to have serve as shade for our house. The men in her family helped us build the house frame, and we filled the walls ourselves with rocks and mud, talking about what we would do in it, and setting shelves and storage areas accordingly. I could not properly marry her until I had a house to bring her to, according to their custom.

Myrddin dismissed me early one afternoon and I decided to carry the hind quarter of a pig to my fisher family as a present. We had received it as a fee for a repair job, and Anna had no need for it. When I rounded the corner of the glen, I saw a dozen people struggling around the cottage. Bran and several of his brothers were fighting with quarterstaves against armed warriors. Saxons! As I ran toward them shouting, a small figure broke away to meet me. It was Bronwyn, but before she reached me, a pursuing warrior threw a double-bladed, short-handled ax overhand and it hit her in the back. She collapsed without life, snuffed out like one of Anna's tall candles caught by the wind. The Saxon was laughing, as he walked to her stooping to retrieve his weapon. Laughing! I reached the man before he was erect and swung the pig's leg into his face, knocking him backward, off his feet. He rolled, got to his knees and attempted to rise again, but I swung the leg underhand so that the force of the blow turned him in a somersault. He had dropped both ax and shield and was attempting to rise a third time when I smashed him to the earth, hitting him again and again until he stopped moving. I picked him up and held him over my head as I ran screaming to the cliff edge and threw him over to light on the sharp rocks of the beach below.

For the first time, I became aware of the blood chant. Myrddin had said it was possible to eavesdrop on people's minds when they were thinking very loudly, under great emotion. I found it impossible to shut out the mental screaming of the warriors for blood.

With that sound filling my consciousness, and the memory of blood spurting from Bronwyn's back as she fell, I had been merciless.

I was suddenly conscious of the silence, and turned to see twenty of the fisher folk armed with staves and long knives. The raiders had been ringed and dispatched as reinforcements came in from the other glens, roused by watchers on the cliffs. I walked through them to Bronwyn, fell to my knees and turned her over to gaze at her face. Her eyes were still open. The last thing she had seen was my coming to her aid, but not in time.

I gathered her into my arms, ignoring the blood that still streamed from her back and cried, great wrenching sobs that tore at my throat as I rocked her back and forth. Someone knelt beside me, his body shaking, and put an arm around me, and one around Bronwyn. It was Bran. I did not wish to release her when the women came for her, but Bran gently tugged on my hands so that I understood what was wanted. I saw tears were streaming down his face when I looked at him and knew his loss was as great as mine. I laid Bronwyn back on the earth and closed her eyes with my hand, kneeling to kiss her lips gently one last time before I rose and turned away.

Ector and his people came running down to where we stood and together we waited for more raiders, watching the smoke rising from Lyoness, and imagining the havoc being wreaked there. I saw Myrddin, Anna, Nithe and Bear with them so my sudden anxiety for their safety was eased. The survivors of our skirmish excitedly told about the fighting and particularly of my role, for one after another of the men came up to me where I sat, a little to one side, and patted me awkwardly. I was a hero, but felt a fool. The expected additional raiders never came.

Ector mounted a watch around the island that night. I stood with Myrddin and the fisher folk, still dazed from the loss of Bronwyn. Men spoke of me often that night as I stood guard with the others. I heard the words over and over, "He is as big as one of the giants of Geen" or "he fights like one of the giants of Geen," and I asked Myrddin about it, for I had never heard of them, except as a taunting reference by the Romans, who still referred to me as "the Geen."

"Who are the giants of Geen?"

"They were men, but of unusual size, who came here in long-boats after the Picts had settled the land, and became their rulers. They built hilltop forts, and took Pict women, for they brought none with them. In time the Gaels came and the Geen fought them, but to no avail. They were overwhelmed by sheer numbers. Now and then a man is born to a Pict woman who appears to be a throwback to that period, and people speak of them as being one of the old giants of Geen."

"Do they think that of me?"

"Yes. If you grow bigger, there will be no doubt in my mind, either."

"And you, are you a Geen?" I asked.

He looked at me, and laughed suddenly, but did not answer except to say, "My mother was not a Pict woman."

Nithe came to me next morning with hot bread and a bowl of soup as I stood guard. "I am sorry about Bronwyn," she said. "You must not blame yourself that she died. It was not your hand that threw the ax." Nithe had realized that I felt responsible when I was not aware of it myself. Having it at the front of my mind helped me to grieve freely, and maybe in time I would heal from the loss. I was grateful to her.

We buried our dead. A dozen of the fisher folk had fallen before they overwhelmed the raiders. Men brought me the head of the man I had killed, as a trophy of the fight. He had been a man of middle years, slightly balding and missing his front teeth. With the approval of Bran and his wife I buried the head at the foot of Bronwyn's grave so that she would have someone to serve her in the afterlife. It seemed to give them much satisfaction. It helped me not at all.

I learned there are always watchers on the hills, men who can control the weather to keep the boats safe at sea, and one of them had seen the flash of oared boats. The watchers sent pillars of

smoke high into the sky to bring the fishermen back in time to
meet the one ship that veered off to attack our island. A few of
the folk met the raiders on the beach, delaying them at the cost
of their lives, and by the time the Saxons had splashed ashore and
cut their way up the cliff path there were sufficient numbers of
men to meet and hold them.

The quarterstaff is as deadly a weapon as a spear in the hands
of a trained man for it can be used to thrust, parry and slash, and
these men practiced with it from childhood on. They would be a
match for the Romans if they could learn to fight under discipline.

Ector's men had been chagrined to find there was nothing for
them to do when they arrived at the battle scene. They felt cheated,
and were quarrelsome, and would have engaged the fisher folk
just to fight someone if allowed, but the presence of Myrddin kept
their irritation at a level where it was not provocative. The fisher
folk were not in a mood to suffer much insolence.

Next day we had a visit from gruff Cador, Duke of Lyoness, to
apprise us of the effects of the raid on the other islands. He had
suffered a number of his people killed and asked Ector, as liege
man to Uther, to prepare us for further onslaughts. Duke Cador's
wife had been killed, along with all his sons. Only his daughter,
a child of Bear's age, had escaped. Between them, the Duke and
Ector arranged for Ector's oldest daughter, a pleasant girl named
Miriam, to become his wife. Cador wanted heirs. He would not
stay the night, interested only in gathering information, and ar-
ranging for a replacement for his duchess before sailing back to
Tresco, the largest of the Islands of Lyoness. He was not a sen-
timental man.

Ector wished to institute military training for all males on the
island, but Myrddin dissuaded him. "The fisher folk will resent
being taken from their daily tasks, and no overall good will be
accomplished, anyway. They managed to contain the raiders well
enough. If there had been more, your men would have met them
and defeated them. They were on the scene almost immediately."
Ector grumbled, but the implied compliment quieted him.

Later Myrddin had words for me that were slightly different. "You need some training, if no one else does. Using a pig's leg as a club, and beating a man to death with it? What kind of a thing was that?"

He was serious, and every morning before we had breakfast I was required to undertake lessons in hand-to-hand combat, particularly in sword use. I quickly learned that I could lock my mind on Myrddin's and anticipate each move. I could not always avoid being hit that way, for he could read my mind as well, but I knew it would be an advantage with most men. Myrddin was aware, of course, and taught me a second lesson as a warning. He hit me harder than I thought warranted several times, and finally once when I was not expecting it and I lost my temper. Immediately I lost contact with his mind, and not being able to guess his moves, found myself soundly beaten. I was on the ground, looking up, dazed, when he finally spoke to me.

"If you are going to use your special gifts this way, you must learn their limitations. Do you think you may have done so?"

I glared at him a moment, but the funny side occurred to me, and I laughed, thinking about it. Myrddin knew me well. I never learn anything except through hard experience.

Next day, a visit from the mainland diverted us from further discussion of this. Brastius Red-beard, the Gaelic cattle-king I once thought was my father, came dressed in the armor of a Roman centurian. He was surprised to find a guarded beach, and Ector proudly explained we were ready to ward off raiders. They were old friends, both having served Uther in times past.

"Uther, the High King, is dead," Brastius said after he was alone with Myrddin and me. "There will be no one ready to assert claim to his crown for a few years. Will you be ready when the call comes?"

"You have seen the boy," Myrddin said, "What do you think?"

"You call him Bear? That's no British name, but he's very promising. In any case, Uther named him heir with his last breath."

79

He turned to me. "I thought it would be you, and not some other child. You were never aware of that, were you?"

"No. I knew your eyes sought me out, but I thought it was because I was your son, and you did not wish to acknowledge me."

"I am sorry for that. I would have been proud to acknowledge you. When Uther decided to sacrifice you to buy more time, I plotted with Myrddin to save you, but I have long thought you dead, having last seen you bleeding like a stuck pig, despite our pains."

I pulled open my tunic and traced the scar with my finger. "I did die, in a sense. Myrddin brought me back to life."

"And well he did so," he said approvingly, inspecting the scar.

"We brought an old friend of yours with us," he said, changing the subject. "Have you seen him?"

"No, Myrddin has kept me busy."

"He's waiting outside." I took the hint and left the two men to talk. Outside waiting patiently was Ulfas, my old second-in-command on the hurley field.

"Ulfas!" I cried.

"By Lud's balls!" Ulfas said, gawking up at me. His grin was as I remembered it, but he was only a head taller than of old, though he sported a short, black beard. "What happened to you?" he asked.

I lifted him in a bear-hug, laughing. "I grew up. How is my mother?"

"Brusen has remarried. She held the woad dyer responsible for your selection by the Oak King, which was wrong, of course, for you remember how little others thought of him. However, nothing anyone could say would budge her, and she went off and joined old King Pelles' household." I had named myself after Pelles. "She is running things there now, last I heard," he continued.

I laughed again. It was like my mother.

"You'd never recognize her," Ulfas concluded. "She has so many tattoos now that it's hard to see the natural color of her skin."

"Does she know I'm alive?" I asked.

"No. She says you died on the black stone, and she's stubborn about it. I think she's afraid if you are found alive you'll be sacrificed again."

"I see. She may well be right." I looked at him again, and asked, "How did you talk your way into the trip here?"

"I'm to be a messenger. I know the way to London, and the way back to Pict country at need. If Myrddin wants to send word to Brastius, I'll find him one place or another."

"You'll stay here then?"

"Yes."

I was delighted. Ulfas became one of us, taking over Myrddin's sleeping cubicle. Anna stayed to cook for us, and for something else. Perhaps it was Myrddin's farsightedness, for Anna was no older than Ulfas, having had her child at thirteen. To give them privacy, when I saw how it was going, I took Bear and Nithe for a boating trip to Lyoness to visit Ector's daughter, and when we returned we found they had become handfast. I was happy for them, but wondered what Bear would think of the noises they made at night. I needn't have worried. He has always fallen asleep when his head touches his pillow, and nothing short of a lightning bolt striking the roof would serve to waken him. I slept little, thinking of Bronwyn, as I also did most of the day, at least at the back of my mind. It didn't get better.

I was eighteen and Bear was seven when Myrddin came into the smithy one morning to ask, "Have you seen Nithe and Bear?"

"Why, no," I said. "Should they be here?"

"I thought they were."

"And I thought they were with you, playing soldier," I said. I hadn't meant it to sound quite like that.

"I see," Myrddin replied dryly. "I wanted to tell you all that I must leave for a while, and wanted particularly to ask you to look after them. First, I guess we'll have to find them."

I was not alarmed at their absence. I was wondering what

Myrddin meant about needing to leave. One of the first places I looked was the beach, for I knew the attraction the water had for both of them. The boat was gone. I ran back up the hill to inquire whether Myrddin had loaned it out, but he had not. Nithe and Bear had taken it. Now, I was alarmed. It was dark before they brought the boat in, and Myrddin and I waited for them on the beach.

"Do not touch that boat again without permission or I will have it sunk," was all he said. It was enough. Myrddin made no empty threats.

That night Ulfas was in Anna's bed, and while I ignored their giggles I decided if I was going to have to worry about Nithe and Bear in Myrddin's absence, I had better keep my mind on it. Nithe would have to move back to the smithy, and Anna could move into Myrddin's little house with Ulfas. I regretted the need, but knew myself unable to act responsibly toward the children unless they were foremost in my mind. It would help me to have something other than Bronwyn to think about.

"I am going to the mainland, and may be gone for several years," Myrddin told us in the morning. "A messenger came yesterday for me, and I must leave with him."

"What is it about?" I asked.

"It is about the business that brought us here," he replied. "Brastius sends word that I must begin the preparations. You will be in charge of the smithy and the children in my absence." He turned to Nithe and Bear. "You understand what I mean by this?"

"Take me with you, Myrddin," Nithe said.

"No. I also leave you in charge. You must watch over Bear while Pelleas provides for you both, as a father would. You must obey him as you would a father, without argument. Will you promise?"

Nithe looked at me sideways. She was now fourteen or fifteen, I thought, and nearly grown, but was still well-padded with baby fat. It was probably time she stopped playing soldier, however. She was no longer really a child. Bear also looked at me, smiled, and nodded his head.

"Very well," said Nithe. "I imagine we'll have some differences, but if Pelleas is not unreasonable, I will obey him."

Myrddin grunted, knowing that was the best he would get. He left that afternoon but not until he took me aside and declared my apprenticeship completed. It had been seven years since I joined him. He told me everything in the smithy was mine if he did not come back, and if he did we would share equally in ownership and responsibility.

"Is where you are going dangerous?" I asked him.

"When you move among kings it is always dangerous," he responded, and embracing me one last time turned and left. I helped Anna and Ulfas move into his house that afternoon and that night we slept as a family again, me and Nithe and Bear.

The new arrangement worked. Nithe became an excellent cook; having watched Anna for years, she knew what was required for plain cooking but, using all of her considerable imagination, she managed to make our monotonous food more than merely edible. As far as Bear was concerned, she was wasting her time. He would eat anything, cooked or raw, with little interest in it except that it filled his belly. He did not become fat, but needed food the way a fire needs wood, to give him the energy to be active all during the sunlit hours. So much for him. Nithe knew I enjoyed it.

Bear and Nithe helped in the smithy, and found as much interest in it as they had in playing soldier. The training phase was over and the young men were standing regular watches so the children could not participate as they had before. I needed help with the bellows primarily, but I made them small hammers to shape the hot iron and when we were not actually working on mending or making things for which there was a need, we made things for fun. They both wanted real swords to replace the wooden ones which they felt were children's toys only, and beneath them. I explained it would take time for them to become skilled enough to make their own, and that no other kind was really dependable when one's life was at stake. They accepted the reasoning, and patiently learned the rudiments of smithy skills, always with the goal of having real weapons in the future.

We reinstituted the sailing days, for they were as important to me as to the children, and I found the work at the smithy less time-consuming than I might wish. Indeed, if we did not fish regularly, we did not always have enough to eat. When there was work at the smithy, we were often joined by Ulfas and Ector's son, Kay. Kay was a true Gael, tall like his mother's people, and full of his own importance as son of the island's lord. Ector had grudgingly accepted my right to be on the island following the raid, and recognized my role in driving off the warriors, but there was still condescension in his voice when he addressed me, and Kay imitated him, perhaps without realizing it. Kay was also somewhat of a bully with Bear, but Nithe was the same age as Kay, and as strong. She permitted little abuse of her ward.

Our sailing excursions took us often to Lyoness, and we were welcomed there, particularly when Kay was along. It became evident that Duke Cador had decided that a good match could be made between Kay and his daughter, Samana. Samana had other preferences, showing a marked liking for Bear, to Kay's discomfort. Bear was unaware of it, at first, which kept hostilities down. Our visits became regular, for we found a market for iron goods at Lyoness, and needed the contact to pick up and deliver items to repair, and the food we received in pay. Our reliance on fish as a staple lessened, to my satisfaction. Fish is not my favorite meal.

Bear was still in his seventh year when the druid came after him, but a few months after Myrddin left. Ector limped over to the smithy himself to introduce him.

"This druid claims Uther has given him Bear," he announced, "though why that might be so, I can't imagine." The Romans had outlawed druidry, and even though the Romans had deserted Britain, as a loyal old Roman soldier Ector still held druids in suspicious dislike.

With a start I turned away from them to pull on my tunic. I

had been working stripped to the waist and wished to hide the scar on my belly from the druid's prying eyes. I was not quick enough.

"I'll take him as well," the tall man with Ector said, pointing at me. "I had heard of a Pict living hidden here from us, one who escaped death on the stone at the hands of the false druid, Myrddin, may the Oak King curse him!" He spat and I pulled the tunic back off, advancing to meet him. It was Cathmor, the druid whose eyes I had last seen glinting in the moonlight in the sacred oak grove.

"Uther is dead," I challenged him. "His need of a new substitute for the debt he owed your dark king of the woods no longer holds. As for me, I belong to no man, not Uther, not Myrddin, not Ector and not you!"

"What say you, Ector? Is this serf free to speak before his better in this fashion?" Cathmor asked, ignoring me.

"He is no serf. He is a master smith, who completed his apprenticeship under Myrddin, and who now serves this island in Myrddin's place," Ector replied in an angry voice. "I am a good Roman and a good Christian. Do not look to me for help in making good your claim here."

The druid stared at him for a long moment before turning to leave. "This is not the end of this, Ector," he warned, but he did not turn back. At Ector's suggestion, Bear and Nithe moved to the manor house where Bear could be better protected. Ector's wife, Lady Ellen, wanted Nithe to learn female responsibilities, something she was not likely to learn from me. Besides, she was getting too old to live with me without scandal; under Roman law, girls are marriageable at fifteen. I was not invited to join them.

Ulfas and Anna stayed in Myrddin's house on the cliff and married quietly with only Bran's family and the rest of us in attendance. The marriage itself was a simple exchange of vows before witnesses, since neither Anna nor Ulfas was Christian. Anna was pregnant again, and blooming with health. When the baby came, not long after the wedding, they named her Myrdda, after Myrddin. Myrddin would have been pleased.

Ulfas fished sometimes with Brig and worked in the smithy sometimes with me, going wherever he was needed and welcome everywhere. Anna got pregnant again almost immediately after Myrdda's birth and seemed more than just content. Indeed, it was difficult for me to be around the two of them.

Bear became aware of Samana when they both turned eleven, and life became more complicated for us all. Kay attempted to keep them apart, without success. Bear insisted on visiting, and Kay would not be left behind, although he was miserable when he went. He attempted to order Bear to defer to him, but got laughed at for his pains. Bear was strong, though not particularly big for his age. He was beautifully coordinated, and completely unafraid. Nithe, who had been suspicious of my interest in Bronwyn, accepted Samana as a proper friend for Bear, and she abetted their conspiracy. Kay was no match for the three of them. It was a settled thing in their minds that Bear and Samana would become handfast as soon as they were old enough to make choices of that sort, and I made no objection, for who was I to stand in the way of a friend's happiness? Besides, I liked Samana and the influence she had on Bear. He steadied under her friendship and grew into a young man both thoughtful of others and responsible for his behavior. Myrddin would be proud of him, I thought, if ever he saw him again.

Ector spoke to me of Kay's disappointed hopes in terms that were insulting, but candid. The interview was harder on him than me.

"Look you, I have no dislike of the boy, but you know his prospects are limited, in reality. We haven't heard from Myrddin in over four years now, and probably never will again. Duke Cador is not going to allow his only daughter to marry some landless man, no matter what his bloodline is. That's not to say he'd believe it in the first place. What I mean is that with my daughter married to Cador now, it would be very fitting to have Kay married to Samana. She's a sunny little thing and will come around when she sees how much her father is set on it, what?"

"Duke Cador is a Christian, is he not?" I asked.

"Well, yes, but what does that matter?" Ector grunted.

"I have heard Myrddin say that the church does not permit marriage between people so closely related."

"Kay and Samana are not related," Ector objected.

"Kay's sister is Samana's stepmother. That makes him Samana's uncle, does it not?"

"But they are not blood related!"

"The church doesn't care. The relationship is one confirmed by the wedding sacrament, and that is more binding than blood."

"You say Myrddin said that?"

"Yes." He hadn't, though.

Ector left, a troubled man. I knew he would talk to Duke Cador about it, and Cador to his priest. If he let the matter lie the priest would not think to object, but the question of succession was too important to Cador for him to do that. His daughter's marriage had to be valid for her child to be his heir.

I was also troubled. Ector was right in thinking Duke Cador would object to a marriage between Bear and his daughter. Bear would not abide by Cador's wishes if they ran counter to his own, and Nithe and I would have to back him, as always. We would probably have to steal the girl and flee.

The ache in the core of my being dulled and I began to visit fisher families where there were young daughters in the household. I was welcome everywhere. I looked for someone with whom I could find the companionship Bronwyn and I had shared and with whom sexual union would be as meaningful. The fisher folk do not shield their daughters in this way. A woman must be proven fertile before she is marriageable but knows to take certain herbs when she does not wish to conceive. I found many pleasant girls, some with whom I could have had a happy enough life, in all likelihood, but having known Bronwyn, it was not enough.

I usually avoided the glen where Bronwyn and I had built our house, and came to it this time only when I noticed smoke rising from the chimney. I was angry that anyone would intrude into my private world. Before I even opened the door I heard singing, and when I looked in I found Nithe, seated before the loom I had built, happily weaving.

"What are you doing here?" I asked sternly.

"I didn't think you'd mind," she said, but from the look in her eye, I knew she was uncertain about that.

"Why didn't you ask permission?" I asked.

"Would you have granted it?" she responded, looking up at me defiantly.

"No," I said.

"I didn't think so. I have no place of my own. I liked Bronwyn and I talked to her mother. She said it would be all right. She even gave me wool and taught me to spin and weave. You're out among the girls so much you didn't even notice," she said, tears welling up into her eyes and beginning to fall disregarded down her cheeks.

I was appalled. I could not remember ever having seen Nithe cry. Each utterance came in a single breath, followed by a sharp intake of air that was almost a sob. I realized Nithe was growing up alone with no one her age to talk to, and little support from her family. Anna and Ulfas were busy with their own small family, and while Nithe was always greeted with affection there by everyone, including several dogs, their boisterous enjoyment of each other only served to underline her loneliness. Bear was busy much of the day with the soldiers, his soldiers in his mind, and Nithe could no longer join him among them. Women do not follow soldiers unless they are willing to serve them sexually, and Nithe was not, nor would I allow it if she were. I was either busy at the forge, fishing or visiting, and while she worked alongside me in the smithy or the boat along with Bear, I did not invite her along when I roamed.

"Look you," I said awkwardly, "among the Picts, houses belong to women. I have always thought of this as Bronwyn's house, and like as not I would have given it to her sister had there been one. But, if her mother says it is all right for you to be here, I give you the house. I had not thought to hear singing in it again, and it eased my heart to hear it."

"Do you mean it? Is it really mine, and not just pretend?" Nithe asked, rising and running to grasp my arms as she gazed earnestly into my face, trying to read truth there.

"It is yours," I said, and she hugged me in thanks. After that she no longer slept in the smithy house, coming in only to cook for Bear and me, and clean the place as needed. From then on when I wanted her for something, and did not see her close at hand, I knew I could find her in Bronwyn's glen. Always she was singing, and her singing became part of my feeling for the place.

Bear drew a soldier's daily allowance of two pounds of flour, either oat or barley meal depending on what Ector's mill could furnish, and he brought it home to Nithe. Others of his comrades did the same when they tasted the quality of her bread, and it became a common thing for a number of them to join Bear and take their evening meal at Nithe's house. I was often gone myself and it was some time before I became aware that they were courting her as they had Anna in time past. I was of two minds about it, but Nithe took such pleasure in having company and Bear was so protective of her that I forbore saying anything that was on my mind. Myrddin had bid me take care of her along with Bear, but they were fast outgrowing the need.

Bear announced his independence on one of the rare evenings the three of us ate together, having spent the day sailing with Nithe to visit Samana. "You are not to call me 'Bear' any longer," he said. "It is not a British name and Samana doesn't like it. You must call me Arthur. It means 'bear' in Welsh."

"You are right," Nithe said, "the word *bear* is Jute, but I named you and my first language was Jute."

"Well," he considered, "you can still call me 'Bear' if you want, then, but nobody else." His tone was insistent, but his eyes were coaxing.

I thought about it. Brastius had objected to his name, and said he must take another to claim his throne. This would do very well. "Arthur," I said. "King Arthur. Arthur of Britain. I like it. It has a certain ring to it." He beamed at me, and I grinned back.

"Get used to it, for you will hear it much in the future," I said, and he laughed aloud.

CHAPTER VI

Myrddin came back, quietly, almost as if he had not been away. One evening he just appeared, walking into the smithy and hanging his harp on its accustomed peg before greeting us. It was Bear's birthday, "Auld Saint Deere's Day," and we were celebrating, with only the family, Nithe, Bear, Anna and Ulfas and their children, and me. Bear was fifteen.

"What's the occasion?" Myrddin asked. No one told him, or if they did, he couldn't have heard, for Anna screamed, Nithe ran over and threw herself into his arms and Arthur and I pounded on his back.

"Cease!" he cried. "Cease! You're killing me!" We were hitting harder than we realized, perhaps, though not that hard. We desisted, however, and merely beamed, but Nithe would not release him, clutching at him as if he were about to disappear again.

When she could finally speak she looked up at him, scolding, "Where have you been? I've missed you!" She had, more than any of us.

"I did not stay away so long through choice," Myrddin said. "Part of the time I was imprisoned, a guest of the Saxons, who broke their word that I was to receive safe passage. They do not understand what a pledged word is, holding a vow only so long as it serves their immediate interests to do so."

"What had you to do with them?" I asked.

"I sought to make an agreement with them at the behest of the chief men of London that they would stay in their lands in Kent, given them and the Jutes by Vortigern the Traitor, but they complained of crowding. Changes are coming."

He would say nothing further, and the party became one of homecoming. Later, at the forge, he told me and Arthur and Nithe more about it. "Saxons do not believe they are bound to standards of ordinary decency when they deal with those who do not share common familial bonds," he said, while carefully shaping a new saxeknife to replace the one he had lost. "They lie to other Saxons outside the family group, steal from them when the opportunity arises, and kill them when they believe they will be undiscovered in the act and thus avoid the penalties of paying the blood price of the victim, all for the most trivial reasons. Of course, they deny all of this when they are confronted with proof of their treachery for as long as they can, bowing only to the threat of superior force.

"Those who are not Saxon, who do not know their capacity for deception and casual violence, are much at risk. Never trust a Saxon, never! Do not trust one with your life, your goods, your honor, or aught else you may hold dear. There is no virtue to be found in them." His pounding on the hot iron had become stronger as he talked, and the blade shaped up more quickly than any I had seen before. I glanced at Nithe, who claimed to be descended from Horsa, the Jute, but she had fixed her gaze on the hot iron she held with the tongs against the anvil for Myrddin to strike with his hammer. I could not tell if the color that rose to her face was heat from the forge or from embarrassment.

Golden days followed; spring was early, summer delightful and fall like a continuation of summer, but changes came, as he warned. Messengers from abroad were the first of them. I learned of it through an argument between Kay and Arthur one morning. There had always been friction between the boys, and Myrddin's return had brought the longstanding quarrel into new perspective.

"You're short and fat. You don't even look like a king," Kay said accusingly, as the two of them walked into the smithy together.

Arthur's hand went involuntarily to his upper lip seeking the few soft whiskers that grew there, but his reply was sure enough, "What is a king supposed to look like?"

"Like . . . like Pelleas!" Kay blurted, and amended that by adding, "But not so dark." Kay is tall and thin, russet-haired and fair-skinned, looking more like his Gaelic mother than his Roman father.

Arthur grinned at me, amused at the slight. "I agree," he said. "Pelleas doesn't look exactly like a king. He looks more like a god."

"Don't tease him," I admonished in mind-speech. Arthur can hear mind-speech, like Nithe, but also, like her, lacks the ability to speak. Myrddin thinks both parents must be mind-speakers, as mine likely were, to make that possible. My mother never spoke to me, mind to mind, but she told me she heard voices when she was young. "What is this about, anyway?" I asked aloud. I was working at the forge, hoping to add to our store of horseshoes before the sun made it too hot to stand before the fire. Kay and Arthur were early. Usually Ector's bailiff kept them at chores until at least midmorning, learning whatever he thought it best for them to know about the management of Ector's lands.

"The Bishop of London sent word last night that there would be a special Christmas Mass at St. Paul's to reveal the successor to King Uther," Kay said.

"Uther has been dead a dozen years," I said. "Why the sudden urgency?"

"The Picts and Saxons have started raiding together, and the Bishop fears for London," Arthur said.

"Myrddin said Arthur is to be chosen," Kay interrupted, indignantly. Arthur shrugged, embarrassed. He'd always known.

"You were eavesdropping," Nithe said, herself unobserved behind them as they stood before me rehearsing their argument. Nithe is

93

taller than Arthur and stronger than Kay, and as hard-muscled as either of them from toil at the forge.

"If Myrddin wanted you to know about this, Kay," I said, agreeing, "he would have told you, himself. If you are smart, you'll let him tell you now before you speak of it in his presence."

We had not long to wait. I put the boys to work sorting the horseshoes into sizes while Nithe pumped the bellows. We work well together, even with Kay helping. I do not permit idle talk in the smithy. People get hurt when they are not paying attention to what they are doing.

Myrddin came upon us quietly, walking with Ector. "I have news for all of you," he said. "We are going to London for Christmas."

"See, I told you," Kay blurted, and flushed as he realized that Myrddin had found him out. He pressed forward anyway, reckless in his outrage. "Why am I not to be king?" he demanded. "I am better born." Ector looked at Myrddin to see how this statement would be taken by the older man.

"You are not to be king because you are not the son of Uther, the last High King," Myrddin replied, calmly.

"King Uther had no sons. Everyone knows that," Kay insisted.

"I know better than that," Myrddin said. "I, myself, took Arthur from between his mother and the wall when he was not two hours old, and brought him here to your father for fosterage. Why else would I, the chief advisor to the High King, come to this island village and be a smith?"

"There is no proof," Kay said.

"Your father has heard proof from Uther's own mouth. Ask him." Kay glared at his father in accusation and Ector nodded and looked away, as though he had somehow betrayed his son.

"Everyone has heard of Uther's hurried marriage and the baby who was spirited away at birth. I will believe that Arthur is that baby, but I won't believe he is Uther's. And if he is, he was conceived out of wedlock, and bastards can't inherit," Kay said, returning to the argument.

"That is enough, Kay," Ector said sternly.

"Let him be," Myrddin said. "If we cannot convince Kay, how are we to convince the rest of the world? It will be enough, Kay, that he is Uther's son, and acknowledged by him, as your father and I will bear witness along with others who were there. Not all of us are Christians and have the feeling, as you do, for the sanctity of marriage. You may even have heard that my father was Satan, himself," and Myrddin raised an eyebrow as Kay nodded briefly, but continued. "Uther had at least one other son live that he acknowledged. I heard him so claim Pelleas before he gave him to the Oak King."

Arthur looked at me with surprise. "We are truly brothers?" he asked.

"By Kay's reckoning, we are bastards of the same father," I said. "Our sinful mothers are different."

Before either Arthur or Kay could respond, Ector went ponderously to his knees before Arthur and said, "Let me, who has been foster father to you these fifteen years, be the first to offer my allegiance, and to demand a boon," he reached out and grasped Arthur's hand. Arthur took a half-step backward, weakly attempting to free his hand from Ector's grasp, but to no avail. He sought Myrddin's eyes in an appeal for help.

"He has the right," Myrddin said. "Grant his boon."

"Well, I will then. Must he kneel?"

Ector kissed his hand in allegiance, ignoring Arthur's discomfort, and said, "There, it is done. Now promise me you will appoint Kay as seneschal over all your lands."

Arthur freed his hand and wiped the back of it absentmindedly on his tunic. "I don't have any lands," he said, misliking the idea of being that closely tied to Kay for the rest of his life.

"You will have," said Ector. Again Arthur looked to Myrddin, who nodded gravely.

"Oh, very well," Arthur said and extended his hand to Kay that he might emulate his father.

Kay's anger burst from him in a torrent of words. "Me kneel? Me kiss his dirty hand? Not bloody likely!"

Arthur's face was as flushed as Kay's was pale. He looked at his hand a moment to determine whether Kay's words reflected some unusual truth, but it was at least reasonably clean. Suddenly his own uncertain temper flared and he stepped up to Kay and hit him sharply in the stomach. As Kay doubled over, the wind knocked out of him, Arthur hammered his fist on the back of Kay's head, driving him to his knees.

"Are you better than your father, then?" he asked, thrusting his hand under Kay's nose. "Now, kiss it!" Kay did, dazed and uncertain as to what was happening. Arthur stepped back and waited until Kay raised his unhappy face and looked at him. Ector stepped over to Kay and rested his hand on Kay's shoulder as if to warn him of the consequences of hasty words.

"Hear, now," Arthur demanded. "You were never friend to me, Kay. Yet I know you will keep your word in most things. I will make you seneschal, overseer over all my lands, if you promise never to deal me falsely. If not, boon or no boon, I will not have you near me."

Kay rose, and Ector squeezed his arm cruelly. Kay jerked it free and glared at Ector before replying to Arthur.

"I swear to be faithful to you as your seneschal, but in naught else," he said.

"Little I care," Arthur said. "There is naught else I would entrust to you."

I mistrusted this exchange. Kay is very subtle and I feared would one day do Arthur an injury. I could feel it. No one asked my opinion, though. Ector was interested in his small concerns, and Myrddin in his large ones and neither would be influenced by mere feelings. Ector and Kay left, Ector to make preparations for the journey to London, and Kay to sulk.

"Pump up the forge," Myrddin said. "We have work to do." He selected several long thin rods of soft and hard iron, thrusting them into the fire. Between us, striking the hot iron in turn, we made the several rods into a single bar. This was hurried crafting. Usually we took time with weapons, but any work from Myrddin's forge was better than the best from anyone else's. We had it shaped in half a dozen heatings, a record even for us.

"Who is it for?" Arthur asked.

"For you."

Arthur's eyes glowed in the forge light. Having his own sword was a goal just less desirous than owning his own horse.

"Can I have one, too?" Nithe asked.

"Whatever for?" Myrddin asked.

"I'm better with a saxeknife than either Arthur or Kay," Nithe replied.

"This isn't for fighting," Myrddin said.

"It isn't?" Arthur asked, crestfallen.

"Of course not. Would I fabricate a fighting sword for anyone, let alone you, with so little care? This is for looks."

It was evening when we finished work, all three of us dirty from the fire. The sword was a handsome four feet long with a deep blood groove that ran almost its entire length of the blade, and a full three inches wide where the blade joined the hilt. It had a simple crosspiece for a hand guard, set with flashing jewels. The hilt was nearly a foot long, counterweighted to balance the blade. Myrddin took one of his specialized tools from the box that opens only to his hand and etched decorative lines on half the blade's length. When it was finished, he laid an inch-thick, soft iron bar on the anvil, and cut it in two with a single overhand blow. Afterward he carefully inspected the edge of the blade to determine whether there had been any damage to it. He smiled finally, a rare event.

"This will do nicely for a show sword," he said. "Feel the balance of it," and handed the weapon to Arthur. Arthur stepped out into the yard fronting the smithy and grasping the sword with both hands set it swinging around his head. I knew it to be as heavy as my great sledge, but in his hands it seemed no weightier than a willow withe. With shining eyes he brought it back to Myrddin, inarticulate as always under great emotion.

"So, you approve," Myrddin said dryly. "I am glad. Now we must build a nest for the bird."

The great anvil is hollow, being no more than an inch thick, which is still enough mass to hammer out the heaviest plowshare. The opening from the base is square, to allow it to be placed solidly on a stout wooden post sunk into the ground. Myrddin picked up the anvil from its post and laid it on its side on the wooden stock table that stands next to the forge. He chose a short piece of steel stock and probed the hollow interior of the anvil, finally tapping it with a hammer, popping out a thin plug that filled a hole built into the anvil when it was first cast. The slot ordinarily receives special cutting tools. A chisel set there, sharp edge up, serves to cut long bar stock into shorter pieces when the iron has been heated white-hot and is struck by a heavy sledge.

Myrddin tried setting the sword into the slot, and it was possible to pass it down the anvil about half the length of the blade. "We'll pour molten lead around the blade and pull it out before it sticks," he said.

I placed a cast iron crucible containing a few small scraps of lead into the fire while Arthur worked the bellows. Myrddin packed oakum around the space where the blade came through the anvil on the bottom side to keep the molten lead from flowing through and then stood the anvil upright on the stock table. He used wet clay to build a small dam around the upper opening to contain the flow and announced himself ready. Nithe stood on the table to steady the blade and Myrddin lifted the iron crucible from the fire with heavy, wooden-handled tongs, quickly pouring a stream of metal into the opening around the blade to the level of the clay dam. At his signal, Nithe freed the blade. Lead cools very quickly, and a moment later Nithe tested the fit by thrusting the blade back into the anvil, allowing it to stand upright unaided.

"That's the easy part," Myrddin said. "Now we face the problem of how to hold the sword in place until we want to release it, and release it in such a way that only someone who knows how will be able to do it. I put some thought to this problem and devised a little contraption that may do the trick. Let's set it up and see." The device looked like a small steel trap, and operated much like one. There was a pressure plate that would release the jaws from where they engage the blood grove in the blade, and with further pressure would spring them shut again.

"When we weld the trap to the anvil, the blade becomes a part of the anvil when the jaws are closed, and you must lift the anvil and anything it is attached to to move the blade. Even that won't separate it from the anvil." He had built the device to an exact fit, and attached it by fitting red-hot bars into holes he had drilled in the anvil to receive them, first threading the bars through holes in the device.

When he judged it was cool enough to hold the weld he righted the anvil again and thrust the blade hard into the slot, releasing the trap to hold it. "Try it," he invited Arthur. Arthur leaped onto the table, grasped the sword by the hilt with both his hands and tugged. It did not budge. He drew a deep breath and tried again, engaging all of his great strength in the task of withdrawing the sword and succeeded only in lifting the anvil. Stepping back he shook his head.

"If anyone can pull it out straightaway, he deserves to win the prize," he announced. Then stepping back to the anvil he pressed down on the handle lightly until he felt a slight click. The mechanism had been set. He was then able to pull the sword from the anvil with ease.

"So, I am to be King of the Britons." He flourished the sword overhead. "Myrddin, I do not know if I will be able to keep a straight face."

"Be sure that you do. You must also not seem to press down on the sword lest you give the secret away."

"I will be careful," Arthur promised. "Will you have need of me tomorrow?"

"We've a few days free while we plan the trip. What do you wish to do?"

"I would take Pelleas as the senior member of my blood family to visit Lyoness. I want to settle things with Samana's father before this adventure starts. He won't believe me, but everyone believes Pelleas, or pretends to," Arthur said glancing up at me, and smiling.

"You will speak for her?" Myrddin asked.

"We have been promised to each other since we were children, but the Duke would not hear of it, preferring some suitor with more prospects. Tristram of Cornwall has been visiting for the past month trying to win her over, with the Duke's approval. She will resist while she can, but in time they will wear her down. I will stop all that."

"The Duke wants an heir. Your first son will have to be pledged to become Duke of Lyoness and not High King of the Britons," Myrddin said, watching Arthur closely.

"So be it," Arthur said.

The breeze was light and Arthur and I rowed half of the distance between Ector's Island and Lyoness. It was pleasant work in the cool air, warming our blood. Each of us handled two oars, a feat ordinary men found difficult, but Arthur was well named "Bear," for his strength at fifteen was not that of an ordinary man, and I, myself, have not met my match since Myrddin stopped wrestling with me when I was twelve. He said then I was too strong to teach, not yet knowing how much pressure was required to break a man's arm. I know now.

Samana met us at the beach, flying into Arthur's arms and hugging him. She had grown into a very pretty girl, with straw-colored hair that hung to her waist, great sea-blue eyes and a surprisingly rounded form for one so young. She had been watching for him from the headland for weeks, she said. "You must speak to my father this day, for he will not wait for me to make up my mind any longer."

"Tristram?"

"Yes. He is King Mark's heir, and a great catch."

"Truly?"

"It must be. He tells me so himself," Samana looked up at Arthur when she said this, and smiled when Arthur laughed, the tension draining from him. He hugged her again.

We found Tristram and the Duke talking privately. The Duke frowned when he saw his daughter hanging on Arthur's arm, but stayed his anger when he saw me with them. I have that effect on some because of my size.

"Greetings, Pelleas. Arthur." He nodded his head as he spoke, barely acknowledging the boy.

"We have private business with you, Duke Cador," Arthur said.

"I have a guest," the duke said.

"I will excuse myself," Tristram said, rising gracefully. "Our business is concluded anyway, Your Grace."

"So it is. I apologize for the abruptness of these visitors. I will be back with you before long." As Tristram left, Duke Cador spoke his anger.

"Samana, go to your room. I have had enough of your disobedience. I have accepted betrothal in your name and expect you to acquiesce when the priest comes for the formal pledging. As for you, Arthur, you were never welcome here as a suitor for my daughter, and I will not hear you speak on this subject."

"Then hear me, Duke Cador," I said. "Arthur is the acknowledged son of Uther the Pendragon, High King of the Britons. Arthur has been hidden by Uther's orders until the Bishop of London should call him forth. That time has come, and we are to set out within a week's time for London to claim his crown. He will then be King of all Britons, yourself included, as his father was, and you will not refuse him anything on pain of his displeasure."

"This is a thin story, perhaps one the druid, Myrddin, has concocted to bring himself close to power. In any case, I have betrothed my daughter to Tristram, the heir of Mark, King of Cornwall, and I will not break my word."

"You cannot pledge me against my will!" Samana declared hotly.

101

"Under Roman law, I can, and I have."

"I am no Roman," Arthur said, "and I recognize no Roman authority here. I claim Samana as a free Briton, and I am willing to enter into any marriage contract you wish, but I will not be put off. Tristram is a latecomer to this contest."

"You are willing to do single combat with Lord Tristram? He is widely judged to be the best swordsman in the world."

"He is not willing," I said before Arthur could speak. "Even if he were, as Arthur's brother and champion I would undertake to contest this issue with Lord Tristram or anyone he might delegate to stand for him. In the meantime, Samana will be going with us, for I do not trust you to keep her free since you do not respect her stated wishes in the matter."

"You will not leave this island with her," Cador said.

"Who will stop me?" I asked, with an edge to my voice. Tristram came up to us and Duke Cador turned to him.

"These men state a prior claim on Samana, and have said they will take her with them."

"What does Samana say?" Tristram asked.

"I would go with them, Tristram. Arthur and I pledged ourselves when we were children, and I have told my father I have no wish to wed any other than he."

"I will force no maiden, Duke Cador. I do not have to. If she loves this youth perhaps I was mistaken in thinking she would be mature enough to take on the responsibilities of a great court."

"You will not urge your claim?"

"I will not. However, I believe I overheard Pelleas say he was willing to undergo combat with me to prove Arthur's claim. Is that true?" and he turned to direct the question to me.

"It is, that," I said.

"We may have occasion to discuss this at a later time," Tristram said.

"At your pleasure, my lord," I replied. I had been trained in combat by Myrddin, and had no fear. I might even come to dislike Tristram enough to want to hurt him.

"Perhaps I was also in error, my lord," Duke Cador said. "I was of the opinion that I was talking with a gentleman who would honor my daughter as his wife."

"What are you saying?" Tristram asked in a silky voice.

"I am saying that my daughter's hand seems to be of less importance to you than I would like, if you avoid fighting for it."

"Did you use the word *avoid?* Surely you do not think me in fear of these country yokels?"

"I will think what I please from your conduct. In any case, we have nothing more to discuss. I regret the time we have spent on what now seems a bootless topic of conversation." A little more of this, and Cador would be talking himself into a fight with Tristram, I thought. Tristram's face was white. He was unhappy to the point where he needed some outlet. Poor Kay provided it. He came puffing up, out of breath from his effort to run up the stairs to the sitting room.

"See here," he said. "The priest says that if I declared myself before Miriam's marriage, the problem of my being an uncle doesn't enter into it."

"Another suitor? Surely no one will question my reluctance to fight all of the swains on your island, my lord." Tristram looked at Kay, who was tall and thin to the point of emaciation. "And in particular such a one as this!" he added, and making an exaggerated bow to Kay, sauntered away, looking fatigued.

"What's his problem?" Kay asked, puzzled when the rest of us laughed.

"You are just in time to witness a betrothal," Duke Cador said, his good humor restored. "We will celebrate that it is not Tristram's."

"You will let us marry, then, father?"

"No, but I will promise not to engage you elsewhere, even to Kay, for one year. If Arthur is king a year from today, we will visit him, and if you are both of the same mind you are now, you will then have my blessing, under one condition. Your first child will

103

be born on this island, and be the heir of Cador and you will stay by his side and raise him here."

"Very well," Arthur said.

"No," Samana cried. "I would be with Arthur always!"

"Hear me, Samana. I have undergone as much of this sort of thing from you as I care to experience today. If you do not accede to my wishes I will lock you in a convent, put Miriam aside in favor of some female who can give me an heir, and you will never see Arthur again." This was no jest. Under Roman law he could do this thing, and Arthur would be barred by the church from interfering. Likely enough she would be sent to Rome, out of his reach, to be sequestered. Samana bit her lip to keep from speaking out again and looked down in submission.

After a pause, Cador continued. "In exchange, I want you not to see my daughter for that year. I know you believe there is no occasion for doubt about the constancy of your affection, but things will change for you, and I do not want my daughter hurt."

"Oh, thank you, Father," Samana cried, hugging him in contrition. "We won't mind the wait, will we, Arthur?" Arthur looked doubtful at this, but was persuaded by Samana to accept the separation in good faith. I was happy it was settled so amicably, except for the enmity we had earned from Tristram.

Arthur wanted to sail all the way to London, but Myrddin would not hear of it. "We have a wagon waiting for us at Exeter. The same one you were so scornful about when I traded it for the boat," he said smiling sardonically at me. "The man promised to exchange with me if I ever requested it back. It was cheaper than paying him to store it." I laughed. Myrddin was complex.

He turned to Arthur. "I am uneasy about the weight of the anvil if we should run into weather. It could shift and plunge through the boat's bottom, which would sink our enterprise, let alone us. The shorter the trip, the less the risk." There was nothing more to be said. In matters like these none of us disputed Myrddin's authority.

I carried the anvil to the cart we used to transport goods to and from the beach. Arthur surprised me by lifting it in his arms and handing it to me as I was about to pick it up. I had not thought anyone else could do that but Myrddin. Out of the corner of my eye I saw Arthur wink at Nithe, proud of himself for his feat, while she shook her head in resigned amusement.

At the last minute we could not find Nithe. All was ready to embark, with Ulfas and Anna and the children waiting on the beach ready to wish us a safe voyage. They would stay behind. Ulfas knew enough smithing to do simple repairs, and the work would be kept up.

Ector had left the day before, impatient to be moving, and Nithe had been relieved, not wishing to travel with Ector's good wife, Lady Ellen, and be scolded for her hoydenism all the way to London.

"Where is that dratted girl?" Myrddin demanded.

"I think I know," I said. "I'll get her." As I had thought, she had gone to bid good-bye to her house. I found her on her knees hugging her loom, in tears.

"What is this?" I asked, but gently, for I knew.

"I love this house, Pelleas," she said. "It's the only place in the world where I have felt at home. Will I ever see it again?"

"Truly," I said, "we will come back, and you know Ulfas has promised to take care of it. Come now, Myrddin is waiting."

I took her hand and helped her to rise and she threw her arms about me and hugged me for a long moment, saying good-bye to her childhood as well. When we reached the beach, Myrddin took one look at her face and gave over saying whatever he had planned. On the journey to the mainland, Nithe kept her eyes on where we had been, but Arthur sat in the bow as if by straining he could hasten the morrow.

We left soon after sunup and were on the mainland before night, driven by a spanking breeze. Myrddin traded the boat back for the wagon to the same man with whom he had once traded it for the boat. The man had been waiting for us as Myrddin had foreseen.

The wagon appeared to be in good condition. The man had been proud of it, and worked it less than we might have ourselves. The oxen were long since dead, and Myrddin bargained for a team of giant horses with full harness. They had been trained for the wagon, but could carry a knight in full armor as easily. They became Arthur's special responsibility. He curried them as if they were pets and they responded with affection.

I touched their minds with my own as I had learned to do while shoeing horses and found these two timid and gentle. They might look like war horses, but they were not.

I spoke to Myrrdin about the horses. "I think it would be well if Arthur had a horse of his own to ride. He's horse-mad, and it might give him something to think about other than this business of becoming High King." Myrddin looked at me intently for a moment, and nodded.

"I have also been thinking," he said. "Arthur is not out of danger just because he's grown. It would be best if we hide him for a while. What think you about making Arthur squire to Kay? Ector plans to bring the boy out at the Christmas tournament, and it will serve as an excuse for Arthur's presence."

"Would he do it? You know how he feels about Kay. I can imagine Kay would use every occasion to humiliate him in front of others."

"I think we can count on his sense of the ridiculous to see him through it." Myrddin was right. Arthur's idea of humor centered on incongruities, and he could be part of a charade like this and enjoy it.

"Very well. Do you want me to talk to him about it?"

"No, bring him and Nithe both in, for we have to settle a number of things." I found them with the horses as I expected. They were arguing, again as I expected.

"Look, when we get to London, I want to look around some. I can't have a female hanging on to me if I want to see anything."

"When did I ever hang onto you? I can take care of myself! I want to look around as much as you do. It's just that Myrddin won't let me go by myself."

"Why don't you dress as a boy?" I asked. "You're taller than Arthur and act like a boy most of the time, anyway. Wear Gaelic trousers and people will assume you are a boy."

"That's it!" she said. She ran over and hugged me enthusiastically. "I can always count on you, Dog's-brother, to help me when Bear gets stubborn. I don't need you, Bear. I'll see London by myself."

"Actually, I don't think that will work," I said. "I think Myrddin expects me to look after the two of you, not that I have any more experience in cities like London than you do."

"Would you come with us?" Arthur asked, excitedly. "If you're with us, Myrddin won't be able to say a thing."

"That's not true," I said. "I'll go along, but let Myrddin force me on you, or he may think of a reason why he doesn't like it. Come with me now, he wants to talk with all of us and sent me to find you."

Myrddin did talk to us, and did order me to watch over Arthur. He also ordered Nithe to go with us.

"I'd have to wear trousers and pretend I'm a boy," Nithe wailed. "I've been looking forward to wearing pretty dresses and looking like a proper woman for the first time in my life!"

"You'll do that, too, but not all the time," Myrddin assured her. "To make it sweeter, I'll buy extra horses so you can ride instead of walk or sit in the wagon."

"Please, Nithe, do it," Arthur pleaded, and Nithe relented. I shook my head, disgusted at their duplicity, but they were very pleased with themselves.

Arthur insisted on picking out his own horse, and one for Nithe as well, when we went to Exeter's horse fair in a field near the town. He took a raw-boned gelding for himself that had been cut late in an effort to improve its temper, to no avail. The animal tried to bite Arthur several times, to be punished so immediately that the beast learned quickly who was in charge. Arthur picked a spirited but gentle mare for Nithe. They liked each other, and Nithe flooded the animal with affection from her mind that washed over all of us. It surprised Arthur's horse into showing better manners for a time. Arthur even found a horse for Myrddin to ride, a huge one able to carry him everywhere. Myrddin named him Blaise, after an old teacher he once had.

"You'll have to stay out of Kay's way when you wear men's clothing or he'll denounce you," Myrddin warned Nithe. "We will travel with Ector's household for protection on the road, and Ector's lady will expect you to act like a lady, yourself."

"I'll be good," Nithe promised, frowning to learn that she would not escape Lady Ellen after all. I decided Myrddin had not been fooled by their pretense.

On the trip to London Myrddin was distracted, fretting that he had so little control over events, but he was, nevertheless, an interesting traveling companion. He knew the names and properties of every shrub and flower, and jumped down from the wagon from time to time to gather specimens. I drove. Arthur, Nithe and Kay rode their horses with Kay being very bossy. He pointed out, endlessly, that Arthur was only a squire on this trip, and that he, Kay was to be knighted. When he attempted to give Arthur orders on the strength of this, Arthur merely ignored him, but Nithe was irritated. It did not help her mood when Lady Ellen called her to ride beside her wagon whenever she strayed off, thinking it necessary to chaperon her with so many men around. Ector had a dozen retainers riding as escorts, Arthur's comrades, not the old veterans Ector had served with. These were Nithe's friends and admirers as well, and of no danger to her, but she could not well explain this to Lady Ellen.

Our wagon had fallen somewhat behind the main party because of Myrddin's practice of stopping to examine any unusual thing he saw and, incidentally, to escape the dust rising from the main party, when a commotion off the road took his attention. It appeared to be a pack of dogs barking and circling a small pile of large rocks. Several men armed with scythes and pitchforks were watching.

"Do you hear that?" Myrddin asked. I listened and my mind picked up an urgent appeal for help. There were no words, but the message was clear enough. Without waiting for orders I turned the wagon and urged the horses to a trot, reaching the group around the rocks in a few short minutes. We saw the dogs had killed a bitch wolf and some of them were worrying her carcass and the bodies of a litter of pups. Other dogs confronted the one pup which was still alive, backed into a crevice and snapping at anything that came close. It was from the pup that the appeal came.

Myrddin was off the wagon in a flash, and I could feel the power of his command of mind-speech that backed the hounds off. The farmers, for such they were, looked surprised.

"Welcome to you, Master," one of them said. "We've found the den where many a chicken has been taken to feed this crossbred litter. Look at them, Master. The sire must have been a mastiff." He was right. The pups had been huge, with heavy bone, and tawny in color. Their fur was longer than any mastiff's, and their muzzles more pointed, but I thought the parentage undeniable. I wondered how a mastiff, the great fighting dog of the Romans, had mated with a female wolf.

Myrddin didn't reply, but walked over to the crevice and soothed the puppy with mind-speech. Leaning over he let her smell the back of his hand. Ignoring the growling dogs behind Myrddin, the puppy came out and sat down close to his feet, craning her neck to look up at him. Myrddin picked her up and strode back to the wagon, climbing up to the seat in silent dignity. He stared the farmers down, one by one, and when the last abashed man muttered something and tugged at his forelock, I clucked to the team and drove the wagon back to the road.

"That was high-handed," I said.

"Wasn't it?" he agreed. "You'd be surprised how often saying nothing is the strongest argument you can make." The puppy was trying to hide by burrowing into his side, attempting to make herself as small as possible, which was ludicrous.

I inspected the animal as I drove. It had the largest paws I had ever seen on a dog. "If it grows up to its feet, it'll be as big as a horse," I said.

"A happy thought, that," Myrddin said. "I'd been wondering what to call her. Horse would be an excellent name."

"Folks would laugh," I objected. They'd laughed at my name when I was young, and I hadn't liked it much.

"Then we'll call her Cavell. It means the same thing but the louts won't recognize it."

By the end of the day, Nithe said the puppy knew her name. It accepted Nithe from the moment she flooded it with love from her mind, but soon it would respond to any of us. Nithe attempted to teach it to recognize me as "Dog's-brother," laughing immoderately at what she claimed was success in the endeavor.

She and Arthur were so occupied in teaching the puppy, or attempting to, for at three months it was too young to learn much, that time passed quickly. We lost sight of Ector's party, except as a distant dust cloud far to the east.

The roads were good, and Nithe changed back to her linen tunic and hose, away from Lady Ellen's eyes, riding in the wagon with us much of the time. Arthur remained on horseback, and his friends circled back to ride with him on a rotating basis so that we always had communication with Ector's group. Arthur would sleep on horseback if Myrddin would let him.

We could see the pall that hung over London long before we could see individual buildings. Myrddin likened the city to a newly opened, and not particularly fresh grave. When we got to within smelling distance I understood the reference; London stank of the sewage of several thousand people. Who would want to be king of such a place? Nithe became pale, her intolerance for bad smells not having lessened over the years.

As we came nearer I ignored what it smelled like in wonder at the place. It was walled with fitted stone, with its only visible entrance a bridge arched over a broad, slow-moving river. I had long since known that there were more rivers flowing into the sea than those of my homeland, but I had never imagined anything like this. This was the mighty river Thames. I wondered why Myrddin claimed London's citizens feared the Saxons. The city looked impregnable. I sniffed again. If all else failed, its very smell would be a defense. I sighed, and drove the wagon over the high bridge into the city, steeling myself for immersion in the filth. I was surprised to find how quickly I got used to it, and I soon forgot it entirely in trying to avoid collisions. These city folk drove like madmen!

PART II

The
Young King

468 ~ 473

In Rome General Ricimer, the king-maker, is the real power behind six emperors in sixteen years. In Britain Myrddin, also called the king-maker, brings Arthur to the throne.

CHAPTER VII

his is even worse than it was the last time I was here," Myrddin grumbled. He drove us to the modest townhouse that Sir Ector owned with his brother, fronting on a muddy, narrow street that led off a mean square. Only the main streets of London are paved with stone. There were no windows on the street side of the wall. Stout double doors, big enough to drive a wagon through, had "Ector" carved into them, so we knew we had arrived, and Myrddin called out.

"Hallo, the house!" There was no response. He hammered on the portal with the butt end of his whip, and suddenly a small panel was opened in one of the doors. A face thrust through, reddened with anger.

"What in Lud's name do you want with all that uproar?" the man yelled.

"I want in, fool. What did you think?" Myrddin yelled back. "I'm with Ector's party." As suddenly as the man's face had appeared, so did it disappear. It was replaced by a large, grizzled head I recognized as belonging to Brastius Red-beard, the Gaelic cattle-king who used to bring his people and his beasts for summer pasture to the high valleys near the Strathclyde. As soon as he saw us, he pulled one of the big doors open and came over to gaze up at Myrddin. Myrddin got down and was enfolded in a bear hug.

"Peace, Brastius!" he cried. "You'll break something," but he was laughing.

"I've waited for you, for a week," Brastius said. "Come, Ector's house can't hold you all. You must stay with me."

Ector limped out to join the welcoming party. "What took you so long?" he asked.

"Arthur insisted on stopping so we could eat. He said he would die of hunger if he had to ride all the way through London on a simple breakfast." It was true. Arthur liked to eat five times a day when he could.

"Brastius is right. You'll be more comfortable with him than here, although I imagine we could bed everyone down," Ector said.

Before Myrddin could reply, a messenger in Roman livery thrust a scroll at him, insistently. "My lord," the man said, "the Bishop of London wishes to see you as soon as it is convenient. He's had me waiting here for days." Myrddin raised an eyebrow. The messenger seemed to think his time was important, and that, somehow, Myrddin had deliberately wasted it.

"His palace is on the way to my house," Brastius said. "We can stop on the way, if you wish." Myrddin nodded, and broke the scroll's seal. He scanned it quickly, and handed it to me. All it said was "Bring the boy."

I read it and handed it to Brastius to share with Ector. When Myrddin made good his vow to teach me several languages he also made me learn to read Latin. He did it by assigning the work to Nithe, who has a gift for languages, and who enjoys teaching. I have never reached the level at which she and Myrddin perform, but I can speak Latin, Saxon, Gaelic and Pictish, as well as read Latin. Not wishing to be taken for country folk, neither Brastius nor Ector spoke anything but Latin while in London, but neither of them read it with much fluency, barely enough to make out simple messages.

Myrddin said, "With your leave, I shall take advantage of Brastius' offer and guest at his house." As though an afterthought, he added, "I might as well take Nithe along, as well as Arthur. The Bishop will want to meet them both, I think." Sir Ector hesitated for a moment, knowing Lady Ellen had counted on Nithe's help, but she was Myrddin's ward, not his. He nodded in agreement, and we soon found ourselves being led through one narrow street after another, until we came to the big square on which St. Paul's Cathedral was located.

"Do you want to stop now, or wait until you're cleaned up from the journey?" Brastius asked.

"Let us wash, and change clothes first," Myrddin said.

"The Bishop is waiting now," his retainer objected.

"Well, he will have to wait some more. Tell him I said so," Myrddin replied, grimly. The man's self-conceit had begun to wear on Myrddin. The messenger gave us all a look of outrage, and stamped off toward the cathedral to report.

Brastius' house was just off the square, in a better neighborhood than Ector's. His street was paved. I gathered he was considerably wealthier. I knew he had been one of Uther's principal followers, but was surprised, nevertheless, by the number of retainers that came out to greet us, and unload our baggage.

We changed our dirty clothes and took sponge baths in warm water brought to us in our room. Myrddin, Arthur and I were together, but Nithe had a small room of her own. The three of us put on dark trousers, and tow-colored smocks. We all had cloaks with dark blue stripes. I was surprised to see Nithe emerge from her room, escorted by a woman from Brastius' household. Nithe had on a short, forest green tunic that came to midthigh, with full sleeves caught at the wrists. An open, sleeveless overgarment hung nearly to the floor, and her black leather sandals were strapped to midcalf with crisscrossed thongs. Her knees were bare. The tunic was cut low in front, and gathered at her breast by a fibula, set with an amethyst. I had never seen her look so female.

117

Her hair was braided in two long ropes that hung down her back and tied with red ribbons.

"You should wear that gear all the time, Nithe," Arthur said. Brastius was speechless.

"It wouldn't be convenient in a boat, or on a horse," she said. A moment later she added, "And stop staring at me, you're making me self-conscious." She flashed a look at me from under long, dark lashes that made me catch my breath. I didn't realize I had been staring, too.

We made a brave appearance as we called on the Bishop. Our horses had been brushed and fed, and were in an amiable mood. No one walks in London who can afford to ride. The streets are too filthy, a long comedown from when it was occupied by Romans, Myrddin grumbled. Since I do not believe any real Roman ever swept the streets, I put their condition down to a lack of organization. I pitied Brastius' lackeys, who escorted us afoot. Brastius, himself, came with us, wearing a cloak with four colors in it, the strips of color overlapping in a way that Nithe assured me was very fashionable.

"Where did you get the dress, Nithe?" I asked.

"Brastius' daughter loaned it to me, to impress the Bishop. She said it would distract him, and make it easier for Myrddin to deal with him." I thought she was right.

The Bishop's palace was a house of two stories, next door to the cathedral. We were ushered directly into his presence on arrival. He was a man of middle years, running to flesh, bald and clean-shaven. He was wearing a white toga, Roman formal dress, and looked to be at least half-Roman himself. After greeting Myrddin and Brastius, he took Arthur aside and turned his face to the light of the window.

"No one who knew Uther would doubt his parentage for a moment. I have seen that very look on Uther's face a thousand times," he said. Arthur was wearing his expression that said he didn't know quite what was going on, but didn't like the way it was going. Hauteur is as natural to him as breathing.

"Have you prepared the test?" the Bishop asked.

"Yes, Your Grace. When do you want it in place?"

"It will still be dark when they assemble for morning prayers, Christmas Day. Set it up to greet them as they come out."

"Are you sure Arthur is the only one who can pass the test?" Brastius asked.

"He is the only one who will," Myrddin replied, and Arthur turned to smile at Nithe, drawing the Bishop's eyes with his movement. Nithe had taken off her cloak, and her pale skin glowed in the light of the hearth-fire.

"You have not met my ward," Myrddin said. The Bishop stepped over, and took Nithe's hand, tugging her gently into the light. His eyes were busy, looking her over. I felt amusement bubble in Nithe's mind, barely under control. So did Myrddin, for he looked sharply at her. Arthur grinned, happy to have attention shifted from him for a moment.

"Allow an old and harmless man to comment on your extraordinary beauty, my dear," he said. He didn't look either old or harmless to me.

"And this is our companion, Pelleas," Myrddin said, indicating me. I stepped up beside Nithe, forcing the Bishop back, in order to look me in the face without craning his neck. Nithe was amused again, partly because she looks petite beside me, instead of like a young Amazon.

"I thought I knew of every Geen in Briton," he said.

"I am not aware of being a Geen, my Lord Bishop," I said. "In fact, I am not sure what one is."

"The Roman historians say they originally lived in the Canarias, the islands off the coast of Africa named after the giant dogs," the Bishop said. "The Greeks knew the islands as the Islands of the Blessed." I must have looked amazed, because he laughed in a self-deprecating way.

"Forgive me, I tend to lecture," he said. "I speak in paragraphs when people prefer to listen in sentences."

"I am grateful, my Lord. Do you believe it?" I asked.

"Not at all, not at all. The Greek word for earth is 'ge.' I suspect that the Geen are earth giants. I mean, they were the original people here," he amplified and turned again to Arthur.

"What can I tell you, young man?" he asked.

"Who am I?" Arthur asked, directly.

"You are Uther's chosen heir, to be named High King of the Britons. I was there when he chose you before he died," the Bishop replied. "He also cursed you if you did not claim his throne. In this claim, you have my support. However, the wild Scoti from Ireland are invading from the west. I do not think they respect your claim."

"They will learn to," Arthur said grimly and the Bishop looked at him in surprise.

"I thank you," Myrddin said, smiling. "I doubt if Arthur quite believed it before. Now, you will have to allow us to depart, for we are all drooping with weariness. The trip has been long and hard."

"Of course. My apologies for bringing you here without rest. I was eager to see the boy. Now that I have, it would be best if you did not come again until after Arthur has been crowned, or men will say we conspired." He winked and then said, "But when you do, bring this charming creature with you," and he took Nithe's arm in such a way that his wrist pressed against her breast as he guided her to the door.

"Do not be concerned," Myrddin said later, as we mounted and rode out of earshot. "He treats all pretty maidens so."

"I do not find that reassuring," Nithe muttered.

One of Brastius' lackeys walked before us, holding a torch. Several others were armed with cudgels to fend off robbers, although a party as large as ours was probably not in any danger of being attacked. As we turned into the side lane, the most appalling sound greeted us. Cavell was howling, a full-throated, wolf's howl. Arthur snatched the torch and galloped off, hoping to reach the dog before someone silenced her with a sword-thrust. Nithe and I followed, leaving Brastius and Myrddin cursing in the dark and exhorting the lackeys.

We need not have worried about Cavell. She was alone in the courtyard, having kept everyone else indoors with the frightful din she was making. She broke off, giving forth with puppy yips and owr-owr-owr talk, delighted to see us again, and forgiving of our error in leaving her. Arthur was off his horse and hugging her when we rode up, with Brastius and Myrddin close behind. Arthur was laughing in the way that he has, which invites everyone else to join in. The annoyance we might have expected to find in Brastius and Myrddin melted at the sound.

"We'll have to take her with us next time," Arthur said. "Can you imagine what it will be like Christmas Day if we leave her behind while we're on our errand?"

"The thought makes me shudder," Myrddin said, but he was amused, nevertheless.

Kay and Ector went their way, and we saw little of them. One of Brastius' pages was about Nithe's size and we borrowed trousers and a smock from him to clothe her. Arthur, Nithe and I walked through muddy London's back streets as three visitors from the country, looking at everything there was to see, ignoring the dirt. Cavell frisked at Nithe's heels. London is about a mile across, not counting the river. It spreads up and down the banks of the Thames from the town center, which is the stone bridge, built two hundred years ago. There are stalls on the bridge where you might barter for anything. There is even hot food to be had, and clothing, shoes, clay utensils, baubles and weapons, as well as various services.

Bold women plucked at our sleeves as we strolled by, offering almost unimaginable experiences if we were to buy their time for an hour or more. They demanded good Roman coin, and we had none. Arthur pretended to be interested to tease Nithe, but as she was not as constrained in pinching and patting as he was, women being less mysterious to her than to Arthur, he soon gave that over. None approached me because my size was so remarkable in this town of Roman descendents, but some of them looked at me from the corners of their eyes, like a horse that has not quite decided whether it will tolerate shoeing. That could change.

Almost always we wound up at the docks, where sailors busied themselves loading and unloading ships. Boats can sail up the Thames when there is any breeze, but they need to be rowed or towed into a slip to avoid accidents. Most days we could find a wrestling match in progress, with apprentice lads, sailors and farmers in for the day laying bets on the outcome. If no one else could be induced to accept a challenge, Arthur would good-naturedly take off his tunic and take part. Although not yet sixteen, he was as formidable as any of them. It was not an entirely safe thing to do, for excited spectators might join in at any time. These adventures stopped after we all nearly got killed.

It happened that one day in particular, when Arthur was feeling especially full of himself, he challenged all comers. "Anyone, anyone at all," he shouted. "I'll bet my knife of good steel that I can take anyone in three straight falls!" I looked at Nithe, and she shrugged, and loosed the saxeknife in her sheath. Free to act, she can throw or cut with it at need, but the crowd might not tolerate interference from us if bets were taken.

From one of the ships a shout was raised, and from the deck leaped an enormous man. When he landed on the floating dock, it rocked. It was not that he was tall, though he was that, but that his body bulk was immense. Furthermore, he was black, darker than any person I had ever seen. There are black people to be found in London, descendents of Roman soldiers from Africa who have taken discharge here, and prostitutes hanging around some of the better brothels, but they are all of mixed blood. This man was pure black. I glanced at Arthur. He was staring in awe, with his mouth open.

"Let's see the knife," the man said in sailor's Latin.

Arthur handed it over, hilt first, and the man inspected the blade, nodding. He then took out his own and gave it to Arthur to inspect. The blade was curved, with a brass handle, and appeared to be very sharp. Arthur stuck it into a dock piling, and the black man did the same with Arthur's knife. Arthur came to us to strip and rub his body with oil.

"Are you sure you want to do this?" Nithe asked. "This man looks big enough to kill you."

"He can't be very fast," Arthur said. "It'll be fun." And he stepped up to face off against the man, who stripped down even bigger than he appeared clothed. I wondered if I would have to intervene and whether I could handle him if I did.

Arthur took the first fall, diving under the man's outstretched arms, and grasping a leg to flip him on his back. The man rolled and was up immediately, nearly catching Arthur. Arthur was mistaken. The man was unbelievably fast. There was no second fall. Arthur slipped in a bit of fish slime on the dock, and the man was on him. He caught him by throat and crotch, squeezed him in a paralyzing grip and lifted him high above his head. As he slammed Arthur's body toward the earth, he dropped to one knee to break Arthur's back across it. It is a killing throw, and not permitted. Nithe launched a flying kick, caught the man in the face, and knocked him backward so that Arthur only fell stunned to the dock.

Nithe crouched, her saxeknife in her hand, ready to cut the man's throat if necessary, and I picked up a short fending pole from the boat behind us to use as a quarterstaff. Fortunately, Arthur was popular on the waterfront, where many of the dock workers had won drinks betting on him against sailors. Sailors in the crowd tried to push forward, protesting, but I was watching the man, who was looking at Nithe with death in his eyes.

"Try it," she invited, beckoning him with her left hand, her knife hand moving in restless circles. "I'll show you a foul blow that will spoil your fun for the rest of your life. Come to me, little one."

He moved backward on his butt, kicking Arthur as he rose to his feet, and strode to the piling to claim the knives. I stepped beside him and grasped his wrist as he reached for them, and the crowd quieted, looking for another fight.

123

"You forfeited the stakes," I said. "Killing falls are not allowed in dock fights."

He tried to brush me off so I squeezed, surprising him. Years at the forge have given me a grip beyond the average. "Leave it," I advised. He had to look up at me, an experience that must have been uncommon for him.

"Would you like to wrestle?" the man asked, smiling a fighting smile.

"Not with you," I replied. "I will kill you if I have to, however." He shook his head, but stopped straining against my grip and I released him. He looked back at Arthur, who by this time was on his feet, white and shaken. He had picked up the fending pole I dropped and was holding it like a pike, more than willing to ram it into the man's liver. Nithe was standing with her weight on both feet, one hand on her hip, and the other casually flipping the knife up in the air and catching it without looking. She kept her unblinking stare on the man, but was cursing Arthur in flawless Latin. Color slowly came back into Arthur's face, as the insults mounted. It was clear he would be all right. The black man shook his head again, turned to his boat, leaped back aboard, and disappeared below.

We walked home in silence, Arthur finally having become angry enough at Nithe's jibes to demand that she shut her mouth. She did, and refused to speak to him for the next two days until he apologized. He did so by giving her the knife the black man had forfeited, and she liked it so much she promptly attached it to her belt. By then it was Christmas Eve, and we retired early, to be awakened by Myrddin when it was still dark. Brastius and I harnessed the draft horse to take the anvil to the square, while Arthur picked up the anvil and carried it to the wagon, showing off. Nithe lifted the puppy and put her in the wagon. I wondered if she had the blood of a Geen dog in her ancestry. She already weighed fifty pounds and was but a few months old.

We could hear Matins chanted as we drove into the square, stopping before the marble base that had once supported some

Roman emperor's statue. The statue was gone, but the stone was too big to move easily, and had been left in place. Myrddin placed the anvil, fastening it down with a thick chain to bolts sunk into the stone drilled originally to fix the statue in place. When the anvil was anchored, Arthur stood on the stone and slid the sword into the slot made for it, setting the trap mechanism and releasing it once, to make sure it was working properly. Myrddin then quickly painted a message on the side of the block.

We left with the horse and wagon, and Brastius waited until we were out of sight before entering the church. He interrupted proceedings with the news of the miracle outside. He told us later that the Bishop gave a short prayer of thanksgiving, reminding the congregation of the promise to reveal the new High King before leading them out to view it. He allowed no one near the stone, saying that a full mass must precede any attempt to gain the sword. He counseled those who would attempt the feat to confess themselves before they put hand to the task, and with one thing and another it was midmorning before anyone did.

We joined the crowd gathered around the sword in the stone. Men from the Bishop's household held back the folk, with short, thrusting pikes. They warned them it was possible to die if they accidentally touched the stone without the Bishop's blessing, and no one tested the premise. We saw Kay and Ector. Ector waved, but Kay didn't.

It was amusing to watch the nobles shoving each other in an attempt to be first to try the sword. The Bishop frowned and waved them back, but scant attention was paid him until Myrddin stepped to the stone, holding up his hands for silence.

"Painted on the stone is a message," he said. "Whosoever pulls this sword from this stone is rightful King of the Britons." He pointed to the words. "The Bishop will make the first try. After that, it will be by rank." He stepped away, leaving a space for the Bishop to stand. A bench was brought so that the Bishop might step on the stone, next to the anvil. Despite his secret sponsorship of Arthur, the Bishop gave an honest tug on the sword, testing it to assure himself it would be no easy task.

Proud King Lot tried next, claiming precedence due his age, as well as his rank. He had truly aged in the years since I had seen him, his hair and beard turned gray, but he was still in the full flower of his strength. I wondered how old he was, and whether it was life with Morgause that had changed him so. King Mark of Cornwall and King Ban of Armorica bowed to each other, offering precedence until finally Mark tried and failed, and Ban attempted it, and also failed. Others pushed their way to the front, being barons and earls from country holdings, and not giving way to anything but superior strength.

King Pellinore was late, not having attended mass. He thrust himself to the front, displacing others with slight courtesy, and set hand to the sword. He was big, bulkier than I, and as tall as Myrddin. The effort he made held Myrddin's full attention, and when it failed, in its turn, I could see Myrddin relax. No one would pull it out by sheer strength.

"What is he king of?" I asked aloud.

"He's the High King of the Picts, one of those Geens, they say," a citizen told me, glancing up at me and moving away, his mouth open in awe.

So that's what a Geen looks like, I thought. He wasn't much bigger than I am.

The sword did not so much as budge all that day, though I had feared it might break from the fierce twisting it was subjected to. Arthur did not attempt to pull it out, under Myrddin's orders. When all others had failed, the stone was left under guard once more, and the crowd drifted away.

That afternoon a tournament was scheduled. Kay sent word that he intended to participate, with the hope of winning his spurs on the field if he did well. He asked that Arthur attend as his squire, as had been agreed.

"Will you go?" Nithe asked.

"Oh, I suppose so. It is not dishonorable to help in this way, and Kay is not so bad. Isn't that so, Myrddin?"

"Go, by all means, if you wish to. Take Nithe with you. I have work to do," which meant only that tournaments bored Myrddin. I was sent along to keep an eye on Arthur, as Myrddin quite unnecessarily reminded me.

We left from Ector's house, Nithe dressed as a female to accompany Lady Ellen. Kay lost his temper a dozen times in the bustle of departure, until even Ector was exasperated.

"Oh, do give over being such a puppy, Kay. Your being cross is not making it easier for anyone," he finally said.

Kay was not used to being checked in public, and thereafter sulked, not speaking to anyone. Consequently, we were near the tourney grounds before he announced that in the excitement he had forgotten his sword.

"It's Arthur's fault, really. If he were a proper squire he would see to that sort of thing," Kay said, bitterly.

"He's right," Arthur said. "I'll go back and fetch it," and turning his rangy horse, set off at a fast pace, scattering late arrivals, with little regard for their dignity. One of these was King Pellinore.

"I say, who is that young ruffian?" he inquired, testily. Everyone within fifty feet of him moved out of range of his evident anger.

"My horse don't like being jostled," he declared. "Gets him frettin'. If he's put off his feed, I'll have that rascal's neck under my arm before the day is over." It sounded mild, but coming from a man of Pellinore's size and ill temper, it was serious enough. He rode up to us.

"No harm done," Brastius said. "He forgot Kay's sword, and Kay'll be wanting it for the tournament. You know Sir Ector, don't you? Has a nice place west of here."

"That your boy?" Pellinore asked Ector, by way of acknowledgment of the introduction.

"Not really," Ector said, nervously. "Fosterling, merely. This is my boy, Kay," and he nodded to Kay, who was awed enough to remember his manners.

"It's an honor, King Pellinore. If I might, I'd like to ride on whichever side you'll be leading in the melee." It was a pretty speech, and did credit to his upbringing, but it also reminded Pellinore of his grievance. I wondered if Kay knew Pellinore was a Pict.

"Glad to have you," he growled. "Don't know if I'll ride, though. Depends on my horse. If he settles down, I'll be with the green party." And he moved through the crowd, the weight of his mount parting it like a full-laden ship sailing through muddy water. We followed after him, locating the box reserved for Brastius. His lackeys were occupying it, thrusting rival claimants away with their cudgels. They vacated it for us, and stood in front of the box to prevent others from joining us, except by invitation.

The weather was beautiful, bright and crisp. Hides had covered the jousting grounds, and workmen removed them so everyone could see the dry earth, free from snow. The melee field was fast turning into mud from the trampling of the horses. The green and blue parties were already assembling at its opposite ends, with officials tying strips of green and blue cloth to the helmets of each man to distinguish one party from another. Our horses were led off by Brastius' men, except for Kay's. Kay stayed mounted, and paced his animal up and down, asking piteously for help.

"What is keeping Arthur? Someone fetch him! Doesn't anyone have an extra sword? Why does this happen to me?" he asked. He was ignored. He was still chafing at the delay when Arthur dashed up, with Cavell riding behind him on the cantle of his saddle.

"Sorry," he said. "No one home at your house, Ector, and when I got to Brastius' place I found Cavell had broken loose. I had to chase her half across London before I caught her. It was so late then, I found this sword and borrowed it. Will it do?" Above his head he waved the sword from the stone, with a gay flourish, before offering it to Kay. Kay looked at it with disdain, taking it gingerly and holding it away from him as he might a long-dead fish.

"You call this bauble a sword?" he asked. He appealed to the folk in the stands, raising the sword above his head so all could see. The crowd was restless, waiting for something to happen, and as Kay rode along the rail separating the boxes from the field, a hush followed him.

"My squire was sent to fetch my sword from my lodgings, where he had carelessly left it, and returned with this. How can I fight men with a child's toy?" he asked.

I grinned at Arthur, who was still mounted in front of our box. He was not abashed, sitting easily on the tall horse he had chosen from Brastius' stables. He was simply dressed, but no one would take him for an errant squire. When Kay reached the royal box, Pellinore called him over.

"Here, boy! Bring that sword to me. Where did you get it?" Flattered that Pellinore should speak to him, Kay gave him the sword to inspect.

"The same lout who jarred your war-horse brought it to me, in place of my own, which I had sent him for," Kay said.

Ignoring Kay, Pellinore stood up and waved the sword at Arthur. "You, boy! Come over here and explain this!" he demanded in a voice heard over the whole tourney site. His voice was as commanding as his presence, and Arthur could not well ignore the summons. All eyes watched as he rode smartly up to Pellinore's box, coming to a stand in front of it. Their eyes were on a level, the boy on the horse, and the king standing tall in the box. Kay looked out of place.

"Did you steal this sword?" Pellinore asked.

"I only borrowed it, for Kay. He seemed to want one rather badly," Arthur replied.

"Don't evade me, boy. Who did you borrow it from?"

"From no one, sire. I found it sticking in a stone and anvil, in front of a great church. No one seemed to be using it, so I just took it along. I meant to bring it back when Kay was through with it."

Arthur appeared meek and civil enough, but his mind sent out

129

shouts of laughter, which I heard clearly. He was enjoying himself. Kay was incensed that Arthur was receiving attention from someone as illustrious as King Pellinore, and pushed his horse in front of Arthur's, reaching for the sword.

"I want it back, now," he said.

"The other fella said he borrowed it," Pellinore said suspiciously.

"Well, he borrowed it for me, so it's mine," Kay maintained. Sir Ector rode up along with Myrddin on his horse Blaise, looking bothered. I was surprised to see him. Kay looked for support from his father, and Ector looked hopefully at Myrddin, for his interpretation of events.

"No," Myrddin said. "This sword belongs to the rightful High King of the Britons, and can be pulled from the anvil by none but he. It was supposed to be under guard." He glared at Arthur, to bring him to a becoming gravity, and said, "Speak up! Did you pull this sword from the anvil on the stone?"

"Yes," said Arthur. "I meant no harm. There was no guard."

Pellinore waved the sword and called in his great voice, "We have found our king! Ector's son has claimed the sword!" Within minutes a cluster of men, afoot and mounted, crowded near. We were shoved up against the royal box, too tightly pressed to move.

"Get back there! Show some respect!" Pellinore roared. Several horses reared and shied away from the sound of his voice, bumping into folks afoot, knocking them about. Considerable thrashing around and cursing contributed to the disorderly scene. I placed Nithe behind me, and Arthur, Kay and Myrddin urged their horses over to help shield us from harm. Cavell jumped down and pressed herself against Nithe, in the way, as usual. We were in some danger, but the humor in the situation kept Nithe and Arthur from taking alarm. I could hear both of them laughing in their minds. They could not hear each other, which was a blessing, for they would then have been out of control. I called them to order.

"Get serious," I said in mind-speech. "These people are not fools. Myrddin will be very cross if this goes awry." That was true. Both Nithe and Arthur were more fond than afraid of Myrddin and wished to please him, in any case. It was the only effective appeal for either of them. Brastius pushed his way up beside me, and Pellinore jumped over the box rail to help shove the crowd back. We moved away from the stand, and soon stood in the center of a tight circle with two full paces between us and the onlookers.

King Mark, who had shared the royal box with Pellinore, leaned out and said in a clear voice which carried through the crowd noise, "Pellinore, do you say someone has claimed the sword?"

In response, Pellinore grasped the sword by the blade tip and held it high. "See for yourself. Is this not the same sword which we all attempted to release from the anvil?" Those on the west side of the field were nobles and gentry, placed so the afternoon sun would be behind them, and not shining in their eyes. They knew what he meant.

"Who did it? You, Pellinore?" Brastius asked.

"No, it was Ector's son," he said, and pointed at Arthur.

"Not Ector's son, but his foster son," Myrddin corrected, in a voice whose carrying power quieted not only those around us, but the townsfolk on the east side of the field. The silence following this declaration stretched for half a minute before he continued.

"His true identity has been a guarded secret for many years. Not even he knew who he was until recently. This youth is the legitimate son of Uther, the Pendragon of the Britons, last High King of this land. Only he could claim the sword, for it is his to claim."

Myrddin looked at the Bishop of London, who had entered the royal box. The Bishop stretched out his hands in blessing. "By the all-abiding Grace of God we have found our prince," he cried. "Come up here so all can see you," he ordered Arthur.

Arthur rode to the rail, and stepped up on it, holding his balance with ease. He was bareheaded, and in the winter sun his hair shone like polished gold. Pellinore tossed him the sword, which he caught by the hilt and waved about in high spirits. The crowd

131

cheered him, but the Bishop brought it to silence again by holding out his hands to them.

"This is our miracle which was promised for this day," he intoned. "Let us postpone the tournament and see, with our own eyes, our future king pull the sword from the anvil once again."

The crowd took charge, and Arthur, the Bishop, Myrddin and Pellinore were caught up and swept back to town, where Arthur did pull the sword out again and once again. He was still mounted on Brastius' horse. As he looks his best on horseback, he was believable. I noticed, however, that King Mark had not come with us, nor were there any of the Gael faction present. No matter; this was a king for the Britons.

CHAPTER VIII

rthur spent that night with the Bishop, as his guest. Myrddin was with him, but Nithe and I stayed with Brastius Red-beard, who was worried, and explained himself to us.

"I don't like it," he said. "With no British high king to keep them down, the Gaels have divided Uther's western lands among themselves, and will not be willing to give them up for the sake of an upstart boy."

"Did they acknowledge Uther?" I asked.

"Aye. Uther won his crown with his uncle Ambrosius at his side. There were those of us who believed Ambrosius the better man and sure to be a better king, but no matter. Uther was the stronger of the two and when King Vortigern left the field it was Uther's name that was on men's lips."

"Gawaine, proud King Lot's son, told me this Ambrosius was his grandfather," I said.

"So he was," Brastius replied. "Rome's emperor claimed Gawaine as a hostage soon after he learned of Uther's death, jealous of his rights as Britain's master. Gawaine grew to manhood believing himself Uther's heir. He may still think so."

"Arthur doesn't know about this," I said.

"He will learn of it," Brastius responded dryly.

"Did all the people accept Uther as their high king?" Nithe asked.

"Yes, even the Gaels were happy in him, including King Lot, as a defense against raiding parties, for the Saxons were threatening to overrun us, and they would not stop at the boundary of British lands. No, they would eat them all, Briton, Gael and Pict."

"What changed, then?" Nithe asked.

"The Gaels are stronger now, and in the absence of a high king have crept back into lands that once were theirs; lands that Britons had won from them long before Uther's time. The Saxons have been quiet until recently, but they breed like lice, and they are outgrowing the lands they've squatted on along the coast. In Kent, where Vortigern, then High King, earned the name 'Vortigern the Traitor' by settling the Jutes as a barrier to Saxon expansion, much the same is true. The Jutes complain of crowding, too. We will face Jutes and their cousin Saxons together when they swarm. The wonder is that they have waited so long."

"The Bishop says they wait on the Picts, hoping to bring them into alliance against the Gaels and Britons," Nithe said.

"They will wait long, then. Only a true Geen can unite the Picts to fight under a single leader, and naught else is useful. Pellinore could do it, but he fought beside Uther and would not. Picts are true, unlike the Saxons."

"How will the Gaels deny him?" I asked. "King Lot and his allies?"

"They'll claim finding the lost heir is a trick, and drag out acknowledging him as long as they can. With Myrddin involved along with the Bishop, who could blame them? Two craftier men never lived. In the end, Arthur will have to take his crown by force of arms."

"Why do you believe Arthur is the true king?" Nithe asked.

"I was at Uther's side when he died, and heard him name Arthur his successor, and where he might be found. I was Uther's sworn man," Brastius said simply.

Brastius' fears were well grounded. The next day, when Arthur

134

sat in the royal box to view the postponed Christmas tourney, only Myrddin, Nithe, the Bishop and I sat with him. The Bishop was seated next to Nithe, and she kept squirming in her seat as if something were making her uncomfortable. I could not see that he was patting her unduly, but maybe she objected to any patting. The kings took the field, so they would not have to sit next to Arthur, with Mark and Ban leading the blue party, and Lot and Pellinore the green. We could see that the commoners on the west side of the field were nudging and pointing, recognizing in Arthur the person who wrestled on the docks, but the gentry kept their distance, as if we did not exist. They weren't hostile, merely caucautious.

Kay fought with the blue party, having become angry at Pellinore for ignoring him in favor of Arthur. He did well, and was knighted on the open field by Mark at the conclusion of the melee. We cheered with the others, proud to claim kinship with him. He ignored us, however. The tourney closed, with only Brastius and the Bishop openly accepting Arthur. Even Pellinore had been persuaded to back away from his seeming sponsorship.

New tourneys were announced for New Year, Candlemas, Easter and Pentecost, running the season nearly into June. We spent the time between tourneys walking through London by day and talking with Myrddin and the Bishop at night. Arthur insisted on inspecting London's wall, and we went around it from the outside and from the inside as well, although houses built against the inside of the wall made it less approachable there. We found three gates in addition to the bridge that gave access to the city: Lud's Gate, the Old Gate and the Cripple Gate. I looked carefully at the repairs to the ironwork that gave it its name and told Arthur I could improve on them. All the gates were closed at night, shutting out latecomers, who were forced to find quarters in the cheap inns that ringed the city or do without.

Inside the walls Arthur liked the public baths and the Temple of Mithras best, deciding, as a warrior, that Mithras was the deity he should most honor. He made no effort to seek initiation into the mysteries, however, for he discovered the baths as a place to find girls, and he went there, often as not, by himself.

At night he received instruction in the duties of a king. "A king is the father of a people, almost like being father of a family," the Bishop told him.

"I'm only fifteen," Arthur objected. "What do I know about being a father?"

"Listen and learn," the Bishop said, in an unperturbed voice, "A king must provide his people with leadership, keep them safe, and make them prosperous so they will love and follow him in bad times," and Myrddin nodded in agreement.

"And a queen is like a mother, then," Arthur said, bringing the discussion closer to a subject he found interesting.

"Time enough for that," Myrddin grumbled. Arthur smiled and kept his council.

"This is serious," the Bishop insisted. "You must begin to act like a king, instead of a sailor on shore leave, if you want to be accepted."

"Accepted by whom?" Arthur interrupted rudely. "The gentry do not follow me about to know what I do, but if they did they would learn I have more friends among the common folk of London than any of them." It was true. When Nithe, Cavell and I went out exploring with Arthur, folk spoke to him by name, with affection and respect. He knew the name of every dog in every alley in London, I believe.

"The common people have nothing to do with it," the Archbishop said sternly. "It is the gentry and the nobles you must win over."

Consequently, we went to tourney after tourney, and went abroad in London less often. "Don't you think they're overdoing this a little?" Nithe asked Arthur, at the Tourney of Pentecost. "People will get tired of all this carnage, won't they?"

"Never," Arthur replied. "I, myself, could watch tourneys every day, and when I am crowned I may require them year-round."

"If I were you, I would not say that in public," Myrddin said.

"Some of us who support you now might have a change of heart." Arthur grinned. Myrddin thought tourneys a waste of time, and fit only for adolescent minds. As an adolescent, Arthur was not incensed at his judgment, merely pitying. The real purpose of having one tourney after another all through the winter and into spring became clear, finally. The herald outlined the situation in his announcement before the Tourney of Pentecost.

"Greetings, nobles, gentles and ladies," he cried, after a trumpet fanfare alerted the crowd. The commoners on the west side booed, not happy with being ignored.

"The great London Tourney of Pentecost is about to open," the herald announced. "This is the last in the series held to determine who shall sit in the Council of Britain. Leading the Gaels today, we are honored to have Sir Marhaus of Ireland, winner of the prize as most valiant knight for the Christmas Tourney, and Sir Tristram of Cornwall, winner of the prize at the Easter Tourney. Leading the field for the Britons is Sir Palomides, who won the prize during the Candlemas Tourney, and King Pellinore, his father, and winner of the New Year's Tourney." The crowd applauded with the mention of each champion. None were local so the commoners cheered impartially. The gentry cheered by faction.

"Palomides is Pellinore's kin and Pellinore is a Pict," Arthur said. "Are there no Britons who can lead?"

"None wish to while you claim the crown," Myrddin said grimly.

"As a warning to the ladies," the herald continued, "we expect to see most puissant faynting and foynting and sore strokes this day. Any ladies feeling swoony may retire to the tent behind the stands, where couches and attendants will be provided."

"Faynting and foynting and sore strokes!" Nithe complained bitterly. "This is my fifth tournament in five months. Do all heralds talk this way?"

"You know what foynting is," Arthur said, his expression a mixture of affection and exasperation, "it's thrusting with the point of a sword under the opponent's guard, and faynting is . . ."

"I don't need instruction," Nithe interrupted, "I need relief! Swoony," she muttered. "Lud's balls!"

"What do you have against tourneys?" Arthur asked, mildly. "We've seen some splendid falls, and look at the great seats Myrddin got for us."

"Mostly I don't like the punishment the poor horses take," Nithe replied. "I've seen a dozen deliberate fouls, and nothing is done about them."

"A deliberate foul would disqualify a contestant," Arthur said. "I don't like to see horses hurt any more than you do, but I'm sure no one here has done it deliberately."

"Are you, now?" Nithe said, warming up to the argument. "I've seen King Mark twice thrust a broken lance into the face of an opponent's horse, wounding the poor beast dreadfully each time. Once might have been an accident, maybe, but twice is a tactic."

"Oh, Mark!" Arthur said scornfully. "You know how worthless Cornish knights are. They don't understand honor. You can't judge by them."

"Seems I've heard Tristram of Cornwall is considered the very flower of knighthood," Nithe mused.

"He's a pain in the butt," Arthur growled.

"Same thing," Myrddin observed. The Bishop had joined us, and he smiled at this. This time Nithe sat where she could be between me and the wall of the box, giving the Bishop no opportunity to get at her.

"You're a hopeless lot," Arthur said.

"All of us?" I asked. "I don't remember giving an opinion on the matter."

"True," Arthur said, as I looked around at him, sitting elevated and alone except for Cavell, who had her head on his knee. "What is it?"

"I was about to say that, considering this show is to find someone more acceptable to the Britons as king than you seem to be, you are remarkably supportive." Arthur turned back, frowning, but without response.

The herald came forward again, and called out, "This tournament is sponsored by Arthur of Wales. Let's hear it for Arthur!" Arthur stood to acknowledge the applause, but it was evident that the bulk of it came from the commoners across the way. Only a light spatter of clapping came from around us. Arthur waved his jeweled sword at the crowd, and sat down abruptly. King Mark of Cornwall and King Ban of Armorica sat two boxes distant, and neither of them applauded when Arthur was introduced to the crowd. The omission was not lost on Arthur. He was in a foul mood, therefore, when King Lot rode up.

"Greetings, Sire," Lot said. His tone was mocking. "Why don't you join us on the field? Perhaps you could win a following if you acquit yourself well in the melee." I could feel the anger erupt in Arthur's mind, but his reply was civil enough.

"The suggestion is welcome. I have no party, however, and would have to ride with no one to watch my back. I might fare ill under such conditions."

"I'll watch your back, Sire," Lot purred. "It is too hot for armor, so we decided to fight with blunted swords, shields and helmets only. You will not come to harm." He hesitated and then said, "But, of course, not everyone is up to fighting." It was a deliberate insult.

"I'll fight beside you, Sire," I said, giving him the title for the first time. "We will not wear colors, but strike whomever crosses our paths, without hindrance." Arthur was over the rail and yelling for a horse before I finished. I followed him, and within minutes we were outfitted. He rode his rangy hunter, and I was on Myrddin's horse, Blaise.

"Does it occur to you that Myrddin saw this coming?" he asked me as we rode out to the field. "There was gear suspiciously available."

"He is remarkably longsighted," I said. "We will know by the results whether he will claim responsibility or not." We took station to one side between the blue and green parties, a dozen men in each contingent. When the trumpet sounded, it was obvious that we were the target of everyone, because everyone came riding toward us, rather than at each other. By the time they had committed themselves, Arthur suddenly urged his horse into a gallop on a course between the two lines, drawing men toward him from the far end of the field, and leaving the bunched blue and green riders uncertainly facing each other. I followed him on Blaise, yelling and waving the light, long-handled flail I had chosen for my weapon.

I saw Pellinore and Lamerok pull up, unwilling, apparently, to participate in what appeared destined to be a massacre. We were lucky. Those nearest them slowed and milled uncertainly, indecisive in the absence of their leaders.

"Stay with me," Arthur called, and Blaise was only a stride behind when Arthur suddenly wheeled his horse around and charged back into the knot of men who had come together behind us. "You take the blue and I'll take the green," Arthur called, and we attacked.

The knights were on lighter horses than their usual war mounts, and these horses were not trained to fight. Blaise was, and so was Arthur's horse. I rode against Gaels and Arthur against Britons, by his choice. My opponents were bigger, but not more skillful than his. Most of them had their hands full managing their horses, and they could not also protect themselves against me. I hit them at will, knocking them from their saddles with ease. Their yells and the plunging of their horses added to the confusion. I did not hear the blood chant, and fought coldly, controlling my strength so that I killed no one. I could sense Arthur's mind, and realized he was in a furor. It made me anxious, but I was too busy to do anything about it.

Another presence entered my consciousness. Cavell was beside me, leaping and dragging men off horses, shaking them senseless on the ground. She made only snarly noises, but they were terrifying to the horses. In a few moments the horsemen at my end were fleeing, and I turned to help Arthur. He needed no help. He was chasing his foes, and caught King Lot with a blow on the side of the head from behind, which tumbled him to the ground. The Gaels among them rode off the field when Lot fell.

"Let them go," I called. "Watch your back!" and rode to save him from ambush. I pushed the nearest men away by riding over them, horses and all, and hammered on blue- and green-ribboned heads indiscriminately where I could reach them. I met Kay straight on. He had the courage to charge, humiliated by the rout we were making of the melee, and I struck him a glancing blow on the arm as I swept by. I saw him fall out of the corner of my eye, and hoped he wouldn't be stepped on.

Cavell joined me, and with Arthur fighting like a berserker, the three of us swept the field. Within ten minutes we were in control. Arthur raged, riding up and down, challenging one and all.

"Come out and fight, cowards! Are you afraid of two men and a dog? Look, I'll fight without a shield." He flung his shield away from him. "I'll fight without a helmet!" and he took off his helmet and tossed it away. The commoners swarmed onto the field, cheering and throwing their hats in the air in emulation.

"Arthur! King! Arthur! King!" they shouted, chanting until they reached us and ringed us round, preventing any of the mounted men who might have wished to accept his challenge from doing so. I was uneasy, not trusting the moods of crowds, but these men gave us space, not wishing to come within the sweep of our swords or Cavell's teeth. They pressed us toward the royal box where the Bishop still sat and had put the crown on display.

"Crown him! Crown him!" the crowd demanded, and the Bishop picked up the crown, holding it aloft. An aisle opened, which Arthur rode down to receive the crown from the Bishop's hands. Crowned on horseback, on the demand of the people of Britain. It was a start.

CHAPTER

IX

The door to Ector's house was closed against us. We'd moved back from Brastius' house after Ector's Christmas guests went home, but the door was barred. I didn't understand it. I hammered on the portal, as Myrddin had once done, and the same angry man opened the small door only to turn me away. I am not Myrddin, and I was hungry, bruised from a hundred blows, and out of temper. When he attempted to swing the small door shut, I grasped it in one hand and tore it off. I then thrust my hand through, and grasped his shoulder. A sharp tug slammed the man against the inside of the portal, and he dropped, limply. It was but a matter of moments to put my arm through the open door, seize the gate bar, and lift it from its stanchions. I thrust the gate open, and stopped short. Kay was there, backed by two housemen holding cudgels. Kay's arm was in a sling, and he was in a temper to match my own.

"How dare you break my door! Who do you think you are?"

"I think I'm your father's guest, and have lived in this house for five months," I said.

"You are no longer welcome here, you Pictish horse-eating bastard. Not you, nor your filthy Jutish whore, nor your foul beast."

"Does Myrddin know what you do?" Nithe asked him.

142

"It matters not. My father left me in charge, and you have been my guest these many months. You attacked me from behind and broke my arm this day, and I no longer am required to give you hospitality. By Lud's balls, I will not."

"If you were hit from behind in the melee, you must have been running away like the rest of the Britons," I said, well knowing this was not true.

"I am not running now. If you attempt to enter this house I will have you struck down like common housebreakers. Go." We went. It was his house. I led Blaise, being too weary to remount, and we made our way to Brastius' place. There we were courteously received, and I took Blaise to the stables myself to check him over. He had suffered bruises and small cuts very like mine, but had no special wound. I wiped him down and fed and watered him, with Nithe standing and observing silently, before entering the house.

Cavell was very proud of herself. She cavorted around me, playing leap-leap as if she had not been tearing out throats a few hours earlier. On the other hand, Nithe had not spoken to me at all. She even rebuffed Cavell, shoving her roughly away when she came up to her for praise. The three of us were brought to Brastius' great hall, awaiting his return or the coming of Myrddin. Myrddin had told us to be where he could reach us at need, and we knew he would follow us here after not finding us at Ector's. Myrddin had said he had to supervise the activities around Arthur. They had looked like the beginning of a week-long drunk to me, when we left.

"I don't know why you're so upset," I said, as I had said several times to no avail. This time Nithe looked up.

"Why should I be upset?" she asked.

"Exactly."

"I'll tell you why," she continued, as if I had not spoken. "You all could have been killed out there. It was stupid in the extreme, and you're supposed to be the person who is taking care of everyone so nothing like this happens. If it weren't for you, maybe it wouldn't have happened at all!"

143

"Well, what was so bad about it?" I asked. I was becoming a little irritated at the need to defend myself from an attack that never materialized sufficiently to meet directly.

"You could have been killed. Arthur could have been killed. Even Cavell could have been killed. You didn't even think of that, did you?"

"Actually, no," I said, focusing on a question for which I might have some answer. "I thought you were looking after her. I didn't invite her to come along, you know."

"Oh, sarcasm. Oh, wonderful. Now it's sarcasm. You might have known that Cavell would be in it if you were. She wants to be just like you."

"Cavell? You're talking about a dog," I said. "Be sensible."

"Well, she does." Cavell, hearing her name, ran from me to Nithe, where we sat before the fire, warming ourselves against the chill that had fallen. Nithe absentmindedly stroked the dog's head, to Cavell's delight, and broke the silence. "I was worried," she continued. "I would have been out there with you, myself, but Myrddin forbade it. He said you and Arthur had to work it out yourselves."

"Myrddin wasn't worried about us," I said. "You know he doesn't worry about anything. Arthur is just another of many responsibilities he's taken on, over a long lifetime. He takes the view that if we're any good, we'll survive. If we aren't, we weren't supposed to."

"He doesn't think that way, at all," Nithe said, scandalized.

"Well, almost," I temporized. "Look, I'm covered with bruises and cuts, and I want a bath and something to eat. Is there no one in this house but lackeys?"

"I doubt it. Let's go back to the kitchen and take care of ourselves." We found a couple of kitchen maids who helped us fill a huge copper basin with hot water, and I stripped and bathed with the help of all three women. One was younger than Nithe, and inclined to giggle, but I ignored her. Nithe grumbled over the condition of several cuts, swearing they would infect. The hot water was soothing, and eased the soreness. Nithe insisted on putting stitches in one cut on my elbow, because it wouldn't stop bleeding.

"You know how fast I heal ever since Myrddin forced that stuff on me, Samhain night," I said. "It'll be all closed by morning."

"It will not, then! The cut you had that night Myrddin and I sewed shut before we put you in the wagon, or your guts would have slopped all over Strathclyde."

"I didn't know that," I said. "I'm not even sure I believe it now."

"Believe what you will, but hold still. This won't take a moment." I don't like being sewn up. Nithe has doctored me since we were children, and I never liked it then. I've never found a way to stop her, however, so I sat in the tub and let her work on me, while the kitchen girls brought more hot water.

We ate bread, still warm from baking for the next day's use, and strong yellow cheese. We washed it down with beer, cool from the cellar. When I finally dried myself on an old linen cloth, I was feeling very well, but sleepy. We had not been given a room, so we went back to the great hall, and stretched out on the bear rug before the hearth. I covered us with my cloak, and Cavell rested nearby. Hours later I awoke. Nithe had turned her butt into my side, and pillowed her head on my outstretched arm. She was clutching it fiercely, with both hands. I was glad of the stitching after all. Cavell's great head was on my chest, which accounted for the dream of being buried alive that had awakened me. I tried to move her, but she growled her objection, and I went back to sleep, laughing to myself.

In the morning Brastius woke us and apologized. "I am sorry a guest should be without a bed under my roof," he said.

"Never mind," I said, sitting up. I was naked under the cloak. My breechclout was dry, so I stood up and put it on, and plucked the cloak away from Nithe. She resisted, and woke up protesting.

"Why do you always take the covers?"

"It's mine," I said.

"Where's your tunic?" Brastius asked.

145

"The one I was wearing was in shreds," I said. "Kay would not let me in to get another."

"Myrddin will speak to him. Kay is Arthur's sworn man, and will have to receive you again."

"He called me a dirty, horse-eating, Pictish bastard," I said. "I will not go back."

"Nor will this filthy, Jutish whore," said Nithe.

"It was that bad? Very well, you are welcome here. I never knew why you left in the first place," Brastius said.

"Oh, Myrddin thought Ector was feeling put out," I said. "Thank you for the offer, but I believe Arthur plans to bespeak a smithy. He said as much the other day. We will live there."

"And if he does not, we will find one ourselves," Nithe said.

"Indeed. Have you some place in mind?" Brastius asked.

"Yes, I do," she replied. "There is a vacant building down by the docks that would do very well. I think it belonged to the Romans, and no one has had authority to use it until now."

"I think that is the Imperial Warehouse you have in mind," Brastius said. "You'd have to apply to the Town Council for access to it."

"So be it. Arthur is king. We'll have him do it."

"Will he?" Brastius asked.

"He will if he wants arms for the troops he must have," I said. "The Gaels will never accept him as High King of the Britons and master of the Gaels if the Britons are not behind him. He must be strong in arms to achieve even that much. I can't imagine he'll be able to raise money to buy them, so it will be up to us to make them for him."

"Of course. Excellent! Will you leave this matter in my hands, and be my guests in the meantime? It so happens I have some influence with the Council, and might prevail upon them. I'll tell them that they'd have to loan Arthur the money to buy the arms, otherwise. That'll open the warehouse for free."

"We'll have to be able to do custom work as well, if we're to eat," I said.

"Trust me. I'll make them pay a bonus for every weapon produced. You could get rich on it. In the meantime, I might have
a tunic that will fit you. Come with me."

It didn't work out quite the way Brastius expected. Arthur con-
fiscated the warehouse as representative of the Roman Emperor.
We were moved in the next day, and the dock workers, who had
crowned Arthur king, turned out to clean the place up for us. The
dust was so bad I had a sneezing fit; Nithe borrowed a boat and
took me fishing to clear my head.

Arthur was the center of a whirlwind of activity. As king he met
with the principal men of London, offering them royal charters in
exchange for tithes. The church exacted its tithes, and Arthur's
needs were as great. The idea of tithing craft groups was Myrddin's,
and it worked because Arthur gave something in return. Myrddin
brought in the four established smiths in London and urged them
to band together to set standards for the quality of goods, the
terms of apprenticeships and the prices to be charged to vendors.

Under Arthur's charter they would be able to limit competition
from itinerant smiths, unless they met craft standards in tests devised
by the town smiths and supervised by Arthur or his representative,
me. The value of this to the trade was so obvious that they
immediately subscribed to the concept, and it was soon expanded
to the drapers, the masons and the bakers. Other groups sought
the same status, but Myrddin advised to hold back until Arthur
built a reputation for taking care of these constituents before trying
to serve others.

Kay collected what was due Arthur and reissued the goods from
stores kept in rooms at one end of the smithy. He was in better
temper than ever I remembered him, though he avoided me and
I did not seek him out. What we could not use he traded for
materials we needed, pressing on Arthur the pleas of one or another
group of tradesmen who wanted the same protection, for Arthur
was as good as his word, regulating commerce so only established
craftsmen were allowed to sell, at fair prices, within a day's ride
of London.

Arthur was also given gifts as a matter of course, above and beyond the tithing, to plead for special treatment. Most of these were handed over to Kay without comment, and used as any other supplies. However, when the proprietor of the public baths sent him a slave girl to induce him to restrict the baths to gentry and prosperous tradesmen, allowing the baths to be turned into brothels again as they were in Roman times, a different kind of treatment seemed called for. Arthur brought us into conference.

"I don't want her slinking around the place," Nithe said, dirty from the forge and eyeing the perfumed girl with a critical eye. "This kind of distraction will get someone hurt, someone who is not paying proper attention to the work," she explained. She looked at me suspiciously, but since I agreed with her I returned the look calmly enough.

"Send her back," I advised. "Nithe is right. The girl is out of place here." The girl's eyes filled with tears suddenly, as she came to understand our remarks, and she appeared younger than perhaps she was.

"Why don't you ask her what she'd like to do?" Myrddin asked quietly.

"What does that matter?" Kay replied, seeing some difficulty arising that might keep him from disposing of the girl as he did with other unneeded material. I thought the same objection had occurred to Arthur independently, but being voiced by Kay made it unacceptable to him.

"You heard the man," Arthur said to the girl, "What do you want?"

"I want to go home," the girl answered, in a nearly inaudible voice. It was unexpected, and changed the tone of the discussion.

"That, at least, is impossible," Kay said. "She came on one of the boats, tribute to Rome that was sold at the dock before even entering the city and transshipped here to market. Lud knows where her home was. If we could return her she'd just be sold away again by her family."

"Is this true?" Arthur asked. She nodded mutely, tears running down her face.

"That does it," Nithe announced. "Can't you help her, Myrddin?"

"I can, of course, but her case is just one of many. What about the larger issue here?" he replied.

"What is that?" Arthur asked, as Kay threw his hands into the air and walked out in disgust.

"Are you comfortable with this business of giving folks away as presents without considering their wishes? With this buying and selling of people as if they were objects?"

"It's always been done," Arthur said in amazement. "Men are killed and their heads taken as trophies while women and children are carried off as slaves. You know that!"

"Since I taught you, I guess I know it is done, but did you ever hear me say it was right? A king must dispense justice to all his people equally, as a father to his family. The question is, is this girl a person?"

"I'll free her, then," Arthur said. "You can go and do what you will," he said to the girl. She raised her manacled wrists and Nithe snipped the slim, iron bracelets from them with the pincers from the forge.

"Where will I go?" the girl whispered. "What will I do?"

"Wherever and whatever pleases you," Arthur said grandly, whereupon the girl sunk to the floor in a fit of weeping.

"Whatever is wrong now?" Arthur asked Myrddin in the tone of a man who is panicked by a woman's tears.

"In Roman law, a father has life and death power over any child born to his wife until he names it. With that act, he endows it with rights that he may not transgress without penalty. He may not then, for instance, have the child exposed on the hillside to die, as he might have before.

"A slave is like an unnamed child. Its owner may kill it, rape it, flog it, starve it or maim it without recourse. When you free a slave, however, it is like naming a child. You endow the freed slave with rights, and become responsible for it as a father for a child. You have freed this slave. She is now a person, and you may not abandon her or turn her out-of-doors."

"Well, I won't then, but Nithe won't allow me to keep her here," he added resentfully, for she was very pretty.

"You could always marry her," Nithe responded dryly. "Maybe we can teach her to smith." The girl looked up in alarm but perceived that Nithe was only teasing.

"No, he could not," Myrddin growled, on seeing Arthur's face brighten up. "Marriage should be the one thing farthest from his mind right now. I will send the girl to friends where she will be taken care of, but Arthur might be thinking about the role of slaves in his new kingdom."

He gently lifted the girl to her feet and led her out. The rest of us stayed and talked, and without Kay to protest, we decided Arthur should be king of a free people and give justice to each person without regard to birth or rank. We returned to work with new determination.

We had set up four anvils around a central forge and Myrddin, Arthur, Nithe and I, all stripped to the waist, hammered hot iron into knives, spearpoints and shield and helmet rims. We used the stock Myrddin had brought with us, but had dock workers on the lookout for more stores, which they reported to Kay. We never ran out.

I invented a weapon modeled on the dock workers' hook. It looked like the tool they use, but I added a short, pointed prod sticking straight out the end, and mounted it on a handle six feet long. After work, Arthur put on padded armor and let them pull him off his horse to test the design. The dock workers loved it. They particularly liked the way he thudded, grunted and cursed when he hit the ground, but Arthur was play-acting. Wrestlers know how to fall without being injured. The padding was to avoid being cut by the weapon's two points.

The dock workers asked to be formed into a special group to fight against cavalry, and he formed them into Arthur's Irregulars.

He gave the training of them over to the young men who had escorted Ector's party to London. Myrddin had arranged passage for Ector and Lady Ellen on a trading ship bound for Cornwall, and he could well spare the men. Arthur needed them. They considered themselves an elite force, and named themselves the King's Own Guard. Arthur loved it.

The Irregulars could handle knives as well as anyone, and the hooks better, but swords were awkward in their hands. I remembered how effective my light iron flail had been in the melee. I am not as skilled with a sword as Arthur and had found the flail an easy weapon to use. I made some and they practiced on an oaken post planted into the ground. After watching them at practice I pitied the men who would have to face them.

Myrrdin called a Council of War after we had been living under Arthur's rule about six months, and had crafted enough weapons to field an army. He opened the Council, saying, "We have heard that the Gaels will not give up our lands they have seized following Uther's death. These lands belong to Arthur and the Britons, but to take control of them we'll have to fight. At the present time, we have nothing to fight with."

"We've built a fair armory," I said. "We have flails, my new prodhooks, spears and knives enough to equip two companies along with the Irregulars. We need only fit the iron helmet and shield rims with hide and wood and they will be ready."

"We need more," Myrddin said. "We need horses, and men to ride them. We need archers to harass the enemy. They have them, and we must match them."

"Why must we?" Arthur asked. "We need to counter what they have, and have something they can't counter, but we don't have to have the same thing."

"Explain it more fully," Brastius said.

"You remember the Tourney of Pentecost? Pelleas and I, on heavy horses, along with Cavell, panicked a score of men lightly mounted and drove them from the field. I'm not suggesting we try that again, but if we can figure out a new way to panic them, we might neutralize their horsemen."

"We could get more dogs like Cavell," I said. "She's old enough to breed, and breeding her back to a wolf might give us extra large and fierce fighters."

"Could we control them?"

"Yes. Wolves hunt in packs. If we become their pack, they'll fight with us. I get along well with wolves. I'll find some of those, too, if you'd like."

"What do you think, Myrddin?" Arthur asked.

"Why not? Even a few might frighten the horses. We should work against them and leave the riders to the Irregulars."

I nodded. It was up to me to provide these since I had volunteered, and I immediately began planning on where I would go to seek them.

"There are a number of old veterans who would follow me even if they are not ready to follow Uther's son," Brastius said. "These are archers from the hills, and I might raise a company of them. They'll need pay, but I can cover that."

"Good," said Arthur, "I am grateful. We will still need some horsemen to keep from being run over. Would the Britons of Armorica come to help?"

"I could get King Ban to come, I think," Myrddin said. "The last time I talked to him he told me he would consider helping in exchange for a promise to help him at his need. The problem would be in transporting the horses."

"I know a way," Ector said, slowly stroking his jaw. He had returned when word of Kay's conduct reached him, and Kay was only slowly earning his way back into acceptance as a member of Arthur's party by hard work and faithful service. Ector had thrashed him in private, beaten him so severely that he wasn't seen in public for weeks while the bruises faded. He rarely spoke up in Ector's presence, but now he echoed his father's words.

"I know what Father means. We transport horses that way in the islands, and never lose one."

"How is it done?" Arthur asked. Kay looked at his father for permission, and then replied.

"You must rig a leather harness under the horse's belly, and hang it by a davit from a roof beam in the hold of the ship. If the horse loses its balance in a heavy sea, it won't break a leg, because its weight will be supported by the harness."

"That sounds like it might work," Brastius said.

"It does work. I'd be willing to sail to Armorica with Myrddin and show them how it's done."

"Fine," Arthur said. "Any other ideas?"

"I could get you some Pict slingmen," Ulfas said. He and Anna had come with Ector when he returned, at Myrddin's request. "Not everyone likes Picts around, though." Ulfas watched Arthur closely to see if there was any hesitation in Arthur's reply. So did I, but there was none.

"Excellent! They'll do more damage than so many wild boars. How many can you get?"

"Two double handfuls, maybe. I'd be sure if Pelleas came with me. Picts like to see Geens in charge of things." I was surprised. This was the first time Ulfas had ever called me that.

"I will go with him. The wolves of the Caledonia are bigger than those here, anyway," I said.

"And I will go with Myrddin to Armorica," Nithe said. "Someone has to keep an eye on him so he doesn't forget what he is about in the wonder of discovering a new flower."

Myrddin looked at her and smiled, but said nothing.

"Everyone plan to be here by Easter. That will give us seven weeks to Pentecost. We'll announce a tournament in honor of the anniversary of my crowning, and that will bring out the Gaels like hornets. We'll meet them up-country, somewhere."

"It will take Ulfas and me longer than that," I objected. "We'll meet you up-country before the battle, if you can be a little more specific."

"Caerleon in the west, then, where the Roman legion encampment was. The barracks may no longer be fit to use, but it should be possible to provision troops in the area. The Romans found it so. We'll build a hill fort on the Usk River and make them come to us."

"We can find that," Ulfas agreed, and I nodded.

I said good-bye to Nithe with foreboding. "I wish you were coming with us," I said.

"Why?" she asked, looking up at me from the corner of her eye.

"I am not comfortable when I don't know what you're up to," I said, after pondering the question a moment or two.

"Not good enough, Dog's-brother," she said, coldly. "Not nearly good enough."

"What do you mean?" I asked.

"When you think you know the answer, ask me again," she replied, and slammed the door to her room, effectively cutting off further discussion. I didn't see her again before we left.

The trip Ulfas and I took back to the Strathclyde on good horses was faster and less eventful than the trip out had been, with one exception. Cavell came into heat, and we had dogs from a dozen villages following us. She seemed not interested in mating, punishing severely several males who tried forcing her. At night she lay with her head on my chest, growling continuously, and about once an hour would leap up, snapping, to chase some overambitious suitor away, awakening me in the process. Ulfas thought it amusing. I got cross from lack of sleep and Cavell seemed broody. When I touched her mind I sensed confusion, and irritation. The first heat did not last over a week, for which we were both thankful, and she had not permitted any of the suppliants to mount her.

When we rode into the valley I grew up in, I was surprised to see how small it was. I had been a boy of eleven when I fled with Myrddin, hidden in a leather sack. I was returning at twenty-six as the acknowledged brother of the High King of the Britons. I wondered how I would be received. I noticed Ulfas seemed unnaturally calm, a pose, I thought, to mask other feelings. He still had family here, and he was barely a year older than I and subject to the same qualms. The Gaels had left the summer pasture and there was a hint of snow in the air. The Picts had expanded from their palisaded home site, and encroached on the pasture land. I wondered what the Gaels thought of that. We stopped at the largest house, a stone-walled, thatched-roof affair that was new since my time.

"Hallo, the house," Ulfas called, in Pictish. A stout, heavily tattooed woman came to the door, and called back.

"Welcome, stranger. Come, eat with us." At least that hadn't changed. We climbed from our horses, giving the reins to a small boy who ran up, and approached the door. The fire's heat was cheering after hours in the saddle.

"Come in, come in," the woman urged. "You're letting all the hot air out."

The house seemed roomier inside than I would have expected. A slanting ramp led to a sunken living space in the middle of which a fire-trough had been dug, and in which a roaring blaze worked. Sleeping shelves were arranged against the wall, with piles of furs stacked on them. In the rear of the house were bundles and pots filled with stored goods. They appeared ready for winter. We had noticed rows of cut wood at the back of the house, along the north wall. The door faced south, to take advantage of what sun there was.

Seated before a loom was a small, active, older woman, who appeared familiar except for the tattoos that covered her face and shoulders.

"Mother?" I asked.

At the sound of my voice she looked up, quickly, and a moment later was clutching at the front of my tunic, pulling me down so that she could gaze into my face.

"Dog's-brother?" she asked. I lifted her so that her eyes were on a level with mine, and she squealed, and threw her arms around my neck, hugging me with a deathlike grip.

"You didn't die on the black stone, then, did you?" she said, accusingly. I couldn't find breath enough to reply, and finally had to gently free myself.

"You'll make up for the Oak King's oversight if you don't let me breathe," I said, lightly placing her on her feet. She stepped back to look at me, cocking her head to one side in the gesture I remembered. The difference was that now I was looking down at her, rather than up.

"Are you not glad to see me, then?" I asked, teasing.

"Much you care," she said. "Whatever did they feed you to grow you so big?"

"They say I'm a Geen, whatever that is," I replied.

"They run in my family," she said. "My older brother is a Geen. You didn't know that, did you?"

"I hear you married one," I countered.

"Ah, that. No, I married old King Pelles, a man like other men. He could adopt you if you like. We have no boy children of our own, and he wants an heir."

"It is not necessary for me to be adopted," I said. "I have made a place for myself."

"What is it, that you would refuse to be a king's son?"

"I am a smith," I said. "I serve the King of the Britons, Uther's son. We have been friends for many years, and I am not free to leave his service now."

"I have heard of him. Not all believe him rightful king, I have heard."

"That is why I cannot leave," I said.

"What brings you here?" she asked, sitting back at her loom and beginning to weave again. The colors were wonderful, bright and cheerful, and her skill surpassed anything I had seen.

"We seek help from the Picts for Arthur, High King of the Britons, Queen Brusen," Ulfas answered, giving my mother her proper title. "We want slingmen to offset the Gael horsemen."

"There will be some who will go with you just to throw rocks at the Gaels," she said, laughing. "My husband will be home from hunting by dark. You must stay with us, and ask him."

"We will," Ulfas said. "If you will excuse me now, however, I would visit my own family. I will be back after supper to talk with the king." We watched him go.

"He was ever your friend, and seems not to have changed in this," she said.

"Do you find me much changed?" I asked.

"No, you were independent at eight. I remember asking you to cut me a switch and bring it to me so that I might punish you for running off to play in the woods, against my orders. You did as I bade, and gave it to me saying, 'You can beat me if you want to, but you can't make me cry.'

" 'I'll bet I can,' I said.

" 'Not unless you kill me,' you replied.

" 'In that case, I suppose there is no point in it, is there?' I asked.

" 'No, none at all,' you replied, and glared at me. I thought it was funny, unfortunately, so I let you off, and never tried to punish you again, satisfied you had to learn everything the hard way. So, do you think you've changed?"

"No," I said. "A friend told me just before we set out that I had to figure some things out on my own. I suppose this is what she meant."

"She?" my mother questioned, but she laughed, not seeking an answer, and shook her head.

When Pelles entered the house I looked at him with interest. I had never seen the man I had named myself for, only heard stories of his bravery. He looked older than I would have thought a Pictish king was supposed to look, but his voice was strong. Young men challenge old leaders among my people. Only vigorous men are deemed fit to lead a vigorous people. The hunt had been successful, and he was in a good mood.

"Wife," he said, "be sure you have this soaked in a good red wine for a few hours before it is cooked. You know I don't like the wild taste in the meat that will be there else."

"Wasn't it I who taught you that?" she asked in an amused

tone of voice, but she left her loom to tend to the catch, glancing back once.

"I ran into your friend Ulfas on the way," he said. "He tells me he has come to enlist slingmen in King Arthur's cause against the Gaels."

"It's his mission, not mine," I replied. He let the matter drop and we talked of other things until mother called us to eat.

"You know Lot and his followers still come to the valley some summers," Pelles said to me after dinner. "I do not want trouble with them."

"All Picts look alike to the Gaels. King Lot will never know where ours are from," I replied.

"That's true enough," Pelles said, ruefully, "but he may still find out some other way. He is very subtle."

"It will do you no harm to have King Arthur's gratitude, and Lot will not press the proof in any case," I said. In the end, Pelles decided to put it to the Council so they would share the blame, and we were stuck in the village until they met, sometime after the first big snow.

We made friends with the young men, because Ulfas was sure the Council would say no, and be able to claim that any who joined Arthur did so against the Council's wishes. It was up to us to convince enough people that it would be an adventure, with the hope of loot, so there would be those who wished to defy the Council.

Before the big snow came, we heard a hunter had captured a great wolf and caged him in the old town. I went to look, because I had found no fresh wolf sign in my travels through the nearby woods. This wolf was very old, and gaunt. It had a lame foot.

"Don't you know your brother?" a taunting voice asked. It was Korlac the Hard-handed, who had beaten me as a child, looking older, skinnier and meaner. "This is the same beast you freed from my trap years ago," he continued. "He is finally mine, and I defy you to touch him again." Korlac was drunk.

I walked over to the cage and peered in, moving my mind out

to reach the prisoner. I pictured the last time I had seen him and the wolf stood and came to me, wagging his tail. Cavell whined beside me.

"What will you do with him?" I asked.

"I will beat him and starve him and finally, burn him," Korlac said. "He has robbed my traps for years, seeking out mine, and no others. I will have my revenge on him."

I put my hand through the bars and let the wolf smell it. He licked it once to bring out the odor and wagged his tail again, expectant.

"I will buy him from you," I said. We had done well, smithing in London, and I had a purse of good Roman coin for the first time in my life. Wonderful how it gives one confidence.

"You want to free him again?" Korlac laughed, a grating sound. "This is amusing," he said. "It will add spice to watch your face as the wolf suffers, as suffer he will," and he suddenly thrust the blunt end of his spear hard into the wolf's side.

Almost before I knew what I was about, I grabbed the spear and yanked it from him, breaking it in my two hands. He drew his knife, but Cavell had his wrist in her teeth and flipped him to the ground before he could use it. I turned and seized two of the bars, wrenching them apart, opening the cage for the wolf.

"I offered to pay you," I said. "Now, I will fight you. Be here tomorrow, sober, with whatever you wish to use for a weapon, and I will make you wish you had accepted the gold."

Cavell released Korlac at my command and crouched at my feet, growling. Korlac neither spoke nor moved. I turned to the cage and extended my hand to the wolf, palm down, for him to smell once more.

"Come," I said, and backed away. The wolf leaped lightly down, and the gathered crowd opened a path for us. I stalked away, with Cavell and the wolf following.

King Pelles put his hand to his knife when he saw the wolf enter his house, but the wolf ignored him. Cavell retired to a corner and lay down and the wolf followed her, smelling her all over before settling himself. He walked in a tight circle as if he were trampling down grass before he took his place beside her.

"I may sleep in the hunters' hall tonight," Pelles said.

"Not without me," my mother countered.

"There will be no trouble unless Korlac makes it," I said, "and certainly none from this beast."

Ulfas burst in and cried, "You should have seen it! We'll have more recruits than we can use!" He glanced apologetically at Pelles, and gave a somewhat exaggerated account of what had occurred in the square.

"It would appear Ulfas is right," Pelles mused. "What weapons will you take tomorrow?"

"It doesn't matter," I said indifferently. "I can beat Korlac with my knife against his sword, if necessary. I think I would prefer to do that."

Pelles and Ulfas came with me to the duel. So did Cavell and the wolf. Even my mother put aside her weaving to accompany us. Korlac looked blear-eyed, but he was sober. Most of the older hunters were with him, all armed.

"What are you prepared for?" Pelles asked.

"If the wolf does not stay quiet, they will kill him, and his master, as well," Korlac stated.

"They will not, then," Pelles retorted. "I forbid it. The wolf ate my salt. So has Pelleas, my namesake. I formally claim him as my son and heir. You must treat him as you would me." I looked at Pelles with surprise.

"I understand you claim to be a Geen, Dog's-brother," Korlac sneered. "Geens are reputed to be great fighters, but you are no Geen or you wouldn't try to get out of this by claiming kinship to the king."

"I don't wish to get out of it," I said.

"Where are your weapons, then?"

"I need only my knife against such as you," I said. "Come at me if you are so eager to die," and took a defensive stance. Cavell whined, but I reached her mind and the wolf's, giving them calm

160

thoughts so they both relaxed. Then I locked on to Korlac's mind to learn what he planned to do. I was able to anticipate each move he made, deflecting spear jabs and swinging sword cuts with equal ease. He angered quickly, and reached too far. I grabbed his spear and held it briefly while he tugged frantically, letting it go suddenly to put him off-balance. He swung the sword in panic, and I stepped inside the swing, catching his wrist in my hand. I struck him on the forehead with my bare fist, weighted by my saxeknife. I stepped back and let him fall to the ground. He was unconscious, but I thought not dead. It is not good to let a fight go on too long. I could slip as Arthur had on the dock, and a man such as this would kill me.

"Is it over, or must I finish him?" I asked his friends.

"It is enough. If he lives, we will bind him to a pledge to seek no revenge." They dragged him away to the hunters' lodge.

I did not test their resolve. I was ready to move out of the village that morning, but Pelles detained me, saying he wanted to show me something. We went to a small, fenced pasture in the mountains, where Pelles kept his stallions away from the mares. One horse stood out, a giant, bigger than Blaise.

"I wish to give you this great horse," he said. "He should be able to bear your weight better than the ones you were riding to get here." It was true. I had to change mounts every half-day to avoid breaking them down. This one would bear a warrior in full armor.

"Is he gentled?" I asked.

"No. That's another reason I'd like to give him to you. The other stallions are afraid of him, and he's apt to kill one of the fools who try to ride him. You have a way with fierce animals and may be able to tame him."

"Good," I said. "I will take him with thanks. I would also thank you for accepting me as your son. My blood father claimed me only to betray me. I cannot tell you how long I have waited for someone to acknowledge me. I had given up on the idea of ever having it occur."

"It pleased your mother, which is of importance to me," Pelles said. "For myself, I have long wanted an heir I could claim. Some of the younger men have been looking at me sideways of late, wondering if I could survive a challenge. Now they'll have to start with you, and I just may live forever." He laughed and clapped me on the back, delighted with me and with himself.

I turned my attention to the horses. They had caught scent of the wolf, and were bunching up nervously and milling about. The big horse advanced toward us. I touched his mind and calmed him, slipping through the fence to approach him. He allowed me to walk up to him, and stood quietly while I ran my hands over his legs, inspecting them for flaws. From his teeth I judged him to be about four years old. He was even bigger seen close up, heavily muscled in a way that I marveled to see him move so lightly and gracefully.

I vaulted to his back, still touching his mind, and urged him into a walk. It was strange to him, and I could tell he had not been ridden before, but he permitted it. I brought him to a halt, and slipped down, making much of him and letting him smell me as he would. I called up Cavell and then the wolf, introducing them, holding their minds in touch through my own. It took no more than that.

"I will spend the night here," I said. "I will say good-bye, for I must start my quest. Ulfas will stay until after snowmelt, but I must go."

"What do you plan?"

"I must seek wolves. It is in my mind that they will have left the hills at this time of year, so I must travel into the mountains to the east and north. Once I find them, I will get them to accept me as their leader and train them so they can be managed in battle. That will take some months."

"I would have thought it would more likely take forever," Pelles said gravely, "but that was before I saw you with the stallion. I will not be believed when I tell the story in the village, not even by your mother. Will you not see her again before you go?"

"Tell her not to worry. I have been delayed here too long already, but I will return when I can. Once Arthur is firmly on his throne, he will not need me. I do not like the Gaels who cluster around him, and would rather be with my own people."

"I will tell your mother. It will make her happy." And grasping me by the upper arms, he looked into my eyes before turning and walking off. Cavell, the wolf and I watched him until he was out of sight. I turned to the horse.

"What is your name, then?" I asked. He whuffled at me, blowing through his nostrils, and rubbed his face against my chest. Cavell and the wolf lay down in the grass, watching closely.

"I think your name is Mountain," I said. "No other horse is as big or as strong as you, and a lesser name would be demeaning." It fitted.

I did not name the wolf. He was not mine. I called him "friend," and he looked up at the word, so it served in place of a name.

We moved the next morning, with Mountain walking beside me, and Cavell and the wolf ranging ahead and to the side. They jumped a deer and ran it up to me by midmorning. I was able to bring it down with my sling, and we ate. The horse moved away from us and grazed, not interested in our meal. The wolf gained weight over the next two weeks on regular meals, and when Cavell came into heat again, she accepted him. Soon after, we went into the mountains to find our wolves.

CHAPTER
X

On a high meadow in the Grampions we located a small, south-facing cave that had been half-walled with stone by shepherds, but had not been used in years, for the sheep dung on the cave floor was dried to powder. Cavell sniffed all over it and checked the surrounding territory, while Friend watched, and Mountain grazed. I took a nap. When I awoke, Cavell had moved in, and Friend was lying in front of the cave entrance. Cavell was within a week of delivery, and needed a safe den. She had found it. That night we heard wolves.

I had ridden Mountain a little each day, getting on and off his back several times in the process, and making much of him. I cured a deerhide using the deer's brains and urine and laid it over his back, tying the legs together under his belly and padding it with moss so the shock of my bouncing up and down would not jar him so much. Finally, I fashioned stirrups to better control my seat, modeling them on what Myrddin had told me he saw the Huns use in his travels east. They were a great aid and allowed me to grip with my knees, freeing my hands to hold both shield and weapon. Arthur would be fascinated.

The second and third nights we heard the wolves come closer. Friend stood in front of the cave, howled a few times, and settled down, ignoring the chorus of voices that replied. Mountain didn't like it, and neither did I, but I realized it would be necessary to contact the wolves if I were to recruit them. Cavell went about her business. When I touched her mind I found it focused in upon itself. If she were aware of my effort, she gave no indication. She also ignored Friend and his nightly challenge as being no concern of hers.

The fourth night the wolves made contact, coming into the meadow, and close enough to the fire for me to see their eyes shine. I went to Mountain and gentled him, letting him know he had nothing to fear. He was quiet, but uneasy, watching. Friend made no attempt to greet the other wolves, until one came close and made owr-owr sounds. Friend rose and walked slowly to the other wolf, wagging his tail quietly, until he was quite close, at which time the other wolf broke into excited yips, and licked Friend's muzzle, the greeting a pup gives an adult. The rest of the pack came up, and the adult wolves all made much of the meeting. A number of half-grown beasts held back. I guessed this was Friend's old pack, and except for one large male and the youngsters, they all knew and welcomed him. Probably the half-grown ones were a new litter, and the male had moved in as leader after Friend left the pack.

Cavell came to the door of the cave to watch. Friend yipped, and she came slowly out to meet him. The pack greeted her with interest, sniffing at her politely, including her belly where teats were forming. She ignored the process, standing very still, an impressive figure a full inch taller at the shoulder, and twenty pounds heavier than any of the wolves, even Friend. If wolves had a bitch goddess, she would look like Cavell.

Off in the distance, a wolf barked, and the pack turned as a unit to face the sound. At the second bark, followed by excited yipping, the pack ran off into the dark. Friend went with them, but Cavell walked back to her cave. That evening she gave birth to eight pups with only me to help her. They came within half an hour of one another, six males and two females, all healthy and lively within a few minutes of birth. I was in the cave with her, patting her and telling her what a good girl she was, when the pack came back. Friend stuck his head in the door of the cave and waited until Cavell answered his whine before coming to inspect the pups. He left, coming back within minutes with fresh deer liver from the kill the pack had made. He laid it in front of Cavell, and nudged her muzzle until she acknowledged the gift by licking at it. I left them alone.

Within a few days I could identify individual wolves. There were twenty in the pack, though I never saw them all together. They were always coming and going on private business, hunting mice in the tall grass of the meadow, drinking from the spring, or sleeping out in the sun. The half-grown ones were very curious about Mountain and me, and together we led them out hunting. The older wolves watched us go, but paid little attention to us. Within an hour the pups jumped a deer, and I brought it down with my sling. They were tearing at the body with ferocious growls when we rode up, and I touched their minds, moving them back. I hung the deer, opened it, skinned it, and cut pieces of the liver to toss to each of them in turn, sitting in an eager circle. All of the soft parts I fed to them, giving the bloody skin to them to worry while I packed the rest of the meat on Mountain to bring home.

The young wolves scampered after us as soon as they discovered us moving toward the cave, abandoning the deerskin. I arranged them in my mind the way I wanted them to be, and they moved into two groups, paralleling our progress, one on either side. It was easy. They didn't object to being manipulated, as they had no deep patterns of their own. I had found the older wolves more resistant to direction, and worked with them through Friend, except for the big male who had taken over the pack in Friend's absence. When I touched his mind, I found him confused, and open. Whenever I could, I made eye contact with him, sending soothing messages. Wolves do not make prolonged eye contact with creatures other than prey or enemies. This one did not know how to classify me, so there were numerous opportunities.

This wolf was also curious about Mountain, and watched him graze with an intensity that made Mountain nervous. When he made up his mind one afternoon and attacked the horse, Mountain was waiting, and kicked him with a hind foot solidly in the ribs. I seized his mind with comfort before he hit the ground, and drew him to me while he was dazed and hurt. Once my hands were on him, he was mine. This one I gave a call name, Hair, the Pictish word for wolf. That night he slept at my side, and his presence, and my acceptance of it, kept the others away.

My training of the young wolves proceeded more quickly with Hair to aid me. I included him in my mind structuring, and he did not allow deviation from his perception of my desires. Then when Friend and the other wolves joined us on the hunt, they fanned out in front and to the sides of our tight group, which I directed from the center. I looked forward to the time Cavell would be able to run with us. I thought we would be formidable, indeed.

The wolves loved Cavell, and were fascinated by her pups. As soon as the pups were able to open their eyes, she brought them outside and introduced them to the pack. All of the wolves brought them food, regurgitated to make it easier to eat and digest. They were fat and fuzzy, with enormous feet. I waited for Cavell to bring them to me, and at about forty days after their birth, she did. She watched the pups crawl over me as I sat against the cliff wall, near the fire. Satisfied they were in good hands, she went off with Friend for two hours, returning to nurse the pups just as I was beginning to wonder if she would return at all. At midwinter, she weaned them, and left them in my care. I shared the responsibility for them with the young wolves, and we began to include them in our daily drills. By the end of winter, they were a part of our unit, taking their place on either side of Mountain as we rode, and able to run for hours at a time in pursuit of game. I had been alone for five months. It was time to return.

I had had much to think about during the day when the wolves were resting, and at night when sleep wouldn't come because of the penetrating cold. Among other things I wondered what Nithe had meant when she refused my request to accompany me rather than Myrddin. I thought back on our time together from the first days when I was eleven and she was seven and realized she had been an important part of my life almost for as long as I could remember. Sixteen years! I knew her in ways I had never known Bronwyn, and she was not less dear to me. I would have much to speak to her about when next we met.

We traveled south through the mountain country, keeping out of the way of men. I had calculated the Easter moon, and knew we had seven weeks to Pentecost when we were to meet Arthur to join him in battle against the Gaels. We began to see signs of the movements of large groups of men, as many as twenty at a time, coming from the northern Gaelic villages. They were armed, and carried provisions on packhorses. Even though they did not stop to hunt, their movement sent the game into hiding, and we found it scarce. The necessity to find food for three dozen carnivores outside of their own territory made delay inevitable, but we were able to reach the Usk valley five full days early. I circled the camps of the Gaels already assembled, and brought my wolves to the south of the area where there was little disturbance from their passage. Game that had run ahead of them were in the southern hills, and my wolves ate well.

I found an abandoned hill fort with second-growth trees on the slopes that would serve to shelter the wolves. A small stream in the valley flowed into the Usk. I left the wolves in the valley, rode downstream to the Usk and north to Arthur's camp, followed by Cavell, and one of her pups that refused to stay behind. I was greeted by a hail from the wooden lookout tower on the hill, and minutes later saw Nithe running down the path toward me. I dismounted as she came up, and stopped Cavell from going to meet her. Cavell whimpered, wagging her tail madly. When Nithe threw her arms around me and hugged me I lost control of Cavell, and she pawed at the two of us while the puppy barked and jumped about, adding to the confusion. Nithe disengaged herself, and patted Cavell into something less boisterous. The puppy smelled her outstretched hand and licked it amiably.

"I was in despair of ever seeing you again," Nithe said, without looking directly at me. "What kept you all this time?"

"My charges had to eat. Also, I had to wait until Cavell's pups could travel, and could obey orders before I started. Were you and Myrddin successful?"

"No," she said. "King Ban will send observers only. It depends on how Arthur conducts himself. If he needs help, he won't get it. If he doesn't, he will. Ban's son, Lancelot, wanted to come and lead his own knights beside Arthur, but he has to convince his father first."

A note in her voice, a studied, careless air that I associated with Nithe telling stories that are something but not precisely near the truth, caused me to look at her sharply. She turned her face away, bending over to let Cavell's pup smell her hand and changed the subject, saying, "This is one of Cavell's? She won't reach her size by half. What was the male like?"

"It was the old wolf I let out of the trap when I was a boy," I said.

"Surely not. What's her name?"

"I haven't named the pups. Some of them will be killed in the battle, and I don't want to feel worse than I would anyway," I replied.

"May I have this one?"

"If you wish," I said. "I can't guarantee she'll stay with you. She's the only one that won't mind me."

"Hmmm," Nithe said, still not really paying that much attention to what I was saying, making some plans of her own, as usual. "I'll call her Lucy. Does she look like a Lucy?"

"She's very pretty," I said, as indeed she was. She was white underneath, with long, soft, dark guard hair on her back. She had great amber eyes, outlined in black like those of a Saxon whore.

"I thought you'd be thin," she said glancing sideways at me

from where she knelt, petting Cavell and Lucy. "You're even bigger than when you left. Did you find your mother?"

"Yes. She is Lady Brusen now, Queen to Pelles, and tattooed blue as a pike. I hardly knew her."

"Ulfas is back. He says you are a prince yourself."

"Pelles adopted me as his son, which I appreciated, and named me his heir, which is naught to me. He had reasons of his own. I am a smith as I always was."

"Arthur insists on your joining his court officially, now that you've been acknowledged."

"I'll think about it, but I doubt it."

"He thinks that it will help enlist men to have it known that a Pictish prince is on his side."

I grunted. I did not want to be a member of his court and pretend not to notice slights directed at me. Harmony between the Gaels and Picts would have to be achieved some other way.

She stood up to look Mountain over. "Oh, what a beauty he is. He must be the biggest horse in Britain."

"I guess it's possible. Pelles said he was not ridable when he gave him to me, but I've found him gentle and tractable. The wolves respect him, however, for he kicks any who venture into range of his hooves."

"You have wolves? Will they serve?"

"Yes. I will have to bring them to battle, however, and not wait with Arthur for the charge. I've been thinking how best to do it."

"Arthur will listen. He does a lot of that now." She hesitated a moment, then continued, saying, "It's Kay you might have trouble with."

"Not likely," I said. "He's one of the reasons I don't wish to be a member of the court, however. I find I don't like scribes who work with numbers instead of people. They seem not touched by human concerns."

"He's worse than ever, now that there are supplies to hand out, and equipment to account for."

We walked to the fort with Nithe holding on lightly to my

deerskin tunic with one hand and patting Cavell and Lucy with the other, alternately, as they took turns pushing up against her. Mountain followed us in his docile way, pausing to snatch a mouthful of grass from time to time, but not really loitering. We were met by Kay.

"I hope you don't intend to draw grain for that horse," he said, by way of greeting. "I'm sure he eats enough for six ordinary horses, and he is not officially on the rolls—or are you planning on making him a present for Arthur?" This last was said in a different tone, as he considered how magnificent a beast Mountain was.

"No, and I don't intend to draw anything from you. You may have forgotten when you turned me from your door, but I haven't. If I have to come to you for anything, I'll leave," I said, looking him in the face.

"That won't please Arthur," Kay said smugly.

"It pleases me," I said, turning away and walking by, with Nithe at my side.

"He can cause you trouble," Nithe said as we moved out of earshot.

"How? I'll tell Arthur myself," I said. I did just that a few moments later when we found Arthur on the training grounds, stripped to the waist, and demonstrating the way a proper guard should work against the attack of two men.

"Pelleas," he yelled, throwing his sword down and grabbing me by the arms to look up at me.

"By the very gods, you are a Geen! And look at the horse." I could contain Cavell no longer. Of all of us, she had come to love Arthur best. Her greeting was overwhelming, even for one of his strength. She had him down in a twinkling, and ruthlessly licked bare skin everywhere while he laughed helplessly, holding her off with difficulty. I let them alone until Arthur regained his feet and came up to look Mountain over with a professional eye.

"It's the first horse I've ever seen that's up to your weight. Can I try him?"

"Pelles said he was unmanageable. That's why he gave him to

171

me. Too many of his men were getting hurt trying to ride him."
I should have known better. Arthur was on his back in a moment,
and almost as quickly back on the ground.

"Are you all right?" I asked, anxiously. I really was concerned.
I stepped between Cavell and Mountain to prevent the dog from
getting kicked. Cavell was crouched over Arthur, growling at the
horse.

"Wow. He's fast. I'd still like to ride him."

"You could if you took the time to make friends. I talked to
him first," I added in mind-speech, so Arthur would know how I
talked to him.

"Really?" The three of us and the animals were alone, the other
people having moved away to give us privacy. Arthur worked on
the horse, rubbing him down with a rough cloth and listening to
me report on the wolves.

"I know enough about how they hunt to realize they'll never
make a direct attack on mounted men. We can ambush a cavalry
charge, however, and drive it into Strathclyde. If you know where
they'll come from, we can lie in wait."

"Perfect. They'll be so busy with their horses, they'll be ineffective.
When they reach our Irregulars, we'll have them down in moments.
It couldn't be better. What'll you need?"

"I've already seen Kay. I need to have him kept away from me.
Aside from that, I can provide for myself. Nithe will act as courier
for me. When you want us to move, send word. If I'm not with
the wolves, they'll scatter." Aside from making a wry face at the
mention of Kay, Arthur only nodded. Soon others claimed his
attention, and I took Nithe behind me on Mountain to ride back
to our camp.

It was pleasant to ride along with Nithe's head leaning against
me, and her arms around my waist. The two dogs trotted on either
side of us in the formation they had learned, and Mountain went
on without complaining about the extra weight.

"I'm glad you found your mother," Nithe said.

"Umm," I replied, waiting to see what was in her mind. She never went directly into a conversation.

"I found mine, too."

"The water sprite?" I asked, remembering a conversation we had once had as children.

"She isn't really. She lives in a fine cave, not far from here on the bank of the Usk. The cave has a secret tunnel in the back which leads down into a small lake. She can appear and disappear in the lake at will by entering the tunnel. The cave can't easily be seen."

"It must be inconvenient in the wintertime," I said.

"Be sensible. She doesn't do it very often. The local people call her the Lady of the Lake, and it suits her purposes to be known so."

"Well, was she happy to see you?"

"Mildly. She doesn't seem to be very maternal. I found I had no clear memory of her when we met, and she was not much more certain of me. Myrddin brought me over, and she hugged him with a certain lack of reserve, I noticed. He seemed quite at home."

"How does she live?" I asked.

"The cave is large and comfortable, but a fort on top of the hill has a number of young women who seem to be under her protection. They call it New Avalon, because of the apple trees that lie in the small valley below. Myrddin said Avalon once was on a small island near the coast in the western sea, but King Pellinore made them move. He owns the island, and didn't approve of what went on there. Seems Uther once visited and seduced Pellinore's sister, who was an acolyte at Avalon, and ran off with her." I waited; it was my mother, Brusen, Uther had run off with. I hoped to hear more, but Nithe said only, "They don't seem to be acolytes any more."

"So, what are they?"

"Young widows. Distressed gentlewomen. Lonesome people, mostly, looking for company. Finding it, too, I would judge." I decided not to inquire further, because Nithe's body had tensed, although her voice remained casual.

We reached our own hill fort, a circle of stones with trees growing in the clearing. The place had not been used in many years, but the walls would keep our fire from being visible. The two male wolves were waiting for us, Friend and Hair, ignoring each other. Both of them carefully inspected Nithe, and she touched their minds with good thoughts. They wagged their tails, like dogs. Friend greeted Cavell and she reciprocated by licking his muzzle. Hair greeted me with affection.

"Friend is her mate," I said. "It really is the same wolf I rescued years ago from the trap. The other is named Hair. He was pack leader until Friend came back, and now he is my beast."

The wolves looked away from us, intent on something happening in the valley. We went to the edge of the stone ring and peered over. It was a rider on horseback, coming from the direction of Arthur's camp, and headed due west toward the mountains.

"Only Arthur rides like that," I said, "but it isn't his horse, or his armor."

"It looks like some kind of emergency," Nithe said. "Maybe he's looking for us." Arthur took a path north around our hill, and Nithe said, "My mother's cave lies that way. He's probably looking for Myrddin. Maybe we ought to follow him to find out."

Mountain came at my whistle, and we were off, with both dogs and the two wolves. I had instructed the rest of the pack to stay out of sight until summoned, but I knew we were observed, and would be followed.

We took the same path Arthur took, along a small stream, and came in sight of him entering a small wood. When we came up to him, Arthur was on the ground, and a huge knight stood over him with a sword at his throat. Arthur's sword had been cut cleanly in two, and lay at his feet. Myrddin was talking urgently to the standing knight, and a tall, flaxen-haired woman stood to one side, watching with amusement. Her arms were folded over her breasts, and she appeared to be but lightly clad.

"You can't just kill him," Myrddin was saying.

"He's trespassing. He's brought his men onto my land, taken over one of my hill forts, and now challenges me beside my own spring. Why can't I kill him?"

"He can be a friend to you. He will restore your lands."

"I don't need friends among the Gaels and Gauls. No one has taken my lands."

"They will if you don't find allies. They're coming down here to depose Arthur and take over everything in sight."

"I have allies, too," the knight said.

"Do you just? Old King Pelles is sending six hundred Picts against Arthur. Don't count on them," Myrddin warned.

"I am King Pelles' heir," I said, riding up to them. "Who do you say claims to lead Picts against Arthur?"

"His war leader, Korlac the Hard-handed," Myrddin said. His eyebrows went up on seeing me, but his voice showed no surprise.

"Korlac? He's a hunter, not a war leader," I replied. "Only Geens are war leaders. Too, King Pelles would not send men against Arthur. Korlac is acting on his own, and will not be able to deliver men to Lot's cause."

The knight stepped back, and lifted his visor. "You are heir to Pelles?" he asked.

I dismounted and lifted Nithe down, then walked over to him. I was a bare hand's breadth taller. I could see the partially concealed face was that of King Pellinore. I had not seen him since he rode from the field at the Tourney of Pentecost rather than join in the attack on Arthur and me. He had not remained long enough to see us drive the rest of the knights from the field, with Cavell's aid.

"Greetings," I said. "I am Pelleas, son of Brusen, King Pelles' queen. He adopted me."

"Brusen, is it? You are a Geen," he said.

"So I am told."

"You're that smith fella," he continued. "One of Uther's bastards."

"I'm getting tired of hearing that," I said.

"No offense," he said.

"Really?" I said. I was offended right enough. Arthur broke up the discussion by moaning and sitting up.

"What happened?" he asked.

"You ran into King Pellinore's sword. Lucky you aren't dead," Myrddin said. "Whatever possessed you to come here in that gear, anyway?"

"I was hunting with my falcon, and found Sir Griffith and his squire not far from here. He had jousted with King Pellinore, and was near death. I promised to avenge him."

"That was stupid," Myrddin said. "Pellinore is an experienced knight, and you aren't even in your own armor. Look at that sword, broken. You know better than to fight with such poor equipment."

"It's Griffith's," Arthur said. "I thought it better to take care of this right away. If I went back to arm myself properly, someone like you or Kay or Pelleas here would try to stop me, and my honor was closely engaged. Griffith is my squire."

"Griffith is a fool," Myrddin said. "We go to battle in a few days, and he sets out to get himself too banged up to be of any use, just out of boredom. I wish I didn't have to work with such children!"

"He wouldn't have been of much help anyway," Pellinore observed. "He couldn't parry the simplest backhand swipe."

"Why did you hit him so hard?" Arthur asked, looking up in indignation.

"I didn't mean to hurt him. I have to stand here every few months to maintain my claim to this place, and he challenged me. What was I supposed to do?"

The tall woman came over and said, "I'll have Griffith picked up and brought to Avalon. If he lives, we will take care of him." She bent and examined the bump on Arthur's head where Pellinore's sword had struck. The force of the blow was such that the helmet had barely saved his life.

"We'll have you along as well. You have a concussion, and won't be able to walk, much less ride, for several days unless you're taken care of. Fortunately, I have some experience in taking care of men. Bring him, one of you," she said, and turned to walk off, but stopped on seeing Nithe.

"My dear!" she exclaimed and held out her arms to her. Nithe hugged her, looking somewhat surprised, but I noticed her mother was looking at me, not at her.

I stepped to her side and Nithe introduced me. "This is Pelleas, Mother, my comrade, and Prince of the Picts, Heir to King Pelles. Pelleas, this is my mother, Hilda, the Lady of the Lake."

"Oh, yes! Myrddin has spoken much of you," she said, giving me her hand, but keeping her arm about Nithe's shoulders. "Are you interested in my daughter, then?" she continued, a teasing note in her voice.

"He's interested in wolves and boats and iron," Nithe said before I could respond.

"I see," she said, looking thoughtfully back at Nithe. "I see. Well, that should change," she added. Nithe slanted a look at me and I felt myself flush with embarrassment.

"I must see to my charges," the Lady Hilda said, giving Nithe a last squeeze and me a calculating look before she dropped my hand and walked off purposefully. I gazed after her until Nithe poked me sharply in the ribs.

"Is your mother's place far?" I asked, moving to pick up Arthur.

"We'll take him up to the hill fort," Myrddin said, overhearing the question. "This way." And he strode off after the lady.

I looked at Pellinore, who shrugged. Without further question, I picked Arthur up and carried him like a child, following Myrrdin, with Nithe beside me leading Mountain. Arthur protested being treated so, demanding to be put down, and I did so, barely catching him as he fainted and nearly did himself further injury.

"Here, what are you about?" Myrddin yelled, turning at the clatter.

"Arthur just discovered he can't walk on his own," I replied, and picked him up again, carrying him the rest of the way without hindrance.

Cavell and Lucy were with us, but the wolves circled the clearing, keeping out of sight. When we broke through the fringe of trees, we could see the hill fort a few yards away, and found the lady's retainers waiting to receive us. I delivered Arthur to them and grinned as they struggled to place him on a stretcher and staggered off into the fort. It took four of the young women to handle the load. We were not invited in.

I vaulted onto Mountain's back and lifted Nithe up behind me. Mountain looked around at this, to assure himself we were comfortably seated before he walked off. I could feel Nithe's relief at finding Arthur not greatly harmed, though she tried to contain herself; it is not always easy for her to mask her emotions.

Myrrdin came to us that evening. The wolves heard him, but watched without showing any alarm. We guessed it was he from their lack of response.

"Hail, the fire!" he called from the darkness.

I was waiting there for him, and spoke quietly, "Welcome, Myrddin. Let me escort you in." Both of us felt Nithe's mirth as we approached the fire.

"I must be getting old to have been caught out like that," Myrddin grumbled. On hearing Myrddin, Nithe's laughter pealed out, and I grinned. "What's put you in such spirit?" he asked. "You've been moping for months."

"I've missed Pelleas," she said. She glanced up at me from under a lock of black hair that half obscured her face, and I felt my stomach lurch. Myrrdin did not give me time to reflect on it.

"Arthur's head will be all right, but his self-confidence is badly shaken," Myrddin said in a worried voice. "He thought he was invincible, and will need to hold that view in earnest over the next few days."

"What are the chances?" I asked.

"Our scouts tell us that the northern Gaels and some of the Britons have joined forces against us. You were right about the absence of Picts under Korlac, by the way. They didn't come. We will have the Invincibles, Brastius' archers, Ulfas' slingmen, your wolves and help from King Ban, maybe."

"Ban's men? They've come? I thought they had decided not to get involved," I said, glancing at Nithe.

"They are not committed, but King Ban led them over. They have their own scouts out to determine who the participants are, but I doubt if they'll show up in time, unless they think their presence will turn defeat into victory. We'll have to wait that out, and that takes courage. Arthur has lost his."

"Did Lancelot come?" Nithe asked, interrupting. She could not quite conceal the interest in her voice.

"Yes. He it was who brought the news."

There was a small silence. I shrugged, trusting time to inform me what was transpiring here, and asked, "What can we do to help Arthur?"

"The lady Hilda and I have thought of a plan. Arthur needs a battle sword, anyway, as you remarked some time ago," Myrddin said, nodding toward Nithe. "We'll give him one that won't break, with fitting mystery, so he will believe it has unusual virtue."

"You have one set aside?"

"The lady Hilda holds a sword I made for a friend from long ago. He will not be back for it, and I believe he would approve of the use we plan to put it to. It is an exceptional weapon. What we must do is devise a dramatic way of giving it to him."

"Have my mother do it," Nithe said. "She can turn a walk in the park into the event of a lifetime." I looked at her to see if she were serious, and observed the quirky eyebrow raised slightly, which always indicated sincerity.

"I agree," Myrddin said. I wondered again what there was between Myrddin and the lady Hilda.

That evening Arthur came to see us at Myrddin's request. He seemed to have recovered from the blow on his head given him by Pellinore, but he seemed quieter, somehow. We took him to the shore of the small lake, where a boat had been drawn up on

179

the beach, not far from where the cave tunnel opened under water. In the gloaming, as we watched, a bare arm was raised from beneath the surface of the water, brandishing a sword in the air. The dying sun caught the blade's surface, and turned it into a flashing light.

"This is what I hoped to see," Myrddin said. "The Lady of the Lake has chosen you as the guardian of Excalibur."

Arthur needed no instruction. He jumped into the boat and rowed to where the apparition had appeared. He plucked the sword from the surface of the water where it floated, tied to a dried piece of ashwood. The scabbard was with it. I admitted to myself that the sight was impressive, even when I knew it was a sham. For Arthur, who had always been willing to believe in the agency of gods and demons, this was not hard to accept as a true happening. I wondered how far Hilda could swim underwater.

"The Lady of the Lake has disappeared, but she left this for me," he exclaimed, as he neared shore. We inspected it closely, Myrddin being particularly interested in the runes that had been engraved on the scabbard.

"These say, 'Whosoever wields this sword in justice will be victorious, and whosoever wears this scabbard will never die of a battle wound.' The scabbard would appear to be more valuable than the sword, by that account."

"Not to me," Arthur said. "Why is it named Excalibur?"

"It was named in a land far from here. I do not know the language," Myrddin said.

"You know the history of the sword, though," Arthur said confidently. "Where did it come from?"

"Even that I may not say," Myrddin replied. "It is enough to know it has always been borne by heros and used in good causes. You will be invincible with it."

"We march tomorrow," Arthur decided, and left us at a run, catching up his horse and galloping off.

"What does Excalibur mean, really?" Nithe asked skeptically.

"Nothing, so far as I know," Myrddin said. "I just made it up.

If Arthur believes he has a magic sword, though, he will have enough confidence to perform to the limit of his potential, which is considerable."

"He can get hurt," Nithe said darkly.

"So can we all, my dear," Myrddin admonished. "This is not a game we're playing."

We found Ulfas and about thirty Picts waiting at the camp, under scrutiny from the wolves. The men stood closely together, alert for any possible attack, and moving very little.

"It has been a longer wait than I was comfortable with," Ulfas said as we came up. "I knew there were wolves, but I didn't know how many."

"There will be enough," I said. "Arthur marches tomorrow. Will you fight with us?"

"Yes. The Picts wish to fight under a Geen," Ulfas said. "They are more willing to take orders when a Geen leads."

"Very well. Let me bring the wolves close, and introduce them. Tell the men there is no need for fear, and in fact, fear can be smelled and will make the wolves nervous."

"Good. I would not like the wolves to mistake me for an enemy," Ulfas said, and instructed the men in what was about to happen. It was easier than I thought. I brought the wolves in, and with Nithe broadcasting good feelings, and Myrddin helping me with the mind contact, we had individual wolves selecting individual men to make friends with. We would make a formidable attack force.

"Where will Arthur want us?" I asked.

"Where we are," Ulfas replied. "As soon as he starts to move away from the hill fort, the Gaels will move as well. Arthur will lead his men in this direction and the Gaels will counter by rushing down this valley to cut him off. After they go by, we will attack, and drive them into his prepared forces in an undisciplined rush."

"Will they not suspect an ambush?" I asked.

"From wolves?" Myrddin asked in return. "Whoever used wolves in battle before? They will suspect nothing. They will know there are wolves here, of course, for we will let them be seen, but that will be enough for them not to send out flankers. They won't believe men could ally themselves with wolves and control them in battle. Where wolves are thick, there should not be men. Common sense tells you that."

"I only hope we can control them," I said. "We don't know much more about how they will perform in battle than they do."

"You've hunted with them," Myrddin said.

"That is different," I said. "In battle, I will not be as calm as I am in the hunt, and I may forget what I am doing with the wolves."

"I will be with you," Nithe said, unexpectedly. "I will remind you, if necessary."

"Battle is no place for a female," I said.

"Oh, hear that," Nithe said. "Saxon women fight beside their men all the time. So do the Gaels. I handle a sword as well as you do, and you know it."

She was right. Myrddin had trained her as he had trained Arthur. Furthermore, she had spent untold hours at the forge, and was as strong as most men. I said no more.

We saw the first Gaels at midmorning the next day. They were on horseback, for the most part, although there were foot soldiers among them, carrying long pikes. They drew their scouts in as they entered the valley, and we allowed a wolf to show from time to time to keep them close. Our men remained hidden until the supply wagons and spare horses came by, and then the Picts started a barrage of stones, using their slings to throw fist-sized rocks high in the air to fall on men and horses alike. The wagon drivers swore and slashed at the horses with their whips, further confusing things. Into this, I led the wolves, riding Mountain, with Nithe and Ulfas mounted on hill ponies riding behind me.

It was a rout. The loose horses, with wolves snapping at their heels, overran the warriors. Panic gripped them, and the Picts stationed on high ground flanking the Gaels used their slings with deadly effect, attacking the head of the column. When the Gaels reached the open ground at the end of the valley, Arthur was waiting for them. His line of warriors opened to let them break through and closed as they went by.

We cut the wagon train off from the main column, bunching the teams and wagons so they were running into each other. I rode into the heart of the tangle, calling the wolves to me and engaging the few guards who had managed to remain mounted. The wolves would not let me near enough to strike, swarming around me like bees on a badger, but the warriors went down.

One horse was screaming, with its leg caught in the wheel of an overturned wagon, unable to free itself. I dismounted by it and calmed it with my mind and hands. The horse relaxed beyond my expectation and I glanced up at Nithe who was still behind me, her head back and her eyes closed, concentrating. She sent out such a wave of emotion that all the wolves and warriors within fifty feet stopped struggling. The driver crawled out from under the overturned wagon, under the influence of her mind, and held the horse while I knocked out wheel spokes with my fist. I cut the traces, and the driver looked at me reproachfully, for mended leather is never as useful as before, but the horse was freed and had not, seemingly, any bone damage.

I remounted and watched the driver's face as he realized he was exposed when Nithe withdrew her concentration. He gazed at me with horror, so I gave him a wolfish smile. He dove back under the wagon, and the horse bolted. I looked around. A few stragglers were fleeing, still followed by wolves, but the rest were dead or had thrown down their arms. It was over.

Nithe and I rode up a small hill and looked out on Arthur's battle with the main column. The Gaels were fleeing, and Myrddin was restraining Arthur from pursuit. I could feel disappointment oozing from Nithe like wine from a wet sponge.

"Whatever is wrong?" I asked, craning my neck to look at her face. "Arthur has won his first battle, without the help promised by the Britons from overseas. He will not be a client king."

"Lancelot did not come as he promised," was all Nithe replied.

Of my own activities, I remember little. It is always that way when the blood chant starts in my head. I asked Nithe about it. "Did I do aught amiss?"

"You don't know?"

"No."

"You're a bloody hero, Geen. Look at the way the Picts regard you." I did. It was embarrassing.

CHAPTER XI

e withdrew from the battle scene. Nithe and I took the wolves hunting far from the valley to find clean meat. I didn't want them to taste human flesh for fear they would kill men for food in the future. I also wanted to get away from the memory of the blood chant. Nithe asked me what was bothering me.

"I hear a pulse when I'm fighting that beats 'blood, blood, blood,'" I said. "I try not to surrender myself to it, but I find I have little control over it. That's why sometimes I can't remember what I've done in battle."

"You're a berserker!" Nithe exclaimed, clapping her hands in delight.

"Whatever it is, I don't like it. It's why I don't fight in tourneys. I'm afraid I'll kill someone, maybe even a friend."

"I see. That's why you won't join Arthur's court, for fear you'll have to enter tourneys like the other knights?"

"Yes. It's difficult to explain," I said.

"No, but not everyone would understand," Nithe replied.

When we returned to the valley, the slain had been stripped of armor and ornaments and the bodies laid in two rows, Arthur's men in one, and Gaels in the other. There were many more dead Gaels than Britons. Wood was piled over them, and priests were chanting over the corpses. Only those with Roman connections claim to be Christians. Bishop Ninian works among the Picts and has converts. Other missionaries are with the wild Scoti in Ireland and the Britons in the midlands, but only chief men among them have become believers, as much for evidence of Roman sophistication as for any other reason.

"Has Arthur turned Christian?" I asked Nithe.

"No, but he allows the priests freedom to exercise their rituals if the men want it. You'll notice some are off drinking and carousing, and some are praying. He's with the drinkers."

Among the drinkers we saw numerous women, and I was amazed to recognize Morgause, proud King Lot's wife. She was sitting with Arthur, and stroking his thigh with her bare hand. I remembered spying on the wanton creature playing naked in the sea with the young men nearly twenty years ago. She appeared not to have changed, except for a certain languor in her movements, which may have been only that of repletion. We rode up to the trestle table which had been set aside for them.

"Greetings, Arthur," I said.

"Join us, Pelleas," he replied, while Morgause looked lazily over her shoulder at me.

"I am sore in too many places for ease," I replied. "I'm going to have water boiled for a bath."

"Perhaps we'll join you," Morgause said. "It sounds like fun."

"That is not its purpose. This is a healing bath," Nithe explained in an offended tone. "When Pelleas gets beaten up he expects me to oil his bruises and bind his wounds. Big as he is, it takes time, and his patience wears too thin for company."

We drifted away to the kitchen which Kay had set up to feed the men, and commandeered a large tub, and apprentices to carry water. Nithe sewed up the more substantial cuts, which had closed but opened under the hot water. I endured her ministrations with more than usual calm. It amused her.

"What do you care what I say to Morgause?" she asked.

"What does she want with Arthur, and what is she doing here?" I replied, evading her question.

"I imagine she followed her husband, King Lot, down here, don't you? And now that he's been sent off like a beaten dog with the other Gaels, she is trying to make friends with Arthur with the hope of accomplishing in her way what Lot could not in his."

We saw much of Morgause for the next week, until Kay insisted Arthur dismiss the troops and return to London. Our supplies were running out. Ulfas' men were already on their way home, laden with the spoils of war. Shortly after Kay's warning, Arthur led the Irregulars back to London, and Myrddin went with him. Morgause didn't, somewhat to Arthur's relief.

"She's insatiable," he said to me, privately. "I couldn't carry on an affair like this much longer. I'm grateful to Kay. Will you be coming with us?"

"I will come down when I have settled the wolves. Some of them went with the Picts, who partnered them in hunting, but I still have the young ones that bonded to me, and all of Cavell's pups."

"It would be well if you could keep them," Arthur said. "We have not seen the last of the Gaels, and the effect the wolves had on their cavalry was as good as a company. If we had not had them with us, the defection of the overseas Britons might have been disastrous."

"Nithe seemed to think Lancelot was committed to you," I said.

"King Ban's son? I don't know him well, but I gather he may still join us, together with some of his cousins, on a private basis. His father doesn't wish to do more than show awareness of the problem at this stage. Myrddin thinks if King Lot had been successful in his push against us, King Ban would have entered the fight in earnest, but in his own interests, rather than mine. I would no longer be a player."

"Lancelot would be only an observer here, then, instead of a warrior or leader of men?"

"Very like, I should imagine."

"Why is Nithe so sure it's something more?"

"Probably because he gave his pledge to her, rather than to

Myrddin, I think. Everyone else made a real contribution to the victory, even Kay, and Lancelot was hers."

I thought over his words and shook my head. It didn't sound right. Was Nithe in love with this foreign prince? I didn't even like his name. Lancelot! "About the wolves," I said, going back to the main conversation, "I wish to travel with them separately. They are nervous so close to this many men. If they get too uncomfortable, they will just fade back into the woods and I'll lose them." Arthur nodded and went about his other business, while I considered further the strange behavior of Nithe without getting any closer to answers that satisfied me.

Nithe left with Arthur and Myrddin, and I had opportunity to talk to Morgause with no one around. "Greetings, lady," I said, coming to the pavilion where she was lounging, looking for all the world like a mare after being serviced, inward dwelling, pleased with having fulfilled some private goal.

"Hello, Dog's-brother. I would know you anywhere, but how did you grow so big?"

"You know me, my lady?" I asked, surprised.

"Of course. You're the one who spied on me bathing and spilled that information, along with your guts, on the black stone. I heard about it from Lot for years, every time a young man looked at me."

"I meant you no harm, lady," I said lamely. "I didn't think of it as spying. I just followed you around, even to church. I had never seen anyone so beautiful."

"That's all right, then. No matter. Lot will not be happy to learn you are alive, and that you were the main cause of his defeat, or so Arthur assures me," she said, smiling. "I would not give him a second chance at your belly, if I were you."

"He didn't see me with Arthur at the Pentecost tourney?" I asked.

"That was you? I forgive you for the misery you have caused me, for telling me this. When Lot spoke to me of it, I'm afraid I laughed. He hit me, and I had him thrown out." Her eyes glowed briefly at the memory. "The Merrick country belongs to my people.

188

Lot had to go back to Lothian and the cold Orkneys and eat snow."

"You did not support him here?" I asked.

"Never. I came to assure Arthur of that. I will send him my sons. You remember Gawaine and Aggravain, do you not? They were much of your age."

"Yes, lady. They would be cousin to Arthur and find high favor with him," I said. She looked smug, and I felt depressed. What I said was true. Morgause was sister to Igraine, Uther's wife, and Arthur would be overjoyed to win such allies. I remember Gawaine as being arrogant and hasty-tempered, Aggravain as sneaky and having snot constantly running down his face, which his searching tongue licked off with every appearance of relish. I don't know which of them I had disliked the most.

I rode Mountain, and exercised the wolves, Cavell, Friend, the pups now half-grown and of formidable size, and the young wolves now adult, who regarded me as leader. When we got near London, I found an abandoned hill fort that would serve as a central place for our wolves. Raiders from the sea had burned it, leaving only the defensive mounds and trenches, and a few stone walls standing. It would do very well since the valley was abandoned as well as the fort, and the game was thick. The road through the valley had washed out in several places, discouraging cart traffic although it was less than an hour from London's east gate.

I left Cavell and Friend in charge of the base, bringing only Hair with me to find Arthur. Lucy had gone with Nithe; she would not be left behind. I reported to Arthur, and then set up the forge in the old warehouse on the Thames, finding much to do. Every few days I visited our wolves, hunting with them to keep the contact strong. Arthur had asked Nithe to act as hostess for him, and at Myrddin's urging she reluctantly became a part of the court. It gave her little time for me, and she had no time at all for the wolves.

I continued working with Ulfas at the forge we had established in the old Imperial Warehouse. Anna ran the household. None of the three of us were comfortable in Arthur's court, which he had set up in the old Roman-built public baths. Myrddin had recommended it because the sewage drains still worked. Almost the first people I saw there, on one of my infrequent visits, were Gawaine and his brothers. They had not changed much except to become bigger. Gawaine was tall, arrogant and handsome, and Aggravain was shorter and moved without Gawaine's grace. He looked dangerous. Remnants of old meals could be seen in his beard, reminding me of the snot-faced child he had been. He was a rarity, a dirty Gael.

"Dog's-brother!" Gawaine greeted me in mock enthusiasm. "Now we can say we have a truly cosmopolitan court. We have our own Geen!" He made it sound like it was an almost satisfactory substitute for a court fool.

"Greetings, Gawaine," I said. "I see you're still accompanied by your stalwart brother." He flushed slightly at my tone, and the smile died on his lips. It had never reached his eyes. Gaheris put his hand up to touch a scar across his ear as he looked at me, and his dull eyes lighted up as he remembered I had given it to him on the hurley field. I noticed he was beginning to bald. Aggravain was built like his father, King Lot, and effected the same proud, strutting walk and posture. Perhaps he was the only son of Lot's body, and Gawaine was reckoned his merely by courtesy. The Gaels have a saying, "the child belongs to the man who owns the bed."

"Come, this is excellent!" Arthur said, not aware of the nuance in our greeting. "With my brother at my back, and my cousins by my side, who shall stand against me?" Myrddin, who did know from watching us all as children, merely shook his head, and Nithe looked troubled. I avoided the problem by staying away as much as I could without causing remark, but I missed Nithe.

A few weeks after we arrived, the light from outside dimmed as a big man entered the smithy. He drew his sword and laid it on the anvil. "Put an edge on this, smith," he ordered. "Arthur requires me out on a quest, and I may have need of it." A smaller man, dressed as a squire, had followed him into the smithy.

"You'd better have him put a point on your spear as well, Lord Tristram," the squire said. "They say she's still a virgin, and like as not you'll split her open." They both laughed, and I looked at the big man more carefully. It was Tristram, with a new thick mustache, and about twenty extra pounds, the same Tristram who had courted Samana, the girl who was pledged to become Arthur's wife.

The sword was good steel, banded like one of Myrddin's, and needed only touching up with a file to make it sharp. I set to work on it, making enough noise to drive Tristram and his companion back out into the sunshine. They did not return until the noise stopped.

"It will serve, now," I said. Tristram inspected it, and snapped it into the bronze-bound scabbard hung from his belt, with a grunt of approval. He started to walk out.

"Wait, my lord," I said. "The fee is two pennies." Arthur had asked me to mint bronze market coins to facilitate small trade. It also put his face on coinage where all could see, along with the words "Arthur Rex." It would have been more impressive in silver or in gold, but we had none of that to spare. I made change from the barrel of pennies I kept by the anvil to help spread the new money.

"Let Arthur pay your fee," the squire said, pushing me to one side to follow Tristram. "It's his quest."

I do not mind so much the arrogance of persons like Tristram, since I understand a good self-conceit is important to a warrior. Squires are another matter. I grabbed his shoulder, turned him around, and slammed him into the great post that holds up the roof. It shook. He turned green, his eyes rolled up, and he slumped against my hand. I jerked his belt purse loose with my other hand before letting him fall to the floor. I calmly extracted a silver coin before looking up to meet Tristram's eyes.

"What are you doing, fellow?" he asked in a quiet, menacing voice, fingering the handle of the knife stuck in his belt.

"Collecting my fee," I said.

"A silver coin seems high to me," he replied, in the same tone.

"It would have been less had I not found it necessary to insist on payment," I said.

"Put it back," Tristram said.

"No, my lord, not likely," I said, and before I had finished, he had his knife at my throat. Somewhat to his surprise, it went no farther, for my hand was around his wrist. I twisted it slowly, until he was kneeling at my feet, his face contorted with pain and fury.

"Hear me, Drustan," I said in Pictish. "I know you for a Pict, even with your fancied-up name. Now, know me. I am Pelleas, heir to old Pelles, King of the Picts. Hear me. If you ever draw a weapon on me again, I will kill you." I leaned my face close to his and watched his eyes. I touched his mind and saw that he understood the words. I was right! He was a Pict, a Geen, like me! I carefully plucked the knife from his nerveless fingers with my free hand, and raised up, jerking him to his feet and propelling him backward, throwing him out of the smithy so that he lay on his back like a huge dog, rolling in carrion. Hair was beside me, crouched and growling, watching him intently. I jammed the knife into the post.

Tristram struggled to his feet with the obvious intention of reentering the smithy, his sword half-drawn from its scabbard. Fearing for Hair, I picked up the squire, who was beginning to stir, and threw him out with both hands, hard enough to crash into Tristram and knock him down again. I watched. After a few moments they rose unsteadily, supporting each other, and made their way down the wharf. I shrugged, and went back to work on a new sword Brastius had commissioned. I was intent on my work, and unprepared for the small whirlwind that swept into the smithy, hammering me on the back with surprising force.

"Here," I said, reaching around and imprisoning Nithe's fists. "What are you about?"

"How dare you involve yourself in my affairs uninvited?" she stormed.

"I never did," I protested.

"Do you deny you attacked Tristram and his squire?"

"Tristram drew a knife on me, and I took it away from him. You may recognize it," I said, pointing to where I had stuck it into the roof post. She went to claim it, but I was still angry when I put it there, and even I might have difficulty releasing it now. She couldn't free it and turned back to me, still furious.

"You're just angry because I'm going away with Tristram to rescue Arthur," she said.

"I know nothing of it," I said, staring at her. "What trouble is Arthur in?"

"He's been lured into the forest by that witch, Neeta," she said. "He didn't come back last night."

"He'll not thank you for interfering, like as not," I said. "Arthur has discovered sex, and doesn't need his sister looking over his shoulder every time he follows some maiden into the forest."

"She's no maiden! Besides, he's in trouble."

"How do you know?" I asked.

"He told me," she replied, but her eyes were not quite candid.

"You lie," I said. "You can't hear his mind at all. Furthermore, if he were really in trouble you would have come to me. You just want an excuse to go off with that Pictish lout."

"He is not! He's a king's son. You're the one who's a lout. You're not even knighted."

"I know a Pict when I see one. He's a Geen, same as I am. I spoke to him in Pictish, and he understood. Besides, Arthur has offered to knight me any number of times, as you know. You also know why I refuse."

"You're lucky I made Tristram promise not to hurt you," Nithe said, and stomped out, leaving me to hammer Brastius' sword into shape in about half the time it usually takes. I worked all night, ignoring the calls for silence that I heard, and was putting a fine edge on the blade when Arthur himself showed up next morning.

"Nithe tells me you had a fight," he said, to open the conversation.

"She should know," I said. "Here, see if this is good enough for Brastius." And I handed him the weapon I was working on. He gave it his professional attention for a few moments, and nodded, handing it back.

"It's a beauty," he said. "Nithe is mad at me, too. Seems she objects to everything that doesn't suit her just so these days."

"Whatever possessed you to invite her to play hostess?" I asked. "You must have remembered what a bossy little thing she was."

"She was all right until she left you," Arthur said. "I think she's frustrated by your eternal slowness. Don't you care for the girl at all?" This came as a surprise, and I considered it carefully.

"It doesn't matter what I might feel," I said. "She has no use for me. She thinks I'm a lout. Living with you and your friends has turned her head, I think. Why don't you ask Myrddin what's wrong with her?"

"I did," Arthur replied. "He agrees with me." I shook my head.

"Did she and that Pictish hero rescue you from Neeta?" I asked.

"Pictish hero? Tristram?"

"Tristram is a Gaelic version of Drustan, which is his real name in Pictish. I asked him."

"He admitted it?"

"Not willingly, but it's true enough."

"Not willingly? No wonder he's so hot about you!"

"Nithe was furious," I said miserably.

"If you wonder how Tristram happened to come to your smithy, you should know that Nithe sent him," Arthur said.

"Whatever for?" I asked.

"To alert you to the fact she was going away with him, ostensibly to look for me, fool," he said in an exasperated voice. "She knows what a braggart he is."

I thought it over. Truly, she had seemed to believe I knew of it. Perhaps she was angry because I did not demand an explanation of her. I really did not understand Nithe. No Pictish woman would look to a man for permission to do anything. I shook my head.

"To answer your question," Arthur said when I did not respond to his comment, "I found Neeta was only a talker and I was on my way home when I ran into them. As I said, Nithe was not pleased, somehow, but Tristram was even less so. I think his mind was more on servicing Nithe than being of service to me."

"Nithe needs a keeper," I agreed. "I'd take the job on if I thought she'd let me. What I am sure of is that I have to get away from here, or I'll do something stupid. I think I'll take some time off. What do you think of my going after Sam? Your year's up, and her father will have to let you marry, if you still want to."

"I do," Arthur said, "but she might not be any happier here than Nithe seems to be. Her father only offered a limited marriage contract, you know. One child, only, and then Sam has to stay on the island to raise him up an heir."

"Something is better than nothing," I said, "and anyway, he may change his mind."

"You're right. Go get her. I'll work on Nithe while you're gone, and try to soften her up. Anyway, with Sam here, I won't need Nithe as hostess."

"Two more things," I said. "Cavell's mate is getting too old to hunt safely. I want to leave the pair of them with you. I'll take the pups, except for Nithe's bitch, and Hair, along with the half-dozen young wolves that are bonded to me. We'll use the boat, if it's all right."

"Will they travel that way?"

"I guess we'll see," I said.

"What's the other thing?"

"I want to leave Mountain with you. Kay will grudge him fodder, so you'll have to take him under your personal protection."

"I will do that. If you have no objection, I'd like to ride him."

"You will, with or without permission. Just be careful," I said, and Arthur grinned.

He wished me a good journey, and in the morning I brought the wolves to the hill fort, leaving Cavell and Friend, and taking the rest of the animals to the boat. It was in good repair. Supplies were kept aboard for a journey of the length I expected to make, and Ulfas and Anna and their children went with me for crew. Ulfas did most of the work of sailing while I played with the animals and kept an eye on the children. Anna cooked. By journey's end, the wolves were comfortable aboard boat, and the children great friends with them. This is not to say they were quiet. They were not. The wolves, with the exception of Hair, were only six months older than Cavell's pups, and they occupied themselves with constant play. Hair lay on top of the small cabin, and refused access to anyone but me. I expected him to challenge me also, in the way of wolves, but he did not, perhaps because I did not come between him and the young animals. Ulfas sat at the tiller, and Anna stayed in the cabin out of the way. From time to time I found it necessary to go overboard to rescue one or more of the beasts or children who became careless in chasing one another.

Ector's Island came into view the second day, and we reached it that night, but lay offshore to keep the animals from scattering. There was some doubt in Ulfas' mind as to how welcome we would be with our retinue. Ector, himself, came limping down to meet us, and offered to send a messenger to Sam and her father, requesting an audience. He looked askance at our passengers, but I assured him they were under control, and that I would make good any damage done by them. To keep him sweet, I offered to do repairs on any broken tools that needed fixing, and found myself busy before our midday meal.

Ulfas absented himself to do some tasks around his house, and I went out to look Nithe's house over. It was secure, just the way she had left it. I found myself spending time there, thinking of Bronwyn and of Nithe and wondering if my difficulty in starting a family stemmed from the Oak King's anger with me.

I fed the pack daily and made them sleepy, so they sprawled around the old smithy with little appearance of being what they were. Young wolves look less fierce than grown ones. There was no mistaking Hair, though. I judged him to be about four, and he was nearly as big as Friend. Friend, slowed with age, would be no match for him in a fight.

It took a week for us to hear from Samana, and then she came with her father, Duke Cador, in a large boat loaded with baggage.

"Oh, Pelleas, I am so glad to see you!" she cried, hugging me. "You have come to take me to Arthur, haven't you?"

"By his order, Sam," I said. "He has fulfilled the conditions your father laid down, and is king of all the islands' Britons."

"I will abide by my pledge, and insist he does the same," Duke Cador said. "As soon as she is pregnant, she is to return here to give birth to my heir, and is to stay to raise him in a way a duke's son should be raised."

"Would you not consider letting Sam and her child reside with Arthur? If it's a boy, he would also be Arthur's heir, and some day rule in Arthur's place."

"I care not for that," the Duke said. "I seek an heir for my islands." Sam looked troubled, so I dropped the discussion. Time enough to worry about that when she found herself expecting a child. I believed she would be reluctant to admit pregnancy when it happened, but all things come in their season.

"We do not have room enough for your gear," I said. "Would you be content to send it on separately?"

"That is our plan. Sam and I will travel with you, and the barge may follow as it will."

I agreed. The Duke was much at home with hunting dogs, and was delighted with my pack. Using wolves as hunters represented a departure from practice that might give me a bargaining lever when it was time to settle Sam's future. The half-grown wolf-dog crosses were just slightly smaller than the full-grown wolves, and were as eager to please. They pleased him.

Arthur met the boat as we sailed up the Thames. He had kept a watch posted and was ready to greet us at the smithy warehouse dock where we usually kept the boat. I had never seen him as royal, with his crown, scepter, attendants and a wagon with gilded wheels for Sam to ride in. She spoiled the gravity of the scene by squealing, and running the length of the dock to throw herself into Arthur's arms. He didn't seem to mind. The hunting pack followed after her, causing some of the attendants to unsheathe their swords.

"Stop!" the Duke ordered, coming after the animals as quickly as he could. "Stop! Don't hurt them! They're only playing!" He was already attached to them.

I docked the ship with Ulfas' help, and joined the group. Arthur was so wrapped up in Sam he could spare me but a smile before he walked off with her. Ulfas found men to carry our gear into the warehouse, and Anna brought her brood inside to feed while the Duke and I bedded the wolves down in a small shed on the dock we used for overnight storage. I convinced them they would be safe there, but I left the shed door open so they would not feel trapped. Hair lay in the opening, making it impossible to close, anyway. When I left to join Ulfas and Anna, the Duke was reluctant to leave them alone. I agreed we would take them out to the hills next day, and the Duke joined me on one of Arthur's horses when we left.

I had expected to see Nithe at the dock, but she didn't come. I didn't see her at all for days. She stayed in the bathhouse that had been converted to royal quarters, with Sam and Arthur, and Myrddin told me the three of them were always together. I was invited but was too busy to go, and Duke Cador spent more time with me and the wolves than he did with his daughter. Sam was pregnant within a month, but hid the fact for weeks until her morning sickness gave her away. Duke Cador was content to wait until the seventh month, but then he insisted on taking Sam to the islands. I tried to talk him out of it.

"Who will hunt with you on Tresco?" I asked.

"There's little hunting there, except with falcons," he said. "I hunt by myself."

"If you stay here, I'll let you run the pack. They know you well enough to work for you."

"It's almost enough," he said, "but not quite. I am aware that they tolerate me in your presence, but only then."

"That's nonsense," I replied, as indeed I thought it was.

"No, I've visited the old hill fort several times without you, and have never seen a wolf. They only appear when you come." I had not known of that and found no easy answer.

When they did leave, Nithe went with them, to keep Sam company. She would return after the birth to bring Arthur the news. I gathered she considered us completely estranged for she did not say good-bye to me. I don't believe I had occasion to speak to her a dozen words all year, though I had been conscious of her mind touching mine from time to time. What was wrong with her? I was twenty-eight and she barely three years younger. When did she plan to settle down?

Word came from the west that Saxons were harrying the coast, and had made a landing in the small kingdom ruled by the Pict king Grance. Arthur received a message from Grance, begging for help.

"Go," said Myrddin. "You legitimize your rule when you are recognized by peers."

"Will you come?" Arthur asked.

"No. Take Pelleas with you and listen to him," Myrddin replied. We were sitting at the forge where they had sought me out with questions about military stores when the message came. Kay had not requisitioned any military stores from me for Arthur's armory in his role as steward, but I made long swords for pleasure, perfecting my art, and had a quantity set aside.

"I would go if only to find some new thing to look at," I said. "Perhaps I will find some females who do not look at me as if I were some kind of animal."

"Who does that?" Arthur asked.

"Who does not? Your British females are a puny lot."

"We won't be chasing skirts," Arthur said. I looked at Myrddin and he grunted in disbelief.

"It doesn't sound like much of a war, then," I said. "However,

Sam has been gone two weeks, and based on the past, I would have thought that was about your limit for celibacy."

"I'm a married man," Arthur protested.

"Actually, you're not," Myrddin said, "and a good thing, too. I don't believe in young men getting tied down at too young an age."

"Sam and I are married, no matter what you and her father believe," Arthur said.

"There are twelve different kinds of marriage contracts. Yours is legally over, no matter what you and Sam wish to think," Myrddin replied.

"That's what Gawaine says, too. He says I ought to make an official marriage with some patrician, as soon as possible, to gain recognition from Rome."

"And what good would that do you?"

"He says without recognition from Rome, I'll never be more than a usurper."

"Gawaine spent his youth in Rome and brought back some ideas that do not fit the reality of Britain," Myrddin replied. "Rome abandoned her interests here when she withdrew the legions."

"Gawaine says that the other kings in Britain will never accept me until Rome does. Lud knows they don't now," Arthur said grimly.

"They do not," Myrddin agreed, "but toadying to Rome is not the way to gain their acceptance. You would be better advised to make yourself useful to them. Go help Grance. It will do you more good than any number of Roman wives. As it is, you can only keep your mind on one thing at a time, and the less time you spend bedding females the more you can spend on establishing yourself as King of all the Britons. You have plenty of time; you're only seventeen!" Arthur did not reply, but reddened and left, obviously angry.

"Why do you talk to him so?" I asked. "Surely you know how it upsets him to be treated as a boy."

"He is a boy. It's time he grew up," Myrddin said impatiently.

"You will lose your influence over him if you keep scolding him like that. As it is, he spends more time with Gawaine and his rowdy friends than I like to see."

"Well, you keep an eye on him, then," Myrddin retorted. "He listens to you." I shook my head in disbelief, but let it go.

Arthur's temper improved as we made arrangements to march to the relief of Grance. We took the London Irregulars, loaded in wagons drawn by horses Kay had brought over from Brittany, and Gawaine and his friends, who still insisted on fighting from chariots. I rode Mountain at Arthur's left side, as his shield-bearer. He was riding his raw gelding. Days later we found Grance camped in a meadow dominated by a hilltop fort.

"Well met, Arthur, King of the Britons!" he cried. "I am the Lion of Grance. We have these rascals penned up like so many sheep. Now we can shear them." He embraced Arthur like a brother, and from the extraordinarily grave look on Arthur's face I knew he was on the verge of laughter. Grance was a small, peppery man with a wispy beard and the nervous mannerisms of a scribe. His chain mail looked too heavy for him and was certainly originally made for a larger man. It appeared that the lion title was honorific.

"Will they come out at our call?" Arthur asked.

"No, and there's the rub. I can't think how to entice them."

"How many warriors have they?"

"These are not warriors. They're raiders, with no sense of honor or decorum."

"Let us set up camp, and we'll ask for a parley," Arthur said.

We did not approach the hilltop until the next morning. Arthur and I, along with Grance and a few of his men, rode up within a few furlongs of the wall. The fort was made of crisscrossed logs set straight into the hill. A row of boulders lined the top of the wall, providing ammunition for the defenders against attackers attempting to climb the steep hillside. I could imagine being crushed by one rolling over me and doubted that we had been well advised to climb within shouting distance of the warriors inside.

"Hallo, the fort!" cried Arthur.

Several heads appeared above the boulder fringe, and one of them spoke, saying, "Hallo, yourself. What do you want here?"

"We have come to invite you to a parley," Arthur called. "We pledge no violence to you."

"What is the goal of the parley?"

"We will permit you to depart without injury from this, the land of the Lion of Grance. We cannot permit you to remain and must remove you if you do not go willingly."

"We have that message already, and we are still here. What is your interest in this matter?"

"I am Arthur of Britain. King Grance, my liege man, has requested my help, and I am bound to come to his aid."

"Well, Arthur of Britain, we do not intend to leave and think you had better do so yourself." Immediately he and others shoved the boulders over the edge of the wall. We turned as one to race our steeds down the hillside before the boulders could catch us, barely escaping serious injury in the process. Arthur was furious.

"We will burn them out," he said, and ordered a catapult be assembled. Kay was instructed to find some local source of peat and have several wagonloads at the camp within three days. Arthur seemed as grim as an old man, and no one questioned his orders as they might have felt free to do at home. When the catapult was ready, he had practice started, throwing big rocks at the fort. The rocks that reached the top of the hill soon appeared on the wall, ready to be rolled back down. We could hear faint cheers greeting each successful launch. Twice we heard screams, quickly silenced.

Kay returned with two wagons weighed down with peat. "There is more on the way, but I wanted to bring this as soon as possible," he said when Arthur greeted him. Arthur had them unload the turfs near the catapult.

"Dig a pit here, and start a fire," Arthur ordered. "I want this peat burning well by nightfall." We had three hours of daylight left and, working without break for rest or food, we were able to comply with his instructions. I dug with the men while Arthur went off to glare at the fort.

An hour after dusk, Arthur ordered the catapult sling wet down with water from the stream. He then took a pitchfork and loaded burning peat into the sling pocket, sending up a cloud of steam. Before it could catch fire he released the great arm and an arc of fire blazed through the air like a falling star. It smashed against the wall of the hill fort and live coals stuck to the exposed timbers, setting them on fire. Arthur worked with the men, loading and shooting fire across the darkening sky until the hilltop glowed with the light from burning huts inside the fort.

"The whole fort is burning," I said. "The timbers imbedded into the hill are on fire. If those people don't get out of there, they'll be roasted like pigs."

"Rouse the men," Arthur ordered. "Have them waiting for an attempt to cut through the lines. Spread out." I led the Picts and wolves to the far side of the hill to cut off retreat. They came at us, rather than making a frontal assault on the catapult as Arthur had hoped, masking their escape by leaving a rear guard to taunt Arthur, standing on the front wall of the burning fort and cursing. Those were brave men.

At the rear of the fort we could see the Saxons slipping over the wall, against the light from the burning fort. I had a quick memory of using my sling to drive the sons of Ector's men away from the smithy years ago. It was much the same this time, except there were thirty of us, and when the few men remaining upright reached the foot of the hill, they found themselves surrounded by wolves, and men with knives, and iron-shod staves. They surrendered. I sent a man for Arthur, who returned with the Invincibles, all carrying torches. They went up the hill, and drove down those who had been stunned by rocks, finally working around to the front wall and taking the rear guard. We assembled them all near the catapult.

"Who is your leader?" Arthur asked in good Saxon when he came up as he looked over the prisoners.

"He died on the hill," one of the men answered. "He was slow in making up his mind to leave the fort, so we made it up for him."

"You killed your own leader?" Arthur asked.

"We deposed him first," the man answered. "He had lost his right to lead. We follow only victors."

"How many of them are left?" he asked Kay, who keeps track of things like that.

"I have counted twenty-seven," Kay replied. "Several are badly wounded and need to be dispatched."

"See to it," Arthur said. He turned back to the Saxons, closely watched by victors and vanquished alike.

"Why did you come here in the first place?" he asked.

"We seek gold," their spokesman replied. "Our leader promised us we would find riches here worth the effort of sailing a month through bad seas."

"What luck have you had until now?"

"None. It is all of a piece with this night."

"I can use seasoned fighters. Any of you who would follow me I will spare and reward like my own men."

"What will happen to the rest of us?" the spokesman asked.

"I will turn you over to Grance. What he will do with you I do not know, but I do not think he seeks warriors." I noticed that neither Grance nor any of his men were around.

"I do not wish to be hanged," the man said. "I am Hjort. I will follow you, until you lose," and he knelt in front of Arthur to kiss his hand. Men lined up behind him, following his example, some seemingly happy about it, some resigned, but none showing reluctance.

"I would not count on these men in a hard fight," I said in Pictish. Myrddin had required Arthur to learn languages along with Nithe and me. "If they think the battle is going against you, they might switch allegiance to be sure of being on the winning side. Myrddin has warned us that Saxons are treacherous."

"They will never be in a position to hurt me," Arthur said.

"They will make splendid shock troops and will be happy to have the place of honor. They will live longer," he continued, "at the forefront of battle than in the hands of Grance. It is a fair contract."

Grance was not happy when daylight came and he found the battle over and the prisoners enrolled among Arthur's men. "Why was I not called?" he asked.

"Why did you retire from the field?" Arthur countered.

"It was bedtime," Grance said plaintively. "Only barbarians fight at night."

"That may be why the Roman legions had so much difficulty with the Picts," Arthur said. "Picts fight like wolves whenever the opportunity offers, and hide and rest when the enemy hunts. It makes sense to me."

"It is uncivilized," Grance replied stiffly.

"So be it. When next you find yourself in difficulty, find a Roman to help you."

"No offense," Grance said, "but we are not used to caring whether other folk are sensitive about things like that."

"What other folk?" I asked, in Pictish. "You are Pict, as I am. Do you pretend to be a Roman?"

"I am a citizen of Rome, as my father was," he replied haughtily. "No one rules legitimately in Britain unless he is a citizen of Rome, or has an alliance with a Roman family."

"What then am I?" Arthur mused.

"You are the son of Uther Pendragon, a Roman citizen. Were he not a Roman, he would not have been a king. Were you not his son, you would be a barbarian upstart."

"Perhaps I need an alliance with a Roman family, like Gawaine says, to silence doubts about my proper station," Arthur said doubtfully, looking closely at Grance for his reaction.

"It would not hurt," Grance said. "I am not ungrateful for your help, and I apologize for my bad temper. Put it down to disappointment that I was not able to be in on the kill. Some say my daughter Ettarde is of unusual beauty, and I have a ward who is the daughter of Vortigern. If one of them pleased you, I would welcome you as a son."

"Vortigern the Traitor? He was Uther's old enemy."

"True, but in his time Vortigern was acknowledged in Rome as King of the Britons, as was Uther later. Vortigern lost support of Rome when he put aside his wife, one of the daughters of Maximus, to marry Rowena, daughter of Hengist the Jute. Vortigern gave Kent to Hengist as bride price. When Vortigern died, Rowena and her daughter, Guenevere, came to me for protection. My wife was sister to Vortigern. By rights, Rowena should have gone to Hengist's brother, Horsa, but Horsa's wife objected. Rowena was still attractive and Jutish women lack easy ways."

"What does she look like?" Arthur asked. It was not a proper question for a king seeking to strengthen his throne, but Arthur was seventeen and the matter was of importance.

"Guenevere? She looks like a Jute," Grance said, shrugging. "As Pelleas reminded me, I am a Pict, as well as a Roman, and I prefer my women small and dark. Guenevere is tall and blond. But come, you will go home with me and you can see for yourself."

Kay told us that two more wagonloads of peat had come in. Arthur had them dumped to make room for the wounded. We took them, along with all the gear and baggage belonging to the siege, to Grance's castle. It was stone, two stories high at the gate and palisaded. The enclosed space was upwards of two acres, all situated on a pretty hilltop near a good spring.

"The stonework is Roman," Grance said with pride. "Your catapult would not touch us here."

"How fortunate for me that we are allies," Arthur said lightly.

Until we had settled and fed our troops, we were not free to attend to the main business on Arthur's mind. But finally we went to seek Grance's daughter and ward. I followed Arthur into a large, pleasant room to which we had been directed, with its own fire and two windows to permit a cross breeze in summer. The windows were shuttered, and the firelight augmented by rush torches set in wall sconces. On a low bench fronting the fire sat two young women, quite unlike but each beautiful.

"Which of you is Ettarde, daughter of the Lion of Grance, and which his ward Jennifer, the daughter of Vortigern the High King?" Arthur asked, smiling courteously.

"One of us is one and one the other," was the pert reply. Arthur's is not a playful nature, but he tried.

"A riddle? I am not good at riddles. What is the answer, Pelleas?" he asked.

"One of them is Ettarde, the daughter of Grance and the other is Guenevere, his ward, whom you have called Jennifer," I said.

"Ah, I had gotten that far myself," he said, "but which is which?" He was still smiling, but now with a certain tension. Killing is anxious work and not everyone takes to it. The fight had not lasted long, but it had been brisk, though Arthur was too late to enter the fray. His blood was still up.

The women smiled back, but did not reply, waiting for Arthur to continue with the riddle. "I'll ask you for help once again, Pelleas," he said, as I did not tell him what I thought was obvious. "I'm afraid I'll not get to the bottom of such a mystery unaided."

"If it's bottoms you're interested in, young lord, you should have said so," the small dark girl exclaimed, and jumping up on the bench, turned her back and lifted her skirt. Her bottom was round and shapely, putting me in mind of my mother's husband's younger sister, who used to tease her suitors in much the same way. I could see the blood flush up Arthur's neck and knew he thought he was being mocked.

Ah, naughty Ettarde, I thought, a true Pictish lady. "Surely this one is Grance's daughter," I said. "Only a Pict would act so, and we have assurances that Guenevere has the manners of a Roman lady."

"Then, Jennifer," Arthur said to the other girl, ignoring Ettarde, who was laughing at him, "I will talk to your guardian directly. My business is serious, and he will inform you of it in his own good time," Arthur turned and strode out. I let him go, watching the girl lower her skirt and turn to her companion.

"Well, I've run him off," Ettarde said ruefully to Guenevere, "but he still seems determined to speak for you. What shall we do?"

"I am at a loss, but if he thinks I will answer to Jennifer, he's mistaken."

"It's an honest British name," I told the blond girl. "I think he was trying to be friendly. He knew your names, but had not made up his mind which of you he would speak for until your friend became so outrageous."

"Well, my name is Guenevere. I am not a Briton, and I will not answer to a British name. Advise us, Sir Pelleas, what shall we do?"

"I am not Sir Pelleas, but only Pelleas, the King's shield-bearer. What do you want to do?"

"We want to stay in Somerset. Ettarde and I were brought up together, and have had only each other for company. We will not be separated."

"You are surely never sister to this naughty Pictish lady," I said.

"What do you know about naughty Pictish ladies?" Ettarde asked.

"Much," I replied. "My mother is Pictish."

"You are the biggest Pict ever I've seen," she said. "Why do you carry the King's shield?" and she slipped over to feel my muscles with small, busy hands.

"He trusts me. I've known him since the day he was born. He's been in my charge, one way or another, all his life."

"Are you a servant, then?"

"More like a steward, a caretaker," I replied.

"Are you married?" Guenevere asked.

"No."

"If you were to speak for Ettarde, we could stay together, for you will be close to the King. Do so. I can tell she likes you."

"Pictish ladies speak for themselves, in my experience," I said easily. Ettarde left off petting me and stepped back.

"You are right. My sister and I will talk of this and let you know, but don't count on it too much."

I had offended her. If I had agreed, she would have been pleased, but would still have made up her own mind. As it was, there would be little I could do to influence her in my favor. I was not unhappy about it, though she was very comely.

Arthur arranged with Grance for a betrothal to Guenevere before we left for London. I think her unwillingness made him unhappy, but no less determined on the match.

"Myrddin will not be pleased," I said to Arthur.

"Myrddin would be pleased best if I shaved my head and became Christian," Arthur grumbled.

"Surely not," I replied. "Even excepting the light regard he holds for any religion, he said you were too young to know your mind, and any warm body would do as well as another. My feeling is that this body will not be that warm. You would do better with Ettarde."

"She is not Roman. Grance is right. Without some connection outside of being Uther's son, I will never be accepted as King by the Britons. Marrying Vortigern's daughter would help."

"He was deposed," I objected.

"Ah, but before he was deposed, he was king," Arthur said. "The blood is there."

CHAPTER
XII

Myrddin was angry. More than that, his outrage exceeded any umbrage of his ever I had witnessed.

"You young jackass!" he shouted at Arthur. "Do you not listen? Did I not tell you that you were too young to marry? What do you use for brains, boy?"

"I am not a boy," Arthur said, with a shaking voice. He was barely able to keep himself under control. "I need no advice on the subject of whether or not I am too young to marry. I gave you the courtesy of listening to you, as I always do, but in these matters I must judge for myself."

"The girl is completely unsuitable," Myrddin said.

"In what way? Guenevere is of noble blood. Her father was Vortigern, acknowledged by Rome as High King of the Britons and her mother was Rowena, daughter to the Jute king, Hengist."

"I am well aware of her bloodlines," Myrddin said. "Her father was an attainted traitor to the British people, and her mother's father a noted butcher. You could not have chosen one less able to rally Britons around you if you dredged the Thames."

"Grance says I must be allied to a Roman house to be accepted as a legitimate ruler by Rome."

"What in Lud's name do you care for Roman acceptance? Will they send legions to support your cause?"

"I need none."

"A good thing. If they came they would pull you off the throne and birch your butt for presumption."

"Grance has given me his knights."

"You'll feed them, and bring them to his aid at his request? I'd give you mine under those conditions, had I any."

"He's giving me his great round table as a wedding present."

"He has no room big enough to put it up. That's why he takes it on campaigns. You'll need the greatest hall in Britain to house it."

"Then I'll build it. I'll build it near the Usk River, with access to the sea."

"You'll do it without me," Myrddin said grimly, and left the room.

"I'll talk to him," I said. "Maybe he'll change his mind."

"Don't bother," Arthur said, and I was left alone. I found Myrddin packing. Nithe was with him, arguing.

"Don't leave him this way. He can't take care of himself."

"He told me he didn't want me. I have other projects that need my attention."

"Tell him, Pelleas," she appealed to me. It was the first time she had spoken to me since I threw Tristram in the mud.

"Winter is coming. Where will you go?" I asked.

"Back where I came from," Myrddin said.

"I'll go with you," Nithe said. Myrddin hesitated a moment, and nodded. Nithe ran from the room, and Myrddin turned to me.

"Nithe will return. Take care of her."

"As much as she will allow," I said. "Will you also return?"

"Perhaps, in time. The gold we have saved is yours. Be sure Nithe has a suitable dowry. Better yet, marry her yourself."

"You know how Nithe feels about me. She says I try to run her life without her license. I am fond of the girl, but she will not accept me as a suitor. I do not plan to change my ways to accommodate her, anyway."

"Think about it," he said. "You may have misread her." He was silent for a moment and then looked me full in the face. "I have taken pride and pleasure in our friendship, Pelleas. I wish you well. I do believe we will meet again," and he embraced me. I saw tears in his eyes, a thing I had not seen before. Nithe came dashing in.

"Will you bid me good-bye, Nithe?" I asked her. She looked at me oddly.

"I am not through with you yet, Pelleas," she said, unexpectedly, but threw her arms around me and kissed me soundly. I was surprised. "Come, then, Myrddin," she said, "if you are so eager to leave, let us go." Myrddin cocked an eyebrow at me, but said no word as they walked out of the room, and out of my life.

Arthur moved back to the River Usk in the spring, and began work again on the hill fort he had started before the battle. He planned to make it into a permanent castle with stone masonry. Myrddin had built a small model of what the fort would look like when finished and now Arthur studied it, determined to better it, if possible.

"He named it before he left, did you know?" Arthur asked me.

"Another of his mysterious names out of his murky past?" I asked lightly.

"Maybe. He called it Camelot. Here it is, right on the model."

"That's nice," I said, considering it. Camelot. Camelot. "What does it mean?"

"He didn't say," Arthur answered, looking miserable. He missed Myrddin.

The model appeared to be a figure eight when viewed from above with the top loop planned to enclose about four acres with equipment and food stores and living space for several hundred warriors. The larger circle would have houses to shelter Arthur's folk at need, tradesmen and farmers and their families. That loop enclosed about ten acres, with space enough for animal pens and stables. I noticed a smithy was located near the armory, but I preferred a location outside for regular use, near a small brook that ran by the hill into the Usk.

When I suggested it to Arthur, he considered it a moment and agreed. "There will be a village built around the foot of this hill in a few months. Pick the spot now that suits you best before the good locations are all taken," he said. "The fort is for emergencies, and for barracks. The men will be under better discipline if I can keep them apart from the folk."

There are woods with deer east of Camelot and I settled Hair and the young wolves there, visiting them when I could. The old pack stayed near London, except for a female who had accepted Hair as her mate. Together, they led the pack, and I was not really needed. I was always welcomed, however, when I came to see them and sometimes, to strengthen the bond, I hunted with them.

I chose a small hill next to the Usk to build my smithy and was soon turning out ironwork needed for the fort, great hinges for the doors being the first responsibility. Myrddin had assembled tools and stocks of pig iron and charcoal, so there was no need to look for supplies. I slept there, the better to watch things. I didn't know many of Arthur's people, but the ones I did know had little regard for the property of common folk, taking what they came upon for their own use, scorning protests as being the whining of so many curs. They did not win many hearts for Arthur.

I had some discussion with several of them about this, and convinced them to leave me alone. Two warriors, armed with long swords hung on baldrics, and wearing chain mail and helmets stopped by the smithy not long after I set up.

"Here, villein," one said. "I want you to drop whatever you're doing and make me about a dozen lance points."

I looked at him in surprise, and then at the man with him. They were twins, well set up men and not unhandsome, except for the look of arrogant petulance on their faces.

"I am sorry," I said in a civil tone, "but I have been instructed not to honor individual requests. You'll have to go to Kay and get a requisition if you want war gear."

"That's Sir Kay, varlet," the other brother said. "You let me worry about him, and do as you're told."

"Well, that's just what I can't do," I replied. "There's only so much iron, and so much time to work it, and Arthur has set priorities. I have no choice in the matter."

"Did you hear that, Balan?" the first said in a deceptively mild tone.

"Indeed. I've been told he was a stiff-necked Pict who doesn't know his place, but I never dreamed he was this bad. We must do something about this."

I took a long iron bar from the fire, one end glowing red, and advanced on them moving it from one to another. "I am very busy just now," I said. "I have no time for this sort of thing. I want you out of my smithy."

They backed away, but the first brother said, "This is not the end of this, Pict. You have made a mistake, and will learn what it is to respect your betters."

"I do respect my betters," I said. "The error is yours in assuming that's what you are. Don't come back, even with a requisition, for I will not honor it."

Kay was down to see me before an hour passed, out of breath and red of face. "What do you mean by insulting Sir Balan and Sir Balin?" he asked.

"What do they mean by insulting me?" I asked. "They started it."

"Ridiculous! They are gentlemen."

"And I'm not, is that it? We've had this discussion once before, outside of your door," I said. "This is my door. Get out."

"But you don't understand," Kay blustered. "These knights are from Brittany, part of Lancelot's troop. They are to have anything they want."

"Not if it has to come from me," I said.

"I'll take this matter to Arthur," Kay warned.

"Do it and be damned to you," I said. "Now, do you want to leave on your own, or do you need assistance?" I looked up, and perhaps something in my face convinced Kay to leave, for he did.

Arthur referred to it in passing when he came to ask for more shovels to start a well to be dug within the fort for water during a possible siege.

"Thank you for the hammers and chisels," he added. "We're hauling rock from the deserted Roman barracks at Caerleon to build with, but some of it has to be reshaped. Kay has found some masons who know how to work stone Roman style. I have had the men dig down to bedrock to anchor the foundation, and we can start the keep now."

"I was happy to do it," I said. "You can have anything you want for the asking."

"I would appreciate it if you could work with Kay," Arthur said apologetically. "I really should supervise the building."

"I don't mind except when he comes in to explain how important it is that I not offend every jackass that brays in the street outside my door."

"I was sorry to hear of that incident," Arthur said. "I've explained to Lancelot that he is responsible for keeping control of his men. He said he would do it, but I admit he seemed surprised I thought it necessary."

"Why do these overseas Britons act so?" I grumbled.

"Oh," Arthur sighed, "they all claim descent from the legions Maximus took from Britain and settled on the continent to guard his rear when he marched on Rome to claim the title of Emperor. They say no real warriors were left here, only cowards, old men and children."

"And Picts," I added, laughing.

Arthur relaxed. "I've decided to enlarge the feasting hall Myrddin designed," he said, "making it round instead of rectangular, so Grance's table will fit inside."

"The table seats one hundred and forty men," I said. "Grance told us it's forty Roman paces across when all the sections are joined together. The hall will have to be pretty big. How will you span the roof?"

"I'll leave the center open like a Roman atrium, using two rows of columns like Stonehenge and roof over that part where the men will sit. The center will be paved and have drains against the rain. Do you think it will serve?"

"I think you may have solved your problem," I said, smiling, and he left whistling.

The warriors Grance had promised joined us, along with the London Irregulars and the Picts that stayed with Ulfas. Arthur put them all to work. Gawaine brought his brothers and cousins to help in the building, and I asked Ulfas to work with me to keep up with the demand for great bolts to tie the wooden frame to the stone foundations. By late summer we were well into the work when Nithe came back with Lucy but without Myrddin. She paid me a visit to see if I were still living alone, so she said.

"What happened to Myrddin?" I asked.

"He didn't take me with him after all," she replied moodily. "He just wanted to spend some time with me before he left. It didn't help."

"Where did he go, then?"

"He said he had to go north to find out if we could expect more folk like the Saxons and the Jutes on our shores in the near future," she said.

"Good for him," I said. Nithe looked lost. "We could use help around here," I offered, indicating the pile of bolts Ulfas and I had turned out that day. Ulfas grinned at her, but she made a face.

"Arthur needs looking after," she said. "I can keep busy with that," and she left, apparently satisfied with what she had seen. She must have been kept as busy as we were, for we saw as little of her here as we had in London. I heard, though, that she was spending time with the young men who were coming in to serve with Arthur, younger sons of noble houses, ambitious to make a name. They strutted around showing off for the ladies who had come with them, or perhaps had followed them. They were not good company for a person like Nithe.

Arthur claimed Mountain as his own war-horse when I told him I didn't need him any longer, but Myrddin sent Blaise back with Nithe to be placed in my care. I wondered how I would be able to keep him from gaining weight. I had little time to exercise him myself and had hoped Nithe would ride him for me, but she appeared not to be interested in geldings. I visited Blaise evenings for the company as much as anything, and it was usually dark when I returned to the smithy.

A few weeks after Nithe returned I came back from the stables to see the smithy lit up with torches and was surprised to find a dozen young knights milling around inside. I recognized some of them as among those who had commissioned fancy armor from me. Real fighters insist on smooth joints with nothing protruding to catch a lance head, but these fancy boys wanted spikes and ridges to catch the sun, and the eyes of the ladies. When I came to the open door, I saw them crowding to get close to the great square anvil. On it was standing Nithe, drunk and but half-dressed, wearing neither hose nor shoes. Her long hair was unbraided, surrounding her face like a black cloud. I stood outside the edge of light cast by the rush fires and listened.

"Come, who will top a hundred gold? Remember, a true virgin, or your money back. I need a dowry, and orphaned as I am, must supply my own. One year's service. Who's bidding?"

"How about a sample?" one of the men asked, and clutched at her. She was holding the curved knife Arthur had given her and swished it under his nose backing him off.

"You know my terms. Look but don't touch. Cash on the barrelhead. Single offers. I will not be common to an army. First claim on marriage rights after a year's service." The men were gazing at her owlishly as I walked in. They were drunk. I gathered they had been partying with Nithe.

"Ah, another customer. How much would you bid for my services, Dog's-brother?" she asked, looking at me in what was almost an anxious way. She was more than half-drunk. I had never seen her in such a state, wild-eyed and angry. Myrddin's leaving her

217

had hurt her more than I had understood before. I eyed her knife hand. She could throw as accurately as she could thrust, and I had no need to be spitted.

"I saw a better woman sold for seven gold," I said. "I would pay no more than that." The sudden silence, during which I could feel her anger flair against me, was broken by an uncertain laugh. Nithe could only broadcast emotion, not direct it. Any punishment of me would have to wait, or her whole following would be driven off.

"Maybe what you need is something to heat your blood, Pict," she said. With a sinuous gesture she hiked her skirt with her left hand, and half turning, looked at me over her shoulder and wiggled her bare butt at me. She had been talking to naughty Ettarde.

"Two hundred gold," a small, dark man gasped.

"Done, Pynel!" Nithe cried, never taking her eyes from me. "I've always fancied Picts."

A very angry Arthur pushed his way up to the anvil, followed by Tristram and Gawaine. Pynel stood his ground, full of bluster, and no one tried to move me back.

"You're too late to bid, Arthur," Nithe said, dropping her skirt. "Pynel has purchased my services for a year for two hundred gold." Arthur turned and glared at me.

"Actually, not yet," I said. "Terms were cash on the barrelhead. There's mine," and I laid seven gold coins at Nithe's feet, ignoring her saxeknife. "Where's your two hundred gold?" I asked Pynel.

"I don't carry that weight of coin with me," Pynel protested.

"You beauties don't carry anything yourselves," I said.

"I'm willing to postpone the delivery until tomorrow," Nithe said. "Eager as I am to consummate the sale tonight, I'll just have to wait."

"Well, I'm not willing to wait," I said. "The terms were yours. I accepted them. I bid, and paid my money down. You're bound by the conditions." I turned to Arthur and said, "This woman has sold her services to me for a year. She is my property."

"You never should have been allowed to bid," Pynel said. "You're a tradesman. This is a tradesman's trick, not the behavior of a gentleman."

"Do gentlemen buy young ladies in your experience, Arthur?" I asked.

"His blood is as good as mine," Arthur said to Pynel. "We are brothers." Turning to me he asked, "Whatever do you intend doing with her?" His blue eyes shone in the rushlight, and his young brow was still furrowed with rage.

"Do, brother?" I asked. I was fully as angry as he. "I'll do whatever I think best. I may stake her out in front of the smithy and sell her services until she's had her fill of whoring. And then again, I may not." I stepped away from the forge to avoid losing my head to Nithe's knife, and caught her wrist, tumbling her to the ground. The fall dazed her, but I took no chances, placing the hand that held the knife under my foot.

"Will you lead these folk out of here, Arthur? I have work to do," I said.

"Well, I can't permit it," Pynel said, grabbing my arm to pull me away. I brought him forward, catching him by throat and crotch, and pitched him out of the side window. A short time elapsed before anyone moved, and then a splash signaled that Pynel had reached the river. Gawaine started forward, but before he could reach me, Arthur stepped between us.

"Stop!" he commanded, freezing everyone again. "We'll discuss this later, but it is treason to pull weapons in the presence of the King. I have warned you." The knives disappeared, and the young knights left by twos and threes, glancing back at me, their faces eloquent of their anger.

"If Pynel is hurt, you will answer to me, Pelleas," one said.

"If one of you challenge me, I will choose to fight on foot with the mace. You will lose," I said. It was true.

"You damned Pict," Arthur said, turning on me, no longer able to hold his anger. "You fight one of my knights, with mace, hammer or dung-fork, and you'll truly answer to me," and he stormed out.

"Well, Dog's-brother, you may have bought a poor bargain,"

Nithe said. "If you'll take your great foot from my hand, maybe I'll eventually regain the use of it. A one-handed slave is not of much use."

I strode to the wall and pulled a fur robe I sometimes slept on from its shelf. "Here," I said. "Use this." I then lifted the anvil from its stand, and looked into the hollow it covered. Myrddin and I stored our gold there, coin as well as ornaments. No one had ever moved it unaided but the two of us, except for Arthur. Selecting a gold torque, I slipped it over Nithe's neck as she stood beside me and pinched the ends together, so they could not be pulled asunder.

"This will remind you that you are owned. A slave collar need not be cold iron," I said. "Your pallet is still in the corner. Go and sleep off the drink."

"Do you think you can keep me here against my will?" she asked.

"You will stay here this night if I am forced to spike you to the wall," I said. "I will not debate with you. You have no choice but to do what I wish, and that is what I wish." I may have sounded more harsh than is my usual tone with Nithe, for she crept into the corner, and curled up, wrapped in the old fur robe against the chill.

I decided to fabricate a mace. I had offered to fight with such a weapon but had none of my own. Tomorrow, I might have need of one. I started the forge fire from the coals that still lived in the ashes. In the scrap metal pile I selected worn-out wheel rims and discarded slave collars—the rims for toughness, and the collars for a flexible, bitter meld. The rims had thousands of blows from the road that had hardened them beyond the patience of a smith, and the collars would provide layers of soft iron that would bend without breaking.

It took me half the night to fashion the strips of metal into long, thin rods. I welded them together, piece by piece, reheating the whole with each new strip. I alternated the hardened rim steel to the softer iron until I had a single bar an inch and a half thick

220

and four feet long. Each end I heated until the metal melted and formed a ball. When I was finished with that, it was done, and needed nothing more. It was daylight, but I had my weapon.

I did not sleep. Nithe had not moved, and her eyes were shut when I looked at her. How she could have slept in the din I made, I do not know. In a few minutes I had moved the anvil again, and scooped out the gold that lay therein. I put it all into a stout leathern sack, and placed it back on the anvil. I then took Myrddin's mail-coat from a chest where he kept it away from moisture, and put it over my linen tunic. It would serve to turn a knife edge aimed at my back. I fastened on his light breast and back plates and tried on his helmet. It fitted. Picking up the mace and the sack, I called Nithe.

"Wake up," I said. "We are leaving." She was with me in a moment, but I didn't look at her. I walked straight to the keep gate, and into the great, round hall, coming upon Arthur as he broke his fast with some twenty of his knights. Hair followed me, along with Nithe's bitch.

Arthur frowned as he looked at me.

"We are not pleased with you, brother," he said. Gawaine glared at me but was silent.

"I am aware of that, Arthur," I said.

"Have you come to beg pardon, then?" he asked.

"Would a damned Pict do that?" I asked. "No," I answered myself. "I have come to say good-bye, and to charge Kay with a responsibility." I took the bag of gold and jewelry and placed it on the low table before Kay.

"This treasure was left in my care by Myrddin to be Nithe's dowry," I said. "As seneschal to this court you must receive and hold it in Myrddin's name, for I am leaving."

Kay untied the mouth of the bag and spilled the contents on the table. It was the richest dowry any British princess had ever had pledged for her marriage. There were gasps as the knights leaned forward from their places to view the glitter.

"This is an immense fortune," Kay said. "How did you come by it, and who will make Nithe's contract?"

"Some part of it was Myrddin's, and some little part was mine. I am the best smith in these islands and have gained much wealth to match that which Myrddin left in my care. No one will contract for Nithe until the year she owes me is complete. Then she will please herself, as always. Who would dare to speak for her?"

"I will, if she will permit it," Arthur said.

"You will not, then," said Nithe. "I know nothing of this dowry, and will not accept it. Give it back to Pelleas."

"You have no say in this," I said sternly. "These were Myrddin's instructions as well as my command. You will hold your tongue. Seeing what can happen perhaps you will not be so eager to sell your freedom again." For a wonder, she looked down and did as I bid her. What I would have done if she defied me, I do not know.

"What do you plan to do, then?" Arthur asked, his anger fading before his curiosity.

"Why, I believe I shall become a knight errant for a while. Perhaps I'll find something in knighthood that has escaped my notice up to now."

"Will you finally let me knight you?" Arthur asked.

"No," I said. "You have cursed my mother's blood. I will find a Pictish king to serve, who will know my worth."

"I am sorry for the slight I put upon you. I would not have us part in anger. In token of this, I give your great horse back to you to help you on your way. I know you for as true a man as any here. A true man is a true man whether he be Pict or Briton, Gael or Saxon. A man can rise above his birth."

"I have never felt the need," I said. "In truth, I've always thought my Pictish blood the better ancestry." Gawaine sneered at this, but I paid him no mind, my eyes on Arthur.

"Let the surly dog go," Kay said, aloud.

I turned away from Arthur and addressed Kay, who was within reach of my hand had I so desired to touch him.

"I trust you where property is concerned," I said to Kay, "but in naught else. Your judgment of men, or of women for that matter, is full of error. Arthur was condescending to me by consenting to overlook my Pictish blood, and I answered him in kind. We deal at arm's length. You, however, are not my peer. Open your mouth once more, and I'll deal with you as one does with an inferior. Do you yearn to know what that is?" I held his gaze with my own until he looked away, silently. I looked back at Arthur.

"Take care of Nithe, as befits your honor," I said to him. "I will leave Blaise for her. I will return within the year to see how she has fared and perhaps release her from her collar."

"You cannot leave me so," Nithe said. "You hold my contract, and I will serve no other man, not even Arthur."

I shook my head and having said what I wished to say, I left, followed only by Hair and his pack.

Part III

The King's Shield Bearer

473 · 477

Alaric the Visigoth sacks Rome and breaks the power of the Empire in the West. In Britain Arthur the King, establishes his rule and begins building the legend of the Round Table.

CHAPTER
XIII

It was good to be with Mountain again, riding through the fall leaves. He was glad to see me, and touched noses with Hair in greeting. I rode out along the path that eventually would lead to Pellinore's spring, hoping to find him there since he wasn't at Camelot. It was dusk of the third day when we rode into the clearing around the spring. His horse heard us and shifted its weight from foot to foot as we entered, awakening Pellinore from a doze. He was mounted and in full armor, awaiting challengers and in danger of falling off his horse. I had seen Pellinore fight in several of the tournaments before Arthur was crowned and knew he was faster than he looked and as strong as he appeared to be from his size. He was a true Geen.

He pulled his visor up to stare at me, and urged his horse into a walk to approach us. "All who enter here are obliged to joust with me," he declared.

"Why?" I asked, riding forward.

"Because that's why I'm here," he said. "Defend yourself, or I'll run you through."

Before he could turn away to set himself for a run at me I moved my horse up until we were side by side.

"I don't have a spear," I said. "Besides, I'm not eligible to joust. I haven't been knighted."

227

Pellinore glared up at me. Mountain stood two hands higher than his own horse, and my sitting height is a full four inches taller than his when we are seated on a level. It couldn't have happened to him often, and may have been responsible for his reconsidering his position.

"Why do you go riding around in that gear if you don't intend to joust?"

"I'm looking for someone to knight me," I said. "Arthur offered, but I'd rather have a Pictish king do it." Pellinore stared up at me more closely.

"You're that smith fella," he decided. "You're one of the big Picts, like me. Are you sure your mother isn't named Brusen?"

"That is her name. Did I deny it?"

"Not at all. I mentioned I had a sister once, ran off with Uther. Always wondered what became of her. If you're her son, I'd be happy to oblige you, if you'll stay over. I'd appreciate the company." He hurried on to explain in case I had misunderstood, "You have to stay awake all night, and watch your arms, you know, without eating or drinking."

"You're my uncle? Why, well met!" I said. "And I'd be glad to stay over, but why no eating or drinking? We should celebrate."

"How should I know? It's done, that's all," he replied testily. "The knight business is British, not Pictish. Sometimes I wish I'd never heard of it."

"Why don't you give it up?" I asked.

"If I don't come down to this spring once a month and defend this piece of ground, I lose control of this whole region, and half my income is gone. I can't afford not to be a knight with all the thieving Gaels and Britons around."

"I see." I considered that for a moment. It sounded like a lot of trouble. "Can't you have some of your own knights defend your spring?" I asked.

"You know how small Picts are. There are only four of us big enough to handle Gaels and Britons, one on one. Me, Palomides, my son Lamerok, who still needs a little growth, and that lout,

Drustan, that's Latinized his damned name. You know him, Tristram."

"I know him," I said. "I'll make one more, maybe."

"Maybe. You're big enough. Are you any good?"

"Myrddin taught me and I taught Arthur," I said.

"Is that a fact? Say, could I interest you in taking over some of
these nearby islands for me? Maybe Mona and Man? You could
be Lord of the Islands. You'd have to hold under me, of course,
and I'd get a tenth of your revenues, but it would give you something to do. It'd also relieve me of the necessity of riding up the
coast once a year, meeting all comers. Bad for the joints, at my
age. Damned cold on that north coast."

"That would tie into Pelles' holdings. I'm his heir," I said. "Yes,
I'd like to be Lord of the Islands. I think I'll just attend a few
tourneys, though, and get a reputation so I don't have to fight
every ambitious, landless knight in Britain."

"You're that good? Well, let's have some supper and talk about
it, anyway," Pellinore said, and led the way toward a tent pitched
at the edge of the clearing. His squire helped him off his horse,
an ungainly venture that both obviously dreaded. The squire was
a Pict of average size, and King Pellinore was not only huge, but
encased in heavy jousting armor. We had a pleasant supper,
between us eating three braces of pheasants, a large salmon and
the loin cut of a pig.

"Where do you get fresh meat out here?" I asked.

"Oh, I have men who pretty much spend their time hunting
and fishing when I'm out like this," Pellinore replied.

"This is not wild pig," I objected.

"That so? Something wrong with it?"

"Not at all," I said.

"Then eat it and shut up," he said. I gathered from that his
hunters were not above foraging in farmyards.

It was several flasks of wine later that he said we'd have to
begin fasting until morning. I was stuffed, and at least half-drunk,
for as a rule I drink sparingly, and wondered what I would do if

I were required to eat and drink the rest of the night, rather than fast. Pellinore, however, fetched forth a heavy sigh, and I realized that going through the night with not even a light snack to sustain him would be an ordeal of no small proportion. Staying awake would be my problem. He arranged my mail-shirt, my light but sturdy helmet, and my back and breast plates in a neat pile before the fire.

"Why don't you carry a sword?" he asked.

"This is better," I said, handing him my mace. "I can knock people down without killing them."

"You have some effeminate objections to killing people?" he asked politely.

"It's not something I do for sport," I said. "My personal attitude toward knightly games might offend you."

"Try me," he countered.

"Very well. It's my opinion that most knights are ignorant of anything unrelated to bed, board and arms, and are stupid enough to be content with that. The real reason I refused Arthur's offer of knighthood for so long is that I don't like knights as a class, and could avoid associating with them if I remained a commoner."

"You don't like Arthur?"

"I love Arthur. We are brothers. I am proud of him and was happy to serve him when he allowed it on my terms."

"How was that?"

"In peace I was his armorer-artificer, his smith. In war I was his shield-bearer."

"What happened?" We were sitting before the fire, and Pellinore threw more wood on it, causing us to move back and settle again. Before I could answer he called his squire and said, "Look, you, keep that fire up. One piece of wood at a time will do it. Mind you don't run out. I don't want to be walking around in the middle of the night looking for more."

"I'll be up all night," the man groused. We Picts aren't much on respect.

"So, go to bed, then. Who asked you to stay up?" Pellinore

growled, shaking his head. The man left in a huff, disappearing into the woods where I assumed the Pict hunters were camped.

"Gaels make better servants," Pellinore confided in what he thought was a whisper. "They're cleaner, quieter and more civil than Picts."

"Why don't you use them, then?" I asked.

"Don't trust them. Most of them look down on Picts, even Pictish kings. You couldn't count upon their being around if trouble comes."

"You asked me what happened. That's what happened. Arthur's knights are almost all Britons and Gaels pretending to be Romans. As long as I don't have to associate with them, I don't need to resent being sneered at all the time. Have you ever been called a 'dirty, horse-eating, Pictish bastard?'" I asked.

"Horse-eater, is it? These Britons are all horse-mad! They think Epona, the horse god, favors them, and only barbarian Picts eat horse meat. But, then, I've been called 'man-eater' in my time."

"When I was a boy at the hunters' fire, they used to talk about eating men killed in battle to earn the right to be tattooed," I said.

He laughed. "That's part of the hazing used to intimidate young men. They tried it on me when I killed my first Gael, so I cut about ten pounds from his lower backbone, wrapped it with pig lard, and roasted it over the fire. When I ate it, all of it, there were hunters puking their guts out in the woods away from the circle of firelight. I heard them, but I didn't let on. It was the last time anyone tried anything like that on me."

"How did it taste?" I asked.

"Not bad. Not as good as pork, but better than badger. I'd killed him from ambush so he had no chance to become frightened. You know how fear ruins the taste of meat." That was true.

"I don't know if Gaels pretending to be Romans is worse than Picts pretending to be Britons, or not," Pellinore said. "Like this business of staying up all night. Britons pray for guidance. They're Christians. What's the point of our doing it?"

"Maybe a water sprite will visit us," I said. "This is a holy spring, isn't it?"

"The Britons say so. They believe all springs are holy, but I think they'd draw the line at water sprites," Pellinore said, judiciously. "Immortal, maybe," he mused, "but not holy."

We watched the spring glimmer in the firelight and were both startled when a shape appeared before us from the woods behind the spring. I knew who it was when a familiar dog appeared at her side.

"Nithe," I cried, standing up and holding out my hands.

"Are you sure?" Pellinore asked in awe, also on his feet. "It's a neithe?"

"No, it's my Nithe," I said. She came before me, and rested her hand on my chest, looking up at me. In the firelight, she could well have been a water sprite. Pellinore didn't move.

"Are you pleased to see me?" she asked. The gold torque around her throat glowed.

"I have been thinking for three days what a fool I was to leave you behind," I said.

"That's good enough," she answered. "You're learning, Dog's-brother."

I took her shoulders in my hands and pulled her close, wrapping my arms around her tightly. I spoke to her mind and said, "My heart," nothing more. Her response was such a wave of love that it rocked me. I had no idea she felt that way.

"What is this?" Pellinore demanded. "A neithe walks out of the night and instead of asking her for favors you try to crush her to death."

I released her. "This lady's name is Nithe. She was Myrddin's ward, Arthur's foster sister, and my love. I have no intention of hurting her, and have sought her favor all my life."

"Have you now?" Pellinore asked.

"No, he has not," Nithe answered stepping back. "He is nearly the most stubborn man alive and never listens to me. He is as bad as Myrddin, whom he much resembles. I wish no misunderstanding between us, however, even if I must seek him out, like a truant boy."

"How did you find me?" I asked. "How did you convince Arthur to let you go?"

"Arthur knows better than to thwart me when my mind is made up. You should take a lesson from him. I am to be your squire while you play at knight errant. I promised Arthur there would be no more than that between us until you returned, so I could pretend nothing had happened should I change my mind."

"You can't go traipsing off pretending to be a man," I said. "Too many people in court will wonder why you are not there, and will guess where you are," I said. She took off her cap and shook her head so that her dark hair whipped across her face. She had cut it to come to her chin line. Nithe is broad of shoulder, lean through her hips, and taller than most men. In her blousy tunic her breasts did not show. She could pass for a tall, handsome youth too young to sport a beard. I knew her London-gleaned street vocabulary was foul enough to pass for male speech, if she chose. I had spoken in error. She could be a squire for a knight such as I.

"Would it be so bad?" she asked. "Anyway, Arthur threw a tremendous fit to impress everyone and ordered me confined to the tower," she said, continuing her narrative. "Everyone believes I'm still there. Ulfas is the only one allowed to see me. He brings food to the tower, which he then must eat. We can depend on him not to tell."

"Ulfas would not object to the extra rations," I said, to say something. I didn't want to admit I was wrong. Besides, it was true. Ulfas had been a round boy, and had developed into a round man.

"What are you doing up so late?" she asked, sensing she had won and dropping the argument.

"We are keeping vigil," Pellinore said. "Sit with us and help keep us awake. I'll knight him in the morning. I don't want anyone questioning the propriety of the ceremony, and it's good to have a witness. Even we Picts know what's fitting."

The night passed and with the sun's first light I knelt before Pellinore and he whacked me on both shoulders with the flat of his sword. "If I'd used your mace, I'd have broken both your collarbones," he said. "Arise, Sir Pelleas, and be a faithful knight."

As I rose, he asked me, "Will you swear fealty to me and hold the island's tribute from me?"

"That I will," I said, and knelt once more to kiss his hand.

"Then I name you Sir Pelleas, Earl of Mona, Baron of Man," he said. He took a heavy gold chain from around his neck and placed it around mine.

"Now, let's get something to eat," he said. "I'm famished."

The Pict hunters brought in fresh trout for breakfast. We rolled it in stone-ground wheat flour, and fried it in bacon fat on a griddle that Pellinore's squire produced from somewhere. I gathered he hid utensils in the wood to make camping near the spring easier. We ate with good appetite, washing down the trout, the bacon and hard bread with ale.

"This is one of the good things about being a king. You eat well," Pellinore said and winked.

"I may take to it," I said, and Nithe grunted, her mouth full.

"Where do you plan to travel in your errantry?" Pellinore asked.

"I hadn't thought much on it," I said.

"Well, if you'd like some advice, I'd say go south. The knights of Cornwall are valiant, slow and stupid. A good man can make a quick reputation there. They gossip all the time, so it won't be long before they're speaking of you as another Tristram," and he spat into the fire.

"I don't know as I'd like that," I said.

"Don't worry about it. He'll hear about it and arrange to meet you in a tournament, to add your reputation to his. He does it all the time."

"Is he any good?" I asked.

"Yes, he's very good. He's tricky, too, so never turn your back on him."

"We've had words in the past and did not find comfort in each other's company," I said. I glanced over at Nithe to find her watching me with a look of cold disdain on her face. She turned away without speaking.

"Probably he'll handle me with ease. I'd be well advised to get some practice in before that happens." I glanced at Nithe again, but she kept her face turned away. Pellinore watched this byplay, and winked. I guessed he'd heard about the affair at the smithy.

"I notice you don't carry a spear. I have a couple that are a little heavier than I like anymore that you're welcome to take with you. You carry one, and your squire carries the spare."

"I find them unwieldy for hunting anything but boar and bear," I said.

"Nevertheless, they're part of a knight's equipment. If you're challenged to joust, you have to have a spear."

"Very well," I said. Pellinore nodded to his squire, and the man went off grumbling to bring the spears mentioned from wherever he hid such things.

I stood and looked them over. They were well made, with good ash shafts, and slim, sharp heads. They were about ten feet long and balanced nicely in the hand. Ordinarily they are not used for throwing, but I aimed one at a tree to see how it would sail. I hit the knot I aimed at, some forty feet away.

"Hey, you're not supposed to do that!" Pellinore objected.

"I know. I'm as Pict as Tristram, and as tricky, come need. I hope I'll never have to throw one of these at a man, but who can tell?" I sent the other spear to within a hand's-breadth of the first.

"I'll take them, and much obliged," I said.

"Can you handle one on horseback?" he asked.

"Oh, yes. I could cook a meal on horseback, if I had to," I said, and Nithe grunted again.

"Have you thought about designating a lady to be the recipient of all this honor you propose to win?" Nithe questioned.

"No, I have not."

"Can't be a knight without a lady," Pellinore objected. "Can't use Nithe, either. It's supposed to be a platonic relationship, so you pick some married woman."

"I don't know any married women," I said. "Furthermore, if my wife had that kind of attention from some lout, I wouldn't like it much. Besides, I notice you said the relationship was supposed to be platonic, as if sometimes it isn't?"

"Don't you listen to any court gossip?"

"I told you, I don't hang around the court."

"Well, I do," Nithe said, "and I can tell you that not one lady in a dozen actually keeps her paramour at arm's length as she should."

"Then, I don't want to do it."

"Have to," Pellinore said. "Tell you what, I have a niece, actually a cousin's daughter, who is a fetching little thing, newly married to Segwardies. She hasn't been married long enough to be bored, and I'd like to see Pictish ladies get more attention. If you get famous, it would make her look good."

"You already know her," Nithe said. "She is the daughter of the Lion of Grance and was Guenevere's companion when you met the two of them with Arthur. You said you liked her well enough, then," she added, looking at me.

"Well, I did, but I'm not sure she'd be safe to be around, new husband or not," I said lamely. "She impressed me as being very naughty."

"I'll look after you," Nithe said.

"What's her name, again?" I asked, trying to appear casual. I knew it, right enough.

"Ettarde," Pellinore said.

"That was it. Gull," I translated into Latin for Nithe, whose Pictish is not as good as some of her other languages. "Very well, we'll do that. I hope it works."

We set off that afternoon with two of Pellinore's Picts to hunt for us. Nithe had brought four others with her, on Arthur's orders, but we sent two of them back to Ulfas, with permission from Pellinore to build a hill fort on the site of our wolf lair. I sent the young wolves back with them, keeping only Hair and Nithe's bitch with us. Pellinore was lord of all land in the area, including Arthur's hill fort. It rankled in his breast that Arthur had never even inquired who the local owner was before he began to construct Camelot. It was his complaint on the subject that brought the matter to mind.

"You'll need a place to send all those knights who yield to you in single encounters. I can't use them, and Arthur doesn't need them. Start your own army," he advised, and so I did. It was not more than a few hours' ride from Camelot, and might raise a few eyebrows, but I could make it right with Arthur later.

On the road I had a chance to talk with Nithe. We were ostensibly alone, for the Picts were out ranging on either side and in front of us, scouting. "I never had a chance to ask you before," I said. "What happened to Myrddin?"

"He didn't take me with him, after all," she said.

"But where did he go, really?"

"Like I told you," Nithe explained, "he said he had to go north, where the Saxons come from, to find out if we could expect more folks pressing on us in the next few years as the Saxons do now, either more of them, or folks like them. We stayed in a cave high in the mountains, an old living site of his where he had hidden equipment and supplies, long enough to outfit him for travel. It is only a half-day's walk from my mother's cave, I might add, which may be the reason they seem to know each other so well.

"We spent a week with her just before he left, but what they had to talk about, I never found out, for they talked in private. That's a strange place, by the way. They call it New Avalon on the Hill. I gather old Avalon was the island Myrddin was planning to take us to when we left the Strathclyde. Pellinore drove the people out, angered about something concerning his sister, and they settled upriver of Camelot."

"The island is called Mona. Pellinore just gave it to me, and don't change the subject. New Avalon is not a particularly strange place at all. It's a high-class brothel," I said.

"You know that?"

"Everyone knows that."

"Well, everybody is wrong. Have you ever been there?"

"I have not. What about Myrddin?"

"He left without bidding me good-bye, almost before I knew it. He talked to me most of the night before, telling me I must return to New Avalon and take up my duties there as the daughter of Hilda, and train to become the mistress of New Avalon, the Lady of the Lake, if you will, against a time when Hilda would no longer be able to act in that capacity. I couldn't tell you about it, because I didn't think you'd believe me, the way you feel about me."

"How is that?" I asked.

"You think I am light-minded and frivolous."

"I do?"

"Yes," she said.

I didn't reply. She knew better than that. I tried to understand what she had been saying. Myrddin had always an otherworld air about him, but this was not credible. Nithe doesn't lie much, however, in my knowledge of her, not direct lies.

"Let me understand this," I said. "Myrddin told you to train to take over this brothel?"

"I'm trying to tell you, it isn't really a brothel. Some part of druidic training, that the Romans outlawed, was in the study of natural sciences. That's what they do there. There are unattached women at Avalon, true enough, but they are seekers of wisdom, just like the druids. Some folk can't understand that, and would fear it as witchcraft if it were known. So, to protect them, it has developed the reputation of being a brothel, which everyone understands and accepts."

"Then it isn't a brothel at all?" I asked, not convinced.

"Well, just enough of one to justify the reputation," Nithe said, grinning at me.

"I don't think it is a very good idea," I said slowly, trying to picture Nithe in such a setting.

"Neither did I. That's why I ran wild when I got back to Camelot, trying to find another destiny. I'm still not reconciled to it."

We talked about it until we had nothing more to say and put the subject from us. I continued to think about it, however, and I'm sure she did as well.

It took us days of riding to come to Grance's castle again in the lovely summer country men call Somerset. We found a surprise visitor, Kay, in the company of several other knights, among them Pynel and Balan.

"What are you doing here?" Kay asked, abrupt as ever.

"We are looking for Ettarde," I answered. "Our business is with her."

"It will take you some time to conduct it, then," he said with satisfaction. "Segwardies came for her, and she went away with him."

"Where did they go?" I asked.

"Segwardies is one of King Mark's knights. He will have taken his new bride to meet the king," Kay said.

"A king's knight?" Nithe asked, innocently. "Sir Segwardies?"

"Well, yes, but knights from Cornwall are not much regarded. They have a reputation for cowardice."

"And besides, he's a Pict," I added. Kay looked at me and flushed, but said nothing. Perhaps he was remembering he had been knighted on the tourney field by King Mark of Cornwall.

Grance bustled up to us. "Well met, Pelleas," he said. "I did not know you were a member of the escort group."

"He's not," Kay said. "We have only knights with us."

"Pelleas was knighted by King Pellinore," Nithe said, airily. "He also made him Lord of the Isles. King Pelles had already named him Prince and Heir of Strathclyde. He would grace your escort."

"Well, this is wonderful," Grance said, rubbing his hands together. "You must take charge of the party."

"See here!" Kay blustered.

"I have no idea what party you are talking of," I said, ignoring Kay.

"Guenevere is going to King Arthur," Grance said. "He wants to make her his queen."

"So soon?"

"He was quite insistent but Guenevere will not be rushed. It may take some time to get them together," he observed gloomily.

"I see. I am sorry, but I was not included originally, and Arthur is aware I am a knight errant," I said. "I will have to decline the invitation." I noticed Kay was having a visible effort containing his ire. "What I really wish to do is to find your daughter, Ettarde," I continued, "and offer her my knightly fealty."

"What an honor for her," Grance said sincerely. "She will be at Segwardies' castle, in all likelihood. You'll find it on the River Tamar in Cornwall, west of here a few days' ride."

Grance was hospitable to a fault, insisting that we spend a few days with him. We did, and Kay snubbed us, spending his time with Guenevere, telling her of Camelot, and the plans Arthur had for it. He took his role of herald with the seriousness with which he took all of his roles, and it seemed as though Arthur had chosen well to have him as spokesman. We saw little of Guenevere, but before we left she called me to her.

"My guardian says you go to seek Ettarde's permission to call her your lady love. That is most romantic," Guenevere said.

"The rules are strict about choosing a married woman," I replied.

"If you were to wait a few weeks, I would be eligible," she said, teasingly.

"I am bid by my liege lord, King Pellinore, to seek a Pictish maiden," I said. "He suggested Ettarde. She is his niece—really his cousin's daughter."

"I thought Arthur was your liege lord. Did you not come here as his shield-bearer?"

"Arthur is my brother, Lady," I said. "I watched his back as a brother should, but he is not my lord."

"You have a most handsome page, Sir Pelleas," she said, eyeing Nithe. "One might take him for a girl."

"One might," I said.

"One is," Nithe amended. "Arthur wouldn't let me follow Pelleas around unless I dressed like a squire. He said it would cause talk."

"You're Arthur's sister, then. I'm happy to meet you," Guenevere said, and she rose and kissed Nithe very prettily. "You must tell me how to please him. I'm afraid I annoyed him when last we met."

"He doesn't really like being teased," Nithe said, "but he'll share jokes with you, if he thinks you're not laughing at him. And, I'm not really his sister. We just grew up together."

"He's very young," Guenevere sighed. "Kay tells me he has no sense of humor at all."

"Kay? How would Kay know? Anyway, Kay is wrong," I said. "Kay and Arthur do not like each other, and Arthur shares nothing with Kay."

"He trusted him to come after me," Guenevere said.

"Kay is his seneschal, and the marriage terms had to be settled with your guardian. Arthur is no good at that kind of thing, and Kay is. There is no other tie between them."

"Kay said they were boys together," Guenevere said, perplexed.

"True, but they didn't like each other as boys, either," Nithe said. "You must form your own opinion about Arthur, and not rely on what Kay, or Pelleas, or anyone else says."

"Oh, I will."

"Is it true," I asked, "that your mother was Rowena, wife to Vortigern?"

"Yes. They say I look much like her, but I don't remember her very well."

"I didn't know that!" Nithe exclaimed, staring first at me and then at Guenevere.

"That I was Rowena's daughter? Should that be surprising?"

"But, I know of her!" Nithe said. "My mother's father was Horsa the Jute, brother to Hengist."

"Your mother was Hilda, the one who ran off with the priest?" Guenevere asked. "I'd heard that from servants, but is it true?"

"Not just a priest, a Bishop," Nithe corrected her. "Bishop Ninian is my father."

Guenevere burst out laughing and hugged Nithe again. "I am so happy to have found you. We'll be like sisters. You do live with Arthur, don't you?"

"Sometimes. Right now, I am in disgrace."

"What terrible thing did you do?" Guenevere asked, still laughing.

"I sold myself for a year to get a dowry to attract a husband."

"You didn't!"

"Indeed I did. Pelleas bought me out from under the noses of a number of handsome young knights, and scandalized Arthur almost beyond forgiveness."

"How could you?" Guenevere asked me, amused at my discomfiture. "Never mind, I'll stand your champion," she told Nithe. "I'll make Arthur forgive you, and welcome you back. I'll need a sister among all those strangers.

"As for you, Sir Pelleas, you should not go seeking after Ettarde with a beautiful lady like this in your train. Whatever would Ettarde think?"

"Much or little," I said. "I have to do knight errantry and make a reputation big enough for ambitious fortune hunters to leave me alone. I speak of land-hungry knights," I added, at her look of surprise, "not ladies looking for a rich husband. Pellinore says otherwise I'll spend all my time fighting adventurers looking for a quick and easily-come-by domain. He gave me the islands of Mona and Man for my own, if I can hold them. Nithe tells me it is imperative I have a lady to dedicate victories to as part of the process of building a reputation. That way the bards will have something to sing about, and the word will spread."

"Victories? You're counting on victories?"

"There's no other point in going through this," I said.

"Very well," she replied, "Go straight to King Mark's castle. He has tourneys every Sabbath, and Tristram always wins. Beat him, and your reputation is assured; my sister Ettarde can bask in the glory of being chosen by the foremost knight in Britain, and Nithe can come home and help me learn to be a queen."

"That sounds good," I said. "You agree, Nithe?"

"Oh, by all means. Start with the best!" She turned to Guenevere and said, "I will take my leave of you until we have done all that is needful to keep Pelleas from being bothered." She and Guenevere hugged again, both on the edge of laughter, and we left in good humor, Nithe because she had found Guenevere, me because Nithe was happy.

Our trip was all too short. Mark's castle was on a flat hilltop like others in Cornwall, but somewhat larger, and with stone walls rather than wooden palisades. The central building was a round keep like Camelot, though not as large. It was apparent that a tourney was in process as we rode up. The commons was crowded with tents and people. A large open meadow in the center was the tourney field and stands with pennants floating in the breeze and facing away from the sun had been set up for ladies.

We rode up to the herald.

"Has it begun yet?" I asked.

"The general melee is over, and the folks are waiting for challenges to the principal knights."

"Who is here?"

"Segwardies, Palomides and, of course, Tristram," he said. "There are also a number of worthy local knights. What is your name?"

"I am Sir Pelleas, Lord of the Isles," I said. "I would challenge Sir Tristram."

The herald looked up at me condescendingly, and said, "That really wouldn't be proper. He never responds to challenges from unknown knights."

"Are you sure?"

"Oh, yes. No one ever does that any more except those who

are not aware of his prowess, and he is too much of a gentleman to take advantage of their ignorance."

"He is the most famous knight here, isn't he?" I asked.

"Yes, and he shows little mercy."

"Do you think he ought to challenge the field of local knights first?" Nithe asked the herald.

"You don't think I can win over him, do you?" I asked Nithe, ignoring the herald.

"He does nothing but tourneys. He is very skilled."

"Ah, well, perhaps you're both right," I said meekly. Nithe frowned, not liking this change in demeanor. "Would you announce me, please?" I asked the herald. "Say I'll fight anyone, and we'll see who comes out."

The herald shook his head, but walked off. He didn't think much of this approach. Mountain and I rode into the lists, with Nithe, Lucy and Hair behind us.

"Keep the dogs out of this," I said, and left her on the sidelines, taking my position at one end of the lists.

"The Honorable Sir Pelleas, Lord of the Isles, challenges the field," the herald announced. The crowd rushed to the lists to close in the area, and get the best places for viewing what they thought would be a slaughter. A few minutes later a knight came out, and leisurely mounted his horse, a well set up stallion, before turning to the lists. He was armored in breastplate, backplate and closed helmet, and carried a spear and two swords, one long and one short. He set his horse moving toward me, spear leveled, without preamble.

I waited until he had run about halfway to the center and slowed his horse before starting Mountain, so he had lost his momentum and was at three-quarter speed when we met. I caught him fairly at the center of his wooden shield, picking up splinters as the head of my spear cut into the wood, just a split second before he reached me. My blow pushed him off balance, and his spearpoint missed my shield, just grazing Mountain's neck.

I was angry so fast that it surprised me. I turned Mountain, pursued, caught and pulled the knight out of the saddle. Before he hit the ground I was on him, my mace drawn and ready to smash his head in, but I stayed my hand. There would be no satisfaction in striking him while he was helpless. He rolled and came to his feet, sword drawn and at the ready.

"False knight," I said, "if you can't handle a spear so it doesn't hurt horses, why do you use one at all?" My mind closed on his like a hawk's foot on a hare, and I parried stroke after stroke with little effort, until he was panting with fatigue. I slammed him in the stomach with the end of my mace, to take what was left of his wind, and banged him on the helmet so that he dropped at my feet, dazed and panting.

I cut the laces on his helmet and jerked it off in one swift movement, tilting his face upward with the end of my mace.

"Do you yield, or do you wish to give me the pleasure of smashing your head in?" I asked.

"I yield. What's wrong with you? This is a tourney, not a war!" he said in an alarmed voice.

"The next time we meet, and you cut my horse, it will no longer be sport," I answered, and walked away from him, back to Nithe. Mountain followed me, docilely. He wasn't even breathing hard.

I remounted at the end of the lists, and found another knight already in motion, running toward me. If I hadn't turned in time, I suppose I would have been speared in the back. I was beginning to get irritated.

I hit this one hard to teach him a lesson, and when he had yielded, I asked him a question. "Is this why Cornish knights have such a reputation for cowardice?" This taunt was commonly addressed to local knights by the Gaels and Britons from Arthur's court and had the effect I desired.

This time I mounted in the field, and rode back, glancing over my shoulder from time to time. Squires helped the knight to rise and walk off the field, and he must have reported what I said, because there was a sudden boiling of activity. It looked like I would have to fight several at once. I urged Mountain into a run as soon as someone was in the lists, and caught the man only a quarter of the way down the field. He didn't move after I knocked him off his horse, so I didn't get down. I trotted to the midline, and took my post a few steps beyond, waiting for the next one. The crowd was beginning to come to life, and the jostling for position set another knight in motion. I knocked him and his horse over before they were more than a dozen strides down the lists.

This time it took a while for some agreement on who the next opponent might be, so I rode to the end of the lists and talked to Nithe.

"Do you have any water?" I asked.

She offered me a flask. "Are you enjoying yourself?" she asked.

"Not really," I said. "I didn't understand how serious people were about this."

"They don't like you much," she said.

"I guess building a reputation doesn't make you popular if you're doing it in someone else's backyard."

"Look who's coming out," Nithe said. "It looks like they have convinced Tristram he needs to uphold the honor of Cornwall. Is Mountain tired?"

"No, he's just warmed up. Tristram is in trouble," I said.

I was wrong. Tristram and I broke spears on each other, not once, but twice.

"I don't have any more," I said to Nithe.

"Then, I guess you lose by default," she said.

"Damned if I will," I said, and I dismounted, drew my mace and walked down the lists.

"Come back, you fool. You'll get killed."

"Watch me," I said. I assumed Tristram would accept this as a challenge, and fight on foot. I was wrong again. He tried to run me down three times before I broke his spear with my mace, and even then, he didn't dismount. So, I spoke to his horse's mind.

"Whoa!" I said, and the horse came to such a plunging stop that Tristram went over the horse's head. He hit hard. I tapped him on the head as he struggled to stand, and he collapsed. The crowd booed, and might have mobbed me if I had not turned and walked back to Mountain. Nithe was laughing, her head turned away so I couldn't see her face, but I knew.

"Don't say anything," I advised Nithe.

"Why would I say anything?"

"Because you always do. I won't have my horse fouled and hurt by any cow-hearted poltroon. I know he would have thrust his broken lance in Mountain's face the next run. So, don't talk about it."

"I'm not talking about it."

"Well, you're thinking about it. I know how you feel about that lout."

"Oh? How do I feel?"

"I said, I don't want to talk about it," and failing a rejoinder, we rode away in silence. No one followed us.

That evening, Nithe said, "I don't think you have the right attitude to be a tourney hero. Maybe we ought to rescue damsels, kill dragons and the like."

"Are you being funny?" I asked.

"Not at all. I'm sure there are plenty of useful things to do."

I decided that it would be necessary to go along with this, so I said, "I don't mind hunting bandits. They prey on the common people, and generally make their lives miserable. That's useful work."

"Most of the bandits are knights," Nithe said. "Being a knight doesn't pay at all well, and the poor dears have to make a living some way. Are you allowed to beat up on other knights?"

"I guess we'll find out," I said, and directed our route to the nearest village. We sought out the local tavern, and engaged the tavern keeper in conversation.

"Are you bothered by bandits in the neighborhood?" I asked. "I'm looking for something to do that will build a reputation and won't disrupt peoples' lives."

"You look like a nice enough fella, and I don't mind admitting we could use a little help with Bad Breuse."

"Bad Breuse?"

" 'Sir Breuse Sans-Pite' is the way he calls himself. He's a terrible nuisance around here, and any number of knights have tried to fight him, with no luck."

"Why is that?" Nithe asked.

"He has the fastest horses in the country. Prides himself on it. No one ever catches up with him."

"I think we might," I said. "Where is he likely to be this time of day?"

"He's likely to be hanging around the spring, hoping to catch a girl after water. He's a great one for a little rape in the morning."

Nithe changed into the green dress she had used to impress the bishop in London. I noticed it was a little tight, but declined to point this out to her, thinking she would not be grateful to hear it. She staked herself out by the spring, with Lucy for company, and I took the horses out into the woods to hide. Hair was with me. I took a little nap until Nithe screamed, which was our arranged signal. I had little fear that Sir Breuse would do her any harm, but I hurried to the spot with Hair.

"Whatever do you want?" Nithe was saying to him as we came up. Lucy was growling, crouched between her and a tall, weedy-looking man, dressed in green-dyed leather.

"A little company. It won't take long. Call off your dog, or I'll be forced to kill it." He pulled his sword out.

"Down, Lucy," Nithe said, and walked toward Sir Breuse to put some distance between him and Lucy. Sir Breuse flipped his sword, and cut her dress to the navel, exposing her breasts, as soon as she was close enough.

"That's the only good dress I have!" Nithe said, suddenly angry. "Why did you do that?"

He didn't reply, but grabbed her and threw her on the ground. Nithe struggled, cursing him. I move quietly when I wish to and was within touching distance before I spoke. "Are you Sir Breuse?" I asked.

He jumped up as one bee-stung, and vaulted to his horse's back with the ease of long practice.

"Take him!" I cried, and Lucy leaped for him while Hair attacked the horse. The horse reared. Sir Breuse was a superb horseman, but Lucy took his rein hand in her mouth, and pulled him from the saddle. His horse bolted, and Hair bit his other arm as he lay on the ground. He dropped his knife.

"Let him up," I said, and they backed off a step, looking at him intently. Nithe came to join me.

"So this is Bad Breuse," she said, rubbing her arm where he'd grabbed her. "He is stronger than he looks!"

"What is this outrage?" the man asked. "What do you mean by attacking me this way? I'll have you hanged for it!"

"You feel abused?" I asked.

"I am a knight!" he responded.

"Do knights go around raping young ladies, then?" Nithe asked.

"Of course not! Ladies don't haul water."

"You make a distinction between a lady and a common female?"

"Doesn't everyone? I have first rights over all the common women in this valley. I choose to exercise them before they enter into marriage contracts, not to put a pall on the wedding ceremony. It's considered a sensitive thing to do."

"By whom?"

"Why, by husbands, of course. What did you think?"

"I believe it," Nithe said, dryly. "However, I'm not from here, and you have no rights over me of any kind."

"You had only to say," Sir Breuse said. "This appears to me to be a misunderstanding, a serious one, considering who I am. If you don't both wish to be penalized to the full extent of the law, I suggest you surrender yourselves into my hands immediately."

I pulled a strip of leather from my saddlebag, and bending over Sir Breuse, captured one wrist and looped the thong over it while Nithe sputtered in indignation, attempting to pull her dress together.

"Here, what are you about?" he complained.

"I'm tying you up," I said, and did so. I pulled him to his feet and examined his wrists. The animals had been careful not to break the skin. "I'm taking you into the village to check your story. It differs from what I have been told." I tied him to my saddle, and led him into town, listening to him protest all the way.

"You'll be sorry for this," he said. "I am the lord of this village, and my villeins will tear you apart." I ignored him and tethered him to a post in front of the tavern when we reached it.

"I have Sir Breuse," I said to the tavern keeper, and he and his customers came outside to view the prisoner.

"That's him all right, in the flesh," the tavern keeper said. "I'll get you a bit of line," he added. I thought he meant to tie him more securely, but he came back bearing a stout rope tied as a hangman's noose.

"I saved it from the last execution Sir Breuse held, from the tree right in front of the tavern here. It should fit him as well as it did poor Jack."

"You can't let them hang me," Sir Breuse protested to me. "You're responsible for me."

"In what way?" I asked.

"I yielded to you. You are honor bound to protect me."

"You did not yield to me. You tried to flee."

"Do you really think you could defeat me in single combat, if I wished to fight?" he asked, amazed. "Of course I yielded to you."

"Would you prefer to be killed in single combat than hanged?" I asked.

"It would not happen. I am the finest swordsman in the south of Britain."

I looked at the tavern keeper, and he nodded. "Sir Breuse is good, all right. That's one of the reasons he's never been captured. He fights free."

"This is silly," Nithe said. "If you fight him and he wins, he gets away. If he loses before you kill him, he can yield and you will be responsible for him." She was right.

"I can see I won't get any praise for this, no matter how it turns out. Do what you want with him," I said to the tavern keeper, and we rode off. I didn't look back.

"Do you have any other suggestions?" I asked.

"I asked where Segwardies' castle is while you were playing judge," Nithe said. "We could visit Ettarde, though the way things have been going, she might not want to have anything to do with you."

She was right again, but I thought maybe I could talk to Ettarde, so we called on her. I was wrong about that, too.

"Dolt!" Ettarde yelled, when we first came into her presence. She jumped to her feet, bouncing up and down in rage. She was still small and dark and beautiful, but more richly dressed than when I first met her in Guenevere's company. "You embarrass Tristram in front of everyone," she yelled, "and he is carried from the field and doesn't make me queen of the tourney. He promised he would do so."

"If you will accept me as your paramour, I will dedicate any number of tourneys to you," I said.

"You will? No, you will not! I want you off my grounds. Leave, or I'll have you thrown off." I didn't think she could do that, but I didn't want Nithe endangered, so we left. We camped a few hundred yards from her castle and talked about it.

"If I can't get her to change her mind, I may as well give up on this whole business," I said. We were talking over our supper, a few hares that had fallen to my sling earlier in the day, when a visitor rode up. It was Ulfas.

"How did you find us?" I asked, after our greetings had been exchanged.

"You leave a visible trail," he replied. "Inquiring after you could get a person killed."

"What are you doing here?" I asked, handing him a spitted hare to roast over the fire.

"Arthur wants Nithe to bring in the rest of King Ban's Britons to Camelot from Exeter, where their ships have landed. His son, Lancelot, is their leader. He knows Nithe, and will listen to her and believe she comes from Arthur. Arthur hears King Lot and his followers among the Gaels will be coming against him again, and he needs help. Lot's people are assembling near Tintagel, Gorlais' castle."

"Arthur's mother, Igraine, still lives there," I said. "Is she part of this?"

"Who can say? Arthur isn't even sure if King Ban is on his side."

"He is, or Lancelot would not be with them," Nithe said confidently. I looked at her, but spoke to Ulfas.

"When will they attack?" I asked.

"Not for a few months, probably, but he wants to get ready."

"I'll go," Nithe said. "Are you coming with me?" she asked, looking at me strangely.

"No," I said, on consideration. I didn't like this. "I may as well try to talk to Ettarde again. I promised Pellinore," I continued without conviction.

So we parted, with Ulfas and the Pict hunters going with Nithe. The next morning I went to Ettarde's gate and found a dozen men waiting for me, armed with spear, sword and cudgel. They attacked me, and I was forced to beat them down to save my life. Hair bit several of them, and Mountain kicked one. We didn't actually kill anyone, but I may have hit a few harder than needful. When they were all quiet, I spoke to them.

"Things will go better if you but listen," I said. "I am willing to disarm myself, and suffer myself to be bound, so that you can present me to Ettarde. All I want is a chance to talk to her. Stay with Mountain," I told Hair, and he moved a few paces back from the gate to wait for me. It might have been a mistake. Several of those who had suffered bites and bruises were too angry for me to calm down with mind-touch, and I received a few late hits myself, once I was tethered. I escaped the possibility of real harm by breaking my bonds to show I could do it before allowing myself to be tied again. They brought me before Ettarde. She was still angry.

"Pig!" she screamed at me. "I want this man beaten and sent

away," she instructed the leader of my captors. "Who said he could be admitted into my presence?"

"Listen," I pleaded, "Pellinore sent me. He wants me to serve as your paramour so a Pictish woman can gain glory."

"Does he think I need you? I have Tristram, and there are some of King Arthur's knights, like Sir Blamore, Arthur's own cousin, hanging about, waiting for a turn. My husband is furious as it is. With you he'd become a laughingstock."

I was escorted, ungently, to the gate, and pushed out. I broke my bonds, and went back to the campsite. I wished there were hot water to bathe the bruises I had, but lacking that I slept until next morning. After breakfast, I found Ettarde's retainers rushing my campsite, with a number of reinforcements. I repeated the previous day's activities, and was being brought, bound, back to Ettarde when a knight approached us. It was Gawaine, proud King Lot's arrogant son, from whom I had won a fine steel knife playing hurley as a boy. I still didn't like him.

"May I be of help?" he asked politely.

I wondered at it. "No," I said. "I'll be back in a little. You'll find my camp under those trees. Wait for me there, if you want to, and I'll tell you about it later." One of the villeins jerked on my bonds, so I broke off the conversation. Nothing had changed. Ettarde had me thrown out again, with her curses ringing in my ears.

"What are you up to?" Gawaine asked, when I returned to the camp.

"Why would you be interested in my doings?" I asked. "You never were before." I was not in a good mood with Nithe gone, and I was aware what a ridiculous spectacle I must present. If Gawaine chose to laugh I would have something to release my anger on.

"I was not previously aware that you were Arthur's brother," Gawaine said simply. I decided to accept this for truth.

"I'm trying to get Ettarde to reconsider being my paramour," I said.

"By getting beaten up?"

"That isn't happening. Her men attack me. I subdue them, then allow myself to be bound so that I can be brought into her presence. I can't think of another way to see her."

"The world is full of women, many of them willing for anything. Why this insistence on Ettarde?"

"I promised Pellinore." I said. "She's his niece."

"I have to see this paragon," Gawaine said. "I'll call on her and sing your praises. Maybe she'll change her mind. I seem to have a measure of success in such cases."

"This happens often?" I asked.

"Most damsels at least pretend to be reluctant, in my experience. Wait here, and I'll see what I can do."

Three days later Nithe returned. I was sitting by the fire when she rode in on Blaise.

"It seems you were in the same position when I left," she said. "Is nothing going on?"

I told her how things stood. She thought for a bit, and asked, "Have you looked for Gawaine? If Ettarde is as rude to him as she is to you, he may be lying injured somewhere."

I hadn't thought of that, but it made sense. We looked and found a pavilion set up under a tree by a small stream, near a postern gate to Segwardies' castle. When we peeked inside we saw Gawaine and Ettarde, stripped and asleep, a flagon of wine nearby. I carefully drew Gawaine's sword from its scabbard, and placed the naked blade between them before we slipped away. Out of earshot, Nithe laughed so uncontrollably that I realized I would have to do something about Gawaine.

"Let us leave," I said. "If I talk to him now, I may do him an injury."

"But, what about the reputation you want to build?" Nithe asked, her eyes still bright with suppressed mirth.

"I'll think of another way," I said.

"It's just as well," she replied. "Pellinore wants you to come back. He's going to fight beside Arthur, and it will be sooner than we thought."

We rode back to camp, and I said something to Nithe that had been on my mind for a long time.

"I don't want to wait, as I agreed to do. Am I wrong in believing what Myrddin and Arthur say is true? Do you love me, as I have you these many years?"

Nithe was silent for a moment, and then took my hand as we sat on flat rocks I had placed before our cooking fire.

"If you had made this declaration a week ago, I think I would have had no hesitation. Lud knows, I've chased you shamelessly for years."

"What impediment has arisen?" I asked.

"I'm not sure. Let me try to tell you. When Myrddin and I went to Brittany, you know we met Lancelot and we were both charmed by his eagerness and innocence. Well, while Myrddin tried to convince King Ban of the rightness of Arthur's cause, Lancelot and I spent much time together. He sings as well as Tristram, and when I couldn't get him to do that, I told him stories about Arthur as a boy. He's fascinated by the idea of the Knights of the Round Table. He wanted to become one of them. He's very romantic, and the idea of riding about doing good thrilled him. He promised he would win his father's permission to come to fight beside Arthur, and, when he didn't come, you saw how disappointed I was." She looked at me anxiously to see how I was receiving this story, but I nodded impassively, trying to show no emotion.

She sighed, having read something there I did not wish her to see, but continued with her recital. "When I saw him just now he told me he could not leave because his mother fell ill, and she begged him not to go. He is her only child, and he was very close to her. She died, and this is the earliest he could come to fulfill his promise. He was so sad! I was drawn to him irresistibly these past few days. Until I find out why this is, I would not wish to make a commitment of the kind you have a right to expect from me."

I had no comment.

"He is unlike anyone I have ever met before," she continued, having waited for a response from me. "Most of the men I have known well have been quiet and strong outside, and fiery inside. Lancelot seems to shine. From a distance he seems bigger than a man ought to be, and it isn't until you get up close that you realize it's a combination of the way he moves, and his extraordinarily powerful body that gives the impression of size." She looked at me. "You are so well proportioned that you look to be about fifteen stone until you come close, and it is apparent that you might scale twenty. With him, you'd expect twenty, and realize fifteen is nearer the mark.

"There is a kind of purity about him I'd love to sully," she said in a meditative tone. Suddenly flushing, she added ruefully, "That doesn't sound very nice, does it?" She looked full into my eyes and explained, "You know I have always been enormously attracted to you physically, as well as in other ways. This is different. I doubt if he's ever been with a woman."

She continued holding my hand and gazing at my face. "Are you terribly disappointed?" she asked.

I found my voice. "Yes," I said, aloud. Mind-speech seemed too intimate.

"Are you hurt?"

I considered that a moment. "That, too," I said.

"I will sleep with you before I go, if it will help," she said. "I am very sure how I feel about you."

"You are going to him?" I asked.

"I found Lancelot at Exeter; he's waiting for reinforcements. Arthur wants me to bring him in, along with his men. He'll need them, but I don't have to leave right away."

"I think perhaps it would be best if you did, though," I said.

"Being with you would give me joy," she said.

"Being with you, and watching you ride away to another man, would be more than I could bear," I said.

Nithe rose, and looked down at me. "I may not have the right to ask this of you, but by the love I bear you, I will."

"What is it?" I asked.

"You must promise me that you will never fight Lancelot."

"I never fight anyone, except at need," I said.

"That is not good enough. Promise."

"Why?"

"One of you would be killed. He is very cool, very professional. His reputation is of the sort you were seeking a short time ago."

"He could not hurt me, then," I said, quietly.

"Perhaps, perhaps not. I have seen you fight. I don't want either of you hurt over me, and that's the only reason trouble could rise between you."

"I promise I will not fight him for that reason," I said. "I don't know him. He may be all you say, and he may not. If he is, he will have nothing to fear from me."

"That is good enough," she said, and bending, kissed me on the forehead like a child. I reached to the torque around her throat and pulled the ends apart so that I could slip it off. I put it on my arm, above my elbow. I then took the gold chain Pellinore had given me from my neck, and placed it on her own.

"You are free," I said. "Do what you will."

"Ah, Dog's-brother, you will break my heart," she said, standing and looking down at me.

"No," I said, thinking it over. "No."

I watched her ride out of camp with her Pict attendants. She did not look back.

I wandered throughout late fall and early winter in the woods of Somerset, hunting when needful, but mostly just thinking. There may have been Pict scouts around me, for I saw movement in the brush from time to time and Hair would watch without growling. No one spoke to me, and it was just as well. When the first snow fell I turned north to Camelot, not wishing to spend the cold months in a cave.

CHAPTER
XIV

found Camelot a beehive on my return. Stone masons had completed the round tower up two stories, and constructed a massive gate to one side of it. The hinges I had made to hang the gate were set into the stone with bolts that went completely through the wall, and the wall was an integral part of the tower. It ran an additional twenty feet beyond the gate where it was attached to a palisade of giant oak posts. I wondered if Arthur had managed to cut into druidic glades in his quest for timber of adequate size. If so, he was making enemies. The palisade now enclosed four acres on the hilltop. When I looked for Arthur I found him in the tower's second floor along with Pellinore, my liege lord, who jumped up and hugged me.

"Did you see Ettarde?" he asked.

"Yes. She rejected my suit," I reported, and he nodded gravely, which led me to believe he had already heard about it.

"I'm glad you're back," Arthur greeted me without preamble, but with the smile that bound men to his service. "Can you get your wolves together?" The second floor had become Arthur's armory, treasury and bedchamber, and in the middle of the floor, where light from the narrow window apertures shone equally from all sides, was a square table with the model Myrddin had built of the plan of Camelot.

"There will be some wolves at the hill fort with Ulfas but not over a dozen, probably," I said.

"They will be needed if the Gaels fight from chariots this time," Arthur said.

"I don't think we can trap the Gaels twice the same way," I said. "We can use the wolves in scouting, though." Arthur nodded and changed the subject.

"We'll use your hill fort as the assembly point for the Picts. Pellinore will be liaison. It's best if we keep the Picts out of the way of our Saxon allies, if we hope to have enough of either contingent left to fight the Gaels."

"Hill fort?" I asked.

"You might be surprised to see what Ulfas has done there," Arthur said. "I certainly was."

"I gave him permission to build, as I did you," Pellinore remarked, in an ironic tone.

"I know you did when I finally had sense enough to ask," Arthur said. He smiled. "If we were not such firm allies, I would be worried about the hill fort Ulfas is building for you, though. It's too close to Camelot for comfort." The relationship between Arthur and Pellinore was as peer to peer despite the difference in age between them. Pellinore was over fifty, and Arthur barely twenty.

Arthur looked up at me from where he was leaning over the model to ask, "Is Nithe bringing in the rest of the overseas Britons?"

"So she said," I replied. He glanced at me sharply on hearing the tone in which I had answered the question, but looked down again, as if he had found a reason for it in my expression. I have difficulty in masking my emotions.

"How did your knight errantry go?" Pellinore asked. I suspected from the too bland tone of voice with which the question was phrased that he knew.

"I don't seem to have a gift for it," I said. "I guess I'll just have to make a reputation some other way."

Arthur laughed. "That isn't necessary. I find from Pellinore that you are a creature of legend already." There is no suitable retort to a comment like that, so I made none.

"I'll be where you can find me," I said, and left. Ulfas' hill fort was a surprise, as Arthur had said. There was a tower, not big around, but thirty feet tall, with a man posted on top as lookout. An acre of the hillcrest was palisaded, and a ditch had been built in front of the palisade, pushing the walls up to twenty feet. It could not be taken by assault without overwhelming numbers. Arthur was only partly jesting about allies. In the hands of an enemy, it would be much too close to Camelot.

I was hailed from the tower, and a dozen Picts came to greet me. Ulfas was one.

"I thought you were with Nithe," I said.

"I was not needed there," he replied. Anna came to me and hugged me, along with a number of other women and several children.

"Welcome home, Dogs'-brother," Anna said, teasingly.

"Ah, Anna," I said. "Have you finally come to realize you took the wrong man when you chose Ulfas over me?"

"Indeed," she said. "You've become so grand, fighting in tourneys and all, that I would never see you if I had chosen you."

"I'm home as much as Ulfas is," I said.

"Not by half, or we wouldn't have four children, would we," she responded.

"How do you know about tourneys?" I asked. "Particularly since there was only one?"

"All the Picts know," Ulfas said. "You took the wind out of Drustan. It was nobly done."

"Will he be joining Arthur?" I asked.

"If he intended to fight at all, he would be with King Mark, his uncle, and Mark's with Lot. Drustan doesn't really fight in wars, though. He enters tourneys."

I nodded. "Are the wolves around?" I asked.

"Yes. They patrol the walls at night when they're not out with the hunters. No one could sneak up on us with sentries like them."

He reached out his hand to Hair, and the wolf sniffed it politely. "I'm happy to see Hair is still with you. His presence will keep the others here."

"Yes. We'll be out tonight to renew ties," I said.

Hair and I found our pack waiting for us when we left the fort soon after full dark. There were a dozen beasts, half of them Cavell's pups. They swarmed us licking Hair's muzzle and my hands, giving forth with whines and wild tail-wagging. I touched their minds, and found them filled with joy.

Cavell's pups had grown to be as large or larger than the other wolves, and at four were fully mature. Both males and females must have weighed between eight and ten stone. We went hunting with them, and ran down two deer within a mile of the fort. I cut out the liver of one and fed them by hand, as in the past, before allowing them at the carcasses. The other liver I roasted slightly over a small fire and ate myself.

Next day Ulfas and his men constructed a den for the animals at the sharpest corner of the palisaded enclosure, where they could sleep during the day. We put in two entry ports for them from the outside, one from the den into the fort, and covered the whole den with poles and mud. I had the roofs of the other buildings in the fort changed from thatch to poles with mud also, remembering Arthur's trick that burned out the Saxon hill fort.

In a week, the changes I ordered were completed, and I had come to know everyone in the dozen families. There were thirty men of fighting age, some of them single, and there may have been as many children as adults, most of them young. The smallest children, with no chores to perform, followed me around whenever I was in the fort. I offered to work, but it made the men uncomfortable.

"Geens don't work," Ulfas declared.

"What do they do?"

"Whatever they want, but not what other men do."

I played with the children, and surprisingly, that was acceptable, but I remembered that the hunters had also spent their spare time with the children in my village. I had never been accepted by the hunters after I freed the wolf from the trap and had missed much of the closeness of village life. It was good now to be able to tell the children stories and listen to their problems as if I had no other cares in the world. They were fascinated by my size, but not fearful, and I felt at ease with them.

At night I ran with the wolves, reforming them into a hunting band. We picked up several local wolves I had not known before, and after they accepted Hair they accepted me. I worried about Friend, who was increasingly stiff and no longer accepted as pack leader, but Cavell insisted on running with us, and Friend would not be left behind.

Some Pictish hunters who had bonded to individual wolves came with us. Their superior night vision made them a welcome addition. I thought of the Gaelic saying, "Never trust a man with brown eyes," and I wondered if it had originated in fear of the night vision of the brown-eyed Picts. Together we stalked deer far from the hill fort, feeding the wolves and bringing the excess back to feed the men working on Ulfas' fort. I let Kay worry about feeding Arthur's men. It was his job, and I felt no desire to help him do it.

"How did you talk so many people into joining you here?" I asked Ulfas one evening.

"I told them a Geen would live here," he said. "I said there was ample room for fields; there were fish in the streams and deer in the hills. It wasn't hard."

"Why is a Geen important? I've never felt so before."

"There aren't many, but they've always been shepherds of the Picts since any can remember," Ulfas said. "The people feel safe with you here."

"How did you know I would come?"

"I talked to Pellinore, and to Arthur. They both said you'd be back when you came to your senses."

"What is that supposed to mean?" I asked.

"You know. About Nithe."

"I see. I may have come to my senses about Nithe too late. She's become interested in that new knight from Brittany."

"That won't last. All the women are swooning over him. Even Anna rolls her eyes whenever his name is mentioned. Some lady will get him in her bed soon, and the tension will be over. Women just hate to see unattached males. It gives other males a bad example."

"I just hope it isn't Nithe," I said. "I'm surprised to learn he has been here. I thought Nithe was to bring him in."

"Oh, he came some weeks back with Balan and Bors and a few others and left again to meet men in from overseas. Nithe was off with you, but there were plenty of other women around to gawk and talk."

"What do you think of him?" I asked.

"I don't know. Arthur held a small tourney to welcome him, and he rode a few times. He's not as big as Tristram, but he's faster, and sits a horse well. If he fights the way he plays, he's very dangerous." I thought about this over breakfast, and went fishing.

Scouts found me, and brought me back to the hill fort with the information that two columns of Gaels had been sighted, one directed toward Camelot, and a smaller one coming toward us. We were waiting for them when they arrived. We would have had but a few minutes' warning if our hunters had not seen the enemy, barely enough time to send word to Arthur. We had not sent out scouts because Arthur's Saxon spies had assured us there was no need, and if the Picts had not planned on a feast to welcome me home, we would not have had hunters out in the afternoon and would have been caught unaware. As it was, we brought all the folk, and some of the cattle, into the hill fort in time to keep them from dying on spears. I hoped Arthur had not been surprised. The Gaels ringed the fort, out of range of our slings. I recognized their leader by his bearing. It was proud Lot in the seven-colored cloak of a high king. He rode up to the fort and hailed us. "Ho, the fort!" he called. "Open your gates to us, and we will spare you!"

I appeared on the parapet and called back. "Ho, Lot! What mean you by this show of force?"

"Is it Dog's-brother? Is this your fort?" Well he must have known. His spies had been among us for weeks.

"I am called Pelleas, and heir of old King Pelles now," I informed him as he rode almost to within sling range. "I have the use of this fort from King Pellinore, whose land this is," I added. "He will not be pleased to see you in this guise."

"Let me talk with him. We are old friends. He will see things my way."

"He is not here," I said. "You'll have to talk with me."

"Let me in, then," he said. "I don't want to take the time to reduce this fort, although I can send for siege engines and bring down your walls at leisure. Lay down your arms and open your gates, and we will forget past insolences. I have been chosen leader of those who would depose the usurper, Arthur of Britain. We will remember those who oppose us as well as those who aid us."

"No," I said. "Our gates will remain shut to you. We are in Arthur's service, and you'll have to take us. Otherwise, while you're besieging Camelot, we'll be cutting up your supply trains. You can't afford to leave us alone to deal with at leisure." It was true. Lot knew it, and I wanted only to apprise him of the fact that I knew it as well. Arthur would come, given enough time. I needed only to delay Lot.

Lot retreated to discuss the matter with his generals.

Ulfas was apprehensive. "Do you trust these Gaels?" he asked, glancing at me sideways. "Have you ever known them to keep their word when it's given to a Pict?"

"Never," I said, smiling grimly. The men clustered around, no longer pretending not to be interested in our conversation.

"Lot will lie to us, and betray us if he can," I said. "I know nothing good about him, except that he has a reputation for personal courage, and is a skilled fighter. Think, though; if Lot is delayed here with us, his forces will be split, and Arthur will have a better chance to defeat those who come against him. If Lot can be made to believe he can win here hurriedly, perhaps he will not join with the other column of Gaels in time to be of use to them."

Lot came back close enough to shout but out of range of our slingmen. "Will you send a champion out to fight, hand to hand?" he called.

"To what purpose?" I asked.

"If we win, you will open the gates. You win and we will leave you alone, now and later."

"We will consider it," I shouted. "You must wait while we discuss it and decide."

We watched through a hole in the palisade as he became more and more impatient. When we saw a rider coming from the direction of Camelot, probably a messenger from the Gaels fighting Arthur, come to insist on Lot's help, I showed myself from a parapet and called out, "We will fight! I will champion the Picts. If you have a man in your cowardly following willing to face me, send him forward, and I will come out."

They went back into conference, a dozen different men vying for the opportunity to win glory in single combat. Lot brushed off the messenger, impatiently. I had challenged the Gaels to single combat in opprobrious terms, and they could not risk losing honor by riding away, no matter what the circumstances. For us, there was no choice other than me, although several men offered to go. Hand-to-hand combat, Pict against Gael, could have but one outcome, ordinarily.

We saddled Mountain, and I took with me one of Pellinore's spears, a big shield to deflect javelins from Mountain, and my mace. I already was dressed in Myrddin's mail, helmet, and breast and back pieces. A shout led me back to the parapet, a scant half an hour later.

"We have chosen," Lot said. "Marhaus, son of the King of Ireland, will represent the Gaels."

"Pelleas, son of Uther, heir of Pelles, Lord of the Isles as liege man to Pellinore, High King of the Picts, will represent the Picts," Ulfas called, acting as herald.

"Are they all one person?" Marhaus yelled. "No matter. I'll fight any number of Picts." He was standing in a two-wheeled chariot, pulled by two small, sturdy ponies. A driver handled the team. With a flourish, he wheeled them away to a level place between Lot's men and the fort.

We opened our gates, and I rode Mountain out, followed by Hair, and a dozen Picts with bows and slings to guard the opening. I rode slowly down to face Marhaus some fifty paces off. One of the ponies screamed a challenge, and Mountain reared, trumpeting in reply.

"Is your prick as small as your pony?" I shouted from Mountain's back, insults being traditional before dueling, and a great time-user if done right.

"I think I heard your horse fart," he yelled back, and Mountain reared again at the touch of my heel. Marhaus was urged by Lot to get on with it, so before Mountain's hooves were on the ground, he set his chariot in motion. Marhaus threw three javelins in rapid succession, but I caught them on the big shield, deflecting them. I veered before Mountain crashed into the chariot team, and thrust my spear between the spokes of one of the chariot's wheels, into the ground. It took the wheel off, and spilled Marhaus and the driver.

I pulled Mountain up and dismounted, as the watching Gaels groaned in shocked dismay. I walked slowly toward the wreck. Marhaus and the driver were unhurt and rolled free, both with weapons. Before the driver had moved five steps, however, Hair had him on the ground, and he fought Hair for his life with his bare hands. Mountain reared again and attacked the ponies, chasing them both into the crowd of Gaels, dragging the broken cart, before returning to stand behind me. He stamped his right hoof impatiently.

"It's you and me, Marhaus," I said. "My friend wants to get this over with."

Marhaus charged, swinging his long, two-handed sword in an overhead slash designed to cut me in two. I caught the sword with my mace and pushed it to one side, pulling him off-balance. It was the same tactic I had used on the tourney field and I realized what a useful training ground the tournament system provided. Before he could raise it again, I punched him in the belly just below his breastplate with the end of the mace in three short jabs, bending him over, gasping for breath. I tapped him on the helmet to put him asleep. This was too easy. I turned and looked at Lot.

"Are you ready to leave?" I asked. "Your champion is."

"And you're a dead man!" he cried. "Kill him!" he yelled. I was standing too close to Marhaus for them to use arrows without hitting him, so the whole line started running at me. I whistled up Mountain, and easily kept ahead of the Gaels as I rode toward the gate, but before I reached it, the Saxon berserkers' yells drowned out the battle cries of the Gaels. From the wood, Arthur's Saxon shock troops came streaming into the back of Lot's forces, cutting their way through. Before Lot could turn his men to meet the thrust, the Picts let the Saxons through the gate into the fort. I waited until the last man was safe before I entered, just ahead of the Gaels.

The Picts on the wall showered the Gaels with stones and arrows and insults, driving them back.

"Is Arthur coming?" I called in Saxon.

"He is right behind us!" one of the Saxons answered. I marked him well, a big man of middle years.

"Hold the fort, then," I ordered. They were winded from the run. "Get your breath, and follow as soon as you can." I waved at the Picts. "Open the gates, and come with me," I ordered. We were through the gates and among the Gaels before they knew it. They were trying to form against Arthur's main forces that had followed the Saxons out of the woods. The Gaels didn't see us coming. The Picts do not use battle cries, but our wolves do. In short minutes the Gaels were fleeing and Arthur's forces pursuing, and only Ulfas tugging on my arm turned my attention to the fort. The gates had been shut, and there was screaming.

One of the Picts was shouting from the parapet, "The Saxons are killing us!"

I knew it! I knew it! As soon as I heard the words, I knew it! The damned two-faced, double-dealing Saxons had changed sides! Hadn't Myrddin warned us? We turned away from the battle to the fort. I grasped one of the two great gates, and tore it from its hinges, pushing it down. Someone put my mace into my hand, and I was among the Saxons, striking left and right. I did not hear the blood chant. I was in a cold rage where every move was planned, and every blow to kill. There was blood everywhere. The Saxons had slaughtered women and children as they caught them, and turned from this only to meet our charge. Where were Anna and her children?

I sought the man who had called to me that Arthur was coming, holding him responsible for this, irrationally but understandably. I had to focus my rage somewhere. I found him rising from a woman's form, her tunic ripped open and her eyes glazing in death as blood gushed from her slashed throat. One of her hands clutched a baby's leg, a baby whose head had been smashed, and her face was turned away from the Saxon and toward the child. It was Hjort, the leader who had sworn to serve Arthur when we captured the hill fort for Grance. I drove the ball end of my mace into the Saxon's open mouth, breaking his teeth and driving his body off the woman and against the wall. His eyes bulged from the pressure inside his skull as his brains squashed. It could not have been a happy death.

Had we been either in fewer or greater numbers the fight would have been over quickly, but we were evenly matched, and the battle seemed endless. Our men were so angry they threw themselves on Saxon blades to reach Saxon throats, and hand-to-hand struggles were everywhere, Pict against Saxon. The wolves slashed enemies, distinguishing friend from foe by smell. I was aware when the Saxons broke off to defend themselves in a corner of the palisade. I waded into them, leading the wolves who fought by my side and the Picts who were still standing, until I choked the life from the last Saxon with my bare hands. I looked back. A handful of us were left, none of them Saxon.

It took hours to bring out our dead from the houses. Women had been raped, while dying. Children had been split open like fish to bleed to death. I knew them. I tried to put them back together, knowing how foolish it was, but having no other way to resist accepting what had happened. In the end, Ulfas, five warriors, and two of Ulfas' children who had been playing wolf and lain hidden in a den of barley bags, were all that survived.

I left the dead to the Picts, and walked out of the fort, bringing the wolves and Cavell's get with me. A number of them were hurt. Several had been killed. Outside the fort were men dead and dying, and the sounds of battle in the woods. It had nothing to do with me. I turned back, and began to carry Saxons out of the fort, to dump them among the other dead. I didn't want them with ours.

We had found Anna and her two oldest children dead in one of the small huts built against the inside wall of the fort. The body of a Saxon warrior lay across her with a knife in his side, her last defiant act in life. The dead children had evidently tried to defend their mother, and apparently had been swept aside almost casually. They lay crumpled against the wall with broken necks. The two youngest boys were huddled in a corner in shock, and I left Ulfas with them while I carried out Anna and her children, weeping like a child myself.

Pellinore came to us that evening, tired and worried.

"I didn't know what had happened," he said. "After Arthur's charge, we saw nothing of you, and the word is told you fled the battle to hide in the fort."

"When Saxons allied to Arthur came among us seeking help, we offered them shelter in the fort," I said, coldly. "Once inside they turned on us and killed our people while we were out fighting the Gaels. We returned on hearing the cries of our dying women and children. Look about you, King of the Picts. See what alliance with Arthur has done for us."

We had dug a great hole in the fort on the highest ground of the hill, and were laying our dead in it. Each man carried his own. Those without kin to bury aided others in the task. I had carried no few myself, and if the way I felt was any measure, Pellinore was in danger. He came to look upon our dead, and without a word turned and left, with tears streaming down his face. I walked with him. When we came to the Saxon dead I had carried out, I pointed them out to him. One groaned, and I delved into the pile to pull out the man.

"What has happened?" he asked in a thick voice.

"Your master was bought with Gaelic gold," Pellinore said. "He sold himself to Lot to capture the Pict fort. Is that not so?"

"He said Arthur couldn't win. We only follow winners," the man gasped.

"Follow him into hell, then," Pellinore said and struck the man with his closed fist, breaking his neck.

"Is that what happened, Pellinore?" I asked.

"When you let the Saxons into the fort, you lost your people and won the battle. Arthur was supposed to throw his plan away and attempt to rescue you. He would have been destroyed, but he never knew you were in trouble."

"Who did it?"

"Probably Gawaine, King Lot's son. There is no proof, and will likely never be, but I am certain it is he. Usually he is around bragging about what he intends to do before a battle. I didn't see him this time." We picked up our horses and rode to the castle without further talk while I considered what he had said.

We found Arthur's hall in the midst of celebration, but the noise quieted as we entered. Nithe ran up to me. I thrust her aside, advancing to where Arthur sat among his men. Gawaine was on one side, and a man I thought to be Lancelot on the other. All three rose as we walked up.

"Where were you?" Gawaine asked. "Hiding under a manure pile somewhere?"

I grabbed his tunic with one hand, pulled him across the table, and saying "traitor" in Pictish, struck him across the mouth twice with my free hand and threw him violently away. He didn't move, sprawled where he lay like one in death. Lancelot reached behind him for a weapon, with his eyes on me.

"If you touch that spear, you'll never live to use it," I said, holding his eyes with mine. Slowly he put both hands in sight, on the table. I touched his mind and found only the excitement of challenge, no guilt, and no malice.

"What is wrong?" Arthur said, quietly. "You look like death itself. You're bleeding in a dozen places. Do you know that?"

"I know only that men and women who came to this land to place themselves under my protection have been slaughtered by your allies. Myrddin warned you of the treachery in the heart of the Saxons, but you would not heed him. I hold you responsible for what has happened now. I want blood price for my dead, and I don't think you can pay it and live," I said, glaring at him, and working my hands as if I held them from his throat by sheer will power.

"The Saxons slaughtered all the Pict women and children in the fort while Pelleas led their men in fighting the Gaels," Pellinore said. "The Saxons took gold from the Gaels to turn their allegiance."

"I know nothing of this," Arthur said, aghast. I tested his mind. He was telling truth.

"Where is Lot?" I asked.

"I killed him," Pellinore said, "either me or Balan, for we struck as one. I regretted it until now. If he were still alive, I would kill him again." He turned to Arthur, as angry as I, and said, "This matter closely touches my honor, Arthur. Why was Gawaine, Lot's son, sitting at your side?"

"He fought with us," Arthur said. "He and Lancelot led our troops."

"I saw him not," Pellinore said.

"He came late to battle, with Gaels that had pledged themselves to him."

"Against his own father?"

271

"Even so. You have struck at an innocent man," he said grimly to me.

"Picts would not turn against kin, even in a good cause," Pellinore said doubtfully. "It will take much to prove Gawaine's innocence to me." Gawaine groaned and attempted to roll over, but no one paid him any attention.

"Even so, it is true," Arthur said. "Sit," he said, turning again to me. "We'll have warm water brought to cleanse your wounds, and drink to hearten you, while we suspend our victory celebration. We would not sing while our brothers weep."

Pellinore said, "I will stay, but Pelleas will not. His place is with his people this night. Tomorrow, Arthur, you must come to the battlefield to console them."

I turned and walked out. Nithe attempted to delay me, but I brushed her aside again. I was not rough with her. I just didn't want her near me. Her Jute blood made her too nearly Saxon.

CHAPTER XV

We buried our dead, and I patched up our wounded, both men and dogs. My own wounds were tended by Ulfas, with many cluckings. I may have slept, and I may have passed out. I became conscious of daylight and found I had been covered by a woven mat against the cold. Ulfas and his boys huddled near, watching me, and smiled as I awoke. One of the boys ran off and came back with barley porridge in a wooden bowl. He shyly gave me a horn spoon to eat it with. Others came and sat in a semicircle, watching me carefully. No one spoke until I had finished, and given the bowl and spoon back to the boy.

"What will we do now, Lord?" the oldest man asked.

"We will wait for Arthur," I said.

We waited for Arthur inside the fort, with the gate shut. Hours passed without talk, as each of us relived the last hours in our minds.

"Ho, the fort!" a voice called at midmorning. "Let us enter."

"Friend or foe?" I called back, without showing myself.

"Friend."

"Shall I let him in?" I asked.

"Whatever you wish, Lord," the older man said. I looked at him. His name was Gondar. He was the village shaman.

"Do you accept me as your leader, then?"

"Aye," he said, and each man nodded.

"I will lead you far from here."

"To what end, Lord?"

"To kill Saxons," I said.

"Lead on, Lord."

I lifted the broken gate, which had been propped against the sound one, and beckoned Arthur and his following in. Pellinore was there. Nithe was not. Lancelot, looking concerned, followed Arthur, and one other, Ettarde. Naughty Ettarde, subdued in aspect for once.

"I have brought my kinsman, Lancelot, to witness my words," Arthur said, "and these worthy Picts to console your people."

"There are but few of us left for that," I said. "Our village lies under the mound," and I pointed to freshly turned earth.

"You have been betrayed through no fault of mine, except that I believed Saxons when they said they would be true."

"Yet, that was enough," I said. "In truth, you knew better."

"Yes," Arthur said sadly. "I am sorry. When kings place their trust wrongly the innocent suffer. I will make what amends I can, and that you will allow. What do you intend to do?"

"I will go to the islands, and clean my holding of Saxons, and their kindred," I said. "If I find Gaels there, or Britons, they will be sent away. The islands are Pict."

"The Orkneys are Gaelic," Lancelot said. "They belonged to Lot, and now to Gawaine." His Latin had a foreign sound to it. He seemed to talk through his nose. I noticed he moved with the grace of a trained fighter, and had come armed and alert, fearing treachery.

"I was not speaking of the Orkneys, but I will now," I said. "I will not have my people weep alone. They do not belong to him any more," I said. "Tell him I said so."

"Gawaine is one of Arthur's men. An injury to one is an injury to all," Lancelot insisted coldly.

"Your kinsman's insolence is out of place here," I said to Arthur.

"Pelleas is my brother, sprung from the loins of Uther," Arthur said. "Whatever he does, I will not gainsay him." Thus rebuked, Lancelot blushed like a girl and shut his mouth.

"What of the children?" Ettarde asked, kneeling and holding her arms out to Ulfas' boys. "Surely you won't take them on the war road."

"I will find some decent family among Pellinore's people to take them in," Ulfas said.

"Give them to me. I have no children, and am not likely to have any. I will raise them as my own."

"Are you then ready to settle down, Lady?" I asked. "I thought you the ornament of King Mark's court."

"That is past," she said. "Tristram vowed I was his lady, but Blamore abducted me some months ago, and Tristram let my husband attempt the rescue. Poor Segwardies was wounded so severely he will be of little use to me or anyone else again. When finally Tristram was persuaded by my maid to help, he found me with Blamore, but they decided between them I should not stand in the way of their regard for one another. I was let go my way while they went off together, their arms around one another. I have had quite enough of paramours." She looked at me directly and said, "I apologize for my treatment of you, Pelleas. If I had it to do over, I would do it differently." She was wrapped in a cloak, muffled to hide most of her face, and her eyes were luminous with unshed tears. Picts are quick to feel emotion, but only our women are expected to show it.

"Very well, then, Lady," I said. I turned to Ulfas.

"What is your wish in regard to the lady's offer?" I asked.

"I accept it," he replied, in a barely audible voice. "I will be back for them when I have done what must be done to quiet Anna's spirit. For now, I am grateful."

"Ettarde is my niece, and I will also watch over them," Pellinore said.

"Something good may come out of this," Arthur said, and turning to me asked, "Will you stand with me as a brother at my nuptials? I had meant to speak to you about it before."

"When is it to be?" I asked.

"As soon as we can clean up the mess," Arthur said. "Perhaps in ten days."

"One last service, then, Arthur," I said. "For now, we will go hunting, but we will return in time. Pellinore, I give you back your fort. Treat its ghosts with the respect you would your own."

"I will," he said. "They are."

They left, and we made no move to hinder their going, sitting around our small fire through that day and the next, leaving only to care for personal needs. Finally I rose and said, "It is time. We have much to do and far to go."

Ulfas was so grim I did not attempt to speak to him as we readied ourselves for the journey. He and Anna had been so close I wondered if he could survive without her. I thought only the possibility of vengeance was keeping him alive. My own guilt was so deep I was unable to bring it to a level where I could even think about it. The spectacle of the murdered women and children was with me whenever I had a moment's repose. I tried to stay busy.

I rode Mountain to the coast, beside Ulfas and Gondar on their ponies. The rest of the men ranged out of sight in the woods, with the wolves as hunters and scouts. Ulfas was usually silent when around older men and even more so now, so most of the time I talked to Gondar.

"Do you think Gawaine, King Lot's son, was the betrayer?" I asked him. "Pellinore seemed to think so."

"It was either Gawaine or someone else in Lot's confidence," Gondar said. "How many people would you trust if you planned to betray a king?"

"Gawaine would not be one of them. He talks too much and too easily. I would be afraid he'd brag about it to impress some woman," I answered.

"In that, he is like his father was. We knew him well. His family has a long history. They have always been oath-breakers."

"What will Gawaine do to Pellinore for killing Lot?" I asked.

"Nothing directly. It is not his way. If I were Pellinore, I would not sleep soundly, however, for fear someone would stop my snoring forever."

"You think he will be attacked in secret?"

"Yes, but not for years, probably. Gaels have long memories, and do not forget injuries. Lot's spirit will not rest until Pellinore is dead by his son's hand."

"There is another brother I think more likely to commit secret murder," I said. "Aggravain certainly would be capable of it."

"Pellinore says he isn't worried."

"Nor is he," I agreed, "but he keeps his Pict guards out when he travels. Ambush would be difficult. Perhaps he has no cause to worry yet."

We reached the coast in two days, and found a village across from Mona. There were a number of curraghs there, and we traded Ulfas' and Gondar's horses for one, in bad condition, but with the promise of help and materials to make it seaworthy. I know enough about boats so I could insist on certain repairs, and Gondar was a fisherman, along with being a shaman. Even Ulfas' experience on Ector's Island was useful. When I was sure the changes I wanted—mainly a small cabin, and a half-deck to keep from swamping—would be incorporated in the finished boat, I left the men busy, and returned to Camelot. I refused an escort.

"Who will attack a mounted man, armed and surrounded by wolves?" I asked.

"I will go back with you, Lord," Ulfas said. "Gondar can handle things here, and you may need me." I realized Ulfas did not wish to be alone with his ghosts, any more than I did mine, so I permitted it. He rode double with me on Mountain, the great horse taking no notice of the extra burden.

In Camelot, we found everyone busy preparing for the wedding. I was greeted with affection by Arthur, whom I found in the stables, and was given clothes more fitting the occasion than my hunting leathers.

"We cannot have the brother of the groom looking like a country yokel," was the way Arthur phrased it. One of Kay's assistants found garments from somewhere that could be altered to fit. I left them in his hands after he had made sufficient measurements to make a horse harness, let alone clothes, and I escaped to the hill fort as soon as I could. Pellinore had already moved in, and the enemy dead in the field had been buried. Sod had been cut and set over the mass grave within the fort and a low wall of cut stone built to set it apart.

"This is sacred ground," Pellinore said. "My people will let children play here, and lovers will keep tryst, but no strife will be allowed near it." Pellinore's people were everywhere. The houses had been cleaned, and were already occupied by families. I could barely keep from protesting to see folks so blithe.

Pellinore brought me to one house set aside for military stores. It held spoil from the battle before the fort, as well as the Saxon weapons. "I saved the Saxon weapons for you," he said. "You can use the spears, saxeknives, shields and helmets to arm your Picts. I'll keep the axes and trade you a heavy wagon and team for them. Your Picts wouldn't use them for anything but chopping wood."

"You plan to live here, yourself?" I asked, for there were masons busy, shaping stone for foundations. Other workers squared logs for more house frames.

"I am no longer comfortable in Camelot, and I feel my people will suffer fewer insults from Gaels and Gauls if we live separately."

"You plan on building another Camelot?" I asked.

"Arthur is too busy to superintend his masons at this time, so I am using them," he replied. "Yes, I will build a castle here, and name it Terrible in memory of what happened. You can have my castle on Mona in exchange. I will never go back, and it can be a home base for you. Any further north gets very cold in winter."

"Do you think my plan to turn the islands Pict is possible?" I asked.

"Yes. Some of the Picts here will go with you. They are from the islands, and want to go back. Others will come to you once you start your campaign. I may lead them."

"I do not wish to stay long in Camelot, either. I will be in trouble as soon as I run into Gawaine again."

"He is not much in public. You blacked both his eyes when you hit him, and he does not wish to appear until the bruises fade. If you stay here nights, he will not be able to have you killed in your sleep, and no trouble will come to you during the day."

"Gondar worries about you the same way for the same reason," I said.

"We know the Gaels," he said.

"When will the wedding be?" I asked. "I'd like to leave soon."

"Kay should be back with Guenevere soon. Nithe, Lancelot and Ettarde went to meet them and she and Arthur will be married as soon as she arrives. Bishop Ninian has come to perform the ceremony."

"Guenevere is Christian?" I asked.

"Oh, yes. That was the chief reason Kay was chosen as escort."

I had not long to wait. They arrived that afternoon, with Kay bustling around importantly, and Nithe ignoring me. She seemed absorbed in something. I only knew it wasn't me. Of the Gaels I knew only Gawaine and his brothers. I also recognized Nithe's mother, the lady Hilda, with the Bishop Ninian, once her paramour, watching her from the corner of his eye. Guenevere looked tired and nervous, and was whisked away to rest as soon as Arthur had made her welcome formally.

The wedding party gathered next day, with little ceremony. Arthur had grown impatient. He, Lancelot, Nithe, Guenevere, Ettarde and I stood before the Bishop Ninian in the open center of Grance's round table, set up under the open sky of early spring where the feasting hall was beginning to rise around it. Lancelot and I were witnesses for Arthur, and Nithe and Ettarde for Guenevere. Before Ninian could lead them in reciting vows, however, a party of druids walked in, chanting. Among them I recognized Cathmor, the arch-druid who had presided over the Samhain sacrifice when Myrddin spilled my guts on the black stone. He was dressed in the formal red hooded robe of an arch-druid. His beard and hair had turned white in the years that had passed since I last saw him, but my mouth dried with fear as he turned his piercing icy-blue eyes on me. I was distressed to see that he knew me as well, though I was but eighteen when last we met on Ector's Isle thirteen years ago.

"Halt!" he shouted. "The king of all the Britons must be married by druids. He must be consecrated to the eight-year cycle."

"We can do that later," Arthur said, stepping toward him. "This ceremony is for Guenevere. You are welcome here as guests, but you must observe silence."

"Not so," Ninian said. "This is a holy sacrament binding on you as well as Guenevere. It would be sacrilege to perform it a second time with druids, Satan's helpers."

"Your reign will not be blessed by the gods unless the sacrifices are performed," Cathmor argued. "We have the children here." And druid priestesses showed the babies they carried. "We have eight, one for each of the first eight years. At the end of that time, you will owe your life to the Oak King as is the custom."

"It will not be binding unless one is of Arthur's getting," I said.

"Do you think that because you cheated the Oak King, Dog's-brother, that we would?" Cathmor asked scornfully. "Uther paid the price by having his life cut short. We would not have Arthur risk that fate."

"Is Sam's child in this group?" Arthur asked. "I have sired no others I know of, and may not claim hers, under the terms of the marriage contract, nor would I do her this injury if I could."

"This is not your concern," Cathmor said, "but Duke Cador's heir is not among them. Accept my pledge that it will be a ritual acceptable to the Oak King and one necessary to a successful reign. We have a surrogate."

"He speaks the truth," Lancelot said. "The overseas Britons will never recognize a marriage or a reign not blessed by druids."

"And I will never enter into such a marriage," Guenevere declared coldly, staring at Lancelot as if at some stranger. "I am a Christian, and will have only Christian sacraments!"

The lady Hilda stepped forward and spoke, "I am only a guest at this ceremony, but I speak for the Great Mother. She will not bless a union launched on the blood of babies. This is an evil thing, and must not be."

"Horsa's daughter? You here?" Cathmor asked, pointing to where she stood. "At last you are within reach. Kill her!" he ordered. One of his attendants, who had drawn his sword before entering Arthur's presence, stepped up and struck her with a full swing, barely missing Arthur in the process. It was Balin, one of the twin brothers who had confronted me at the forge. The force of the blow cut her head off so that it flew to one side, coming to rest against Cathmor's feet before anyone else could move. For a moment only she stood erect, the blood spouting from her neck like a fountain and staining Guenevere's white dress with spreading spots of red, before she collapsed in a tangled heap. Balin spurned her body with his foot, and Nithe screamed in protest, scrambling over the table that stood between them, her hand thrust forward to ward him off. She slipped in spilled wine and fell to her knees beside her mother's body. Even the druids seemed stunned. The blood dripped from Balin's sword as if from a leaky roof. He didn't move, but his eyes sought Arthur's.

The Bishop Ninian thrust people aside, picked up Hilda's severed head and carried it gently back to her sprawled corpse, setting it near where it should have been. He ignored the tumult around him, acting as one in a dream, kneeling beside her with his hands clasped before him, and bending over her with murmured words that were not Latin. Tears streamed down his face, unregarded.

Arthur was the first to speak. "This is treason," he said, in a barely audible voice. "That lady was my benefactor. Bring that man forward." And Pellinore seized Balin and dragged him to the edge of the table.

"The woman was a witch, Sire," the man said, blustering, but frightened at the look on Arthur's face. "She bewitched my brother, and brought many knights to evil ends. I have not acted in treason, but to protect you."

281

"Who are you?" Arthur asked, still barely above a whisper, leaning toward him, straining to see some possible explanation for the man's outrageous act.

"Balin. My brother Balan is one of your knights."

"Spare him, Sire," Balan said, edging through the crowd, "He speaks the truth. He came to join you at my request."

"Spare him? For your sake?" Arthur said. "Do you overseas Britons have no sense of what is fit, then? Spare him? I will spare him ever setting foot in our presence again. I will spare him the opportunity of ever being admitted to the Fellowship of the Round Table. He is banished! If ever he is found on any land over which I rule, I declare his life forfeit!"

"Then I must go, too," Balan said. "I am grieved that you feel this way, Sire, but do not question your right."

"Go and be damned!" Arthur grated out. "Are there any others of the overseas Britons who wish to leave with them?" and he glared around him.

In answer, Lancelot stepped forward and raised Nithe to her feet, cradling her in his arms, and half carrying her away from the scene. She clung to him, weeping uncontrollably. His look of compassion was hard to read, but I judged he loved her in some fashion.

The brothers left, unhindered, a smirk on Balin's face, and a look of exasperation on Balan's. This was not my affair, but I thought Arthur had handled it badly. I would have had Balin's head. I would not worry about the need to keep Lancelot's friendship so much that I would allow such a crime in my presence, were I Arthur. For that matter, Lancelot would have better served justice to have executed his own man, sparing Arthur the necessity of making such a gutless response.

"This woman who has been killed was daughter to my father's brother," Guenevere said. "I will not marry today, nor will I marry tomorrow. I will not marry until I have buried her and mourned her. I may not marry at all. I do not take it well that you have let her killer walk free." And she pushed through the circle and out of the hall, followed by her ladies. I admired her.

"You can find a new queen, one who will honor the old ways," the arch-druid said, extending his arms in a blessing gesture.

"You brought this evil here," Arthur said, his temper breaking through. "You will leave this castle, and never come to me again. Furthermore, you will leave the babies here, for I will not have more innocent blood spilled on my account."

"We may not do that," Cathmor said. "We answer to a higher authority than you."

"There is no higher authority in Britain," Arthur said, advancing on the arch-druid. I followed him to the gap in the table, watching him take the man's robe in his hands. He shook him violently, throwing him to the ground. Cathmor's other attendants drew swords, but they were surrounded and disarmed by Arthur's knights, happy to have something to do within their compass. Other hands took the children from the druid priestesses.

"This will bring the wrath of the Oak King on you!" Cathmor shouted, rage purpling his features.

"One more word, and I'll hang you and cut down every oak grove in Britain," Arthur said in cold rage, holding himself in check with difficulty, once again.

Cathmor rose and opened his mouth. Before he said that fatal word, a curse, by the look on his face, I grasped his throat, cutting off his wind, and pushed him backward to the gate. Once outside, I released him and said, "I have just saved your life, Arch-druid. Go, before I repent!"

His people came and surrounded him, taking him away, with many a backward glance and many a muttered curse. I watched them out of sight. Pellinore stood by me.

"I'll have them watched by Picts. True Picts are loyal to the Great Mother, and won't be afraid of Oak King curses," Pellinore said. I doubted that but did not respond. I am a true Pict, and I fear the Oak King.

We wrapped Hilda in a linen shroud, and brought her to the

barge she had come on, to be taken to her hill fort, New Avalon on the Usk, up the river from Arthur's castle. Nithe went with her, and Guenevere, and Ettarde, with Ulfas' two boys. The babies were taken by Hilda's ladies, and the whole party left us standing on the shore.

"You have no more luck with women than I do, Arthur," I said.

"If it's as bad as that, I must be in trouble," he said, with a faint smile. "Perhaps I was not really ready for marriage, anyway, and Myrddin was right after all, but if I do marry, it will be to Guenevere. Wasn't she splendid, Pelleas? Wasn't she?"

"That she was," I said, picturing her in my mind as she had looked as she stormed out of the hall. Lancelot, Pellinore and Kay were standing with us. They nodded as one.

"There seems nothing more for me to do here," I said. "It appears there will be no marriage for some time. I am sorry to leave you thus, but I must get on with my work."

"When will you return?" Arthur asked, his hand on my forearm.

"When I can sleep a night through without hearing children screaming in the agony of their murder," I said. "I do not know."

I should have known better. I was still trying to gather supplies and equipment six days later when Guenevere changed her mind at the entreaty of Grance, and agreed to go through with the wedding. Lancelot stood with me as Arthur's witness as before, and Nithe and Ettarde for Guenevere. Nithe never looked at me.

I spent my time at the hill fort waiting for my supplies, and there it was Kay found me. "The High King Arthur wants you to escort Queen Guenevere and some of her ladies to the woods to look for spring flowers. The Jutes make much of spring, coming as they do from a cold land."

"I'm busy," I said, ungraciously. Courtesy is wasted on Kay.

"Nithe asked for you specifically," he said, watching me.

I looked at him directly, gauging his truthfulness, but he could always lie without any evidence of guilt. I felt a singular distaste for probing into Kay's mind, so I merely asked him, "When will my supplies be ready?"

"They will be here when you return," he replied, and in this I could trust him, for it dealt with things, not people. Lud knows how long I would have to wait if I didn't agree to honor Arthur's wishes, or, more probably, Kay's wishes, in this matter.

"I will come directly," I said, and he left.

"Do not bring your wolves," he called back over his shoulder as he rode off. "The Queen is afraid of them."

Taking only my mace as a token symbol of playing guard, I found Guenevere's party and set off to the wood with them afoot. Nithe was not among the ladies, I was not surprised to find. Of the knights of the guard I knew only Kay and Aggravain, the snot-nosed little brother of Gawaine, grown to much resemble proud Lot, his father. Someone had made him bathe for this occasion.

I was civil, but paying little attention to what was transpiring, when shouts mingled with screams brought me to where a number of heavily armed men were struggling with the other guards. I rushed them with my mace in hand, looking for their leader. A man on horseback was directing the attack, and I made for him, to be forestalled by foot soldiers, armed with spears and saxeknives. They melted away before my charge, but the knight circled, keeping people between me and himself, and laughing.

I broke spears thrust at me as I swung my mace in tight circles, backing toward Guenevere and her ladies, wishing I had ignored the request to leave the wolves at home. I saw Kay go down. Aggravain was fighting stoutly, but he, too, was overwhelmed.

"Stop!" Guenevere cried. "I yield myself. Only spare my knights and ladies," and she stepped outside of her ring of defenders and surrendered, grasping the knight's stirrups imploringly.

"Cease!" the knight shouted. "Cease, or I will kill your queen!"

I looked around. Of the ten of us chosen as guards, only four were standing, three others and me. They threw down their swords, cursing roundly as the ladies shrieked incessantly. I lowered my mace.

"Drop it, Pelleas," the queen ordered, "Everyone, throw down your arms! I do not want anyone killed!"

285

I walked up to her, still holding my mace.

"What is this you do, Lady?" I asked.

"Obey me, Pelleas!" she responded. "This is Melligrance. He will spare everyone for the sake of my regard if there is no resistance. We cannot hope to win against him."

She may have been right, but it went hard with me to hand my mace over to a man half my size, and submit to being bound. She and her ladies were rushed on ahead on horses, but the ten of us were dragged along behind them, on foot and with many a needless prod. I was surprised that none of the Queen's guards had been killed. I had bruises that would be days in healing and at least one cracked rib before we reached a fortified farmhouse where we were brought to an underground, stone-lined cellar and chained to the wall. The guards took the light with them when they left, and we were not visited again for some hours.

I tested the iron. The links were big around as my little finger, and the stanchion set into the wall as big as my thumb. I know iron. There was no possibility of breaking free. I went over each link with my fingers, testing for cracks or wear, but the chains were new, and well made. I resigned myself to rest and conserve my strength. It was well I did so.

When light was brought to us, it was in a brazier with glowing coals. "The lady Guenevere resists my suit," the man she called Melligrance said, for it was he. He was a Briton with Roman manners, speaking Latin as a gentleman born. "I have told her how it will go with you, so if you must curse someone, curse her. Your fate is in her hands." Then, in a perfunctory manner, he ordered each of us should be branded on the cheek with a hot iron. He gave no evidence of taking pleasure in watching us or in hearing some of the men gasp and whimper in pain. To him it was only fulfillment of a commitment he had made to the lady.

The next day we were flogged, and the next day allowed to go without food or water so that some of the men were fainting in weakness and despair. Each day he told us the same thing, that the punishment that we would suffer had been told to Guenevere and she still refused to submit to him, requiring Melligrance to have the punishment visited upon us.

On the fourth day we were beaten with staves, the worst yet, and I heard bones crack as some of the men received unlucky blows. My own cracked rib gave way under one such blow, and I feared it would pierce my lung. I lurched to protect it with my head, and was knocked unconscious. When I recovered, Aggravain told me we would be maimed on the morrow, a finger would be struck off and the stump seared over with boiling pitch. He enjoyed the recital, although I would as soon not have known what was in store.

On the fifth day we were fed and given water, and I wondered if Guenevere had finally given in or Melligrance was afraid some of the men would die. Several were no longer conscious, moaning in the delirium of fever. I had not known such frustration and helpless anger since lying on the black stone two decades ago. I would rather have died, fighting the ravishers, than submit to being tortured. I found myself focusing my resentment on Guenevere, perhaps unfairly, but if she had submitted to Melligrance finally, why hadn't she done so immediately, and spared us all this?

I was wrong. They came with hot pitch and pincers instead of gruel at suppertime. The men that struggled were knocked unconscious and lost a thumb for their efforts. Those who submitted could choose. I extended my left hand and allowed them to snip off my little finger, taking the first two joints. As a smith I could not risk losing a thumb. It hurt more than I imagined it could.

On the sixth day we were told we would lose an eye, and perhaps this finally led Guenevere to take pity on us for instead of torture we were given extra bread. Only Aggravain, and Kay and I were still conscious enough to eat it. Aggravain made foul remarks about what he imagined Guenevere and Melligrance were doing, swearing to tell everyone he had witnessed it, until Kay finally told him he would report his conduct to Arthur, who would not suffer to hear his queen traduced. I resolved privately to close his mouth forever if he made good on his promise, although the word pictures he painted were not far from my own imaginings.

At the end of the seventh day, the door to our prison was flung open wide, and men came to release us, carrying out those unable to walk. I was able to move on my own, though weak, and pushed aside hands that attempted to aid me. Outside, the light made it difficult to see immediately, and I blinked for several seconds before I observed Arthur, Lancelot, Gawaine and others in armor, confronting Melligrance and his men.

Guenevere was speaking to Arthur earnestly. "I promised him you would let him go unpunished if he did not hurt me or my ladies. I would not have him executed out of hand. People will assume the worst!"

"Are you sure you are not harmed?" Arthur asked in what must have been a question answered previously, for she brushed it aside impatiently.

"I have told you, no!" she said. "Do I appear hurt? We were stripped and chained to the wall of his sleeping chamber, but aside from his requiring us to pace naked back and forth before him, turning as our fetters limited our movement, we suffered no ill fate. He taunted us by showing us blood-soaked rags he said came from the backs of our guards, and saying we could halt their torment if we submitted to him voluntarily, but it was not until he brought us severed fingers that I believed he was actually mistreating them."

"I am most relieved to find you unharmed," Arthur said, "but if Lancelot hadn't found you, and sent his page back for us, I do not know what would have happened. I have men who were so abused they may well die of it, and you would have him spared?"

"Only for the sake of appearances," Guenevere said. "I prayed for the men and grieve to learn they were hurt." She caught sight of me staring at her and something in my face made her go pale, but she continued pleading with Arthur.

"Let me suggest something," Lancelot said. "I will strip the armor from one side of my body, forgo my helmet, and let them tie one of my hands behind my back if Melligrance will stand up against me. If he is still on his feet after five minutes, then let him go free."

"Would you agree to that?" Arthur asked.

"Of course." Melligrance said. "I would be a fool not to."

"I don't agree." I said stepping forward. "Lancelot was not down in that prison. Let me fight him under the same conditions."

"You. Pelleas?" Arthur said. "You can barely stand."

"I mean no discourtesy." Lancelot said, "but if you were so eager to fight you should have done so earlier."

I made no reply to this, waiting for Guenevere to explain the matter, but she kept her mouth shut, though she flushed under my gaze. I turned away, and started walking back to the hill fort alone, through the woods. Being beholden to Nithe's lover, and having been called a coward by him was more rankling than anything that happened in the prison.

I reached the hill fort that night to find Nithe had been there, waiting for me for hours. She had left, promising to return next day, so I had my rib bound and set off without resting, instructing the men to load the wagons with the supplies that finally had been brought in and to leave at daybreak for the coast. I went through the woods with the Pict hunters and the wolves, not wishing to speak to Nithe or Arthur or anyone from Camelot ever again. I would not have Nithe praise Lancelot to my face for any price.

CHAPTER
XVI

I joined Ulfas after I was sure no one had followed him out of the hill fort village. He drove the wagon while I sat on the seat, idle. My broken rib ached, and my maimed finger hurt, along with various other aches, cuts and bruises. I wondered if Myrddin's potion I drank on the black stone was finally losing its power to heal. I saw we had enough saxeknives, spears, swords and helmets in the wagon to outfit our men a dozen times over. I had left Mountain with Pellinore, finding he was able to ride the animal. Pellinore was grateful to have one that could bear his weight without strain.

"Should we bury this gear somewhere?" Ulfas asked me.

"No," I said, "we'll need it."

"There are but a handful of us, if the men are still waiting at the boat," he said.

I laughed. "We have twice that number escorting us in the woods," I said. "Haven't you wondered where the wolves are?"

"They're with Pict hunters?" he asked. "We have hunters, like Pellinore does?"

"Some of them are Pellinore's, or were," I said. "He released them to me, those that wanted to go. Some of them had kin among our dead and seek vengeance. They believe they will find it with us."

"Why do they not march with us?"

"It's not their way. They scout for bandits, game, whatever might help or hinder our progress. If nothing else, the practice is good for them."

"We'll have a full boat, then," he said.

"With luck we'll be able to trade the horses and wagon for another boat," I said. "If we find we need more, we can always borrow one of Pellinore's. He has several in the harbor."

"Why would we need more?" he asked.

"We don't know yet what we'll find on the coast, do we?" I replied, but Ulfas shook his head and laughed. I guessed he did know, but then, I know Ulfas. If he didn't want to tell me, he wouldn't, so I decided to wait and see. We talked of other things.

"I have not said how much I miss Anna," I said. "I loved her almost from the first day she came to us as Arthur's nurse. She took the place of an older sister for me, one I never had. I do not know how you bear it."

"I try not to think about it much," he said. "It's like a sore tooth. If you worry it with your tongue, it just gets worse. At least the Saxons didn't rape her. They never had a chance; she was protecting her children, and died with a knife in her hand. It was bloody." He tapped a knife on his belt, and I recognized it as one Myrddin had given Anna years ago.

"She was a warrior's wife," I said quietly, nodding in agreement. I had seen how Anna died. I thought about the Saxon treachery for a moment and asked Ulfas a question I had continued to wonder about. "Do you think Gawaine would actually betray Arthur the way Pellinore thinks? You know him from the old days, as I do."

"It's hard to say," Ulfas responded. "Arthur ranks Pellinore as senior knight in the fellowship, and Gawaine is jealous of him. Gawaine talks about Geens as if they aren't human, and word of it gets back to Pellinore. All of us Picts have heard about his comments. So, Pellinore is willing to believe the worst about Gawaine. It's difficult to know what the truth is, really."

"Myrddin once told me that the behavior of men is controlled by the consequences which arise from their acts. If they gain their ends once, they will repeat the act in similar circumstances. He said it was as true for traitors as for honest men. If we knew what Gawaine hoped to gain, we could judge him based on our knowledge of him. I know little good of him," I said moodily.

"I think that Gawaine's coming late to battle might mean he was involved somehow in the bribery," Ulfas said on reflection. "I can't think he meant anything bad to happen to Arthur, personally, however."

"He didn't care what happened to us," I said.

"That, no," Ulfas agreed. "You had a chance to see Lancelot close up. You asked me my opinion. What's yours?"

"I don't like him. He's the kind of man for whom everything comes too easily. He has worked very hard to become a trained fighter, and I guess he's good, all right, but he had the leisure to do so, with no other responsibilities. Also, he's too handsome to be trustworthy," I added. "Men with looks like his don't have to develop character."

Ulfas laughed. "Nithe and Lancelot aren't lovers that I could see, if that's what you're thinking," he said. "I believe they are just friends. I would be more concerned about his attraction for Guenevere, if I were Arthur."

"Well, I believe Arthur is still in love with Sam," I said. "If Guenevere has seen that, Arthur has no one but himself to blame if she's looking around. He should never have married Guenevere. He should never have let Sam go back with her father, contract or no contract."

"Do you know Arthur's sister, Morgan?" Ulfas asked. "She would have arranged the marriage contract her way if she had been in Arthur's place. She should have been the ruler, rather than him. She has the kind of ruthlessness Arthur lacks."

"I never met her," I said. "How did you come to know her?"

"She showed up with her aunt, Morgause, just before the battle. Her mother was Igraine, Arthur's mother, but her father was Gorlais, Igraine's husband before Uther killed him. Morgan and Arthur were like strange dogs, very civil to each other, but hostile. Morgan came down with her aunt to complain that Morgause's baby had been stolen by the druids."

"Was he in the set of eight babies the druids brought to the wedding?" I asked. "I know they took all of the babies with them when they left with Hilda's body. Perhaps she found him among them?"

"Probably. You remember Morgause and Arthur had an intense affair after the first battle, don't you? The timing would be right for her to have a child from that encounter, and the arch-druid did say that they had a surrogate for Arthur. Who else could it be?"

"It makes sense, all right," I said. "Morgause went with Guenevere to New Avalon for Hilda's funeral rites. Like as not they'll work it out there."

"Yes."

"Have you ever been inside of New Avalon?" I asked. "Once Nithe seemed to think it was some kind of a brothel but wouldn't come out and say so, since her mother, Hilda, ran it. Later she had another story."

"It isn't a brothel," Ulfas said. "Hilda was a priestess of the Mother. New Avalon is the center of a fertility cult, so a certain amount of that kind of thing must go on, but I was never invited to participate, and those who do don't talk about it."

"Why not?"

"Sheer funk. The Mother can shrivel your stones if she has a mind. Who would risk it?" Who, indeed?

Our boat was where we left it, but there were two others anchored beside it, and half a hundred men. I was stiff from riding in the jerky wagon, but I forgot that in the curiosity I felt.

"Lord," one of the men said, "we wish to come with you. They say you go to kill Saxons. They say Pellinore has given you the islands. They say you fight like a Geen of old. We would go with you, Lord."

"I have war gear for a large number, but maybe not enough,

after all. Tomorrow, we'll have a muster and look you all over. If we are going to fight Saxons, we'll have to learn to fight and not be killed. I can train you, but I will not take anyone who can't be gone for five years, because that's how long I think it will take to do what I want."

"We're ready, Lord. You'll see."

On the morrow Ulfas and I lined the men up and talked to each one, including the hunters who had come in with the wolves. Cavell's pups at five looked more like wolves all the time, and acted like them, as well, which is not surprising considering that Cavell, herself, was half-wolf, and Friend was the sire of this litter. The wolves faded back into the woods, nervous around so many people; I'd have to bring them out one by one, probably. Most of the men were young, but a few veterans who had campaigned with Pellinore against Saxons were in the line, and we pulled these out.

"You men will each lead squads," I said. "We'll borrow some tactics from the Romans. They have always been successful against Saxons. We'll find they outweigh us, man for man, as much as two stone, and our advantage will come from fighting in pairs. Ulfas and I will demonstrate." We did. Arthur's Irregulars had been trained as pair fighters, and both Ulfas and I had been early adepts.

"One man holds a spear at its balance in his left hand and his shield in his right," I said. "The other holds his shield in his left hand and behind his partner's, and his sword in his right. When an enemy swings with an overhand stroke, his side is unprotected from a spear thrust. When he finishes his stroke, his arm is not protected from a sword slash."

I did not trust real weapons in their hands, for fear of injury, so we gave half the men short sticks and half long ones.

"The use of the shield will come later," I said. "Try to anticipate where I will strike." I moved slowly, allowing them to catch me in the side or on the wrist as I faked a sword cut. Some of them hit hard enough to bruise, but I ignored it in the teaching of the art. Myrddin's potion had worked after all, for my rib had healed in the trip over. If I'd taken a hot bath after being released from prison, and had Nithe sew up the larger cuts, it would have happened earlier.

We divided the men into teams, allowing them to choose partners if they wished. All left-handed men were given spears, along with those who said they could use either hand equally well. The rest were swordsmen. We had twice as many swordsmen as spearmen, but that was all right. We decided to use the biggest as single fighters. All the Picts could use slings, but only Ulfas and I could also use bows effectively. We decided not to attempt to train this skill, thinking it was enough for them to master hand-to-hand combat.

It became apparent, as the summer slipped by, that our numbers were growing all the time, and we merged the new men in with the ones we had been training, telling them to catch up. The neighborhood no longer comfortably contained our numbers, and it appeared we would be a burden on the stored food supplies if we stayed. We decided to capture Mona.

We needed several trips to move our men from the mainland to Mona. The tides were rough and threatened to swamp our little boats. Picts are natural fishers and sailors, however, and nothing was made of the danger.

We chose a sheltered inlet for landing, sending scouts out with the first party ashore. No one had been on the lookout for us, and no one greeted us after landing. A small settlement on the top of the cliff overlooking the inlet should have observed us, but we were lucky. Several of our recruits were from the neighborhood, and we sent them in to alert the folk not to pay any attention to us.

"Come, Lord," a scout said breathlessly to me half an hour later. "The druids have the children. They're going to burn them for the Samhain feast!"

As I listened, the hard core of pain I had carried since the Saxons had murdered the children at the hill fort broke. Tears started rolling down my face, to the astonishment of the scout.

"Where are they? Take me there, now. We must not be too late again. We must not!"

He turned and ran up the path from the beach, with me right behind him. I heard Ulfas order the men to follow and was aware of others, wolves and men, behind me. As we ran through the village, there were women there calling to us.

"Hurry! Our men have already left. They will be killed by the druid warriors."

It was not far. We could see the smoke rising not a mile ahead of us, and speeded up. I had been too late to save Bronwyn from the raiders, and too late to save the children from the Saxon traitors. I must not be too late again, if I were to go on living.

We burst through the trees to see the big druid settlement in the center of the island, sheltered from the wind. We found it palisaded, but the gates were open. The druids thought so little of the Picts that they didn't try to set a guard against them and we were in among them with no alarm raised. From the woods other Picts followed us, armed with hoes and fish-gaffs. These were farmer-fishermen, not fighters, but they were willing to do what they could to save their children.

The druids were in ceremony, sacrificing birds and reading the fates in their entrails spilled on the killing-stone. The children had been placed inside of a huge, hollow figure of a crowned man some twenty feet high, woven of willow branches tied together. There must have been thirty of them, boys and girls together, peering out with frightened eyes.

The arch-druid was that same Cathmor who had watched over the ceremony when Myrddin opened my belly on the black stone and who had cursed Arthur on what was to have been his wedding day. In his hand he held a torch and had just ignited the brush stacked around the wicker figure. One of his guards, armed with an ax, stepped in front of me as I ran up. I thrust at him with my mace, and pushed him off-balance to one knee. Before he could rise, Ulfas killed him with a spear thrust.

"The Oak King will bring you to your knees, Geen," Cathmor

said, seeing and recognizing me. He swung the torch at my head, and I deflected it, picking up the fallen ax with my free hand.

"He has tried before, and failed," I said. "I fear him not." I was lying, but I was angry. "Hear me, Druid, as you failed to hear me at Arthur's wedding. I defy the Oak King! Let him stop me if he can." I thrust the man aside unceremoniously and began to cut the thongs lashed to poles dug into the ground to give stability to the hollow cage. It was ablaze now, and the children screamed with fear. The sound gave added strength to my arms and I ignored the fire and the fighting around me, struggling to free the cage. When I felt it rock, I dropped the ax and pushed it over. I dragged it away from the fire and ran into the cage through the open bottom to help the children. Other men were beside me, their tunics burning, but we freed the children and beat out the flames in their clothing with our bare hands.

One small girl, whom I had found tied to the burning frame, had her face buried in my neck, and would not let go. I held her with one hand, the ax in the other, ready for what might come, as I escaped from the cage. I turned to the fighting. It was nearly over. The wolves had bunched the druids with their warriors in the center of the settlement, and stones from Pict slings dropped them like ripe apples in the wind. The druids were cursing at the top of their voices, calling on help from the gods. They prayed in Gaelic, which most of our Pictish fighters could not understand, so it had little effect. Not a one of their warriors surrendered. Not one survived.

I made no effort to save the unarmed druids, and the Picts slaughtered them all, but I did not see Cathmor, the red-robed arch-druid, among them. I turned back to the children. Women came out of the woods and carried them away. One older woman walked up to me, and looked closely at me and at the child I held.

"You are badly burned," she said. "The child needs help, too. Come with me. I have salves that will take the pain away." I had not been aware of the pain, but at her words I felt waves of it in my hands and arms. I have been burned many times at the forge, but never like this. It was worse than the branding I suffered under Melligrance. I followed her.

She took me back to the village, walking among the other women with their children. In her house I coaxed the little girl to let go and submit to examination. She was dirty from the smoke, but apparently not burned at all. I was amazed. She sat on my lap while I allowed the woman to bathe my raw flesh, and cover it with soothing grease. I could hear children in other huts crying with pain and reached out my mind to them to bring them comfort. As soon as she was through with me, I went to them, with her beside me protesting. The child clung to my hand.

"You must lie down and rest," the woman insisted. "This is not good for you to walk about."

I ignored her, going to the children most in need of help, and staying with them, one by one, until they slept. Their mothers watched in wonder, dressing their burns as the children became quiet. None were badly injured. Every time I sat down, the child I had carried from the fire crawled back into my lap and turned her face to my chest. She had not spoken yet.

"Where is the mother of this child?" I asked my nurse.

"She is dead. The child goes from household to household, staying with one for a while and leaving it for another. We think she has been looking for her mother. She must think you are her," she said, smiling.

I walked back with the woman to her house. "Do you have children of your own?" I asked.

"None. Mine are grown and gone."

"Your husband?"

"Dead."

"Will you be a mother to this one?" I asked.

"Gladly, if she will have me. She has stayed with me before and even talked a little, but never for very long."

"I must see to my men. I will put her to sleep and leave her with you, but I will be back, and we will see what can be done with her," I said. I touched her mind and soothed her until she slept.

Those men who had been in the cage with me had followed me to the village and had found treatment for their burns from the women there. So did the wolves. They all refused to rest until I did, watching me with each child. I had helped our wolves bear pain in the past but had never tried with people. It was much the same. Ulfas came to me.

"Lord, what would you have?" I never got used to hearing him call me that.

"Bury the Gaels who fought for them separately from the druids," I said. "Burn the druids so no ghosts may haunt this island. Place them in their houses, and burn the whole settlement. Let them go to the Oak King in fire."

"Yes, Lord. Will you stay here or go to Pellinore's castle?"

"I will stay here with the children until I feel I can leave them," I said. "Take your men and our supplies to Pellinore's. People here will feed me and find me a bed."

"It shall be as you say, Lord," and he tugged his forelock before he turned and left. I had lost a friend and gained a servant. His respect was mirrored in the eyes of everyone I saw, except for the smallest children, particularly the child who told me her name was Viki. I felt at ease with her and with them and chose them for company when I could. Viki would not use my name but called me "Geen," which brought smiles to the lips of all the adults. When she spoke about me, she called me "my Geen."

The women cleaned Viki up, and she proved to have a mass of curls the color of chestnuts fresh from the hull after a deep frost. Her hair had barely been scorched by the flame. She also had enormous hazel eyes and the look of innocence most markedly in evidence, I found, when she was plotting mischief of the most disastrous kind. Her silence had been shock, as much as anything else, because when she became comfortable around me, she talked all the time. In a few days, we left with Ulfas. I touched the heads of women who came out to bid me good-bye and to give me thanks for the lives of their children. Viki and Hair, who had achieved an understanding, shadowed me. The woman who had offered to mother her watched us sadly out of sight.

My own burns were healed in a week. The potion that Myrddin had given me had lost none of its strength with the passing of time, as I had suspected when my rib healed in the journey over. This, in itself, was a matter of wonder to the men, who had seen the severity of my burns, which added to the legend that seemed to be growing up around me. I attributed my quick recovery publicly to the excellent care I had been given, but it was seen that I was burned more deeply and healed faster than anyone else. My explanation was accepted politely, but not believed.

Viki watched me closely as I started to shave. The burns on my face had made it impossible, and I had the start of a fine black beard.

"Why do you want to cut it off?" she asked. "Geens are supposed to have beards."

"Who says so?" I asked.

"Everyone knows that!" she replied with scorn.

Ulfas walked in and listened to this exchange.

"Ulfas, tell Viki that a beard is a dangerous thing for a warrior. An enemy can grab it and cut your head off."

"Who is going to be able to reach your beard?" she asked.

"Tell her, Ulfas," I said.

"No, Ulfas. Tell him that all Geens have beards."

"It's true, Lord," Ulfas said, grinning. "All the old stories about Geens have them bearded."

"How come I don't know about it?" I asked.

"Didn't anyone ever tell you stories about Geens?" Viki asked.

"No," I said. It was true.

"Poor Geen. I'll tell you stories. But you have to promise not to cut your beard any more."

"It'll be cold where we're going," Ulfas said.

"Are you in agreement with her?" I asked.

"Yes, Lord. There's been talk. Some of the men wonder if you're really a Geen, because you don't have a beard."

"Truly?" I asked, exasperated. "Why didn't you tell me before now?"

"It wasn't important before. Now it is."

I looked at Viki, who had her arms folded over her plump belly, looking stern, and Ulfas, whose amusement was slightly showing through the very correct expression on his face. I decided to be a Geen, in truth. If I served the people as they wished, perhaps I could atone for the deaths of Anna and the other women with their children at Castle Terrible.

"Very well," I said. "Nithe said I looked like Myrddin. I might as well go all the way." And I walked out. They both followed me. We walked over the entire island. A thousand people could live here comfortably. The weather was mild, the soil fertile, and the fishing good. With the druid settlement destroyed, all the people left alive were Picts. I apportioned land to my men, and they took boats back to the mainland to bring in families who had been living as servants to Gaels. There was resistance to their leaving, but bullying a farmer is different from bullying armed fighters. The resistance was overcome and the families brought away before organized opposition developed.

Pellinore's castle was a palisaded house with outbuildings built along the wall. There was room for storage, cooking and servants, whom I did not need. I got them, however, because they were part of the establishment. The main house had three rooms, one large one, ten by fifteen paces, and two small ones, each five by five. Both the small ones had rush mats and furs to serve as bedrooms. I took one and Hair and Viki took the other. Cavell's pups and the young wolves turned the big room into a den and no one was ever better guarded than I. I had a door cut into the side of my sleeping chamber to be able to come and go more freely, but I was never by myself, regardless. There were always one or more of the animals to escort me. How they divided up the responsibility, I had no idea.

301

Food came from our stores and from produce grown by my servants for the household. Ulfas told me they preferred not to have a close relationship with me, for the Picts do not like to think of themselves as servants. I knew them when I saw them but did not speak, out of politeness. They took very good care of me, however, and I could hear them discuss problems related to that among themselves and with others, including Viki, who had definite ideas of what was fitting. They even fed the wolves. When I suggested to Ulfas I could probably take care of myself, he was horrified.

"If your needs are not met, tell me, and I will see to it. But, please don't send them away. They would be crushed. You are king here, a Geen. Serving you is not like serving other men. Serving you is done by choice. That's why it can't be acknowledged. It is something they do for themselves and their own honor."

I guess I understood.

We started the training again, finding new faces almost daily. The men who had been fighting as single warriors needed more work. The saxeknives, used like the Romans used swords, were effective in ways they had not understood.

"Think of it as extending your reach," I said. "You can stab a Saxon who is trying to get close enough to slash you with an ax, and stay out of his way at the same time." It was true. The Romans did not slash with their swords so much as stab. It surprised our short Picts that they could have the reach on the tall Saxons.

"Ulfas, we will have to move on soon," I said, after a particularly successful practice. "There will be more people here than the island can support."

"I've been worried about that, too, and many of the newcomers see it as you do. They want to go with you when you conquer the next island so they can get land for themselves."

Understanding that made planning easier. I told people we would sail in the spring, and everyone settled down for winter. It was after harvest that the first of the women came.

Pict women are free to give sexual favors to anyone they choose, once they have had the rites of passage necessary for recognition of their status as women, and are no longer considered children. Marriage is a contract they enter into voluntarily and leave at will. While married, they are faithful to their husbands, but if they become dissatisfied, they need only to tell their husbands to leave the house and then are free to undertake whatever sexual adventures they wish in search of a new mate. Some of them wanted me.

Perhaps I was a challenge of some kind. Being mother of a Geen must give some special status, although it takes a long time to develop. Being the lover of a Geen is an immediately recognized status, and the fear of being injured during sex an added unknown. Women have always looked at me in a speculative way. Among the Picts, nakedness is common, and there was opportunity for comparisons while bathing in the ocean. It was only a question of time before someone took a chance on me.

I was in bed and asleep when a woman screamed, waking me. Hair had cornered a young woman attempting to creep into my room. He had pulled her down but had not hurt her. I called him off, lit a lamp, and sat her down, giving her wine to drink to calm her. Viki came to inspect the visitor.

"Go back to bed," I said. "I can handle this." Viki gave me a look of amused doubt but obediently went to her own room.

"Whatever are you doing here?" I asked the woman.

"I came to keep you company," she said. "No one told me about the wolf."

"I'm sorry you were frightened," I said and touched her mind to comfort her. She was the first of many. Hair and the other wolves learned not to interfere, and I was soon skilled in the art. The winter passed quickly.

Spring in Mona is filled with the smell of apple blossoms. I ordered the boats hauled out of the water and sealed anew with sheep tallow, working with the men to see that it was done to my satisfaction. It was a relief to leave the beach and be with the apple blossoms after a long day with the stinking grease. When the boats were ready, on calm days we went out rowing and hauling sails, teaching those who did not know boating how to behave on the water. We had ten boats by now, and a hundred men ready to go, trained and eager. Our veterans all decided to stay with us, their hatred of Saxons not cooled by the long winter. We helped the new farmers clear fields and break sod before we embarked, leaving the Picts under the guidance of Gondar, the shaman, who decided not to venture further north.

"I will be your liege man here, Lord," he offered. "I will govern in your name, if you wish it."

"King Pellinore asked me to look after Mona," I said. "It might be well if someone were to settle disputes that might arise in the absence of the druids. If you think invoking my name would be of any use, so be it."

"It will be enough, Lord," he said, and those who had accompanied him, men gray of hair and beard, all nodded soberly.

I nodded back, not knowing what to say to them. I spoke privately to Ulfas, asking him to send a messenger to Pellinore. He was to tell him we would expect Picts to join us in Lothian in the spring to resettle the land. I knew he would lead them himself, for he had spoken to me of his wish to find a land where Picts could be free of their British overlords without fighting other Picts to get it.

Saying good-bye to Viki also proved difficult.

"You must take care of my house like a proper Pict lady," I said. "You are the only woman I can trust to keep it ready for my return."

"Why can't I go with you?" she asked.

"There will be fighting, and I must have my mind free of care for you so that I can fulfill my responsibilities as a leader," I said.

"I could hide," she coaxed.

"You would not be out of my mind even then," I said. "With you here, I won't worry about you or about my house."

She reluctantly agreed to remain behind, and I had Ulfas tell the servants that she was to be treated with the respect my true daughter would have been shown.

"Everyone knows of your regard for the child. She will be watched over with great care," Ulfas assured me.

Everyone on the island gathered to see us off and wish us luck. When I waved to the women on the cliff, a dozen waved back, most of whom were pregnant, according to what they told me. When one knew for sure, she stopped visiting me, and another took her place. The only ones not sure were the last two, who alternated nights, thinking I might leave before they both had turns. I don't suppose it was any merit on my part, but the novelty of my size, that earned me all the attention. However, I tried not to worry about why it was and enjoyed it for what it was. By Pictish custom, none of the women had named themselves to me, relieving me of responsibility for whatever followed. None of them became dear to me.

I missed Nithe, now that Viki was not there to distract me. I had tried talking to the women who slept with me, but they invariably shushed me. They weren't supposed to be there bothering the king, according to what Ulfas told me; the fiction could only be supported if no talk was heard at night. In spite of the comfort I found in the art, I continued to be lonesome. Not even Viki could change that. I felt I had no right to happiness until I had laid my ghosts.

We went north, under sail, two days out from Mona, when Ulfas discovered our stowaway. I thought everything had been arranged for Viki, and that she understood why I must leave her behind. It appeared I was in error. It was too late to turn back, but I was not sure what else I could do.

"Don't you understand that we will be going into battle, and that you can get hurt, even killed?" I asked her.

"Hair will take care of me. You don't need to worry," she assured me loftily.

Ulfas carefully looked away, but I knew he found this amusing, as did the other men. I decided it would have to be as she said. I hoped she was right.

Several of the boats were slow and had the best rowers assigned so they could keep up with the rest. I was in a slow boat since I could handle two oars at once. We had taken only nine boats, finally, with ten to fifteen men in each. Each boat had a wolf or a dog or two, as much to pet as to sniff out land, in case we were blown to sea in a storm and separated. The wind shifted from east to north, and the sails were of limited use. Square sails are not good for tacking.

We were headed for the Isle of Man where we expected to find Picts, and possibly Gaels. Raiders usually come south, down the coast, later in the year, and we wanted to alert the people to the advantages of an organized defense. We carried enough food with us to feed the men, so we would not have to draw on supplies from the winter stores on Man. We wanted to be welcome.

Viki sat beside me, trying to help by pulling on one of my oars, and asking me questions as I rowed. "Why are you not married?"

"I nearly was, once," I said. "Saxons came raiding and killed my betrothed. I have not found anyone who quite suited me since."

"Maybe I'll marry you when I grow up," she announced. "You need someone to take care of you." I didn't dare look at Ulfas, but I heard him snort, and several of the other men chuckle. Picts respect their leaders, but are not overly demonstrative about it.

"Do you have a father and mother?"

"My father was Uther the Pendragon, High King of the Britons," I said. "He died many years ago, and I barely knew him. My mother is named Brusen, and is wife to old King Pelles and sister to Pellinore, High King of the Picts."

"Are you a High King, too?"

"No, I am Lord of the Isles, or will be when I have established the right to claim the title Pellinore gave me."

"What isles are those?"

"Well, there are only two, actually," I said. "Mona, where we

306

have just come from. and Man. where we are headed. some twenty leagues north."

"Will there be druids there who want to burn children?" she asked in an uneasy voice.

"Maybe. but we will not let them hurt you." I assured her.

It took us three days of hard rowing to raise Man. and another day to establish a camp on a shore in the lee of the island. and set out sentries to keep anyone from coming too close. We found there was some opposition to our presence generated by druids, who had heard of our destruction of their settlement on Mona. We met with leaders from a number of Pictish villages to discuss this.

"Listen." I finally said. "I have no quarrel with you. I have explained that Pellinore has given me the responsibility for these islands. and that I intend to exercise it. The first thing I require is that the Gaels leave this place. If they want to serve the Britons' Oak King they will not do it anywhere that I am. I am here. They must leave. Anyone who wants to go with them can do so unhindered. You have until tomorrow to make up your minds. If you continue to oppose me in this. I warn you I will use force, starting tomorrow. and treat you as I intend to treat the Gaels. Come back at daybreak. with your answer."

Under the cover of dark. my men surrounded the largest village. where the druids had a large house and garden. When the village headmen and the shamans came to see me on the beach the next morning. they could not tell that there was anything different. for usually we had concealed half of our warriors. along with Viki and the wolves. in the tents when they were present. At this time the tents were empty. Viki would not stay in the tent by herself. and Hair and the other wolves were with the soldiers in ambush.

"We must not anger the druids." the village headman said. "They will bring the wrath of the Oak King down upon us. and we will die."

"Do you want them gone?" I asked.

"That isn't the point. They will not leave."

"They will now," I said. One of our men carried a battle cornet the Romans had used to signal troop movements. He blew a phrase of music at my signal, and within minutes, the druids were escorted down the path from the village with their hands bound and their mouths gagged.

"Put them in the boats," I said. The village elders were aghast.

"Do you know what you have done? You have condemned us to death!"

"Let the god's curse be on my head and on my head alone," I said. "The Oak King is my enemy. I treat his servants as I will and defy him to do anything about it. You will not suffer for this. In your hearts, you are blameless."

They eyed the arch-druid with fear as he was prodded past. It was Cathmor. "Wait a moment," I said. "You know me, Druid. You have not escaped this time, I see. You have a choice. You will either die by my hand, here and now, or you will promise these people to hold me solely responsible for this outrage against your god. It is your choice. Which will it be?"

He shook his head, so I told the men who held him to remove the gag.

"You, and all who aid you, will be cursed by the Oak King," he said.

"These people did not aid me. They have protested my action. I plan to put you ashore on the mainland, but I can change my mind. I would as soon cut your head off and bury it in a manure pile. Hold these people blameless, and promise not to come back to this island, or you die right now."

"I will not agree not to curse you, Geen."

"So be it. Your curses have no effect on me for you have cursed me before. You have heard me defy your Oak King. Everyone can see that nothing has happened to me, and you are bound and in my power. Why does your god allow this to happen to you?"

"So be it," Cathmor said, and spat on the ground at my feet. "We will see who is the stronger. We will not return to this island until the god has brought you to your knees in sacrifice. The two

308

sacrifices you have robbed him of will come to him in his time," he said, glaring first at me and then at Viki, who hid behind me.

"If he can do it, let it be soon," I said. My show of courage was all on the outside, for who knew if there were not an Oak King who could hear, and act against me? It was just that I no longer cared greatly that he might seek my life. Without Nithe, or Myrddin or Arthur at my side, much that had been precious to me was gone.

After our words, however, the druids left without difficulty, and the people made much of us, all but the shamans who feared the Oak King would punish them at the same time he punished me. We distributed all of the stored goods left by the druids, including the weapons we had taken from their guards. I burned their temple and cut down their oak grove. They would have little to come back to.

My islands were clean of druids. When Ulfas came back from ferrying them to the mainland we called a council of all the folk on the island. Hundreds came, shamans, village headmen, and women in the garb of priestesses of the Mother.

"Pellinore, High King of the Picts, has made me Lord of the Isles," I told the assembled men and women. "He is my liege lord. He bade me to drive everyone from these islands but the Picts, and I have done so. We killed most of the druids and their guards on Mona, for they were sacrificing Pictish children to the Oak King. Those who escaped came here, but this time we were able to capture them unharmed, as you witnessed. If ever they seek to return they will meet a different fate."

"You do not fear the Oak King, Lord?" an old man asked.

"I fear no gods," I said. "As a boy without a Samhain name, I was stretched on my back on the black stone in the oak grove and my gut was opened with a druid's knife. My father sought to fool the Oak King, giving him my life in place of the one he owed, for he was a king in his eighth year. I lived, despite the Oak King's claim. I have since defied him before his priests, and they have been powerless to bring his wrath upon me. They have tried. I will stand between my people and this god of the woods revered by the Gaels and the Britons."

"Do you not fear the Mother, either, then?" the man asked.

"Fear? No. I have nothing to do with the women's mysteries. So long as her priestesses do not feed her human flesh, I will not interfere in her worship."

"We do not do that." an old woman chided. "All life is sacred to the Mother for it all comes from her."

"So be it." I replied.

"Will you live with us here, Lord?" the man asked.

"No." I replied. "It is in my mind to seek out Saxons and teach them the lesson the Gaels have learned these past few days. The men with me have suffered great loss at the hands of Saxons, and seek Saxon heads to bury at the feet of Pictish graves. We will seek them in their homeland as they sought us in ours."

"We know where the Saxons nest, Lord." the old man said. "We have had women taken in slavery escape from bondage among them and return to us. Their homeland is east of the Strathclyde."

"That is Lothian." I said, remembering lessons given by Myrddin around the kitchen table.

"Even so. They hold the coast from Lothian to Kent, so we are told." I believed them. It was the kind of thing fishermen know.

We had arrived in Man in nine boats with five score men. We left for the mouth of the Clyde a month later with fifteen boats and eight score men. I left Viki with fishermen at Man, who promised to return her to Mona where folks would be worried about her. I gave her one of Cavell's sons for company, which she promptly named Slobber, and exacted a promise from her that she would not run away again.

It took us a fortnight to win the mouth of the Clyde, and two more days' hard rowing to bring the boats to shelving land where we could haul them out of reach of the tides that flow up the wide estuary. We left a guard over the boats and supplies and set out on foot to meet the Picts of Strathclyde. At this season of the year we found no Gaels or Britons in our boyhood village, but old King Pelles and my mother had attracted many Pictish followers. They were happy to greet us.

"Let me look at you," my mother said. "You are the very image of my brother, Pellinore, with that beard!"

"You should see them side by side, Lady Brusen," Ulfas said, grinning. "They look like father and son."

"Pellinore would never know you with the wealth of tattoos you have," I said.

"My husband honors me," she said, smugly. "Have you married, yet?"

"No," I said.

"Any children?" she persisted.

"I believe so," I said. "I was busy last winter."

"He never got out of bed," Ulfas remarked.

"Of course," my mother said matter-of-factly. "You look hungry, little one. Come with me and we'll find you something to eat." She led the way into the kitchen and Ulfas and I followed her. She ladled out cool milk from a porous clay pot hanging from a tripod, brought warm bread from a fresh baking, and strong Pictish cheese from a low cupboard before she turned back to us saying, "Stay over with me. I'll find you a nice girl."

"I must be traveling," I said. "I came to ask King Pelles for help."

"Are you in trouble again?" my mother asked, clucking her tongue.

"I have warriors from Mona and Man with me. We are going against the Saxons in Lothian," I said.

"Lothian is King Lot's country," she objected.

"Lot is dead, and Gawaine has not come to claim it," I said. "In the absence of a lord the country is being overrun by Saxons."

"Why do you care?"

"They swarm out of their coastal farms and sail north, around Caledonia, and fall upon my people in the west. Ulfas lost his wife and children to Saxons, and my betrothed was cut down but a few years back." She shook her head, but said no more, waiting

311

for Pelles. As king, it was up to him whether or not warriors would be released to join us. When he came, looking older than ever, he was more interested in what had happened to Mountain than in what might happen to Saxons.

"I couldn't take him with me, so I gave him to Pellinore," I answered his question. "I want men, Pelles. If I can drive the Saxons out of Lothian, you won't have to worry about raids anymore."

"They are in strength in Lothian," he replied. "It will be very difficult to dislodge them."

"As long as they are allowed to stay there, you are caught in a pincer between them and the Gaels in the west. They must be driven out."

"What will Arthur do about that?"

"Nothing, if we hold against Gaels and Saxons impartially. His worry is Saxons, not Picts."

"Maybe we can change his mind about that," Pelles said, eyeing me speculatively.

"No," I said. "I will not move against Arthur. I do not believe he will move against me. I know Gawaine is his friend and cousin, but I am his brother, and am only taking what is mine."

"Lothian is yours?"

"I am the son of Uther, as much as Arthur is," I said, "and by the customs of the Britons would be one of them if I chose to claim that heritage. As a Briton, Arthur will not help the Gaels fight against me." Pelles shook his head in disbelief but did not prevent me from recruiting warriors from among his people. In truth, as his heir, I brought honor to him. The Picts of Strathclyde believed in Geens as much as those of Mona. He could not have stopped me, if I chose to act in spite of him.

I had one surprise. King Pelles and my mother had a child, a girl named Elaine, of perhaps fourteen years. "Why did I not meet this one before?" I asked. She was small and dark in the manner of Picts and as pretty as Ettarde.

"She was off with the Goddess," my mother answered. "You know girl children are taken as soon as they are weaned to learn the chants. They are not spoken of in their absence in case the Goddess should claim them as her own."

"Did you learn the chants?" I asked Elaine as she served us.

"Faster than anyone," was her pert reply. She flashed her eyes, already a practiced flirt. "They wanted me to stay, but Mother wouldn't let them keep me."

"The shamans wanted me when I was younger than you, but she wouldn't let me go either," I said.

"Our mother is fierce," Elaine agreed, laughing.

Before the afternoon was gone, we were friends and my mother smiled to watch us talking quietly together, exchanging confidences gravely. When I asked Elaine if she would like me to find a nice man to marry, she laughed at me again.

"I have found one by myself. He is the most beautiful man in the world, and when he sees the son I shall present to him he will want to marry me," she added smugly. Pictish women breed young. I looked closely at her. Her pregnancy was not far along, but it was apparent if you looked for it. I thought of Nithe, who had been so taken by the beauty of young Lancelot and wished Elaine better luck.

We did stay in Strathclyde that winter. My men spread throughout Strathclyde, visiting kin and recruiting followers for the raid we planned when the weather permitted. I resisted my mother's attempts to have me settle down, mostly by not being home much. Ulfas brought men to speak with me in village after village. I would walk in a week behind him, surrounded by Hair and three other wolves, and stand in the middle of the town. In each village it was the same. The palisaded door would be opened before I reached the wall, and within an hour, I would be given the best quarters available and have men ready to follow me. Ulfas would slip out for the next village.

We agreed to move east in the spring, hoping to reach Lothian before Gawaine could contest us. I didn't want to fight Gaels this season. I was looking for Saxons. It so happened Gawaine was still in the south when we reached the manor house in Lothian that had belonged to his father, but we found it occupied. The mistress was at home and spoke to me.

"Why, it's Dog's-brother," Morgause said. "As I said once before, I'd know you anywhere, but where did you get that beard?"

CHAPTER
XVII

Morgause lolled in a deep chair before the fire, her robe loosely gathered and her hair down around her shoulders. She seemed ageless.

"You look well," I said politely.

"Yes, I do. Tell me, are you being civil because you intend to apologize for disrupting my household, or is it me?"

"I'm always civil," I said.

"Indeed. I have the most alarming reports from the druids that you intend to rape this kingdom and put us all to the sword. In that order, I believe."

"You, personally, have nothing to fear from either eventuality," I said.

"How disappointing. I've never had a Geen before."

"There aren't many of us," I said, "so the opportunity must not have arisen often."

"No, it hasn't. Never." She rose and stretched lazily, and turned toward me.

"You are even bigger than I believed possible," she said. "It should be interesting."

Whatever she might have meant by "it" I didn't get a chance to ask, for a red-cloaked druid burst in upon us.

"What is this? What is this despoiler of the god of the woods doing here? Know, accursed one," he said to me directly, "this woman is protected by the true god. You shall not have her."

"Cathmor! You again! You know you should not say that," I said. "You know I have sworn to defy the Oak King in all things. If I believed you, I would have no alternative but to take her." I was almost willing to believe that druids could fly, for this one appeared again and again, first at Arthur's betrothal, then on Mona burning the children, then on Man cursing me in the name of his god of the woods and now, here.

"I will defend you, Lady," he said, and pulled out a concealed blade. I am wary of druids. Likely the blade was poisoned, and but a touch of the edge would be sufficient to kill.

"Don't be a fool," Morgause said sharply. "The day I need a druid, or anyone else, to protect me from a mere man has not come to pass. Morgause protects herself." She stooped and snapped her finger on the edge of a crystal goblet. It gave a clear ringing tone which brought several armed men into the room.

"Remove this man," she said, pointing to the druid. "Do not let him return without my permission." Cathmor was forcibly ejected, protesting.

"He will resent that," I said. "You will need to guard your back when he's around."

"Much I care. I belong to the Mother, and she watches over her daughters. He has more to fear than I." She came close and placed her hands on my shoulders, measuring me. Her robe fell open, by accident or design it mattered not.

"Do you remember watching me in the surf from the cliff edge?"

"Oh, yes. Ulfas and I considered approaching you then, but feared you would have us whipped, or worse."

"Not I. Very young men I have always found short on performance. However, I would have sent you off to grow a year or two, which you, at least, have certainly done. Are you any good?"

"I am at least enthusiastic," I said. "I have had less time in practice of the art than you might believe, however. Still, I'll venture a trial, if the idea pleases you."

"Oh, it does, it does! Would you think now, perhaps?"

"Why not? If we take a moment or two from conquering your kingdom for more pressing matters, who would fault us?"

"Who, indeed?"

Morgause was not like anyone I had known before. With Bronwyn the act of love was as spiritual as sensual. The bored London whores I occasionally took were shallow and mechanical in the act of love and looked at me with dead eyes and mouths sad in repose. Where I had meant everything to Bronwyn, I had meant nothing to them. Morgause was completely physical, and completely selfish. She talked incessantly, directing me as if I were a well-trained horse, encouraging me to greater efforts as suited her needs.

As a boy I listened with faint understanding to the hunters around their fire when they talked about such phenomena as "snappers," women who seemed to have such control of their bodies that their vaginas rippled in intercourse, giving the impression of independent life. I understood for the first time what a snapper might be, and what an extraordinary hold such a creature could have over a boy like Arthur. I also found out what he meant when he said she was insatiable. I marveled at his lasting two weeks with her, for I was exhausted by morning.

I was lying in a daze, wondering what had awakened me and recalling where I was, when I became aware of the sound of a smith's hammer; the rhythmic pattern of the blows on the hot metal were like a signature. I sat up, ignoring Morgause's sleepy protest and her clutching at the cloak that covered us against the brisk morning air. It was Myrddin! When he works he makes a noise that goes thunk-tunk-tank-tank-tank for he hits with such force that there are four bounces after every blow, the first quite strong, and the last three merely the weight of the hammer falling. Nithe uses a much lighter hammer and she goes tank-tink-tink. The spacing, the time between blows, is also individual, with more time elapsing between Myrddin's blows than Nithe's. So it is with all smiths if one but listens. This was Myrddin.

I left Morgause's room without dressing, picked up the spear I had lain athwart the door jamb to bar entry and nodded to Ulfas, who sat squatted on his heels across the hallway.

"Where is he?" I asked.

"You sleep soundly," he muttered as he rose to guide me.

"For the last hour, perhaps," I responded sourly, following him out of the house and through the gate into the village that lay outside its stout walls. The pounding was coming from a building at the far edge, downstream from the village, where smoke from a fire curled upward. It was distinctly chilly, but I ignored it, striding through the village after Ulfas, with Hair at my heels. Early rising women seized children and dragged them indoors, and a few men as naked from bed as I came running after us, all carrying spears. I ignored them.

Before the smithy a guard, who had been squatting on his heels and yawning, rose to intercept us. Ulfas thrust at his legs and, as he lowered his spear to deflect the blade, I caught him in the throat with the butt end of my weapon, dropping him to his knees, gasping. Ulfas rapped him smartly on the side of the head and he sprawled before the doorway, angering the men behind us. We turned to meet them as they ran up.

"Men of Lothian, look!" I commanded, "your doom is upon you!" and I pointed at the forest edge. From it poured men and wolves, many more than the few defenders in the village. "If you would live, drop your spears and return to your houses. Otherwise you will die!" They ran to do my bidding, casting away their weapons and crying out for pity as they disappeared into the houses, barring the doors. I motioned, and the Picts and wolves melted back into the woods.

Myrddin continued hammering, and I stepped under the shade that had been erected for the forge to look at him. He was bare to the waist, and his back was crisscrossed with fresh welts and lines from cuts ranging from the pink of healing flesh to the white of old scars. He also looked thinner than I remembered ever seeing him, but healthy enough for all that. He glanced at me for an instant with an eye too bright to be as calm as he otherwise appeared. A chain attached to his ankle was looped around the anvil and spiked into the oak post on which the anvil rested.

Out of reach on a table against the one wall were tools for working the iron. I assumed they were given to him depending on what work there was to do, but he was watched to prevent his using a cold chisel to cut his chain. I selected one and returned to him, letting him inspect the saxeknife he was making, and watched him thrust it into the tempering trough before handing him my spear to lean on, while he put his leg on the anvil where I could free him. It took but half a dozen blows to break the shacklebolt. He motioned for me to exchange my spear for his hammer, and picked the saxeknife from the water before stepping outside. I followed him. We found the arch-druid Cathmor, who gave the appearance of having dressed hurriedly. His antler head-dress was askew, leaving him looking oddly vulnerable.

"Beware what you do!" he warned. Myrddin's response was to throw the hammer, crushing the life from him before he could draw breath to utter further threats. Myrddin dispatched him with no more ceremony than a farmer gives a hog before butchering! This was the man whom I had feared for most of my life, the priest of the dread Oak King? Myrddin struck off Cathmor's head and swirled it around in the air, showering his followers with blood. They bunched together, backing away from Myrddin's anger, making the sun sign of Lud with the thumb and forefinger of the right hand to ward off evil.

"Flee!" he roared, and they did so. He tied the head to his belt by the hair, looking wryly at me as he did so. "It needed doing," he remarked in a normal voice.

"I can see it must have," I answered. "How long have you been here?"

"I know not. Some months, anyway."

"I see," I said, "this needs looking into," and led the way back to Morgause's farm. There were armed men at the gate now, and

Morgause was standing there waiting. My clothes were in a pile beside her, folded neatly.

I dressed and spoke to Morgause without looking at her.

"I feel a fool, Lady, but that will pass," I said. "We have business elsewhere, but we will return to burn this farm and the village and everything in it, living or dead." At this I looked at her as I finished tying my belt in place.

"It was known you were coming, and orders given that unless you attacked, the Gaels should ignore you. You outnumber us five to one and could destroy us, if that were your wish, but perhaps at a cost you do not wish to pay. Gawaine is coming in any event, and would avenge us most dearly."

"I have heard you, Lady. Now hear me. I will not warn you again. This farm and village must be abandoned and all your folk prepared for a journey south to start before the moon is full again. It will be three days, by my reckoning. Complain to Gawaine if you wish and to Arthur if you dare, for he will be told of Myrddin's imprisonment at your hands. If I find you or any of your people north of Hadrian's Wall when I return, or ever again after, they will die." I turned and left with Myrddin and Ulfas, going apart to talk.

We found food being prepared in the kitchen and helped ourselves while the terrified serfs cowered against the walls. Outside under a tree we sat and ate while I looked Myrddin over. His anger had faded, but a deep glow of emotion still burned in his eyes.

"Did you find what you went looking for?" I asked.

He glared at me before he responded. "There are no Saxons coming into the north, from what I could see," he finally answered, "but they are swarming on the east coast. They will become a problem if they are not dealt with firmly."

"We will do so, then," I said. "We have been seeking Saxons for reasons of our own." And I told him about the treachery of Arthur's Saxon mercenaries, and of Anna's death.

"I will join you," he said when I had finished.

"I hoped you would. I could not face Nithe again if I let you

320

go off alone again," I added. "Besides, I have missed you these last few years."

He looked at me, nodded, and changed the subject.

"Do you think Gawaine will try to hold this land?" he asked.

"No, I believe that Pellinore and a large detachment of Picts from the south are on their way and will join us. If we do not attempt to drive the Gaels farther south than Hadrian's Wall, the border will be conceded. Arthur needs to know that the north will be sealed against the Saxons before marching on those in the west. He can trust Pellinore and me not to attack his exposed flank."

"Picts will hold the north and the islands, then, Gaels the lowlands and Eire, Britons the south and central lands and Saxons the east coast. Will Arthur try to drive the Saxons into the sea from whence they came?" Myrddin asked.

"Saxons? Likely not. They are thickly settled near their strongholds. If they agree to stay in their own territory it would be enough. What Arthur wants is a period of stability to consolidate his rule of law," I said.

We watched the Gaels start their move south within the three days I had given them, carrying their goods in wagons. We did not show ourselves until they were underway, and then I came out of the forest.

"Greetings, Dog's-brother," Morgause said, smiling, when I came to bid her good-bye. "I thought you might have more time for me than seems to have been the case."

"That sort of thing is better not done, than done in a hurry," I said. "I wouldn't want you to get the wrong impression of Geens."

"One experience is an inadequate sample," she said. "I will need further encounters before I can make a judgment. Do you know other Geens you might refer?"

"Pellinore and his son, Lamerok, are Geens. Lamerok may be still too young to be useful to you, recalling your stricture against very young men. Pellinore's other son, Percival, is normal, I believe. Tristram is a Geen. I gather there is some doubt about his parentage, but Pellinore says he is a true Geen. Tristram doesn't even admit he is a Pict, however. There are others, like Palomides, who might serve."

"My people tell me you are the biggest."

"Myrddin thought so," I replied. "It may even be so."

"What about this Briton, Lancelot, who is in love with Arthur's sister, Nineve? They say he is a big man," she said.

"I have seen him, and he is not a Geen. I am Arthur's brother, and know no one named Nineve."

"I was told she grew up with Arthur."

"No, that is Nithe," I replied. I did not ask further about the relationship between Nithe and Lancelot. Like enough she had that as wrong as Nithe's name. She smiled oddly, pursed her lips, and shook her head.

We disarmed the Gaels before allowing them to go south, and had these weapons, plus the stores in the Lothian village, to arm the extra people who came up with Pellinore. He greeted me warmly on arrival.

"Are we too late for the battle?"

"There has been no battle. We are so numerous the Gaels did not wish to fight unless pressed," I said. "Morgause sent word to the Gaels throughout Lothian to move south. We have scouts watching them and will not interfere as long as they keep moving until they are on the other side of Hadrian's Wall. What do you hear of Gawaine and his brothers?"

"Arthur has promised the Gaels the land he takes from the Saxons, if they but help him. He told me to inform you that he would not lead his men against you and depends on you to respect his borders."

"I plan to do more than that," I said. "I will drive the Saxons out of their new footholds along the coast in Lothian. I will have no one but Picts this side of the Wall. Will he need help against the Saxons in the west?"

"Probably. He will call for it, if it becomes necessary, and I have promised him Picts to give it."

"I am bound by that," I said. "What of old King Pelles?"

"He waits to see what happens. If you succeed in driving the Gaels south, he proposed to step down and recognize your leadership. So will I."

"But you are my liege lord," I protested.

"No longer. The Picts need a hero leader. If I didn't accept you in that role, I would be set aside by my own people."

"I am a smith, Pellinore. After Myrddin, I am the best smith in Britain! Why would I wish to be a king? Half the men I know claim to be king of something or other."

"It is not what you wish, but what others expect of you," he replied. "A High King of the Picts does not hold court like some Roman emperor. He merely leads his people when he must, as you have done, and retires to some quiet spot to wait the call again, as you will when this is over."

I had no response to this, and he expected none.

Pellinore had brought his family with him, his wife and his two sons, Lamerok and Percival. Lamerok at fifteen was as tall as his father and had a big-boned frame that looked as if he would be the true Geen Pellinore said he would be. Percival was still a child, very much his mother's son.

"We will live in Lothian," Pellinore said. "Palomides will move farther north to Caledonia, as far away as he can get from Tristram. They were rival lovers of King Mark's wife, Isolde, and Tristram won the lady's approval."

"Does King Mark care?"

"He pretends he doesn't know, but, from time to time, he tries to have Tristram ambushed, so far unsuccessfully."

"Pelles will stay in Strathclyde?"

"Yes. Your responsibility for now will be the islands from Lyoness to the Hebrides. Your freeing the islands of Gaelic hegemony and druids was the trigger that started this whole migration of Picts. I was not aware how many there were of us until I saw them moving north in such numbers."

"How does Arthur look on this?" I asked.

"He is happy. He wants to bring the Britons and Gaels together

323

against the Saxons, without worrying about the Picts. Moving us away from his strongholds makes it possible for him to concentrate his forces to the west, without fear."

"I would think the Gaels would object."

"Most of them were driven into Eire by Uther in the first place, and have returned here from the west only recently. They were never north of Hadrian's Wall before King Lot came here. If the Gaels truly leave now the Picts will become quiet, and Arthur can concentrate on his real enemies, the Saxons, and settle the Gaels where he will."

I left the supervision of removing the Gaels from Lothian in Pellinore's hands, explaining I had promised to move against the Saxons, and my men were waiting.

We went afoot, for Picts go to war without horses, except as emergency food. There were enough stores left behind by the Gaels that we had no need of that. Besides, Picts prefer oatcakes to meat for travel. It keeps better, and provides adequate nourishment with ease of preparation.

We were but a few days from the first of the Saxon villages, a warriors' outpost as expected in disputed border country. I wondered whether our men could stand against seasoned warriors, and did not share Ulfas' joy at learning we had found them. There was little strategy in our attack. We entered the village at first light, climbing the palisades and dropping to the ground silently. Half our men were fanning out toward the huts arranged in a circle before the dogs first scented us.

We attacked sleepy men, men without armor, and without any idea of what was happening. Our wolves finished the dogs almost before the first man fell. The Picts fought in pairs as they had been trained, with spearmen slightly behind swordsmen, locking shields to provide a defense against Saxon short swords and axes. A dozen older Picts straddled the palisaded fence and rained rocks on the Saxons with unerring sling casts.

I stood in the middle of the advancing line, with Myrddin on one side of me and Ulfas on the other. A tall Saxon threw his ax at my chest, and I deflected it with my shield. It clanged, but did not even dent, which raised the Saxon's eyebrows. I had made my shield of iron forged with carbon to produce hard steel, and tempered it in oil to make it tough. My helmet was of the same material, light and strong.

My opponent was too experienced to be shaken, however, and came steadily up to me. I fastened on his mind, and read each move, until I saw an opening and struck first, knocking him out of the fight. His place was taken by another, even bigger, man, but one who lasted an even shorter time. After the third went down, I had to seek opponents.

Our Picts stood up well. Ulfas fought in fury, remembering Castle Terrible, but held his ground. I had been afraid he would charge, opening himself to attack on two sides. He did not. The size of the Saxons was intimidating, and their shouting calculated to bring fear to the hearts of our men, but our numbers overwhelmed them, and they threw down their weapons, calling for quarter.

The Picts were disposed to give them no more quarter than they gave the women and children of Castle Terrible, but Myrddin strode among them, beating them back and protecting the weaponless men from slaughter, to the surprise of the Saxons, who had believed they would all be killed.

That was but the first battle. We tied the survivors in a long line, some twenty men in all, and sent them ahead of us as we marched on the next village and the next. After the second attack, there was no more resistance. People fled south in boats, looking for safety in established villages. We ceased pursuit when we came in sight of Hadrian's Wall, where the last village had been deserted. We released the prisoners, telling them not to allow Saxons north of the Wall again, and warning them to cease raiding anywhere in Pictland or we would drive them all into the sea. I do not know if they believed us or not, but they were frightened, as men are who have believed their lives forfeit only to have them given back again. Our numbers had grown to more than a thousand, and in their imagination could have been much larger, for the Picts appeared in and out of the forest in such a bewildering manner that they gave the impression of countless hordes.

We burned the village at the wall, after looting it of any useful materials left behind, and did the same for each of the others as we backtracked up the coast. When we reached the limit of Saxon expansion, we moved back inland and began finding groups of Pict families driving pigs, sheep and cattle, and carrying household goods and young children in wagons looking for good land to settle. We escorted some of them to fertile valleys and helped them build palisades to contain the houses they erected. We lost men at each village, men who elected to stay with kin they had encountered, or who were chosen by women as mates.

In the village where we had first found Morgause we now found Segwardies and Ettarde, reconciled and busy. "Dog's-brother," Ettarde shouted, on seeing me. "Come eat with us!" She was dressed as a Pict woman, which is to say with nothing on but a breechclout. It was easy to see why so many of the knights from Mark's and Arthur's courts had striven to win her attention. Two children came from the hut, and ran to meet us. Ulfas dismounted and dropped to his knees to hug them. They had grown under Ettarde's care, but had missed their father.

"Segwardies must be happy to get her away from the Britons and the Gaels," Myrddin remarked as we rode up. "Even Picts, who are used to seeing naked women, should not be trusted around someone who looks like that."

"Arthur chose the wrong wife," I agreed.

Ettarde did not eat with us, but kept up a lively chatter as she served us, and the children responded to her as they reminded her of things they wanted Ulfas to be told. Segwardies looked less often at her than at us. I thought he was apprehensive of the effect her appearance might have on us, but was too polite to say so in front of guests. Segwardies was very tall, but quite thin and awkward. Perhaps Geens come in all shapes and conditions and

I was wrong about him. He had freshly healed scars to mark the wounds given him in his last encounter with Tristram.

"When do you set off for Mona again?" Ettarde asked.

"I have to get back to the coast, find a boat, and visit Man before I go back," I said.

"That's a pity," she said.

"Why?"

"Nithe will be looking for you at Mona."

"I think not," I said, looking at her closely. "Morgause said she was Lancelot's lover."

"Oh, I doubt that," Myrddin said. "They were like children together. Ban wouldn't let his son join Arthur as he wished, for political reasons having to do with Rome. Britain may be too far from Rome to interest the Empire, but Gaul is not. Between them, Nithe and the boy decided if he took a battle name no one would know he was Ban's son. Nithe suggested Lancelot, 'big spear,' and the boy liked it. Ban was not amused. The boy's true name was Galahad, which was also Ban's own father's name, but the boy's mother agreed to the change and there was aught Ban could do about it. Like naughty children, they were."

Maybe he was right, but the thought of Nithe and Lancelot together would not leave my mind. Still, I had to know. Perhaps that is why I moved through my remaining responsibilities with such dispatch. We traveled as fast as I could push our men, visiting Palomides, who had set up a village on the west coast, and begging a ship from him to sail to Mona with little ceremony.

"You may have anything you want from me," Palomides said. "I am a member of Arthur's Round Table, but I have no liege lord. I would swear allegiance to you, if you wish it. Segwardies and I have talked it over, and both of us are willing."

"It is not necessary," I said. "We will work with one another like brothers, helping each other at need."

"We would do that either way," he answered. "My people consider you Pellinore's successor, High King of the Picts. So do I."

"The old term was First Among Equals," Ulfas said, unexpectedly. "Myrddin told me," he added, when both Palomides and I
looked at him. Myrddin smiled in agreement.

"So be it," Palomides said. I shook my head slightly, but there
was nothing I could find to say to him.

As we left I asked Ulfas, "What are we really doing here?"

The dark mood that had haunted him since Anna's death was
gone. His two children would not let him brood. I was happy
Ettarde was willing to let them go, though she cried when they
kissed her good-bye. "Building a kingdom," he responded promptly,
and Myrddin laughed. That was also good to hear. He had not
laughed since his release.

Palomides chose men to row us to Man from among a number
of volunteers and gave us presents of mead, hard barley bread and
dried meat for supplies. I thanked him, but he wouldn't have it.

"It is my duty as well as my honor," he said.

We were greeted on Man as lords, and Ulfas no less than
Myrddin and me. The men Palomides had loaned to me were sent
back home, and a new boat and crew selected for us. While they
readied for the trip, I inspected this island. They had erected new,
stout, sod-chinked houses and started new fields. There were many
more people than I had seen previously, families that had run
away from laboring among the Britons and Gaels.

"There's a difference, Lord, in planting your own fields and
doing it as a serf on some lord's land. We will be sending you
tithes," one of the old men told me.

"That isn't necessary," I said, trying to avoid the acceptance of
this responsibility.

"It is to us, Lord. It shows we are free men, with a liege lord
of our own." Ulfas nodded, and I left the matter to him. We
discussed it later.

"I would be your seneschal here, Lord," he said, "and serve you
as Kay serves Arthur. There will be tithes coming in from the Picts
to show their allegiance to their High King, and you will need a
liege man to receive them."

"What in the world would I do with wealth?" I asked.

"Give it away. There will be other Picts still in the hands of the Gaels who must be freed by purchase if not by arms. They will have nothing of their own. They will want to be sent out to the islands like the others, and will be welcomed if they come ready to help as equals. They must be provided with tools and animals. All that you must do."

He was right.

I talked to Myrddin about it. "Do you think we could set up our forge again on Ector's Island and ship tools north for these people?"

"You already intend to do this," he said. "Are you asking if I will help you?"

"Yes. That is what I am asking," I said smiling.

"Of course," he said. "I need useful work. I didn't even mind smithing for the Gaels so much, it was just being constrained that bothered me."

I knighted Ulfas before we left, at Myrddin's suggestion, rendering Ulfas speechless for the first time in our long friendship. "Rise, Sir Ulfas, Baron of Man," I said, after tapping him on his shoulder with his saxeknife. Ulfas doesn't wear a sword. I had to pick him up with my two hands to kiss him on either cheek, and was astounded to find he was crying. He was touched beyond my expectation. This I should have thought of myself.

We had good weather for the trip to Mona and found the people there were waiting for us on the headland, waving and shouting as we came in. Fishermen from Man had brought news of our coming. On the beach was a small party of greeters, including a short, curly-haired child with her hands clutching the fur of a huge dog. It was Viki and Cavell's pup.

Myrddin had the tiller, and when he ordered the sail down and the oars out to bring us in under control I dove into the water and swam in, beating the ship by a few yards. As I walked out of the surf, Viki came flying down to greet me.

"Oh, Geen! We have a mother," she yelled as she ran. "We

have our own mother!" I picked her up and carried her, looking up at the crowd to see what she was talking about. I hoped to see Nithe, but there were only smiling Picts.

Viki tugged on my beard. "Did you hear me, Geen?" she asked.

"That I did. You said you have a mother," I said.

"No! *We* have a mother, Geen!"

"Oh. Sorry, and who might that be?" I asked, putting her on her feet where she could cross her arms properly as she did when she scolded me.

"You know! Nithe!"

My stomach lurched. I knelt and took Viki by the waist, bringing her to where I could look into her eyes. "Is she here?" I asked.

"Do you see her?" she responded scornfully, twisting out of my hands in an irritated way. Viki did not like to be handled roughly, and I apologized.

"I did not mean to hurt you, little one," I said. "Please tell me where Nithe is."

"I don't know. Someone came and said they had found a wild man and they need her to tame him. She went away."

I looked up at the woman who had promised to care for Viki while I was gone and raised my eyebrows in question.

"It was a messenger from New Avalon," the woman said. "She spoke privately to the Lady Nineve, and took her back with her. She said she would be back when she could."

Myrddin had joined us and I rose and said to him, "Nithe was here. At least I guess she was if she has taken the name Lady Nineve."

"Nineve is her proper name, and with Hilda dead she would succeed to her title," Myrddin said.

When I had told Myrddin of Balin's killing of Hilda soon after we freed him from his chains, Myrddin was very quiet for a time, finally asking, "Why did Arthur permit Balin to leave?"

"Balin is Lancelot's man and he claimed blood feud with Horsa, Hilda's father," I said. "He also claimed Hilda was a witch. Arthur did not wish a breech with Lancelot so he merely exiled Balin."

"Arthur worries too much of what others might think," Myrddin had said. "Hilda was my own sister's daughter, and Arthur has saddled me with a blood feud I could well do without!" and he walked away to be by himself. His statement cleared up the mystery of why he had become Nithe's guardian. I wondered if she knew the reason. I decided that she probably did not, and that it was none of my business. One thing I was sure of was that Balin had a new enemy he could well do without! This was the first time Myrddin had mentioned Hilda since he learned of her death, but I was sure it had been much on his mind.

"I am going to New Avalon," I said. "Will you come with me?"

"Of course, but you have not introduced me to this person," he said, looking down at Viki, grave of face, but with smiling eyes.

"This is Myrddin, Viki," I said. "I've told you about him."

"You're Cavell's daddy!" Viki said with delight.

"I'd like to think so," Myrddin said.

"Nithe told me," she confirmed, nodding her head.

"Well, then, I guess it must be true," he said.

"Oh, yes," she said. "This is her puppy, Slobber," she added, introducing the huge, one-year-old dog to Myrddin. The immense beast drooled amiably on Myrddin's boot as Myrddin bent over to pat him.

Viki turned her attention to me. "Are we going to find Nithe, Geen?" she asked.

"We are going to try," I said.

"Good," she said, and led me up the cliff path to our house.

It was necessary to spend a few days on Mona to confirm Gondar as my liege man for the island. I knighted him as well, surprising him, but not upsetting him as it had Ulfas, having had many honors in his long lifetime. With Gondar on Mona and Ulfas on Man I could be sure my people would be well looked after.

We took a small curragh to the mainland and sailed down the coast, Viki, Myrddin, Slobber, Hair and I. We tethered Viki to the bow, to keep her from falling overboard, since she told us she didn't know how to swim. Myrddin wanted to delay the trip until she had mastered the art, but in our urgency to find Nithe neither Viki nor I thought it a good idea. Consequently, Myrddin fussed over her, sleeping only when he was sure I was awake and attentive. Slobber felt much the same, and between them they managed to make Viki cross, a difficult undertaking had it been on purpose. She spent much of the time on my lap, glaring at the two of them, to their discomfort.

"They think I'm a baby, Geen," she confided.

"They think much the same of me," I told her. "Just ignore it as I do," I advised, and she did, recovering her good humor.

We came to the mouth of the Usk and turned upriver, rowing by Camelot without stopping. If we called there it would be days before we could get away, and Myrddin mentioned Arthur had dismissed him when they disagreed on the advisability of his marrying Guenevere. I think it was more than that. If Arthur had not allowed Balin to go unpunished for his murder of Hilda, Myrddin would have insisted that we stop and pay respects. At the very least he would have wanted to inspect the building going on at Camelot. As it was, it took us two days of rowing upriver before we reached New Avalon.

I had been worrying what I would say to Nithe. Morgause had said she and Lancelot were lovers, but Ettarde had laughed at the notion, as had Myrddin. Nithe had come looking for me after I was released from Melligrance's prison, and again at Mona, but I was not sure she didn't think she owed me some explanation about her relationship with Lancelot. It would be like her to come and explain in person before she committed herself to someone else.

She was not at New Avalon. My sense of disappointment was as keen as that of a child cheated of an expected gift. I had not faced the possibility that I might not ever find her, and the realization depressed me so I became nearly unapproachable. Viki turned to Myrddin for comfort, and he gave her the attention she deserved. I saw it, but was unable to change my behavior.

The people at New Avalon, scholars and shelter-seeking women, made much of Myrddin and insisted he stay, but he pleaded he had made promises to me that bound him elsewhere, and we left after only two days. They loaded our ship with enough food and water to last a month so we would not have to stop for supplies on the way.

"Where did they tell you she had gone?" I asked once we were aboard and sailing down river, for they had told me nothing.

"They didn't know," Myrddin said.

"Who was the wild man she was supposed to take care of?" I wanted to know.

He hesitated a moment before answering, and then said, "It was Lancelot."

"Wild in what way?" I asked grimly.

Myrddin sighed. "Lancelot is competitive beyond normal limits. He cannot bear failure. His father tried to shield him from battle, where failure is as common as success, on the pretext that his kingdom could not risk losing its heir, but it was very difficult, for fighting is Lancelot's whole life. He seems not to suffer so much in tourneys, partly because he is so good that he always wins. Nevertheless, something must have set him off, for he ran away, as he has all his life, to avoid someone or something he found punishing."

"Why would Nithe be involved?"

"He trusts her, and depends on her to shield him when he is wounded. His mother did this for him until her death and now it appears only Nithe can control him."

"You've known this?"

"Yes. What I don't know is how she does it."

"He may be her lover?"

"That's possible. I do not believe it is true, however."

"Will she give her life to this task?" I asked, appalled.

"She will not forsake him. How much of her time it will take, I do not know."

It was pointless to seek Nithe under the circumstances. I felt the loss as I had when she first told me she wanted to find out what it was about Lancelot that attracted her so. Now I knew. He was vulnerable in a way I would never be, and I could not compete with him for her attention if that was his claim on her. I was not afraid of his strength, but his weakness gave him an advantage I could not overcome. I reflected it was not fair, but as Myrddin had pointed out to me at various times as I was growing up, life was not supposed to be fair.

"Let us go to Lyoness and open our forge again," Myrddin said.

"We have no tools there," I objected.

"We can get everything we need at Exeter," he said, and it proved to be true. I remembered when Nithe bought Anna in the Exeter market for seven gold coins Myrddin had given her on her birthday. I saw no wet nurses for sale, or any other people, since Arthur had outlawed slavery under his reign. There were people you could rent by the hour, however, and when Myrddin tried to explain what use they were to Viki, she understood almost immediately.

"They're like Geen's ladies," she said wisely. "Did they pay you, Geen?"

"No," I responded, embarrassed at Myrddin's amusement, "it was more a responsibility of mine than anything else."

"Do these ladies want babies, too?"

"I would doubt it," I said.

"Good. You won't have to sleep with them, then," she decided, and I didn't.

Ector met us at the beach, warned of our arrival by watchers on the hills. He needed a staff to get around now, lamed by age as much as by battle. His men, a new crop of boys, sons of those who had followed Arthur, helped us to unload, and we settled at the smithy again. Myrddin took his old house on the cliff edge, where he could watch the sea, and Viki and I moved into the smithy. I had come here first as a boy of eleven some twenty-four years ago. I didn't feel all that much older inside as I looked around me. Where had the years gone?

There were still stores of iron and charcoal that we had left behind, and with the new tools we purchased in Exeter we were able to start work within a few days. The local people had kept the place clean in anticipation of our return, and stories about our exploits had preceded us. The respect and deference shown us was embarrassing.

With everything else, it was several days before I had time to visit Nithe's house to learn if it had fared well. I would make any repairs necessary in case she ever returned. When we first touched shore I had noticed a hum of expectancy, like distant bees. It got stronger as I approached the glen where Bronwyn and I had built our house. I had the sudden feeling that it was Nithe, broadcasting a welcome to me, but I found the glen was empty, though the house had been swept, the garden had been weeded, and a new weaving was half-finished on the loom. I suddenly realized that Nithe had returned, but with Lancelot, who would not live in a peasant's hut. They were with Ector, as guests. She was not here for me.

I wandered the hills for several days, not eating and not even thinking much. I saw Myrddin at a distance, watching me, but he did not approach, and I brooded alone. It was bad enough last time. I would not bring my foul mood to him and Viki again. When I finally achieved some measure of control, I returned and the routine of rising, eating, working, eating again and sleeping gave me stability. Myrddin spent the evenings with us, telling Viki stories as he had when Arthur, Nithe and I were young. They became very close, and in a sense I lost her as well. I was numb inside.

One morning I woke with my heart pounding, and it was a moment before I recognized the sound of Nithe's hammer in the forge, "tank-tink-tink, tank-tink-tink." I rose and ran to the smithy without dressing, and there she was, working on a knife blank as if she had never been doing aught else. She stopped when she became aware of me, and gently placed the blank back into the fire, laying the hammer on the anvil, all without taking her eyes from me. She walked toward me, but before I could take her into my arms I saw she was not alone. I caught her shoulders in my hands and held her at arm's length, looking from her to Lancelot.

"Oh, come, Nineve, this is too much," he said. "For all his size he's still nothing but a Pict. Look, he isn't even dressed!"

"That isn't quite right," Myrddin said, having come in from his little hut attracted as I had been by Nithe's hammer sound. "Pelleas is a Pictish lord. Pellinore says he is already regarded as the Picts' new High King."

"I suppose even dog packs have leaders," Lancelot said disdainfully.

"Why do you speak so before me, little man?" I asked, in rather better Latin than his. "I gave my word to Nithe not to fight you in rivalry, but I made no promise to accept insult. Do you think yourself so above me that I will not resent your words?"

"I thought you not to understand them," Lancelot said in confusion. "I would not insult anyone thoughtlessly."

"You thought no Pict could speak Latin, let alone understand it?" I asked grimly. "You need a lesson in manners, little man." I could feel the blood pulsing in my ears, and my mouth was drying up. If the blood chant started, I would clutch him in my arms and snap his back. Just one more word; nay, a single look would be enough. But he turned from me to Nithe. I looked at her. She had bowed her head and covered her face with both hands. She had always hated to let anyone see her weep.

"This lout does not love you, Nineve," he said. "Let me give you in marriage to one of my cousins. Bors would take you in all honor if I but request it. If you will not have him, there are others as well or better situated."

"No," I said. "No, Nithe can not leave."

"Surely," he said aloofly, "it is for the lady Nineve to choose what she will do."

"It is not, then," I said. "I gave her that choice once before and she walked away. I will not let it happen so a second time."

"And how do you propose to keep her from exercising her will?"

he asked in a deceptively mild voice, for I could see the tension in him from the way his weight shifted to the balls of his feet.

"With black iron and bright steel and your head hanging from my belt, if needs be," I said. "I will lead her through life like a bear on a chain if I must, but I will not again be separated from her." In the silence I added, "I can not live longer away from the sound of her voice," and I was trembling. Didn't anyone understand?

Nithe raised her head. She was smiling, but tremulously. "Enough of this," she said, and stepped between us, pushing Lancelot back. "I have endured much in friendship for you, Lancelot. I will not risk losing this man to your sword. I have told you how I feel about him. If you value my good regard, you will accept it." He looked at her a long moment, smiled a singularly sweet smile and brushed by me as he left the forge, with Myrddin behind him.

Viki had joined us, and she pushed between us to hug Nithe's legs. "I told you, Geen," she said, and so she had.

Nithe hugged me so tightly I was afraid Viki would be crushed between us, sending out waves of love, but unable to speak. "I will have you know, Nithe, that whatever Lancelot has been to you is in the past and no longer matters," I said.

"My poor Lancelot," she said. "He's almost well, and ready to return to Camelot."

"What happened to him?" I asked, releasing her to pick Viki up, but Nithe would have none of it and placed my arms around her again.

"Old King Pelles' daughter, Elaine, came to court and presented her baby as Lancelot's. She even called him by Lancelot's baby name, Galahad. Guenevere had a terrific fight with Lancelot, for he is supposed to be her paramour, and Lancelot ran off into the woods. Guenevere sent Elaine packing, with orders never to return or to try to see Lancelot again, but the damage was done. When they found him he was eating nuts and berries, and fleeing from all contact.

"The Picts trailed him and found the cave in which he was living, and I was sent for to talk him into coming to New Avalon where he could be looked after. There was too much pressure from Guenevere to return to Camelot, so I took him here where he could find himself again. He has done that. Lancelot and I are great friends, nothing more. I do not think the woman lives who could seduce him. Lud knows, I tried," she said, laughing ruefully.

"What about Elaine, Pelles' daughter?" I asked.

"You still don't understand, do you?" she asked, leaning back to look into my face. "Lancelot doesn't know if he's a wyrtleberry or a frog. He's confused about the birds and the bees."

"You mean he's never practiced the art?" I asked in disbelief.

"You remember the overseas Britons claim to be descended from soldiers in the Roman legions Maximus took to the continent. Roman soldiers, from Julius Caesar to Maximus, himself, supposedly preferred boys to girls as partners in the art. Lancelot thinks that's the way it is supposed to be, although every woman he ever met has tried to convince him differently."

"And that's his problem?"

"It's a big part of it."

I thought of Elaine saying she had found the most beautiful man in the world and wondered. Nithe didn't know much about Pictish women. I decided not to tell Nithe that Elaine was my sister. If Nithe really believed Lancelot had been seduced by some other woman, Lud knows what she might think it necessary to do. I was content not to have her worry about it. I would be happy, indeed, if I never found it imperative to have Lancelot's name mentioned in my presence.

"Well, now," Nithe said, disengaging herself and looking down at Viki, still clinging to her legs, "I want you to find Myrddin and keep him company for awhile. Pelleas and I need some privacy."

"I know," she said, clapping her hands. "Geen is going to make babies. He's good at that." She nodded several times before advising in a confidential voice, "Make him bathe first. He smells awful!"

A smothered laugh drew my eyes to the open end of the smithy to see Myrddin and several Pictish hunters watching us, amused.

"I had wondered about that," Nithe said in a nearly expressionless voice, but holding back shouts of laughter from her mind with difficulty. Her critical comments on the way I smelled in the past were vividly brought back to me.

"It's his bearskin," Viki confided. "He sleeps on it, and it stinks all over!"

"Bearskin?" Nithe asked mildly, eyes dancing, as she turned to the Pictish hunters.

"We were attacked in the mountains, and he killed it with his knife," one of them stated. "We rubbed the bear's brains and urine into the hide to preserve it. Skins tanned by hunters always have a strong smell," he said proudly.

"Well, I would appreciate it if you would get it and take it to Lady Ellen, Sir Ector's wife, and tell her that Lady Nineve requests that the skin be properly scraped and soaked in a mixture of clear water and oak bark for a month, or longer if necessary, at least until the strong smell goes away. I am not a hunter, and I am going to sleep on it from now on." One of them touched his forelock, nodded and left to carry out her orders.

"Now, let's prepare a bath for the mighty hunter, and make him smell more human," she said in a light voice, carefully not looking at me. Several of the hunters rolled out the huge vat we use to hold water when we are tempering plowshares, and others filled iron pails to heat over the forge fire. With everyone but me busy a hot bath was ready before I had made up my mind whether I would have one or not. Myrddin led Viki off, despite her protests, and Nithe dismissed the hunters, informing them she could handle whatever else needed to be done. They thought it was funny.

"Well?" she asked.

I nodded and slipped into the water up to my neck. Nithe took a handful of soft soap and slathered it into my hair vigorously with the result that I soon ducked under the water to try to wash soap out of my eyes, cursing bitterly. While I was occupied, Nithe joined me in the bath, naked, slippery and unhelpful in my trouble.

I soon learned she had other things on her mind. I am good at games, and when I could remember not to open my eyes or try to breathe underwater I was able to master this one, helping Nithe with some of the finer points.

We stayed in the water until it grew too cool to be comfortable, and I picked her up, sat her before the fire and dried her off before I carried her to the house in the glen she had made her own, so filled with love flowing from her mind there was no need for words. For the first time in my life I was truly content.